raging rival hearts

RAGING RIVAL HEARTS
BOOK 4 OF THE LOST CLAN SERIES

COPYRIGHT © 2018 BY OLIVIA WILDENSTEIN

FOR INFORMATION CONTACT:
OLIVIA WILDENSTEIN
http://oliviawildenstein.com

COVER DESIGN BY *ALESSIA CASALI*
EDITING BY *JESSICA NELSON & JOSIAH DAVIS*

CHARACTERS

Adette: Taeewa's mate; the *bazash's* daughter

Addison Wood: Ace and Lily's mother; Linus's wife

Ace Wood: Linus's son; Maximus's grandson

Aylen: Nova's sister; Cat's aunt

Astra Sakar: half-fae; owns Astra's Bakery

Bee: Beatrice; owns Bee's Place; Blake's grandmother

Blake: Bee's grandson; Cat's friend

Borgo Lief: Ishtu's lover; Cruz's "adoptive" father

Cassidy (Cass): Cat's best friend in Rowan; Etta's daughter

Catori Price: main character

Chatwa: Iya's mother; twin sister to Holly's mother, Ley; hunter

Charlotte: mother of twins Cole and Kiera, and Danny; earthly Daneelie

Cole: Charlotte's son; Kiera's twin brother; earthly Daneelie

Cruz Vega: fae; faux medical examiner; friends with the Woods family; Lily's fiancé; Lyoh & Jacobiah's son

Derek Price: Cat's father; Nova's husband; coroner

Elika: Negongwa's mate; Gwenelda's mother; Kajika's adoptive mother

Etta: real name is Cometta; part fae; daughter of Astra; sister to Stella

Faith Sakar: Stella's daughter; bad blood between her and Cat

Gregor: current fae wariff; soulless narcissist

Gwenelda: huntress; first to awaken; absorbed Nova's soul

Holly: Ley; half-mortal, half-fae; Jacobiah Vega's half-sister, Cruz's aunt

Ishtu: Kajika's mate; looked like Cat

Iya: Chatwa's daughter; Cat's great-grandmother

Jacobiah Vega: fae; former wariff; Cruz's father; killed by Lyoh Vega

Jimmy: Cass's brother; Etta's son

Kajika: Ishtu's ex-husband; Gwenelda's brother-in-law

Kiera: Charlotte's daughter; Cole's twin sister; earthly Daneelie

Ley: Holly; Chatwa's "twin sister"; half-fae / half-human

Lily Wood: fae; mute; Ace's sister; Linus's daughter; Cruz's fiancée

Linus Wood: King of the fae

Lyoh Vega: Jacobiah's wife; Cruz's mother; killed her husband; killed Ishtu

Maximus Wood: Linus's father; ruthless, lawless, bloodthirsty leader

Menawa: Gwenelda's mate; Kajika's brother

Milly: mortician; works for Derek Price

Negongwa: revered leader of Gottwa Indians

Nova Price: Catori's mother; Derek's beloved wife

Pete: married to a Daneelie; turned Hunter

Quinn Thompson: earthly Daneelie; Forest Press owner

Satyana: Aylen's daughter; Shiloh's twin sister

Shiloh: Aylen's daughter; Cat's young cousin; Satyana's twin sister; has the sight

Silas: *lucionaga*

Stella Sakar: part fae; daughter of Astra; sister to Cometta (Etta)

Taeewa: Gwenelda's youngest brother; the 13th hunter

Tony: Aylen's husband

Woni: Iya's daughter; Nova's mother; Cat's grandmother

GOTTWA LANGUAGE

aabiti: mate
    abiwoojin: darling
    adsookin: legend
    baseetogan: fae world; Neverra; Isle of Woods
    bazash: half-fae, half-human
    bekagwe: wait for me
    chatwa: darkness
    debwe: truth
    gajeekwe: the king's advisor, like a minister, *wariff*
    gassen: faerie dust
    gatizogin: I'm sorry
    Gejaiwe: the Great Spirit
    Geezhi: day
    gingawi: part hunter, part fae
    golwinim: Woods's guards, fireflies; *lucionaga*
    gwe: woman
    ishtu: sweetness
    kwenim: memory
    ley: light
    ma kwenim: my memory
    maagwe: come with me

maahin: come forth
Makudewa Geezhi: Dark Day
manazi: book
mashka: tough
mawa: mine
meegwe: give me
meekwa: blood
Mishipeshu: water faeries, *Daneelies*
mika: beauty
naagangwe: stop her
nockwad: mist
nilwa: defeater
pahan: faeries
tokwa: favor
twa: men
zava: love
zavagingwi: I love you

FAELI LANGUAGE

adamans: glass flowers as tall as wheat stalks

alinum: rowan wood

astium: portal, door

calidum: lesser fae; *bazash*

caligo: mist

caligosubi: one who lives below the mist, aka marsh-dweller

caligosupra: one who lives above the mist, aka mist-dweller

calimbor: skytrees

capra: slithering Neverrian creature with rubbery skin that can paralyze prey for days

captis: magnetize

clave: portal locksmith

cupola: cage of nightmares

Daneelies: water faeries, *Mishipeshu*

dias: day

diles: venomous Neverrian creature, a cross between a frog and a crocodile

draca: first guard; wariff's protector (dragon-form)

drosa: type of Neverrian rose

duciba: council made up of a member from each faerie race

Duobosi: coupling ceremony

enefkum: eunuch

fae: sky-dwellers

Forma: underground-dwellers, bodiless, *Unseelies*

Fias: child

gajoï: favor

Hareni: grotto

kalini: fire

lucionaga: faerie guards

lustriums: clusters of stars

lupa: wild dog

mallow: an edible plant, faerie weed; doesn't affect humans the same way it affects faeries, and hunters are immune

Massin: Your highness

mea: mine

mikos: Neverrian snake coated in sharp quills

milandi: marvelous

Neverra: baseetogan; Isle of Woods

obso: please

potas: I can't

plantae: plants

quid est: Who is it?

quila: Neverrian eagle with sharp talons and curved beaks

runa: Neverrian gondolas carried by faeries

Seelies: light faeries, *Fae*

sepula: ceremony of the dead

stam: giant flat shells that bob in the Glades

ti ama: I love you

Unseelies: dark faeries, bodiless, *Forma*

vade: go

valo: bye

Ventor: Hunter

Wariff: equal to *Gajeekwe*

wita: faerie dust, *gassen*

FIGHT FOR YOUR FAIRYTALE.

PROLOGUE

From the moment I was conceived, my life was mapped out. My teachers were selected, my friends handpicked, and my wet nurse—Ace's before mine—stationed by my floating crib. The only aspect of my life that hadn't been arranged at birth was the man I would be married off to once I came of age.

Alliances were delicate and timely. And the timeliness of this alliance arose in the sixty-fifth year of my life, the year that bridged childhood and adulthood. Outside of Neverra, in the human world, they call that age thirteen.

I was a mature thirteen-year-old. I did not have much of a choice considering I was the princess of a faerie kingdom and I spent my days—when my tutors weren't pressing my nose into a book about the use of *volitor* wood or the effects of *dile* venom—with Ace and his best friend, Cruz.

I followed them almost everywhere, and never once did they make me feel like one of the wild pups that roamed our mossy kingdom. Taverns and brothels were off-limits, but curiosity would make me peer through the thick glass. I'd watch the scantily-clad women inside and study the way their charcoal-blackened eyes tracked over the customers, the way their cheekbones dusted with shimmery powder from crushed *adamans* petals caught the muted lighting, and the way their lips reddened with a paste made of scarlet *drosas* would slip over the men's jaws.

I hated these women, hated their cloyingly sweet, crushed beetle scent that lingered on men's skin, but I was fascinated by how they enchanted men. More specifically, one man: Cruz Vega.

I wasn't sure when I'd developed feelings for my brother's best friend. *No…that isn't true.* I was born with feelings for him. But like my body, they'd matured over time. Whenever a red-mouthed, glittery-lidded *calidum* approached him, my heart felt like it grew claws.

Sometimes, I would fight the *lucionaga* in charge of my security when he or she tried to haul me away; sometimes, I would leave willingly, unable to endure the pain of seeing Cruz with another woman.

My love for him turned fiercer still when my parents and his mother—the feared Neverrian *draca*—decided to bind our essences together in the Cauldron. I became his betrothed in my sixty-fifth year of life and remained so until my ninetieth.

Four months ago, I released him from the bond that had tied us together, so he could bind himself to Catori Price.

Oh, how I loathed Catori at first.

I hated her exotic beauty that made men gape, and her strange magic that made faeries take notice. I hated that she'd kissed Cruz—twice—and how he'd made light of those kisses by saying our engagement was arranged and loveless. His words had hurt more than when I'd fallen midflight into the *adamans* field bordering the glade, and the sharp, glassy petals had shredded my skin. I hated that Cruz had marked her to know where she was at all times. And then I hated her more than ever when she'd hurt my brother, before I understood she'd broken up with him to protect him.

Why more than ever?

Because at that point, I'd come to like her.

Life is a funny thing.

The girl I'd despised the most became closer to me than all the friends my parents had hired to fill my social card. Weeks ago, she even became my sister-in-law, which was all shades of wild and wonderful.

And the boy I'd adored my entire life became merely a friend. I still loved Cruz Vega, but I no longer craved his attention or his heart.

Another man crowded my mind—a hunter, of all people. I was enamored with one of the people my brethren had taught me to fear and destroy. My nursery rhymes had been songs woven from the dust-thirsty lost clan's most appalling deeds.

How could I possibly desire my worst rival?

I blamed my strange infatuation on my dwindling time. In another two months, the fire burning beneath my skin would extinguish. Unless someone found a way to get me back into Neverra.

When life has an expiration date, you live it differently... dangerously.

Or at least I did.

1

THE PLAN

"*L*ily, are you listening?" Cat asked as she stared at me over the coffee table in her house, which I'd come to think of mine since I moved in four months before—the day I was cast out of Neverra.

I blinked away from the window that framed the graveyard and signed that *Yes, I was listening.* But I hadn't been.

Kajika had told Cat he would stop by after he went to the barn, where he fought illegally for handfuls of twenties. Actually, I had no idea how much he made for each fight. Possibly several hundreds of dollars. Growing up in Neverra, with a limitless access to cash to burn in the human world, hadn't taught me much about the value of money. It was something I was only beginning to understand.

"What did I say, then?" Cat wasn't digging her hands into her waist, but she sure sounded like she was.

I glared at her. Sweetly, but still I glared.

"Aha. You weren't listening!"

I wriggled my eyebrows.

"Lily, we're talking about your life. *Your life!* The least you can do is appear interested in saving it."

I sighed. *Tell me again.*

Cat wasn't fluent in sign language yet, but she was learning.

Besides working to save my life, she'd enrolled in an intensive signing class. Oh, and did I mention she was also studying Neverrian politics with Gregor? Queens must learn how to rule.

Before she could rehash her plan to save my life, which would most probably not work anyway, my hands fluttered through the air. *Do you realize you're a queen?*

She sighed, laying her notepad on her jean-clad lap. "It's still really strange."

I bet Veroli would have an aneurism if she saw Cat wearing jeans. My heart pinched at the thought of my wet nurse. She'd come to visit me after the *Caligo Dias*—the Day of Mist, *i.e.* Neverra's newest Independence Day. The day Cat single-handedly vanquished the mist from our world.

If I died, my greatest regret would be not being able to glimpse this new Neverra. Although I'd stared through the boathouse portal during one of the many failed attempts at bringing me home, the sliver I could see of my world was no panorama. Sadly, phones and cameras didn't work in our world, so snapshots were out of the question too.

"I was thinking we could try a transfusion…"

I gaped at Cat. *I'm made of fire, not blood, doc.*

"I know. But if you heat gases enough, they produce plasma. And that's a fluid."

I blinked. *What is enough?*

"Very hot. It would have to be done in a lab, and then we could reinject that into your veins." She paused. "Don't look so horrified."

I shook my head slowly. I wasn't horrified; I was intrigued, if a tad anxious. *You think it could work?*

"We won't know until we try. I'm going to look into specialized labs tomorrow."

That would be— I was going to sign *incredible* when my palm ignited.

And then it flickered.

I jolted to my feet.

It wasn't the first time the mark I shared with Kajika lit up. Every time he trained hard—which was often—his pulse would speed up and register on my palm as a bright glow, but *never* had it flickered.

The notebook slid off Cat's lap as she too leaped to her feet.

"Where is he?" The urgency in her voice made my stomach constrict.

I closed my eyes and focused on the location of his pulse. *Barn,* I signed, before racing out of the house and shooting into the dark sky. Below me, Cat ran, her black hair ribboning out behind her blurred figure.

My velocity decreased with each flight, an acute reminder that my fire was waning. I cast my mind off my failing body and focused wholly on Kajika. A mile away from the barn, I sensed him and dove down, hitting the ground harder than intended. I landed between him and two faeries whose faces were cloaked by ski masks but whose hands were extended, ribbons of dust winding and unwinding around their fingers.

Kajika was on his knees. The tinny scent of blood tangled with the odor of charred flesh. I wanted to crouch next to him and ask him what happened, but Kajika needed a shield, not a nurse.

I fixed my gaze on the faeries, trying to make out the faces behind the masks. My eyesight had dulled from the months spent away from Neverra. I could still see clearly, but only during the day. At night, I saw like a human…weakly.

Anger flared behind my breastbone. Anger at the faeries who'd carved through Kajika's skin and anger at my useless vocal cords and pitiful eyesight.

"Please move, Princess." The voice was deep, masculine. "We do not want to harm you."

I didn't move.

"We have orders to reclaim the dust the *ventor* has confiscated." The second faerie's voice was a pitch higher, but still a man's.

"Orders from whom?"

Both faeries spun. Catori had crept up behind them, as lithe as a feline. One of her palms was flush against the forearm adorned with the filigree tracks filled with captive dust. Dust she could manipulate. Hunters stored dust beneath their skin, but they couldn't access it. Only Cat had that ability.

"*Massina*," one of them exclaimed.

"Who gave you orders to retrieve dust from this hunter?"

The faeries looked at each other. A split second later, knowing their queen couldn't fly, they sprang upward. Cat ripped the dust from her arm and then fashioned a burning arrow from the blazing ribbons, which she launched at the fleeing faeries. She missed—I suspected on purpose—and the arrow curved back toward her like a boomerang, landing in her fingers.

She watched them until their bodies vanished behind a blanket of clouds. "Did you recognize their voices, Lily?"

I'd been so consumed with rage and worry that I hadn't even tried. I shook my head as I crouched beside Kajika and placed a hand on his back. A growl erupted from his mouth, and he whacked my hand away. I felt the blow deep in my chest.

I snatched my trembling hand back, and as I rose back to my feet, I stared at the muddy ground flecked by tufts of yellowing grass, then at the clumps of mud smudging the white soles of my sneakers.

Another pair of feet appeared beside mine, and then a hand touched my arm.

"He's shaken up, Lily," Cat whispered.

Her words did nothing to comfort me. Truth was, the hunter had never liked me because I was a faerie, and although he was fae too, he didn't consider himself one of us. His loathing for me had grown the night I'd marked him. And for some reason, it had amplified recently. I suspected it was because he felt like I had kept him away from being with his family.

When they'd all left on the *Caligo Dias*, he'd had to stay behind to keep an eye on me. Not only was I a Seelie, but I lived with Catori's father. I was a double threat.

Sometimes, I wished he'd just left.

2

THE ASSAULT

*S*hadows had crept over Cat's brow as she crouched beside Kajika and touched his shoulder. He didn't push *her* away. Even though Cat was now married to my brother, I didn't think the hunter had ever stopped wanting her.

Kajika turned his feral gaze on me. He'd heard me. Ever since I'd marked him, he could hear my thoughts. Having me in his head had increased his loathing for me tenfold.

I didn't step back. I didn't move. I simply crossed my arms in front of my chest and kept my gaze leveled on his, daring him to contradict me.

"Did they get their dust out?" Cat asked him.

Without turning away from me, he said, "No."

There was a disturbance in the air, and then two new bodies materialized beside us.

Cat's brand must've flared to life, because my brother had come.

"Cat!" Ace worried about her first now.

I'd slid into second place months before.

Always second.

I couldn't even fault my brother for it. He loved his wife. *I* loved his wife. I just wished someone would put *me* first. Was that so much to ask?

"Hey, Lily," came a familiar voice.

I squinted at Ace's dark companion. The shock of seeing Silas swept through me, blowing away the pity-party I was throwing myself.

Since the night of Cassidy's birthday party on the beach, our paths hadn't crossed. Ace had made Silas the new *draca*, which kept him busy.

His chest seemed to have expanded, and his arms—his arms were ropes of muscle beneath bronzed skin. Even his eyes had changed. Instead of gold like all *lucionaga*, they'd turned a luminous, almost phosphorescent green. The only thing that remained unchanged was his long hair swept back into his signature ponytail.

I'd had a crush on him once upon a time, but like all of Ace's friends, he hadn't taken notice of me. Silas smiled, and I grinned back. If it hadn't been for the grunts emanating from the still-hunched hunter next to me, I might've asked the new *draca* a thousand questions about his life, but the moment didn't feel favorable for catching up.

"The faeries said they had orders to attack," Cat was telling Ace. She'd risen from her crouch and was now standing closer to him than to Kajika.

"Did *you* send them?" Kajika growled at my brother, amber eyes glinting like forged metal.

Skies only knew how my brother managed to contain himself. He pressed his lips tight before muttering, "Of course not."

"They didn't manage to get any dust out," Cat added.

"Were they *lucionaga*?" Silas asked.

Cat shook her head. "They didn't have golden eyes."

"Whose dust do you carry, *ventor*?" Silas asked.

I hadn't even thought of this... Not only was Silas strong, but he was also smart.

I turned toward Kajika, who was glaring at me. What had I done now?

He shifted his angry gaze off me, and then his mouth moved. "Liv Vargas, Frid Lief, Mallory Thoms"—he recited the names like a priest recited psalms from the Bible—"Sibyl Anders, Vivienne Moss, and Addison Wood."

Cat's black eyes widened at the mention of my mother's name. She rose to her feet, then turned toward Ace. "Could your mother have done this?"

"My mother's in mourning. She hasn't seen anyone since Linus died."

Linus.

Our father.

Since his death, Ace had referred to him solely by his first name, as though avoiding the word *father* could distance him further from the man he'd loathed. I didn't have much love for the man either, but for some reason, I couldn't refer to him by his first name. Not that I thought about him much anyway. When I'd been exiled from Neverra, he hadn't shed a single tear.

I signed: **Frid Lief**. Frid had been Borgo's cousin. Borgo, who took his life after revealing he'd had an affair with Kajika's mate, Ishtu.

"Lily could be right. Frid has political pull and no love for the Unseelies," Silas said.

Ace studied his *draca*. "Return to Neverra and convene a meeting of *all* the people whose dust Kajika confiscated."

"Very well, *massin*." He inclined his head toward Ace, then Cat, then me. Third best. Yippee. "Lily, I hope to see you soon. In Neverra, preferably."

I smiled as he soared back upward.

"Did they hurt you?" Ace asked Cat, running his gaze over her exposed skin.

"No. They didn't hurt me. Ace, I tried to shoot them out of the sky. Not to kill them but to immobilize them. I'm not sure it was a very dignified move, but—"

He pressed a finger to her lips, then tucked her hand in his and pulled her aside. They spoke in hushed tones. He was probably reassuring her that it was okay, that they'd deserved it. I doubted

Ace would ever chastise Cat for protecting her friend, even though my brother wasn't a fan of said friend.

Kajika finally pressed his blood-caked hands into the earth and heaved himself up to his feet. "You did not have to come, Lily," he mumbled through gritted teeth. His tattered t-shirt flapped in the wind.

Your brand flickered.

"You no longer come when it ignites."

I raised my eyes to his. *One, it lights up all the freaking time. Two, you look so* thrilled *to see me when I show up that I'd rather stay away… or spend time with Faith. Even she's friendlier than you. Which is saying a lot, considering how surly she is.*

Faith's mother, Stella Sakar, was a two-timing social climber who'd tried to kill Cat. In the end, Cat had offed her—a detail Faith was still not privy to. She didn't even know her mother was dead. She assumed Stella was off on one of her endless, exotic trips. That was what Stella had claimed her extended absences had been, when in fact she'd been frolicking in Neverra with Faith's biological father, Neverra's *wariff*, Gregor Farrow. He was a cold, cold man with an agenda as thick as an encyclopedia.

Why Ace had kept him as *wariff* still staggered me. My brother claimed it was wiser to keep his enemies close, yet it didn't reassure me. I despised Gregor.

"Did he…*do* something to you?" Kajika's voice jolted me out of my thoughts.

I cocked an eyebrow. *What?*

"The *gajeekwe*, did he hurt you?"

Gregor? I blinked. *He was overjoyed when I was kicked out of Neverra, but he never outright hurt me. I wasn't much of a threat. In his eyes, in most people's eyes, I was only ever a silly little princess.*

Kajika's jaw set so tightly I thought he might be in pain.

Want me to patch you up?

A lock of silky black hair slipped over his brow. "Patch me up?"

You know, close up your wounds? Our fire can injure, but it can also heal.

"You should not waste your fire, Lily. You do not have a limitless amount. Besides, I am a hunter. I heal fast."

Not just a hunter, but an Unseelie. I tried to keep the distinction from my thoughts, but of course it seeped from my mind into Kajika's. The moment my words hit him, he hiked his upper lip in a snarl. He hated to be reminded that his tribe's Great Spirit was in fact an Unseelie spirit trapped in a human body.

When Gwenelda had explained it to him, he'd punched a hole in the drywall of Holly's old cottage. I'd been there because Gwen had brought me in to discuss Cruz's plan of awakening her buried tribespeople with her new clan of hunters.

"How are you feeling, lil' sis?"

I turned to Ace and signed, *Great.* I added a smile so he wouldn't worry.

He had enough to worry about, what with being king. He took my hand in his and closed his fingers around mine. Our bodies used to burn at the same temperature, but not anymore.

"Your skin is freezing."

I pulled my hand out of his so I could sign: *You're just overheated.*

My brother's blue eyes churned, and he grunted. I took it he didn't believe me.

"Have they made progress in locating the lock?" Kajika asked.

"That won't help Lily."

Changing the lock on the portals wouldn't help me reenter Neverra—Kajika knew it...everyone knew it—but it would help hunters return to Rowan. Most of Kajika's tribe was in the faerie world. From what Cat told me, they had settled in and didn't particularly want to leave. Kajika refused to believe this. He was convinced the faeries were keeping his people hostage and mistreating them.

"It very well could counteract her skewed stamp." The hunter was pretending to be concerned about me. I used to appreciate it when I thought it was genuine, but I'd come to realize that my life mattered as much to him as the life of the men he fought in the barn.

Catori bit her lower lip. Unlike Kajika, she was truly worried about me.

Kajika's gaze flashed to me. "That is not true," he said quietly.

I startled. *What isn't true? That Catori cares about me?*

A nerve ticked in his jaw.

"The hunters are working day and night with the *lucionaga* to find the lock," Ace continued.

Uncovering the lock to the portals was the equivalent of finding a needle in a haystack, because the portal lock could be anything, from an *adamans* petal to a doorknob to an insect to a needle.

"If it can counteract her stamp, then it would be unhoped for, but I'm not relying on a hypothetical solution to save my sister."

"What if we cut off her wrist?" Kajika suggested. "It would get rid of the stamp."

It would also get rid of my wrist. I like having a hand. Not that a hand would be of much use to me if I were dead.

Cat hissed at the heinous idea.

"Are you fucking insane?" Ace all but shouted.

Cat closed her fingers over his forearm, as though she sensed he might take a swing at the hunter.

"No one's lopping off anyone's hand," she reassured him, or maybe she was reassuring me. "I had an idea earlier." She filled them in on the plasma injection.

It won her a derisive grunt from the hunter and a deep sigh from my brother. "Faerie fire isn't human fire."

Meaning it wouldn't work.

The corners of Cat's mouth turned down. I had to admit I was pretty crestfallen, too.

I traced the pale lines on my wrist that should've been a circle slashed by five irregular lines. Instead, it resembled a spherical maze.

Ace touched my shoulder. "Lily, I gave you my word…you'll be coming home." His expression was so determined it shrank some of my dread.

As long as Cruz doesn't die, I signed.

Ace flinched, which made me angry, because it meant he was still entertaining the idea of letting his best friend take his own life. If Cruz died, it would annul all the ties he'd forged during his lifetime, thus erasing my awry stamp. I'd rather take my own life than allow him to take his.

Ace needed him.

Neverra needed him.

Who needed me?

"Lily—" Ace reached out for me, but I shook my head and stepped back, and then I shot up into the sky and used what little stock of fire remained beneath my skin to get away from the brother blinded by blood ties, and the hunter irritated by my very being.

3

THE RESEARCH

"*L*ily!" Cat burst into my bedroom a half hour after I'd arrived.

What? I signed, my fingers moving lethargically through the air. I'd bathed, changed into my favorite nighty, and started a new book, but none of these things had done much to brighten my mood.

"Cass just called. Faith went into labor." Cat's cheeks were flushed and her black eyes bright.

I sat up so fast the book propped on my stomach toppled onto the bedsheets.

"I'm going to go to the hospital. Want to come?"

I nodded, then yanked on a long cashmere cardigan that hit mid-thigh, rolled on thick socks, and grabbed my bag.

Faith was prissy and critical, an armor she donned to keep people away. Beneath it, she was a sensitive girl. Well, more faerie than human girl. Cat was toying with the idea of telling Faith about her heritage, but it meant broaching the subject of her missing mother. Announcing you've murdered someone's mother—even in self-defense—isn't a simple thing.

I unplugged my phone from its charger, and then we left the

house just as Derek drove in with the hearse. Cat lowered her SUV's window to tell her father we were going to the hospital.

"How sweet of you girls. Is Stella back?"

Cat became as still as the gray headstones surrounding us.

"I don't know," she said, and I could only imagine how much it hurt her to lie to her father.

Derek was the kindest man in the world, and the absolute greatest father. How I wished my father could've been even a teeny bit like him.

"Cass probably called her," Cat added.

Derek had been present the day Stella died. Technically, he was the reason she'd died. Stella had taken him hostage to recoup her kidnapped dust, but instead of recuperating it in her palms, she'd recuperated it in her mouth. Her own dust had asphyxiated her, and she'd crumbled into ashes in the Prices' kitchen. Sometimes I caught Cat staring at the grout between the tiles and shuddering, as though she could still see traces of Stella. Sometimes, Derek would absent-mindedly rub his throat as though he too remembered the blade that had bitten into his skin and killed him. He had no memory of his death, thanks to Kajika who'd *influenced* him to forget.

Cat powered her window up and rolled past the hearse and out of the gate. For a long moment, we were both lost to our thoughts. But then, I took out my phone and typed, **Are you sure Faith will want us there?**

Cat's eyes flashed to my lit screen. "She'll probably gripe about it the whole way through, but deep down, I think she'll be glad for some company. I can't imagine having a baby all on my own."

I typed, **Like Ace would let that happen. You'll be lucky if you get a second alone once you're carrying his child. And if it isn't him, it'll be Veroli. Or your dad.**

A flush streaked her face. "Really not in a hurry to have any kids." But then she glanced my way and added, "Because you're not going to be stuck to me once I'm carrying your nephew or niece?"

My lips twitched into a smile. I rested my elbow on the door and pressed my cheek into my open palm, staring at the autumn-burnished trees and moonlit asphalt. I would love to be an aunt, but for that I'd need to exist.

"I can hear your negativity all the way to here," Cat said after some time.

I sighed.

She closed her hand over mine. "You're going to live."

I lowered my elbow. **But not at the expense of Cruz.**

She concentrated so hard on her windshield that a small groove appeared between her thin, black eyebrows.

"There has to be a loophole, and we'll find it." She released my hand, but not before saying, "You really are cold."

A full body shiver raked through me as she said it, because I *was* cold and scared of what it meant to be this cold. Did I have another two months in me, or less?

"I want you to promise me something, Lily. I want you to promise me that you're not going to fly anymore. Flying uses up too much fire."

I gnawed on my bottom lip, resenting how pathetic this body of mine had become. An empty, useless shell.

"Promise me."

The urgency in Cat's voice made me nod.

I'd try.

Minutes later we drove into Mullegon, and then we parked in Mercy Hospital's lot. Cat texted Cassidy to tell her we were in the waiting room. We grabbed two coffees and sat on the plastic chairs underneath buzzing strips of too-bright neon.

Cat kept looking around, lips pinched so tight that I signed, *You OK?*

"This is where Stella attacked me," Cat explained quietly. "In this hospital. On the day Astra died." Goosebumps pebbled her exposed forearms.

I touched the top of her hand, then moved my hands through the air, *She's gone.*

"I know." She shot me a quick smile then flicked her gaze to the digital clock hung over the door.

I drew my phone out of my bag. **When are you leaving?**

"Ace wants me to attend a dinner tomorrow night to thank the illustrious supporters of the *Caligo Dias*. It'll give me an opportunity to catch up with Gwen and Negongwa on their progress."

I nodded stiffly. The mention of Kajika's family had me thinking of the hunter again. *Ugh…*

Cat misinterpreted the tightness in my shoulders. "But I'll come straight back."

You don't need to babysit me.

"Babysit you?" she exclaimed. "Is that what you think I'm doing? Because if it is, then you have it all wrong. I genuinely like spending time with you. And with my father. *And* with Cass. And, surprisingly, with Faith. Please don't think I'm staying here out of pity, because I'm not. Rowan is home."

Do you think Neverra will ever feel like home?

"Maybe someday. Maybe when you're there with me. Right now, I feel like too many people there really don't like me…and really don't trust me."

That's because you're an impressive and fearful woman. I mean Daneelie and Unseelie? Hello…explosive mix.

She grunted.

I'm serious. Give them time.

"How much time?"

I shrugged. **A few months.**

"Neverrian months or human months?"

Neverrian months.

"That's years!" She sipped her coffee, then checked her phone for a message from Cass, but she hadn't written back.

Seconds ticked by.

Do you realize your baby will be all three?

She studied the rippling surface of her coffee that was as black as her eyes. "I wish there were other Daneelies," she said suddenly, perhaps to suspend the talk of babies.

A graying man sitting by a vending machine flicked his gaze

toward us. I doubted he knew what Cat was talking about. It wasn't as though Cat had said faeries. *Faeries* was a term humans knew, even though their conception of us was limited to diminutive, winged creatures that flitted around like bees drunk on pollen.

Maybe there are.

She nibbled on her lip again.

"Cruz said he'd never heard of others." She rubbed the edge of her waffle-knit Henley between her fingers. "But Holly mentioned them in her book. She said fishermen had spotted some in Lake Superior. Then again, her book wasn't a book, so I don't know…"

I brought up a map of Lake Superior on my phone. Twice the size of Lake Michigan, it divided the United States and Canada.

"She wrote they were made of copper, which is sort of true."

When Cat swam in the Glades, and more recently in the liquefied mist that covered the Hareni, her skin became coated in tiny, copper scales. I'd begged her to take a dip in the lake so I could witness this firsthand, and under the cover of darkness, she'd indulged me. What a sight! She'd had to wait almost an hour for her skin to stop glimmering.

"But then Holly wrote they defended copper mines." Cat got up to toss her empty cup. She extended her hand, and I gave her my plastic goblet too. "So I really don't know what was fact and fiction."

I typed copper mines around Lake Superior, and lo and behold, I got a hit. A place called Copper Harbor. It could've been pure coincidence.

I was about to show Cat my findings when Cassidy burst into the waiting room, cheeks flushed and blue eyes darting wildly behind her thick, dark bangs.

"It's a boy!" she exclaimed.

Faith had never asked the sonographer for the sex of the baby. She'd been so convinced it was a girl that most of our baby shower gifts had been in various shades of pink and lavender.

"Shit," Cat said, grinning. "I hope she kept the receipt for the dress I got her son."

Cass laughed, while I just smiled, my heart tap-tapping excitedly in my chest. I possessed magic dust, and yet, I believed there existed no truer, purer magic than creating a new life.

4
REMO

aith's son sported a tuft of black hair completely unlike his mother's auburn shade, and a raspberry-shaped birthmark on his temple that we all kissed at least once. Even though Faith's gaze never wandered off her son as he passed from one set of cradling arms to the next, she allowed us to hold him and smiled as we cooed over his tiny, whimpering sounds.

"So what's his name?" Cat tapped gently on the little one's button nose.

Faith smirked. "You mean now that Victoria's out of the question?"

Cassidy laughed.

"Remo," Faith said.

Cat cocked an eyebrow. "Remo?"

"It means the strong one in Italian. After having considered him a girl for nine months, the least I could do was give him an extra-manly name." Faith extended her arms for her son, and Cat delicately placed him in the crook of his mother's elbow. As she gazed down, her blue eyes misted over. "Welcome to this crazy, crazy world, Remo Sakar."

And she didn't yet know the half of how crazy it was.

"Your grandma couldn't make it," Faith continued.

Cat went very still.

"But look at what a hit you are with the ladies already. This is your aunt Cassidy." She pointed to Cass. "And then these are your honorary aunties, Catori and Lily. They all promise to take good care of you—especially at night. Right?" She cocked an eyebrow.

A nurse came in to take mother and son's vitals, and then asked Faith if she needed any help with breastfeeding, which was our cue to leave. After another round of kisses on Remo's birthmark, we hugged Faith, who smelled of sweat, blood, and absolute bliss, and promised to visit in the morning.

Like Cass, I floated down the hospital corridor. Unlike Catori. Even though she shielded her anguish behind a smile, her distress was a tangible thing. I touched her hand, and her smile tightened.

We drove home in absolute silence.

It was only after we'd parked in front of her darkened house that she spoke. "How can I ever tell her?" She raked back her black hair. "She'll never forgive me, Lily."

I squeezed her hand.

I had trouble falling asleep that night, and considering the terrible nightmares that haunted my sleep, I woke up wishing I hadn't closed my eyes at all. I'd dreamt my hair and teeth had sloughed off my skull.

I reached out to touch my head and slid my tongue over my teeth. Had the nightmare been a preview of what was to come? I wasn't an especially vain person, but I really didn't want to lose my hair. Or my teeth. Or any other part of my body, for that matter. Still, I brushed my hair out more delicately that morning.

I got dressed in skinny jeans and a bulky cream cashmere sweater that made my legs poke out like toothpicks, then went to the kitchen.

During the weeks Cat had been in Neverra, I'd wanted to help Derek out, and since he wouldn't accept monetary compensation for taking me in, I'd taught myself to cook and had mastered quite a few dishes. On weekdays, I'd whip up lunch, and Derek, his mortician employee—and friend—Milly, and I would sit at the small kitchen table and sample the flavor of the day.

Sometimes, Kajika would join us, and the whole thing would become a little awkward. Although Derek was still wary of the hunter, he'd softened up since learning Kajika had lost his wife. The only thing Derek still had trouble with was the hunter's fighting gig. He worried Kajika would incur a serious injury.

To comfort him, Cass and I had taken Derek to one of the matches. I usually stood in the back of the barn so as not to distract Kajika with my thoughts, but Derek had insisted on getting close to the ring. Which had been a really bad idea. Kajika, who'd never gotten a direct hit to the face, had been whacked so hard he'd rebounded against the ropes. He still won the fight, but he'd glared so hard my way I'd scurried back to a shadowy corner of the barn.

On our way back into Rowan in Cassidy's bubblegum-pink car, although Derek had clearly been impressed, he mentioned how concussions could really harm a young man's brain, which had Cass telling Derek to save his worrying for Kajika's opponents.

I hadn't attended a fight since, because getting stabbed by one of his arrows would hurt less than his glares.

"What smells so good?" Cat walked into the kitchen, stretching her arms over her head.

I gestured to the waffle iron, speckled in batter.

She sniffed the air again, then banged around cupboards and drawers to set the table. As I plated the waffles, Derek trundled down the stairs, his white-blond hair still wet from a shower.

"You girls are so wonderful." He kissed Cat's cheek, then my temple, and then he took his seat at the table and forked a giant waffle onto his plate.

Cat and I slid into our seats and filled our plates.

"So Faith had a baby boy. Little Remo."

"Oh. Wasn't it supposed to be a girl?" Derek asked.

"She thought it was, but she'd never actually checked."

I signed, *He's so cute.*

Derek grinned. "I'm sure he is." He gazed a moment at Cat, who was pouring maple syrup over her waffle. I bet he was picturing her with a baby. "I can't believe your wedding's in two weeks."

Cat looked up, spilling some of the maple syrup onto the table. She scrubbed it away with her disposable napkin, but bits of blue paper stuck to the sticky syrup.

"Tell me about it," she mumbled.

"You don't sound excited, honey."

Cat finally raised her gaze to her father's. "We're trying to keep it small, but seems like a thousand people are coming, so I'm a little nervous. That's all."

"I'll finally get to meet Ace and Lily's mother."

Derek wouldn't like my mother. *I* didn't like her much. She wasn't cruel or anything…she was just not motherly.

"Will Veroli come?" he asked.

He'd adored Veroli, even after she'd subjected him to watching Titanic three times during her weekend stay. Every time the theme song played, he'd get teary-eyed—it had been his wife's favorite movie.

"Honey, can I ask you something?"

"Sure."

"Can I invite Milly?"

"Of course."

He smiled nervously, which had Cat frowning. She looked at me, and I looked at my half-eaten waffle. Although Milly had never stayed over, I suspected she and Derek had something going on. Obviously, Cat didn't suspect this. Or hadn't up to this point.

Silence stretched out between the three of us, only interrupted by the scraping of forks against plates.

"Are you…are you…is something…going on?" Cat's choppy tone made her father blush.

It had been ten months since he'd lost his wife. I believed he'd been lonely long enough, but I wasn't his daughter.

"When?" Her voice sounded strangled.

Derek shoved a huge bite of waffle into his mouth. After he

chased it down with a long swallow of water, he said, "Two weeks ago. I'm sorry I didn't tell you before. I didn't know how to."

Cat pressed her lips together and nodded. She patted her mouth with her sticky napkin, spreading syrup over her chin. She got up, then went over to the sink and ran the tap.

When she returned, her eyes shone with tears. "I'm sorry, Dad. I'm happy for you." She definitely didn't sound happy. "I promise. Just give me a little time to adjust to the idea."

"If you don't want me to bring her to the wedding—"

Cat tried to smile but failed miserably. "No! Bring her." And then she turned to me. "I'm going to go to the mall. To pick up some boy clothes for Remo. Want to come with me, Lily?"

I nodded. After she left, Derek stuck his elbow on the table and poked at the remnants of his waffle.

I wrapped my fingers around the ones with which he was clutching his fork, then mouthed, *It's OK.*

He raised a minuscule smile that didn't reach his eyes.

AFTER THE MALL, we went to visit Faith and Remo at the hospital. As I held him and marveled at his ten perfect, tiny fingers, Cat discussed the bakery with Faith. Cassidy had quit her job at Bee's Place, to the old woman's great disappointment—Bee had been very understanding though—and was managing Astra's Bakery until Stella returned.

Every time Faith or Cass brought up Stella's return, Catori would flinch.

"I'll still be such a blimp at your wedding," Faith said.

Cat rolled her eyes.

"But at least my boobs will look awesome."

I snorted.

"Talking about boobs, hand him over, Lily."

I walked little Remo to his mom and parted with him reluctantly.

"We should get going." Cat stood up from the chair she'd propped next to Faith's hospital bed. "I have a fancy dinner to attend tonight and need to get ready."

What she needed was to get to Neverra. Although I really didn't want her to leave, I acted all brave and busy so she wouldn't worry about going.

When the sun set, she left.

Derek was hosting a wake that evening, so I was home alone. Which really sucked. I was about to call Cass to see if she wanted to hang when my palm got all glowy. I sighed and tried not to pay it any mind, but it stayed lit so long, it was impossible not to. I assumed Kajika was fighting or working out, but when I zeroed in on his whereabouts, I noticed he was stationary and nowhere near the barn or Holly's farm. According to my inner compass, he was in the woods, two miles or so away from the cemetery.

Curiosity welded to my boredom. I grabbed my fur-lined leather jacket from the coat closet, slid my feet into my black shearling boots, and then traipsed out of the house.

The night was bone-chillingly frosty. I wouldn't be surprised if it snowed soon. I used to love snow, but that was when my body was a furnace. How would I deal with it this winter?

I shivered as I penetrated the dark woods.

I wouldn't be here this winter…that's how I would deal with it.

Branches cracked and bushes moved, which had me walking faster. At a soft growl, I leaped into the air, high enough so whatever animal making that sound couldn't reach me.

Since I was already in the air, I decided to fly the rest of the way. Walking was unbearably slow and tedious. Besides, strolling through spooky woods was counterintuitive if Kajika really was in trouble. I reached the gleaming, cauliflower-shaped lake in under a minute. I squinted into the darkness. When I couldn't see him, I concentrated on his coordinates. He was across the lake from me. Which had me frowning, because the only thing across the lake was a deserted, one-story, clapboard house.

I was wrong.

It wasn't deserted.

A light glowed inside. I glided over the lake and landed on the small pontoon that dipped into the water, then walked the rest of the way to the house. Instead of ringing the doorbell, I went to the window and peered in.

Kajika was there, with his back to me.

Naked.

My heart pitched at the sight of his dark, honed body, at the whorls of dust wrapped around one of his shoulders. I became so lost in the sight of him that I forgot about our little connection.

He whipped around so fast I sprang backward, but not before getting an eyeful of what had gotten his heart rate up. I scrambled away, by foot at first, but that didn't distance me rapidly enough, so I soared up and flew away.

I should've been worried about his reaction to my peeping, or at least, wondered why he'd been inside the lake house in the first place, but I was consumed with a more pressing, crushing question: Who had he been thinking about while he pleasured himself?

One of the two remaining huntresses? Cat? Or maybe one of his fans from the barn? He had so many…

I ended up on the beach, where I sank onto the chilled, humid sand. Knees tucked into my chest, I watched the black surf curl and crash and foam.

Skies, I was pitiful.

Crushing on a man who reviled my existence. And then spying on him during such an intimate moment. How he would hate me even more now.

As I stared at the inky water, I made a decision. One that would lead me away from Rowan. Away from Kajika.

I would go on an adventure.

Alone.

First thing tomorrow, I'd set sail toward Lake Superior.

"What is in Lake Superior?"

My poor, spent heart lurched at the sound of the gruff voice

5

COPPER HARBOR

I'm sorry, I whispered into his mind.

I could feel the full weight of his gaze on me. "Why Lake Superior?"

For nothing.

He grunted.

I need to get out of Rowan, that's all.

"Catori will wring my neck if I allow you to leave."

Allow me? You don't have a say in what I do, Kajika. Besides, think of how quiet your head's going to be with me gone.

He grunted again—the hunter was a man of few words—and sat down next to me. "What is in Lake Superior?"

I'm not telling you, so stop asking. I worked really hard to keep my mind blank, concentrating on the sound of the lapping waves and the briny smell of the lake mixed with the hot, musky scent coming off Kajika.

Hunters usually reeked—at least to faeries—but opal camouflaged their scent. Considering how *not* bad Kajika smelled, I imagined he was wearing the strand of brown leather speared through the rough-cut opal. I asked him once why he didn't wear it on an iron chain. Iron burned faeries, so it would've been a good tool to add to his arsenal of anti-fae weapons. He'd told me that was the way the store had sold it to him, which had prompted me to ask why he didn't restring it, and he'd all but bitten my head off about minding my own business.

"I can wait. The answer to my question will eventually fill your mind."

The one time I wished he'd leave me alone…

I was about to get up and stalk away when I had a way better idea. One that would make him flee without me having to move an inch.

Who were you thinking about back there, huh?

His body became so rigid I could almost hear all of his joints fuse together.

Was it Tracy? Or…what's the other huntress's name again?

I knew exactly what her name was—Diane—I was just trying to get a rise from him.

"I was not thinking about either huntress."

Who then?

"No one, Lily. No one, all right?" His voice was no louder than the growl I'd heard in the woods.

Why were you in that house?

"I bought it."

I spun my face toward him. *You bought a house? That house?*

"Yes, I *bought* it." He emphasized the verb, clearly annoyed by my reaction.

I wasn't implying you'd stolen it or influenced someone to give it to you.

His dark gaze slid to mine as though looking for confirmation of my thoughts in my expression.

Congratulations. It's a great house. Catori loves that house. She always said that— When she'd been a child, Cat had dreamed of living there…

My skin prickled with goosebumps, and I shivered so hard it knocked my teeth together. I returned my gaze to the lake.

He'd bought it for her.

"I did not buy it for Catori." His voice rumbled softly. "I do not have any designs on your sister-in-law."

I ground my knees to my chest.

"Please stop thinking I desire her. Because I do not. Okay?"

Was he expecting me to say okay? His actions said otherwise.

He growled, "I am attracted to someone else."

I squeezed my lids closed. This conversation had been supposed to make him flee, not make him confide in me about his crush.

"You do not know her," he added, because my night hadn't been awful enough.

A long excruciating moment passed. My ego felt like it had just endured one of Kajika's beatings.

I was about to get up when he said, "Silas was pleased to see you."

Silas is a good friend.

"He looked at you as though you were more than a friend to him."

No. We just haven't seen each other since the night Alice...

I avoided thinking the word *died*, but my glance at the patch of sand where Ace had gassed her, and where I had later incinerated her lifeless body, betrayed my thoughts. I'd burned her to prevent any beachcombers from finding her. Plus, I'd thought I would spare Kajika the heartache of burying her.

He'd been so angry with me.

Were you in love with Alice? I asked after some time. I'd never dared speak about her with Kajika.

"In love? You cannot fall in love with someone you just met."

You fell in love with Cat the moment you met her.

He set his gaze on the smattering of stars. "What I felt for Catori was not love. What I felt for her was...complicated. I had absorbed the spirit of a boy who cherished your sister-in-law. And she resembled my mate, whom I—" He shuddered. "Whom I had loved deeply. Part of me was convinced she *was* Ishtu."

As he said her name, he grew even more somber. Which was a

feat considering his mood vacillated between drab and gloomy on his best days.

Ishtu had broken his heart posthumously—a couple months back, Kajika had learned she'd had an affair with a faerie. Not just an affair, but that she'd *loved* the faerie.

"I detest that you know everything about me."

I don't know everything.

"You know more about me than I do about you."

Oh, come on, you can hear all my thoughts!

He fixed me with gleaming eyes, and it made me so self-conscious that I shivered. Slowly, he took off his winter jacket and draped it over my shoulders.

You're going to freeze.

"My blood runs warmer than humans'."

I tried to give it back to him, but he caught the collar of his jacket and buttoned it around my throat, his chapped knuckles scraping roughly against my jaw. As he removed his hands, I caught sight of his knuckles—bruised and scabbed.

Are you angry or frustrated?

He peered at his hands. "I am just training."

Uh-huh. I doubted he truly needed to train; hunters possessed super-human strength.

"So what is in Lake Superior?"

You're really not going to let it go, are you?

"I really am not."

If I tell you, do you promise not to stop me from going there?

He mulled over my demand. "Yes."

Fine. There's a place called Copper Harbor, which was apparently reputed to have copper mines.

A deep groove appeared between his black eyebrows.

Holly's book said Daneelies protected copper caves, and well—I swirled my fingers through the sand—*I was thinking maybe I'd find others like Cat there.*

His eyes widened so much that his lashes hit the black lock of hair that always fell across his forehead.

I shrugged. *I'm probably wrong about more existing, but Cat said she wished there were others, so I thought I'd go check. Besides, I need to get out of Rowan. All I do here is ponder when I'm going to die, and it's getting depressing.*

"Does Catori know about your theory?"

No. And I don't want her to know. I don't want to raise her hopes for nothing.

"You are not planning on flying there?"

No. I promised Cat I would stop wasting my fire.

"You failed to uphold that promise tonight."

I blushed at the reminder that I'd flown away from his house after seeing him— I stopped myself mid-thought. At least my embarrassment had made me warmer. I worked on unbuttoning his jacket, but my fingers kept skidding off the button.

"Can we get there by land, or do we need a boat?"

My fingers froze on the button. *We? I'm going alone. You said you'd let it go after I told you.*

"What I said was that I would not stop you from going there. I never said I would let you leave on your own."

Kajika—

"We either head there together or you do not head there at all."

That's not fair.

"What is not fair? That I accompany you on a trip that could potentially be dangerous and taxing? How is that unfair? Besides, Daneelies are of interest to me as well."

I side-eyed him. *Why?*

"Because I care about all fae species."

Species? I grunted.

"And no, I will not murder them."

I hadn't jumped to the conclusion of murder, but I was glad he cleared that up.

I want to do this alone.

"I will not talk to you."

I snorted. *Because that's going to make your company so much more tolerable?*

"I thought you enjoyed my company."

I had to look at his face then to see if he was serious. He could not possibly think I enjoyed his company.

His company was torture.

One corner of his mouth curled up in an almost smile. The hunter didn't do full smiles. At least not mirthful ones. He'd gotten smirks down to a tee.

I finally managed the button and then tossed him his jacket, no longer cold.

"I will pick you up at seven?"

I'd leave that night. I'd hire a driver and—

A flash of white teeth appeared between his curved lips. "You do that, and I will carry you back to my new home and lock you in my bedroom to keep an eye on you so you cannot escape."

I blinked. He wouldn't.

"I would," he said quietly.

Fine. I'll be ready at seven.

I stood and rubbed the grains of sand off my clammy palms, then started walking away. The quickest way back to the graveyard was through the woods, but the growling I'd heard earlier made me too nervous to head back that way, so I traipsed toward the road.

Kajika matched my strides.

What are you doing?

"Walking you home."

You don't have to do that.

"Perhaps I want to."

Or perhaps you don't trust me.

He glanced down at me and grinned, a broad smile that made me stumble over a rock. He caught my arm to steady me and didn't release me for so long that I had to shrug his hand off and put a full body space between us.

We'd be stuck together soon enough.

6

THE DRIVE

I spent the night preparing for my trip to Copper Harbor. Not mine...*our* trip.

I still couldn't believe Kajika was coming with me. I honestly wasn't sure how I felt about spending the next few days with him. In truth, I was glad not to go alone but wary of his reasons for accompanying me.

He'd been so quick to mention that murdering the Daneelies wasn't his intention. What if that was exactly what he planned? I shuddered. Kajika wasn't a cold-blooded killer. He'd never taken anyone's life since he'd been awakened. Except Blake's, but that had been unintentional.

Unable to sleep a wink, I showered and readied myself early. And then I sat on the porch to await Kajika's arrival. When the sky lightened to the deep gray of dawn instead of the dark black of twilight, it hit me why he'd want to go with me. To please Catori. Sure, he said he no longer cared for her in *that* way, but if he located Daneelies, she'd be so ecstatic...

Tires crunched on the gravelly driveway that snaked through the cemetery, and then a midnight-blue Porsche came to a stop in front of me. I frowned until Kajika stepped out from behind the wheel.

He walked over to me and grabbed the carry-all I was heaving down the steps.

What happened to the pickup?

"It broke down."

So you bought yourself a sportscar?

"I rented it for our trip. It drives fast, so instead of nine hours, it should take us seven in this vehicle. We could be back by tomorrow."

I didn't want to be back by tomorrow; I wanted a longer adventure.

His eyes sharpened tightly on me. "I did not think you would want to spend more time than necessary in my company."

I dragged the front of my boot through the gravel. *You wouldn't have to stay with me.*

He tossed my little suitcase in the trunk, then smacked it shut and folded his body back behind the wheel. I glanced behind me at the house, and then I got into the Porsche.

As I pulled my seatbelt across my torso, Kajika said, "Just so we are clear, I am not doing this to win points with Catori."

It took me a minute to realize what he was referring to. *How far do my thoughts carry?*

He revved up the engine and performed a sharp u-turn that sprayed rocks against the headstones.

"I just have to see you to hear you."

Wow. So he could be standing on the other end of a crowded club and hear me? That didn't afford me much privacy.

"I am sorry, Lily. I wish I did not have this ability."

My own fault. Not yours. I sighed. *Soon I'll either be dead or back in Neverra, so it won't matter.*

"You are not going to die. Ace would never let that happen. Catori will not allow it."

I absentmindedly stroked the buttery leather armrest. I hadn't lost all hope, but I also didn't harbor false expectations. *Kajika, why don't you go to Neverra? And please don't say it's to control the Seelies who come visit Earth, because you have a bunch of hunters who can do that.*

His fingers tightened around the wheel. "I like it here. I understand here."

But don't you want to be with your family?

"Eventually, I will be reunited with them."

That didn't answer my question of why he was even still here.

"I am not going into a place I cannot leave. What if it is a trap?"

I blinked at him. *You still think your people are being mistreated in Neverra?*

"I do not assume anything. Perhaps they truly are as content as Catori paints them to be." He let out a whistling breath. "The same way I am content being here."

Content? You haven't looked content since the day they awakened.

"Because I do not smile and laugh as often as Cassidy does?"

For one, you never *smile. And I don't think I've ever heard you laugh. And secondly, you go around scowling all the time. At everyone.*

Especially at me.

"I am preoccupied, Lily."

What do you have to be preoccupied about? You just bought yourself a house. Your clan was resuscitated.

The light from his dashboard played against his stiff jaw, against his Adam's apple that jostled in his freshly shaven throat.

"I am preoccupied with making money, since that is how the human world works."

I think you figured that part out.

"I am preoccupied with finding the faeries desirous of digging their dust out from underneath my skin."

Ace will find them. He probably already has.

"I am preoccupied with giving the new hunters enough training so they are adept at defending humans from ill-intentioned faeries."

I couldn't help but feel the teensiest bit disappointed that I didn't factor into his preoccupations.

"If your safety did not preoccupy me, I would not have made this trip, Lily."

He said this so quietly I thought I'd imagined it.

My face grew hot, as though all the fire remaining inside my body had converged inside my cheeks. We did not talk after that. Well, he didn't talk. I worked really hard on not thinking any more desperate, silly things.

I watched the horizon lighten, turning lavender and then gold, and then finally blue.

When I was a kid, I petted a lupa—*Neverra's version of wolves.*

Kajika glanced at me.

And by doing that, I opened a telepathic connection with the wild dog. So I know how it feels to have someone inside your head. Except in my case, all the lupa *thought about was food. Which made me so hungry.* I smiled at the memory. I'd hated it so much then, but today, I would give anything to be connected to a Neverrian beast because that would mean I would be home.

Pity leaked from the hunter's expression. I didn't want his pity.

I tucked my cheek against the headrest and closed my eyes. I thought some more about my world, and then I dreamed about it.

And it was a wonderful dream.

I was home.

Kajika was there, too.

7

ZIPLINE

J woke up because the car had stopped moving. I stretched my arms and was about to apologize for being a sucky co-pilot when I noticed Kajika wasn't there.

For half a second, I freaked out, until I noticed the gas pumps and the twenty-four-hour convenience shop. We'd stopped for fuel. Kajika was probably inside. He hadn't dumped me and the car on the side of the road or anything. I took off my seatbelt and got out. The air was brisk and wet, and the sky wooly with clouds. For a moment, the sound of rumbling engines and rattling suspensions faded, and I was back in Neverra, standing below the ribbon of mist that obscured the sun.

But then squeals and gasps snapped me out of my daze.

Three girls, arms laden with chips and chilled soft drinks, were gaping at me. One of them whipped her phone out of the back pocket of her jeans.

"Look who we located off I-75!" the girl shrieked.

I raised my palm to shield my face and turned, scrabbling to get the door handle open, but my fingers skidded off. A shadow fell over me. My heart pitched against my ribs as heat radiated off the adjacent body. I thought for certain the girls had moved closer, but then I heard the deep growl of a masculine voice. Muscles still tensed, I turned and found myself nose-to-spine with the hunter. I peeked around him.

"Delete the footage, or I smash your phone."

The girls' rosy complexions turned pasty. The cell phone slid and fell on the asphalt. The glittery pink rubber case cushioned its fall, but still I heard a little crack.

"Pick it up and erase the images." The muscles in Kajika's back bunched underneath his black cotton turtleneck.

Shakily, the girl crouched and grabbed her phone. When she noticed the shattered screen, she flipped her head up so fast her brown ponytail whipped her gray hoodie. "Hey, asshole, you broke my phone."

"Erase the pictures."

"Didn't you hear me? You broke my fucking phone!"

"I do not care about your *fucking phone*. I care about those images. Must I delete them myself?"

"It was a live video. It's already online," one of her friends said, but then backed up.

Kajika seemed to grow taller before my very eyes. I touched his shoulder blade, and he flinched.

I lowered my hand. *It's okay; it doesn't matter.*

"Get in the car, Lily."

I got into the car.

"What are you? Her bodyguard?"

When the door snicked shut, he stalked toward the girls, who pranced away like a herd of deer, yelling the words "crazy" and "creep." They piled into a compact red car and, tires screeching, took off.

When their tail lights blinked out of existence, Kajika went back into the gas station. I burrowed deeper into the smooth leather. Soon he returned, settled behind the wheel, and handed me a small plastic shopping bag. My stomach growled at the scent of food. There wasn't only a sandwich inside, though. There was also a pair of cheap black aviators and a black baseball cap.

Are these for me?

Kajika nodded as he pulled out of the parking spot and fired the car onto the highway.

Thank you.

"Does everyone in this world know your face?"

I don't know about everyone, but my father loved the Earthly media. It amused him to see how crazed it made people.

"So he subjected you to it?"

It was worse for Ace, but yeah, I got my dose of limelight. I didn't like it. Thankfully, not too many people know I live in Rowan, or it would be a circus. I unwrapped the sandwich and bit into it. Mayo-laden tuna slid heavily down my throat and dropped into my hollow stomach. *So where are we?*

"We are about to cross over Mackinac Bridge."

The bridge underneath which Lake Michigan blended with Lake Huron, their waters gray and frothing, snapping at the metal siding.

Traffic was light, and soon we were rolling along the coast. When I caught sight of a US-2 sign, I pivoted sharply toward Kajika.

Shouldn't we be heading north?

"You said you wanted an adventure. I am giving you an adventure."

Oh. I blinked at the hunter, whose dark gaze was focused on the flat strip of road bordered by drying grass and squat pines. A sliver of gunmetal-gray lake appeared through his window, then flashed out of sight behind clapboard houses and trees.

Mayo dripped onto my jeans and seeped into the material. I hovered my hand over the stain. Blue flames coated my palm and burned away the stain.

"Lily," Kajika chided me.

I rolled my fingers into my palm. He was going to tell me I shouldn't waste my fire.

"Yes."

It doesn't use up much to do that.

A nerve ticked in his jaw.

Fine. I won't do it again.

I had barely finished my sandwich when we pulled up to a park that advertised ziplining.

My eyes widened. *Are we— Are we going to do that?*

"Apparently it feels like flying." His lips flexed with an almost unnoticeable smile. If I hadn't been familiar with his mouth's micro-expressions, I would've missed it completely. "Put on the cap and glasses."

I wiped my fingers on a paper napkin then fished out my incognito get-up. *Don't you think the glasses are going to draw attention? There's no sun.*

"I would prefer you wear them."

I put them on. Since it was still early *and* a weekday, the park was almost empty.

"Have you ever done this?"

No.

As Kajika paid for our equipment rental, I marveled at the thick cables zigzagging through the branches. I doubted it would feel like flying. Flying wasn't fun…at least not for me. It was simply convenient, a way of getting around, like walking for humans. *This* looked like fun.

A bearded man handed me a harness, which he helped slide up my legs. Putting on his own equipment, Kajika watched the man tighten the straps around my waist and thighs.

"So you got two hooks." The man lifted one of mine. "This here's a carabiner, and this one is a track pulley. One of these has to be attached to the cable at all times. When you go down the zipline, keep your hands on your rope, 'cause if you touch the cable, you're going to sear your fingers."

He grabbed two helmets and gave them to us. Even though neither Kajika nor I needed a helmet, we belted them on, and then we headed toward the beginning of the course. I clipped myself onto the first cable and began my ascent toward a wooden platform. The ladder seemed to go on forever.

I secured the track pulley and waited for Kajika to swing himself up next to me. Where it had taken me a full minute to get up, it took him mere seconds.

Show-off.

A smirk appeared on his lips.

I overlapped my fingers on the rope that tethered my hook to my harness, and then jumped off. Wind slapped my cheeks and blew through my loose hair as I soared downward. And then my feet touched another platform. I moved my hooks to the next cable as I waited for the hunter. The line dipped from his weight as he soared toward me.

After his boots found purchase on the tree stand, he said, "It does feel like flying."

How would you know?

His eyes went flat.

I'd asked the wrong question, except now I *really* wanted an answer.

"Your brother once flew me somewhere," he grumbled.

I smiled. *That must've been painful for the both of you.*

He eased his hook off the zipline, then clipped it on the cable wrapped around the thick trunk. "You have no idea," he said gruffly, which made me laugh.

He scowled at me, but it was a playful scowl.

I walked up the rope bridge that led to the next tree, climbed another ladder, and then I was flying downward again, and I squealed a little from the speed and adrenaline of letting go.

Not just of my body's control, but of the worries that clogged up my chest like cotton balls.

8

BIRTHPLACE

*W*e did the entire course twice.

Thank you, I thought as we merged back onto US-2 and continued on our way. *That was really fun.* He pressed on the gas, and it felt like we were flying again. *Was it fun for you?*

"It was."

He said it in a tone that made me think it hadn't been much fun, but I'd spotted a luster in his eyes when he soared through the trees, so he must've had *some* fun.

I have to tell Ace about it. We could implement this in Neverra so the calidum can fly too.

"You have trees in Neverra?"

I placed my sunglasses inside the cap, which I'd laid on my lap. *We have calimbors* and *volitors* and *mallow trees. Calimbors are huge. Like three hundred feet. People live inside the hollow trunks.*

He glanced at me.

Volitors are flying trees. We use their branches to make runas.

A groove appeared between his eyebrows, so I explained what a *runa* was and then told him more about my world. It was the first time he'd shown an interest, and I was starved to talk about it.

"We do not have to discuss it if it is painful."

I'm happy to tell you about it. I want you to understand it, so it won't feel foreign once you go.

He kept his gaze cemented to the road. I told him about the political system next. How the *wariff* controlled the *lucionaga* and the *draca,* but the *draca* was also under the king's command so it sometimes created tension between the king and his *wariff.*

At some point he veered right.

We're going somewhere else? I asked just as I saw a sign that read: Cut River Bridge. I wondered what was so special about a bridge until we were cruising over it. Then I understood.

The bridge loomed up so high that it passed over the tops of the flaming crowns of the trees below. I'd seen many beautiful sights in my life—temples carved in rock, marble palaces, pointy pyramids, and hanging gardens—but the auburn and copper ocean of foliage was breathtaking.

Once off the bridge, he parked the car on the shoulder of the road.

"The gas attendant said there are stairs on the side that lead all the way to the forest floor."

I spun toward Kajika, shocked he'd inquired about sites.

He shrugged. "But we do not have to go if you do not—"

Before he could finish his sentence, I pumped my door handle and got out. Together we descended the fifteen stories that reminded me acutely of the spirals in Neverra.

I never thought being unable to fly would be a good thing.

He frowned at me, his boots pounding heavily on the wooden stairs.

It's forcing me to do things I would never have done otherwise.

———

THE CLIMB back up was steep and difficult. I got a stich in my side halfway up and panted harder than a *lupa.*

"You want me to carry you the rest of the way, Lily?"

I shot him a horrified look that gave him pause. *I'm sorry. It's just that no one's ever carried me before. Well, except for Dawson's uncle, but that was inside a* runa.

"I do not want you to waste your fire."

He had a point. Physical exertion did expend my reserve. I wasn't sure how much of a dent it made, though. Perhaps it wasn't much.

I was evaluating how many floors remained, when Kajika scooped me up. I yelped, then hooked my arms around his neck as he shot up the stairs, moving so fast the world blurred around us. Seconds later, he set me down, and I detached my arms from around his corded neck.

Sorry about my death grip.

His breathing had quickened from the swift climb, which ignited the W on his hand. Palm glowing in response, I leaned over the railing to take in the crashing river and jeweled forest below. Kajika faced the other direction, arms folded in front of his chest.

So what's next, Mr. Tour Guide?

"We can stop to eat something. If you are still hungry, that is."

I wasn't, because I'd wolfed down a sandwich. Without sharing, I realized…

"I ate a consequential breakfast before leaving home," he assured me as we walked back to the car.

The next segment of the drive was quiet. I cradled my head on my fingers and stared out my window until we rolled into a town called Manistique. He parked on the road across from a quaint little café. I put my baseball cap and sunglasses back on.

As we ate golden pastries filled with cheese and grilled vegetables, Kajika gazed fixedly out the window, past the swirly gold logo of the bakery. There weren't many passersby, and the few who walked past didn't hold Kajika's attention.

Are you expecting someone?

He returned his gaze to me. "I once lived here."

In this town?

"It was not a town then." He placed his elbows on the small

table and leaned slightly toward me. "My tribe resided here. I did not realize this until I saw the sign for Kitchitikipi—the Big Spring."

I wiped my hands on my paper napkin. *We don't have to visit it if it brings back—*

"I am eager to show you where I come from." He added a tight smile, as though to convince me he truly was happy about revisiting his birthplace. "I will be right back." He got up, his chair scraping on the ocean-blue tiles.

He walked over to the register and paid for our meal, then asked about places to stay in the area. The aproned lady behind the register twirled a lock of orange hair around her finger.

"I got a room in my house," she said.

Kajika's shoulder blades jolted together like birdwings.

I smiled, even though I did wonder about the woman's ethics. She'd seen me sitting with Kajika. Granted we didn't act like a couple, but propositioning him was definitely ballsy. I got up, slung my handbag over my shoulder, and strolled up to the hunter.

Once next to him, I wrapped my fingers around his forearm. Her gaze dipped to where I touched him. Kajika looked at my hand too and then looked at me.

I didn't let go. *Better pretend you're with me, or she'll hand you her house key.*

A hint of color swept over his jaw. "My mate and I—"

I pinched his arm. *Girlfriend,* I whispered into his mind. *You're not British, and I'm not a dude.*

He frowned, not understanding my addendum. He'd probably never been to the UK... Had he ever traveled outside the States?

Through barely parted teeth, he said, "My *girlfriend* and I would prefer to stay in a hotel."

"Oh. Of course. Well there's the Iron Inn a couple streets—"

"*Iron?* Is it crafted from iron?"

The woman gave him a wide-lidded look. "It's just called that. Why? You allergic or something?"

"My girlfriend is."

Again she looked at me. I expected her to start twirling a finger over her temple any second, but she didn't. Instead, she cocked her head to the side. "You seem familiar... Are you an actress? No you're—"

"She is no one."

Well thanks.

I'd meant it as a joke but I guessed Kajika felt bad for the way it had come out, because he added, "To you, she is no one. To me, she is someone."

I blushed. And it was completely ridiculous. I let go of his arm. *Okay, Shakespeare, let's go.*

The woman made a scratchy sound at the back of her throat, before saying, "Thanks for your visit, Miss Wood."

"She is not Lily Wood."

She winked at him. "My lips are sealed."

Kajika grumbled something in Gottwa as we walked out of the pastry shop.

After we got back in the car, he asked, "Who is Shakespeare?"

Really? You don't know Shakespeare? Romeo and Juliet? MacBeth? Blake must've studied him in school. All human kids study him. I even studied him in Neverra. He was part faerie.

"I have learned to compartmentalize the memories I received from Blake." His pupils seemed to flood his irises. "Already you are inside my head. If I gave his mind free rein, I believe I would *lose it,* as they say."

I bit my lip. Sometimes, I was really sorry I'd invaded his mind. Sometimes, though, what I felt wasn't repentance...it was relief. Relief that someone could hear me. That I existed as more than a noiseless shell.

9

THE BIG SPRING

itchitikipi was a vast conifer swamp. The largest freshwater reserve in Michigan, Kajika told me as we floated atop a wooden raft. There were other people on the raft. Not many though.

"Legend has it," the tour guide was saying, "Chippewa parents came to the pool to find names for their offspring. They would read them in the water's ripples. Another legend was…"

The man's voice faded when I felt Kajika's breath brush the shell of my ear. "It is not a legend. It is how I got my name."

Goose bumps scattered over my neck, but considering the number of layers I wore to ward off the cold, they weren't noticeable.

I hoped.

He leaned back down to my ear, and I shivered. "My mother came here when her stomach was ripe with me, and the spring presented her with the name I was to carry. Kajika meant *arrow* in our tongue."

I shivered again, this time from the cold, and hugged my arms around my jacket. *Arrow.* I glanced up at him. *How suiting.*

His gaze took in my wrapped arms. "You are cold. We should

leave." He turned toward the guide. "Sir, please maneuver the boat back to shore."

Everyone aboard blinked at us.

"The tour ends in fifteen minutes—" the guide started.

The hunter's eyes took on that glow I knew *oh-so-well*. He was about to bend the man to his will. "Now. Steer us back to shore *now*."

I'm okay. I'm not that cold. Let's stay.

Kajika pressed his knuckles against my cheek. "Your face feels like ice."

I wrapped my hand around his and dragged it off my face, then squeezed his fingers before letting go. *I swear I'm okay.*

As the raft docked, it seesawed, and my body bumped into Kajika's.

He steadied me. "I do not know how the cold impacts your fire, so I do not want to take foolish risks."

The people around us were giving us funny looks. I wasn't sure if the hunter's olden speech or the mention of my fire was to blame for the extra attention.

I wet my lips and lowered the already low baseball cap over my bespectacled eyes. *Okay, okay.*

As we passed by the guide, who was rubbing his chin, confused as to why we were docked, Kajika said, "Your account of how the spring got its name is not accurate. The name of the chief was Itchewa. Kitchitikipi was his son. Itchewa drowned in the icy waters, not for the love of his mate, but to save his child who had fallen from the bough of a tree. He was not successful, and the child drowned too. It was a terrible day for the tribe."

The guide's hand froze on his stubbly chin. He stared at Kajika as though the hunter had grown a second head. Clearly, he thought him crazy. From the raised eyebrows of the others surrounding us, I deduced he wasn't the only one who thought this.

Ducking my head low to avoid their curious stares, I strode off the raft and trailed Kajika toward the parking lot.

Did you know Itchewa?

"He was my uncle."

I froze. *It was your cousin who drowned!*

Kajika stopped too. He stared at the clear, bubbling water as though he could see the child's lifeless body floating atop. "He was the same age as my brother so I never met him, but I heard the story. It was told often in our tribe to deter children from playing too close to bodies of water. I only learned to swim when the Gottwas took us in. I used to fear water. I used to believe it was the source of all evil."

Until he'd met faeries. Then *they—we—*became the source of all evil.

"It is true." He lifted hooded eyes to me. "You say you do not know me, Lily, but I fear you know me too well."

I hated that he considered us the source of all evil.

It felt personal. As though he considered *me* terrible. I didn't have an evil bone in my body. Back in Neverra, during one of the royal hunts, I'd once let a *dile* escape because I couldn't bear to kill the venomous reptile. Cruz had had to slay it for me, and then he'd told my father I had killed and flayed it with my own sword. But my stomach had been in too many knots to even look at Cruz peeling away the animal's blue scales. My father had been so proud, he'd had the skin fashioned into a wide belt, which I'd had to don at many glitzy soirées.

I started walking again, shaking my head a little to dispel the memory of the noxious scent of *dile* blood that had spurted over Cruz's gloved hands and reddened the moss.

If Kajika had heard me thinking about the creature, he didn't bring it up.

Thankfully, because I was pretty certain I would've thrown up if he had.

THE IRON INN was not made of iron. It was made of yellowed, flow-ered wallpaper and water-stained hardwood floors. And it smelled musty, the way I'd always imagined the Hareni smelled. It hit me again that it was gone. The underground prison that had been the Unseelies' home was now covered in liquefied mist.

Kajika rolled my little suitcase down the short hallway. He'd insisted on lugging it, even though it wasn't heavy. Did he think I was becoming too fragile to carry my own bag? I stopped in front of room 3 and fit my clunky key into the lock.

The room was small and bare-boned but appeared clean...*ish*.

"Would you like me to find us someplace else?" The hunter's gaze raked over the queen-sized bed that looked as hard as a slab of wood, the canary-yellow-tiled bathroom with a child-sized bathtub, and the square television that dated back to the nineties.

It's fine. I fingered the scratchy bed spread. *It's just for one night anyway.*

He plopped the suitcase down on the desk that was painted a dirty eggshell color.

Where's your room?

"Across from yours."

Okay.

He started back for the door. "I am going to go for a run. Would you like to have dinner when I return?"

Sure.

He was about to leave when he paused in the door jamb. "Unless you want me to stay with you?"

I removed my sunglasses and baseball cap and fluffed up my hair. *Go. I'm going to shower and maybe watch some TV.*

He drummed his fingers on the wood. "Lock your door, okay?"

I rolled my eyes. *I still have dust, Kajika. If anyone tries to break in, they'll regret it.*

"Still."

I'll lock it. Now go run. It's getting dark.

Actually it wasn't getting dark. It was already dark. How I missed long summer days.

After he left, I filled the beige bathtub with warm water and tortured myself by looking up hotels in the Bahamas. Maybe I could head down there after this… Spend my last moments sunning myself on a long strip of white sand. Swim with schools of rainbow-colored fish instead of with Daneelies—who might or might not exist…

What stopped me from booking a hotel was that I would take no pleasure if I were to head down there alone. Maybe Kajika would go with me. I snorted at that awry thought. What had possessed me to think it?

Cat. I'd ask Cat. She'd go with me. But if she were needed in Neverra, the closest portal was in Miami. She had a life. Duties. It would be selfish of me to ask her to drop everything. Cassidy? She'd definitely be up for a vacation, but she was working at the bakery full time now. She couldn't just up and leave anymore. Especially not since Faith had had her baby.

Little Remo.

I scrolled through my phone and found a picture of him.

And then I swiped to the next picture and the next and began to cry like an idiot because of how happy I looked in the pictures we'd taken over the summer. It had possibly been the best summer of my ninety years, because I'd lived each day as though it were my last.

A dripping sound made me look up from my phone. Sudsy water had leaked over the edge of the bath. *Shoot shoot shoot.* I ran to the bathroom and spun the tarnished tap. Normally, I would've burned the spilled water away with my fire, but I was no longer a normal faerie. I pulled the bathmat from the towel rack and laid it on the ground, where it absorbed some of the overflow.

And then I discarded my clothes, turned on the TV so the room wouldn't feel as oppressively quiet, and slipped into the deliciously warm water. I stayed until it turned tepid, and I would've stayed longer were it not for the knock on my door. I wrapped myself in a scratchy towel and walked to the door.

I stood there a moment, a tad self-consciously, wondering if I should pull on some clothes, but it wasn't as though I could tell whomever to wait. I couldn't talk.

Cheeks a little flushed, I pulled open the door. And then I almost lost hold of my towel when I laid eyes on my visitor.

"Hi, Lily."

10

THE VISITOR

*T*he smile on Cruz's lips didn't reach his eyes and lasted a mere second.

Cruz had never been a grinner. He smiled, sure, and he'd once upon a time been happy, but losing his father young had turned him bitter and wary. In a way—in many ways—he reminded me of the hunter: serious, quiet, observant, and cunning. But if I had to compare them to shapes, Cruz was a circle, gentle with no edges, whereas the hunter was a triangle, all edges.

Why in the world was I comparing men to geometrical shapes? I tightened my hold on the towel, rolled up on my tiptoes, and wrapped an arm around Cruz's shoulder, pulling him into a hug. His hands came around me and held me lightly.

"Your skin…it really is cold."

I detached myself from him and gazed into the green depths that had held me captive for so many years. His mouth was set into such a grim line that my pulse scrambled. I knew what that look meant. My state was dismal.

I closed the door behind him and signed, *How did you find me?*

He sat on the foot of the bed and knotted his fingers together. "It wasn't easy. I asked Derek, but all he knew was that you'd left on an errand. I went to find Cassidy, and she showed me this Snapchat clip of you and Kajika at a gas station, and then I puzzled over why you'd go on a road trip. Especially with Kajika. But then I flew over the peninsula and saw the Great Spring. Menawa mentioned he was from there, so I thought maybe Kajika wanted to show you where he'd lived." Cruz studied his overlapping fingers a moment then looked up at me. "Which I still find a little strange, but you're in Manistique, so maybe it's not that strange. And then this woman tweeted that Lily Wood had lunched in her establishment, so I went there, and she told me about this place." He stared around the room. "Where's Kajika?"

He went for a run, I signed.

"Is he staying…*with* you?"

I blinked, then blushed. I shook my head, then turned away from Cruz and rifled through my suitcase for clothes. I was about to explain that it had been my idea to come and seek more Daneelies, but then realized how cracked that would sound. Cruz would remind me there weren't any other Daneelies and force me to return to Rowan.

I didn't want to abort my adventure.

I didn't want to give up hope.

I grabbed underwear, a pair of skinny black jeans, and a gray v-neck sweater, then turned back around and extended my palm to signal five minutes. After spending even less time than that in the bathroom, I reemerged and sat next to Cruz, one leg bent underneath me.

Why are you here? I wrung out my hair that was still a little damp—sadly, it no longer dried as quickly as my skin.

"I came to give you news."

My hands stilled on my ponytail. I didn't dare hope he'd found a way to get me back inside Neverra. And yet, I couldn't help myself from hoping…

"We know what the lock looks like."

I waited.

"A golden acorn. Your mother remembered hearing about it from Linus."

My mother? Since when did Cruz trust my mother? Half the time, she was surfing on some mallow-wave. The other half, she was drinking herself into a daze.

Cruz must've sensed my thoughts because he placed his hand on top of mine. "I know you think she could be making this up, but maybe she's not, Lily. Maybe she truly does remember it. She's been sober for almost a day."

What an accomplishment, I thought bitterly.

In the end, I signed, *How did that happen?*

"Ace locked her in his old apartment and stationed *lucionaga* all around."

My brother did what? Sign language was tedious. Speaking into Kajika's mind was making me lazy.

"Your mom is the one who sent the faeries to retrieve her dust from Kajika, so Ace chastised her."

Mom sent those faeries?

Cruz nodded.

Whoa. That wouldn't earn me brownie points with Kajika. I chewed on my bottom lip.

"She gave us the tip about the lock in exchange for a couple mallow leaves."

So she's no longer sober?

"She is. Ace tricked her. The mallow leaves he gave her were made out of *wita*. They disintegrated before she could rub them against her gums."

My brother was turning out to be pretty ruthless. In a good way, though. Tricking my mother, locking her up, and detoxing her was sure to peeve my blonde genitor.

I seized my phone from the bed and typed: **How is he doing as a king? Do the people like him?**

"The people who wanted change are pleased with him, but the ones who supported your father find him too lenient and young. They favor Gregor."

Isn't that dangerous? Isn't Ace worried Gregor will stage a coup with his backers?

"If he did, Ace would make a public announcement about Faith's lineage. You remember what happens to bastard children?"

They were killed. My fingers tapped on my phone's screen. **Wasn't Ace amending that law?**

"He's been putting it off to enrage Gregor. Especially now that Faith has had her baby. Gregor desperately wants to bring his daughter and grandson to Neverra but won't dare until the law is ratified."

Politics were no more than a game of chess—each move was strategized, its various impacts calculated and analyzed for ripple effects.

We spoke about hunters next, and how they were adapting. They'd chosen to settle in the valley between the Five—five gray cliffs. One of them had flanked the Hareni. I hadn't been a fan of the Valley because of the solitary pilgrimage my father had imposed upon me.

As we talked, I realized how much I'd missed Cruz. Not romantically but as a friend. We used to talk so much, spend hours in each other's company.

A curl of black hair fell into his green eyes, and I lifted my fingers to brush it away, but stopped. His hair wasn't mine to brush away.

I balled my fingers, then spread them and signed, *What about girls?*

He frowned. "Girls?"

Are you seeing someone?

His features tightened. "No, Lily. Once you're safely back—"

Don't stop living because of me.

"Because you believe I can think of anything, anyone else right now?" He reached out and enveloped my hand with his. "I did this to you."

I shook my head, snatched my hand back so I could answer, *Not true. The decision wasn't just yours. It was also mine. Don't blame yourself. I certainly don't bl—*

A knock on my door made me pause mid-sentence. I got up and walked over, imagining it was Kajika, back from his run.

I guessed right.

His black hair was slicked back, wet from a shower, and he'd changed into a v-neck t-shirt that hugged his sculpted chest, and low-slung jeans that revealed the elastic waistband of his briefs.

"Are you rea—" Kajika flattened his palm against the door and shoved it open. "I am interrupting." His already rough voice turned as coarse as the bed sheets.

I shook my head. *Cruz was just filling me in on what was happening in Neverra.*

"What *is* happening in Neverra?"

Cruz stood up and slung his hands inside his leather jacket pockets. "They have a new lead on the portal lock."

They think it's an acorn, I added excitedly.

Kajika would get to see his family sooner than anticipated if my mother's information was accurate.

"A tree nut?" the hunter said, hiking up his upper lip. "Unless it is as big as one of your *calimbors*, that will not be easy to locate."

It's made of gold. Besides, we don't have acorns in Neverra, so it should stand out.

I turned around, suddenly animated with an idea. I turned toward the bed, gripped my phone and was about to type when I remembered Kajika was here. I didn't have to type or sign. All I had to do was ask him to transcribe my words out loud.

Tell Cruz to requisition everyone's jewelry.

Kajika raised a brow but spoke my silent words.

Cruz blinked at me.

Actually, tell him not to seize the jewelry, because if someone does own the acorn and knows what it is, they might hide it. Tell him to throw an Earthly nature-themed dinner where the most original jewel wins a prize. Seelies love those sorts of contests.

Kajika stared at me as though my head had been unscrewed from my neck.

Please tell him.

Shaking his head, Kajika related my thoughts.

Cruz listened. "That's a sound idea, Lily. I will organize it as soon as I get home." He began walking toward the door but paused beside me. "We arrested the faeries who attacked you, Kajika."

The hunter's eyes turned searing. "Who sent them?"

Cruz hesitated. He looked at me, as though checking if it was all right to tell him. When I shrugged, he said, "Addison Wood."

Shock rippled over Kajika's face. "Your mother did this, Lily?"

Cruz shifted to stand protectively in front of me. "Don't take it out on her, or I'll end your little trip down memory lane and fly her back to Rowan."

"Our what?"

"This excursion of yours," Cruz said.

My pulse quickened. *He assumes you took me to visit your home. Please don't tell him the real reason for our trip. He'll laugh at me...or he really will take me home.*

Cruz placed his hands on my shoulders and switched from English to Faeli. "*Vis ade dumu sua?*"

"I would *never* harm her," Kajika growled. "Unlike you."

I peeked past Cruz. *You understand Faeli?* Or had he read it from my mind?

Kajika didn't answer me. He was too busy glaring at Cruz, who'd pivoted to glare right back. Worried he might react to the hunter's implication, I stepped between them and pressed my palms into Cruz's pumping chest. It took several minutes for his heart to quiet.

When it did, I released my hold on him and signed, **Go to Neverra. Find the lock. I'm fine. I promise.**

I pressed up onto my toes to stamp a kiss on his cheek, but he turned his head, and instead of his cheek, my lips landed on his. It caught me by such surprise that I was slow to react. But so was he. When we broke apart, a new light seemed to have flicked on behind his green irises.

I touched my lips and blushed. **I'm sorry,** I signed.

A slow smile appeared on his face. "I'm not."

Oh, no, no, no… Now he wanted me. *Now?* After all those years I'd spent pining for him, he chose *now* to reciprocate. I lowered my eyes to the navy rug that had been bleached in spots.

You should go, I signed.

"I thought…" He didn't tell me what he thought. He simply cleared his throat. "I'll come back as soon as I can."

I stepped aside to let him pass. Only then did I realize Kajika was gone. Skies, I hoped he hadn't jumped to the conclusion that I'd wanted the kiss.

After Cruz left, I took a moment to regroup before crossing the narrow hallway and knocking on Kajika's door. No answer.

Was he avoiding me or had he left the motel?

I knocked again, calling out his name in my mind.

There was only silence behind the flimsy piece of wood.

Glumly I returned to my bedroom and closed the door, then leaned against it and thought about sending him a text message to ask if he still wanted to get dinner, but that would surely come off as needy. I wrapped my arms around myself and waited almost an hour before giving up hope that he would return.

Stomach as hollow as my chest, I tucked myself into bed. Even though I didn't have many nights left, I willed this one to be over quickly.

HIPPIES

$\mathcal{J}$ awakened to thunderous knocking. It sounded as though someone were trying to tear down my door. I shot into a sitting position, clenching my fingers around the abrasive cotton sheets.

I let the hunter's name slip into my mind. *Is it you?*

The pounding stopped. "Good. You are awake. I will wait in the car."

I loosed a heavy breath. What a way to get someone out of bed. I dragged the sheets off my legs and got up, pulled on the clothes I'd worn the night before, brushed my teeth and hair, then splashed water over my face. Like every morning, I inspected my lashes because those would be the first to go once my fire died. That and my hair.

Thankfully, both were still there.

I rid the hairbrush's bristles of the long blonde strands. It felt like there were more of them, but that was probably just my anxiety making me see things. I tossed all my belongings into the suitcase, zipped it up, then put on my leather jacket, baseball cap, and sunglasses, and wheeled my little bag out of the room.

I handed my key back and started for my wallet, but the clerk behind the front desk told me the bill had already been settled.

The sky was a limpid summer-blue, which had me thinking about the sun-soaked beaches lined with palm trees and turquoise water I'd researched yesterday. After Ace and Cat's Beaver Island nuptials, I would be brave and make a one-way trip out of Rowan. It would be easier on everyone if I vanished before *truly* vanishing.

No one *wanted* to see someone die.

The Porsche's engine was already rumbling when I walked toward the trunk and popped it open. I set my bag down next to Kajika's black duffle, then got into the passenger seat.

Thanks for paying for the room.

Kajika grunted, then stomped on the gas pedal.

Can we grab breakfast? I asked, as I clicked my seatbelt into place. *I'm starving.*

He didn't so much as glance my way, let alone answer.

Are you mad at me?

That won me a glance. More of a glare than a glance, really.

My pulse quickened. *You are. Why?*

"You could have told me Cruz was coming."

I had no clue.

He snorted.

I'm telling you the truth. I've had no communication with him for almost a month.

"How did he know where to find us then?"

The lady in the café tweeted I'd eaten at the place.

Kajika's jaw was as sharp as the sunlight pouring through the sunroof.

I waited for you for dinner.

The hunter side-eyed me but quickly taped his gaze back to the road.

We didn't stop for breakfast.

My stomach rumbled, and my mood flattened like the landscape. This was going to be one *long* drive. I toyed with my phone, deciding that I might as well make the most of it. I booked myself a suite in the fanciest Bahamian hotel. I considered booking a flight but decided I would use my residual fire to get down there.

An hour into the trip, he finally talked. "More Daneelies in the Bahamas?"

No.

"Then why are you going?"

I looked at him then, *really* looked at him. *Because there is nothing and no one there.*

"I do not understand."

What don't you understand, Kajika? That I'd want to be alone? How could you, of all people, not understand this? My thoughts hissed out of my mind.

"Why are you in a mood? Did you not have a pleasant night?"

A pleasant night? Are you serious?

"Your fiancé visited."

I shook my head. Kajika knew Cruz wasn't my fiancé, so I wasn't sure why he was tossing this at me. I leaned away from him. A police siren blared. Kajika didn't stop for a while, as though he thought it amusing to have the police chase after us. When he finally hit the brakes, he did it so hard the seatbelt snapped like a rubber band across my chest, almost cleaving me in half. The cop drew out his gun as he approached our vehicle.

Kajika lowered his window and waited, drumming his fingers on the sill.

"License and registration." The cop had a thick voice and an even thicker moustache.

"I do not possess either," Kajika responded calmly.

The cop's eyes almost bugged out of his head. "Put your hands in the air and get out of the vehicle."

Kajika tipped his head to the side. "You will holster your gun and get into your car, and then you will drive away and forget about this encounter."

Of course, the hunter resolved his problem with influence.

As the cop blinked, Kajika muttered, "You had a better solution?"

Not driving as fast.

Once the cop was gone, the hunter pivoted toward me, the

smooth leather seat squeaking underneath his black jeans. "It is a four-and-a-half-hour drive to Copper Harbor, and then we must search the area. Have you even considered how we will go about locating Daneelies?"

Yes. It was a lie, and of course Kajika guessed it—actually, there was no guessing involved.

"Exactly. So unless you want to be prowling around in the darkness and sleeping in another foreign bed, it is best we get there fast."

He merged back onto the road and pushed down so hard on the accelerator that I felt like I was in a *runa,* soaring over Neverra instead of inside a car, rolling over ribbons of asphalt.

Two hours and one more cop encounter later, we arrived on a peninsula of land that jutted into Lake Superior.

Take the lake road. If there are Daneelies, they'd live by the lake.

Kajika finally slowed his pace. We passed tiny town after tiny town. Some of them looked inhabited by ghosts, judging by the eerily quiet streets. We stopped several times along the way to ask about the best swimming spots—which won us many eyebrow raises, considering the season—and whether there were any tight-knit communities of people who kept to themselves.

"You mean hippies?" A woman sporting a skull-and-bones clip in bottle-black hair asked as she handed us bagels topped with lox and cream cheese.

While I bit into mine, Kajika said, "Perhaps."

She cocked a light brown eyebrow that contrasted strangely with the severe tint of her hair. I wondered if the combination of my dark brown eyebrows and wheat-blonde hair appeared as odd.

"There's this hippie community in Eagle River," she said. "A religious sect of sorts. I heard they make their money by selling drugs out of a bookstore."

I froze midbite and stared at Kajika, who stared right back. Finally, I got my jaw to work and swallowed the half-chewed piece of bread and fish.

"I never bought none or nothing. I don't do drugs. I just heard."

Her speech had turned so choppy that I speculated she'd not only bought some but used it.

Ask her if they made her want to have sex.

A hint of color darkened Kajika's bronze skin. "I cannot ask her that."

"Excuse me?" the woman asked, thinking Kajika was talking to her.

Please?

Kajika glowered. "Ask her yourself."

You know I can't do that.

"Type it." He grabbed his sandwich from the countertop and headed back out to the car.

Coward. I fished my phone out of my jacket pocket and typed, **Do those drugs have any aphrodisiac effect?**

My question made her frown. I couldn't tell if it was the form or the content that puzzled her.

The door jingled, and I thought that maybe Kajika had returned, but it was a new customer. A man with a red baseball cap. He removed his cap and scrubbed a tanned hand through a mop of copper hair.

"Did the fish bite, Jack?" the woman asked.

"Caught a couple nice-sized splakes." His gaze slid over me as he approached the counter. "Can I get a BLT, Birdie?"

"Sure thing."

I touched the woman's bony wrist, because it seemed like she'd forgotten all about me in the wake of the fisherman's entrance. She startled. I tapped my phone's screen with a fingernail.

"I told you, I've never done them," she huffed.

Jack leaned an elbow on the countertop. "What haven't you done, Birdie?"

"Nothing." Birdie was slicing through a bread roll so animatedly that crumbs flew left and right.

Jack smiled at me conspiratorially. "Maybe I've done it... What are you interested in knowing?" Although he smelled like fish guts, he was handsome, in a rugged sort of way.

I bit my lip.

"You can ask me anything."

I gave him a grateful nod and then typed: **The hippie community out in Eagle River apparently sells drugs out of a bookstore. I was just asking Birdie if they were aphrodisiacs.**

Jack's eyes seemed to become bluer as they raced over my words. When he raised them back to what he could see of my face behind the sunglasses and baseball cap, they shone with an intrigued glint.

"I'm sure with the right person, they have that effect. I believe my roommate's got some. If you want—"

The door banged open, the glass quivering in its wooden frame. "Lily," Kajika growled my name so vociferously I jumped.

Jack straightened up. "A friend of yours?"

Was Kajika a friend? He hadn't been very friendly recently.

"I am her boyfriend, so back off."

That made me turn pink.

Jack studied my body language. He must've sensed it was a lie, because he didn't *back off*. "She doesn't seem too excited to see you, man."

Kajika's fingers rolled into such tight fists that I lunged toward him and gripped his throbbing bicep.

Stop looking at him like you're going to murder him.

"Perhaps I am," he said, through gritted teeth.

Jack's eyebrows hopped around on his forehead. "Perhaps you're what?"

"Get into the car, Lily."

Ask nicely.

"Get. Into. The. Car."

I sighed annoyedly. *Fine, but, for your information, that wasn't much nicer.*

Before walking away, I typed one last thing on my phone and propped it toward Jack.

Reluctantly, he answered my query. "Forest Bookstore. Ask to see their Marvel collection. Are you sure you're okay?"

Nodding, I pitched a smile onto my face, then mouthed *thank you*.

Once I'd walked out the door, Kajika spun and strode back to the Porsche.

You really have to work on your people skills.

"What do I need people skills for?" He threw the car into reverse and then swerved back onto the lakeside road.

Well, firstly, you'd make some friends. And secondly, you'd most probably land that girl you like.

"I need neither friends nor a girl to complicate my life."

The right girl won't complicate it; she'll make it better.

"I had the right girl, and she did not make anything better. I cannot go through that again."

So you'd rather be alone? That's a pretty miserable way of thinking. I took a large bite of my bagel, watching the deep blue-gray surf foam against the shore. *We've all had our hearts broken, Kajika, but hearts heal. I would give anything to have my heart broken again because it would mean I got to love again.*

THE COMPOUND

A half hour later, we reached Eagle River. We stopped to refuel the car and then headed to Forest Bookstore. For some reason the name sounded familiar. Then again it wasn't highly original, which was probably why it sounded familiar.

The store was small and cluttered with shelves bowed beneath the weight of books. All of the ones in the window display were sun-bleached and lined with dust. Clearly, the person running the shop was not in the business of selling books.

A bald, middle-aged man with a sharp jaw set down the John Grisham book he was reading and stepped out from behind his register. "Can I help you?"

Ask them about their Marvel collection.

The hunter's gaze tightened on the man. Was he trying to tell if he was Daneelie? I wondered if he could. I certainly had no way of telling. They didn't have a distinctive smell like hunters, or a distinctive glow like faeries.

"We are interested in your Marvel collection," Kajika finally said.

The man's eyebrows slanted. "Any specific comic you're looking for? X-men? Thor? Spiderman?"

Kajika glanced down at me.

Tell him we want to see the entire collection.

Kajika gave voice to my silent demand.

The man tilted his head, the naked bulb over the register glinting off his smooth skull. "How did you hear about our *collection*?"

"From a fisherman back in Bete Grise."

The seller absent-mindedly thumbed the spine of the book he'd been reading before returning behind the register. Something beeped and then clanked. A safe.

"Where you two from?" the man asked, his attention on whatever was inside the safe. Only his shoulders shifted as he leafed through his stash. They were impressively wide.

Swimmer shoulders…

Daneelie shoulders?

"Rowan," Kajika said.

The man glanced up, hazel eyes flaring. "You don't say. Small world."

"You know Rowan?" Kajika asked.

He flicked his attention back to his safe. "I know of it." A soft clunk echoed in the small bookstore. He sighed, then placed both his palms on the counter, as if to show us he wasn't wielding a weapon. "I'm all out of Marvels, but I'll receive a shipment this afternoon. Why don't you two come back then?"

He's suspicious of us.

Kajika took a couple steps forward. I caught his arm, knowing that if he acted all tough and spooky, it wouldn't help our case.

The man didn't move, didn't cower. He simply locked his gaze on the hunter's.

"We cannot come back. Direct us to the hippies, and we will leave."

The man snorted. "They don't allow visitors."

Kajika's eyes took on that inhuman gleam. "Forget we are from Rowan and take us there now."

The man frowned, fine wrinkles scrunching his tanned skin. He nodded deeply as though an anchor hung around his neck, and then he walked toward the bookstore's door. He flipped the sign to *Closed,* then held the door for us. As we passed by him, I caught him studying the whorls of captive dust that peeked through the open collar of Kajika's black t-shirt.

"Nice tattoo." He unhooked his keys from his belt buckle and locked up. "Does it symbolize anything?"

"That I am strong."

I cocked up an eyebrow. *Really? You couldn't have thought of another meaning? That's just going to freak the man out.*

Kajika didn't even spare me a passing glance. "We will follow you in our car."

The man zipped up his sleeveless vest. "No unfamiliar vehicles are allowed onto the compound."

Sensing Kajika was about to influence him again, I placed my hand on the hunter's arm. *Let him take us there. If we drive, it'll arouse suspicion. If anything happens, you'll run us back.*

"How far is your home?" Kajika asked.

"'Bout a mile." The man placed a hand on the hood of a rusted red Camaro, and then walked over to the driver's side and unlocked the vehicle.

Kajika folded the front passenger seat. After I settled in the back, he snapped the seat straight and got in.

"I'm Quinn, by the way. Quinn Thompson," he said, a couple minutes into the drive. "And you are?"

Don't give our real names.

"I am Tom, and she is Alice."

I wrinkled my nose. Had he really needed to use the deceased huntress's name for me? Granted, he'd used another deceased hunter's name for himself. *Stellar imagination.*

He turned his head a quarter inch, enough for me to see his pinched expression.

"Have you been living on the compound long, Quinn?"

"I moved there a couple months ago."

I gripped Kajika's headrest to scoot in closer.

"And the others?" Kajika asked.

"What about the others?"

"Are they from here?"

"You are a very curious person."

"Tell me about the others." Kajika's voice had turned tinny and rigid. He was influencing Quinn again.

"Most were born and raised in Eagle River."

"Why Eagle River?"

The man frowned. "Because it's their home."

"Why did they allow *you* into the compound?"

"'Cause I'm related to them."

He hung a left, then drove down a dusty path that ended in a corroded, gaping gate. He got out of the car and shoved the gate wide, then he got back behind the wheel and drove down a sinuous road lined with old campers. A group of small children, dressed in scraps of clothes topped with down jackets that had been mended more than once, stopped playing ball to watch the Camaro.

"Uncle Quinn," one of them squealed, running behind the car.

Quinn lowered his window and waved. "Don't come too close now, Joshua." He slowed just in case.

The kid, a small, pale-haired boy that looked like he'd showered in freckles, gave the car a wider berth before stopping. "Uncle Quinn's got people in the car," I heard him say before we sped down the road.

After another couple minutes, Quinn turned right and slowed before coming to a complete stop in front of the only building that wasn't on wheels. It was made from a hodgepodge of shipping crates. Yellow, red, and green boxes had been parked next to each other. Over them stretched a flat roof made of sheet metal and plastic tarp tied down with what looked like fishing wire.

The sound of our car doors shutting had a tall, skinny woman exiting through the opening of a red crate.

"Charlotte, I've got two customers who'd like to purchase a Marvel comic."

She stared unblinkingly in the direction of Quinn. "You brought strangers here?"

"I—I..." He glanced at us, seemingly confounded by our presence. "Seems like I did."

"You know the rules," she said.

Quinn rubbed the back of his bald head.

Tell her we insisted.

"Why does our presence unsettle you so?" Kajika asked instead.

I sucked in a breath. *She'll toss us out now!*

The little kids, who'd been playing ball, careened toward us, gray dust puffing around their rubber Crocs. All of them panted hard. Some doubled over, palms against thighs.

Charlotte angled her face toward the hunter. "Because visitors aren't allowed on our property." Instead of his face, her gaze set on his chest. She was probably taking in his breadth and bulk, weighing the outcome of turning him away.

Quinn scrubbed his neck. "Excuse my cousin. We don't have many visitors."

Her hands skidded off her hips. "We have *no* visitors. Quinn knows this, which makes me wonder why he brought you here. Did you threaten him?"

"Threaten him?" Kajika's arms pulsed. I caught ahold of one of his hands and pinned it down. "We are not ill-intentioned."

The hunter's muscle jostled underneath my clenched fingers. I had to compress his arm so hard my fingernails surely imprinted tiny crescents into his skin, in spite of his thick thermal top.

Just ask her for the drugs and tell her we'll be on our way.

"We came for your Marvel collection." He shrugged his arm out of my grip and took out a bundle of cash, peeling bills from the batch. "How much does it cost?"

"We're all out," Charlotte said.

Quinn gaped at his cousin.

She's lying.

As Kajika returned the cash to his pocket, he leveled his gaze on hers, or at least he tried to. It was as though she didn't dare look into his eyes, because she knew what he could do.

He approached her. Finally her gaze landed on his.

"You will give us some of the drugs you make," he said with that magical authority of his.

Her tapered nostrils pulsed with annoyed breaths. "I told you... we are all out."

Kajika frowned, but I didn't, because I suddenly understood why his influence hadn't worked.

She's blind.

"Now, Quinn, please escort them off the compound," Charlotte said.

Quinn, who was ruffling the little blond boy's hair, froze. "Um. Okay."

"Could I get a glass of water before we leave?" Kajika asked. "My throat is parched."

I hitched up an eyebrow that got lost in my baseball cap.

"Josh, can you get them a glass of water, please?" Quinn asked.

"Sure thing." He traipsed toward Charlotte, then past her. "Watch out, Mom."

Charlotte instinctually placed her hand on the top of his head as he came back out, carrying a plastic cup filled to the brim with water. "Slowly, Josh. Don't spill."

The little boy moved at a snail's pace after that. It was sort of funny actually, even though I could sense the hunter was growing exasperated.

Are you really thirsty?

"No," Kajika murmured.

Once Joshua reached Kajika, he proffered the cup. "You're really tall."

"And you are very short."

I elbowed Kajika.

"What? I was short once too. And then I grew." He took the glass from the little boy. "And so will you, Joshua."

"You speak funny," the little boy continued.

"So I have been told."

"Why doesn't your lady-friend talk?"

"She cannot."

Josh's little forehead furrowed as he swayed his head toward me. "Why not?"

"Same reason your mother cannot see."

Josh turned toward his mother, then back toward us. "Mom was born that way."

"My lady-friend was born that way, too." Kajika took a sip and then returned the glass to Josh, but the cup slid and sloshed over the boy's upturned face.

The boy let out a high-pitched squeal.

"What?" Charlotte raced toward her son's side. For someone who couldn't see, she was incredibly aware of her surroundings.

"The tall man dropped his water on me."

I dug a tissue from my bag and was about to dry him off when Kajika stilled my wrist.

"I am deeply sorry for my clumsiness, Joshua."

Charlotte turned those unblinking eyes of hers on the hunter.

Kajika wasn't a clumsy person. What he'd done was deliberate. Was he trying to anger the already irate mother?

Charlotte wiped her son's face with her sleeve. "Go get changed, Joshua. I don't want you catching a cold."

He nodded and then scampered away. The other children who'd accompanied him stayed put, ogling us with various degrees of curiosity.

"When will you have more Marvels available?" Kajika asked.

Charlotte directed her spooky gaze at me even though I hadn't been the one to speak. I took a small step back. Even though she was no taller than I was, she was remarkably intimidating.

"You will not let it go, will you?" she asked.

"Once I set my sights on something, I do not let go."

She exhaled an exasperated breath. "Wait here then. Quinn, stay with them."

He shot us a sheepish look. "My cousin is very authoritative."

"I had a sister who was the same," Kajika said.

The hunter never spoke about his family. Cat had told me they'd been murdered, along with Kajika's entire clan, by faeries who wanted to take over the tribal land. Was Manistique the land in question?

"Yes," he breathed without looking away from the entrance through which Charlotte had disappeared.

What was the water about?

"Later," he mumbled.

Charlotte returned holding a brown paper bag, which she handed to Kajika.

He peeked inside. "How much do we owe you?"

"Fifty dollars."

Kajika drew his wad of cash back out and placed a fifty into her palm.

She stroked the bill as though to ascertain it was the correct amount. "Get these folks off our land, Quinn." And then she was gone.

Quinn cocked his head to the Camaro. "Let's go."

As we drove off the compound, I spotted a yellow minivan parking by one of the trailers. A teenage girl with strong shoulders and hair so blonde it was almost white got out of the driver's side. She frowned at us as we passed.

Clearly these people *never* had visitors.

None of us spoke during the ride back to the gas station. It was only once we were in the cover of our own car that Kajika finally said, "The water was to see if the boy had scales."

Cat didn't have scales until she visited Neverra.

"But Cat wasn't pure Daneelie."

Well, did you see anything?

"The boy did not even glimmer."

Cat doesn't shine unless she's in the lake.

"Perhaps, but if they do not shine, then these drugs we bought are not Daneelie scales." He tossed the paper bag onto my lap.

I uncrumpled the bag and extricated a small plastic Ziploc. Inside the baggie was powder the shade of sunset. It didn't glimmer like the one I'd once tried in Neverra on my seventy-fifth birthday— my fifteenth human year—but perhaps Daneelies didn't shine like they did in Neverra.

The sight of the powder brought me back to the eve of my birthday, which had fallen on Middle-Month. With Nadia and Eleonor, my two closest friends back then, we'd headed to the marketplace for some shopping.

We'd sipped sparkling wine while we tried on every jewel crafted by the *calidum*. Even though my mother's vault was full of real jewels, most Earth-made, I favored Neverrian-made ones. Not because they were prettier—they weren't—but because courtiers were sheep who followed in the steps of the royal family. By supporting Neverrian crafts, I was sending a message to the younger generation. They would all flock to the marketplace to purchase what the princess had worn.

In the *runa* that had taken us back to the palace, Nadia and Eleonor had handed me a wooden box—my birthday present. I opened it assuming it was a piece of jewelry, but nestled against burgundy velvet was a tiny vial filled with a powder that twinkled like ground metal. Nadia had told me Daneelie scales would turn me into an irresistible vixen.

On the night of the party, I'd rubbed it against my gums, thinking this was it, the moment I would graduate from baby sister to sexy fiancée. The only thing the powder did was make me desire Cruz more and him want me less, especially after I threw myself at him like a crazed harlot. Even though years had gone by, my heart still shriveled up with shame each time I thought of that night.

I unzipped the baggie, touched my pinkie to my tongue to wet it, then dipped it into the powder. I took a steadying breath as I raised my finger back to my lips. What if it was Daneelie scales? What if I came onto Kajika?

Wasn't I pathetic enough?

The hunter pulled the car to an abrupt halt on the side of the road and grabbed my wrist. Before I could react, he stuck my finger inside his own mouth and sucked off the ground powder.

Shock wasn't a strong enough word to describe the emotion detonating through me. Even after he'd let go, I was still so trans-fixed by his lips that my hand hung limply in midair.

"It tastes like wet earth. Is that what it is supposed to taste like, Lily?"

I swallowed, finally lowering my hand and tucking it between my knees. *No. It should taste like metal. Do you feel any different?*

He raked his hair back. "No."

Emboldened by the fact that he'd taken some and it hadn't affected him, I dipped my still-wet pinkie inside and brought it to my mouth. This time, I touched the powder to my tongue. Instead of dissolving, the substance turned as cakey as wet clay. I gagged, incredibly tempted to spit, but if Kajika had kept it down, so could I.

It's definitely not Daneelie scales.

Like the rancid powder, my deflated hope left a sour taste in my mouth. I pressed the Ziploc closed and tossed it into the paper bag.

Kajika placed his hand on top of mine. His skin was so dark, especially now that I was so pallid. "Do not lose hope, Lily."

I kept my gaze lowered, working on corralling my disappointment.

"We will drive around the coastline. Perhaps we will locate *Mishipeshu*."

I sighed. This hunt for water faeries had been nothing more than a wild goose chase. I removed my hand from underneath Kajika's and nestled it in my lap, and then I stared out the window at the portion of Lake Superior visible between two houses. The surface was just the slightest bit rippled, like poorly ironed linens.

"Could they possibly live *in* the water, Lily? Like fish?"

I squinted at the expanse of water. Could they? And if they did, how could we go about finding them? It wasn't as though we could go exploring Lake Superior's depths at this time of year.

"I have an idea." He turned the car around and started driving back the way we'd come.

THE BOAT

A couple minutes later, we parked next to a harbor where tarp-covered boats bobbed like corks around a cement dock.

Are we stealing a boat? I asked, unstrapping myself.

"I do not care to have my nose chopped," the hunter deadpanned.

His answer was so absurd I tilted an eyebrow.

"That is what happened to Gottwa thieves," he explained, getting out of the car.

I followed him, his long legs eating up the dock so fast I had to speedwalk to catch up. Few people were out, aside from a couple fishermen tying up their boats or cleaning them. We approached a ruddy-faced man who was sorting through flashy fishing lures like a pirate combing through a treasure chest.

"We would like to borrow your boat."

The man raised his eyes toward us, inspected our faces, and then he snorted and returned to untangling his tackle.

"We will offer you compensation."

The man stopped what he was doing and looked up again. "I don't rent out my boat."

"Get out of your boat and hand over your key."

The man blinked as he stood. Brow furrowed, he jumped out of his boat, then dug a key out of the back pocket of his jeans and deposited it into Kajika's outstretched hand.

Kajika took his wad of cash out and peeled off two hundreds. "I will leave two more bills like these and your keys in that box"—he nodded toward the fishing lures—"tomorrow morning. Now walk away."

The man nodded docilely before ambling down the dock. Not once did he look back at us.

Kajika vaulted inside the boat then extended his hand to help me climb in.

I caught hold of his hand. *And the adventure continues...*

A tight smile tugged at his lips. He didn't let go right away; nor did I. No other place on our bodies touched, and yet it felt like we were connected everywhere. Perhaps it was the way he gazed down at me, black pupils so dilated they obscured the brown depths of his irises.

"I feel...strange." His voice was low, coarse, like raw silk.

I took inventory of my own body. I also felt *different*—slightly more carefree and mellow.

"Do you think they could have been Daneelie scales?"

Daneelie scales awaken the senses rather than dull them. What we're experiencing is more of a mallow-high, but since hunters are impervious to mallow, and it only grows in Neverra, I suspect that what we took was an Earthly drug. Pot or something harder. Probably something harder.

Kajika lowered his gaze to the tackle box.

You're feeling calm, right? Equally blissful and lethargic?

"Yes," he said so softly I almost missed it.

He didn't move for a long minute, but then he let go of my hand and proceeded to free the boat from its mooring. And then he swung up the ladder to the cockpit. The boat hummed to life and then it slid out of its slip. I stayed a moment on the stern, watching the harbor shrink and shrink as we maneuvered away from it, and then I climbed up to the cockpit.

How do you know how to drive a boat?

"Blake." Without taking his gaze off the horizon, he added, "I do not like losing control."

We didn't take much. It'll wear off fast.

He squared his shoulders. "How come you know so much about drugs?" Disapproval rang so loudly in his words that it spoiled my fragile high.

Because mallow helps with depression. For years, I was severely depressed.

"What did you have to be depressed about? You were a princess. You never wanted for anything."

I bristled, and the backs of my thighs hit the plastic siding of the boat. *Because everything was handed to me, you think I was happy?*

"I did not mean that." He scrubbed a broad hand over his face, pushing away his long bangs.

I thought you knew me, Kajika, but you still think I'm a spoiled little faerie brat who gets everything she wants. Well, newsflash, ventor—

Sure enough, the Faeli word for hunter made Kajika stiffen, which was my intention. Silly, but I wanted to hurt him like he'd just hurt me.

I never got anything or anyone I wanted. Never. And now...now I'm running out of time. I tried to steady my breathing, but my lungs pumped hectically. I crossed my arms. *This is stupid. We should just go back to Rowan.* A tear slid down my cheek. Instead of wiping it away, I spun my face away from the hunter so he wouldn't see how pathetic I was.

"Lily—"

Don't. Just drive the boat back to the harbor. I want to return to Rowan.

"No."

What do you mean, no?

"I am not taking you back to Rowan yet."

Fine...then I'll just fly back.

Before I could even buoy up, one of his arms snaked around my waist and crushed my back to his chest.

"Stay, Lily. I am sorry. Like you said, I have no manners."

His arm tightened around me as though he didn't trust his apology would get me to stay. He was right not to trust it.

I *really* wanted to leave.

Why?

"Why what?"

I was still facing out. The lake, like my mood, had gotten brisker. Whitecaps now dotted the dark water, and gray, almost purple, clouds obscured the bright blue sky. The weather had shifted so fast that for a second I thought I might have a little Daneelie blood in me —only Daneelies could control the water, and thus the weather— but I knew for a fact that I was pure Seelie. If I'd been even a little Daneelie, I could've survived on Earth.

Give me a reason to stay.

His heart hammered against my spine, setting his brand aglow. Sure enough, even though my fingers were squashed against my elbow, my palm shone like a sun choked by clouds.

You can't think of a single one, can you?

The boat bumped against the choppy water, and cold spray whipped my cheeks. The wind was so strong it caught in my hair and tossed it every which way, and then it flipped my black cap off my head. It bobbed in the v-shaped trail of foam behind the boat before vanishing beneath the water.

"I stayed for you."

I frowned. *You stayed where for me?*

"I did not go to Neverra with my tribe because I did not want to leave you."

His confession jolted me.

"I want to give you everything you want, Lily. I just do not know how to." Kajika's arm loosened but didn't fall away from my waist. "But I am trying."

I held incredibly still, barely daring to breathe. Wind roared around me, and a fierce gust snatched my sunglasses and dropped them into the lake.

"I am failing, though."

I whirled around. His face came in and out of focus. He brushed away a strand of hair that had blown into my eyes, and then he dragged those calloused fingers of his down my cheek.

His skin gleamed with droplets from the lake. "You are delicate, Lily, and I am rough. You are sweet, and I am not."

My arms untangled and knocked against my hips.

A wave knocked into the boat. Even though Kajika flung out an arm to catch me, I flailed backward, and my back hit the metal railing so hard it tore my breath from my lungs.

"Lily!" he yelled, trying to get to me, but the boat tipped and threw him against the throttle.

As the boat jerked forward, I wrapped my fingers around the railing to keep myself upright.

We pitched over the crest of a wave and smashed down so hard Kajika was hurled against the railing. He inched closer to me as the boat tipped again. Finally he reached me and gripped the railing on either side of me, shielding my body with his.

He gritted his teeth as the boat banged against the fierce water. "Fly back to land."

I unhooked my fingers from the railing and wrapped them around him.

"No. Do not carry me. It will be too taxing. I will swim."

Like hell, I would let him swim in this freak storm.

He tore my hands off his waist. "GO!"

Not without you.

"I cannot drown. Do not worry."

The boat dropped over another wave and hit a bulge of water at an awry angle. I tried to grab onto the railing again, but my slick fingers slid off the chrome, and then I went airborne, and not because I was flying, but because I was falling.

"Lily!" Kajika yelled, diving in after me.

The frothing water felt like a wall of bricks and turned my whole world black for a moment. I blinked just as something sharp walloped my head and shoved me beneath the surface. I tried to swim but couldn't distinguish up from down. I blew out air bubbles, but instead of showing me the way to follow, they vanished in the frenzied surf and compressed my lungs.

I began to panic then.

I can't drown. I can't drown.

But I also couldn't breathe underwater. I'd eventually float up, but without oxygen, I would pass out. How long could my body bob atop the frigid lake before it extinguished my fire?

I combed my hands through the water hysterically, trying to move upward, but something banded around my middle and tugged me back.

Kajika had me. I was going to be okay.

When I broke the surface, I gulped in air as though my life depended on it. A wave sloshed into my face, whipped against my open eyes. I shut them but not before seeing something that made the hairs on the nape of my neck rise.

Kajika's body drifted face down, his black hair eddying around his prostrate form like seaweed. If *he* wasn't holding me, then who was?

14

THE SAVIOR

I tried to turn, but the arm dragged me beneath the careening surface. As I was towed away, I screamed Kajika's name in my mind, praying it would jolt him awake.

Again, I tried to twist around to see the face of the swimmer who'd saved me. I assumed it was a Coast Guard, but wouldn't they have a boat? Maybe they couldn't take boats out in this weather.

My savior hauled me back into the murky depths of Lake Superior and then back up and then back down, up and down. I tried to pry their arm off my abdomen, but my fingers were so numb they were useless.

The arm tightened around my middle. My stomach clenched and throbbed. At some point, I threw up, and the jet of warm vomit hit my face and blended with my hair before ribboning off me.

Lightning streaked the steel-gray sky, and icy rain battered the muscular lake. Whoever was propelling me through its opaque blueness accelerated, swimming so fast it felt as though we were soaring.

A crashing sound alerted me that we were in proximity to land. The arm unwrapped from around me so suddenly I sank. But I didn't go deep. My boots hit sand. The lake sucked me back, but then shoved me forward and spit me out onto a bank of sand that felt like solid rock.

My head thudded as I coughed and sputtered. I dragged my knees underneath me and pressed my palms into the gritty sand, but toppled when I attempted to right myself. Thankfully I was still close to the ground, and the blow wasn't as debilitating as it could've been if I'd been upright.

I rolled onto my back to catch my breath. The rain needled my exposed skin and drummed against the packed sand while huge waves crashed at my feet and hissed around my waterlogged jeans.

I started spasming violently, from the shock of the accident and from the terrible cold. A shadow fell over me. Not a shadow. A person.

Kajika?

I stilled.

The figure crouched over me. Long, pale hair dripped water onto me. I scrubbed at my eyes, getting sand into them. Even though it was as dark as night, light rippled over the girl's face.

Thunder shook the ground, or maybe I was trembling so hard it felt like the thunder had penetrated the beach.

Tendrils of steam danced around my face as my fire responded to the cold rain.

"You have finally found us," she said, a note of wariness in her tone. "Cole, get the iron chain!"

No! Please no. She wouldn't hear my silent plea. *Kajika!*

I turned my head to scan the beach for him. If they'd saved me, then they must've saved him. The girl gripped my chin and pinned my head down. Lightning scarred the darkness and reflected on her skin like a torch over a faceted diamond.

I blinked and blinked. Had her shininess been an illusion?

"Cole!" she barked.

"I'm coming. I'm coming. Geez, give me a sec."

The girl stood and stepped back. And then another face loomed over mine—this time a man's. More of a boy than a man. The jaw was too narrow to belong to an adult male. Cole—I guessed—gathered my wrists and wound a chain around them, then secured the links with a padlock. I gritted my teeth and wriggled to slide my leather sleeves between the chain cuffs and my skin, but I failed miserably, exposing more of my wrists to the metal. My skin blistered and smoked.

"Shit. It's burning her," Cole said.

"Duh. That's the whole point. Relax, it won't kill her."

Headlights sliced through the thick darkness and caught Cole's forehead. Like the girl's, his skin sparkled. His eyes widened when he saw me studying him, and he scooted away from the light.

He yanked hard on the chain, bringing me to my feet, and then his hands cinched around my ribcage, and he hoisted me onto his shoulder, where I settled like a ragdoll. As the chain slid down over the backs of my hands, tears sprang up and coursed over my forehead, mixing into my stringy hair.

I didn't squirm, didn't hit him, didn't fly away. I was tired and in too much pain to put up a fight. Besides I wanted to go wherever these people were going.

I'd come searching for Daneelies, but instead of finding them, they'd found me.

15

THE CHAIN

*C*ole shoved me in the back of a van loaded with surfboards, oars, and stacks of wetsuits. I scooted into a sitting position and scanned the dark confines for another body, but there was no other body.

The boy hopped inside and sat opposite me while the blonde got behind the steering wheel.

I mouthed the word *stop*, but the only reaction I got was an eyebrow raise from Cole. I mouthed the word again.

The van rumbled to life and then jolted as it maneuvered from the beach to the road.

"I think she's trying to say something, Kiera!" he yelled.

"She can't talk, you idiot."

The boy's forehead scrunched.

A cell phone rang up front. Kiera picked up. "Yeah?...What do you mean the iron isn't working on him?"

Him. Kajika... They had Kajika. He was alive! Not that he could've drowned, but I was still imagining him bobbing face down in the lake, alone in the vast darkness. As though he heard me sigh his name, my palm glowed, which caught Cole's curious gaze. I rolled my fingers closed.

"Yeah, it worked on her," Kiera was saying.

"Her hand is glowing," Cole said. "What does that mean, Kiera?"

Kiera spun in her seat. "That she's trying to use her magic dust! Wind some chain around her neck. That'll teach her not to threaten us. And put on a mask."

I whimpered and shook my head.

Cole strapped a mask to his face, then pulled out another length of chain from underneath the pile of life jackets.

"His hand is glowing too?" she barked into the phone. "Fuck. You got a mask?...Wrap your shirt around your nose and mouth."

As Cole inched toward me, I rammed my back into the wall of the truck. Tears trickled out the corners of my eyes as I shook my head beseechingly.

Kiera pulled the van to such an abrupt halt I was thrown sideways. The metal chain around my wrists jostled and burned new patches of skin, and the sharp plastic edge of a paddle rammed into my ribs. She stuck the van in park, then climbed into the back and crouched next to me. Even though her hair was still wet, her clothes were dry. How I longed to get out of my soggy outfit.

"What exactly is your friend?" she asked.

I tore my gaze off her cotton hoodie and looked at her. Kiera shoved her cell phone into my hands, but I couldn't grip it, and it fell. She grumbled, then swiped it off my lap and pushed it again toward my hands.

"Type or you're getting a new necklace. What the fuck is your friend?"

I didn't even attempt to move my fingers. They were too numb anyway. Besides there was no way I was sharing what Kajika was with them. Not until they showed me some decency.

Kiera flicked my cheek to get my attention. "Type!"

I wanted to launch my dust into her face. Not to kill her, just to subdue her surliness, but my hands were useless stumps.

Cole touched Kiera's shoulder. "Maybe she's deaf too, sis."

So Kiera was Cole's sister. Her eyes were as dark as his, yet they seemed darker.

"Nah. She can hear fine." She pocketed her phone. "Your fault we'll have to torture the truth out of him," she said before climbing back into the driver's seat and setting off again. "Collar her."

Grimacing, Cole slid the iron chain around my neck. The acrid stench of burning flesh made my eyes water. I concentrated on keeping my hands as still as possible, which was a feat in a moving vehicle. The skin around the chain had bubbled, some had even flaked off, and pale smoke puffed from the open sores.

A peal of thunder echoed outside, making me jump. Every chain on my body shifted, and I hissed. More tears fell down my cheeks and evaporated, blending with the smoke curling from my wounds. My father used to say crying was the most terrible sort of weakness.

He'd tried to toughen me up one year. I was to trek from the valley surrounded by the five cliffs back to the palace with *lustriums* for my only source of light. If I took to the sky, or if the sun peeked before I reached the palace, the lone royal guard hovering overhead had the order to carry me back to the departure point. All Wood heirs went through that pilgrimage, but until me, the heirs had all been male. Never had a woman, let alone a girl, completed the strenuous journey where wild *capra* slithered along the rock, their rubbery skin slick with a substance that could paralyze their prey for days, and where flocks of *quila* circled the sky in search of flesh to peck with their curved beaks.

During my first attempt, I'd climbed the stone ledges, scraping my knees and elbows on the pale-gray rock, while fighting off a pair of mated *quila* with my dust. I lost my first fight, and had to start over in the Valley. The second time, I killed the eagle-like beast, but a few ledges from the top of the cliff, I encountered a nest of *capra*. The creatures drove me to the edge of the rocky shelf, which crumbled, sending me flailing all the way back down into the Valley. Had I not been a faerie, I would've died on impact.

And I'd cried because I would have to make camp and then start my trek over at sundown. I'd been desperate to forfeit, and I tried, but my father wouldn't hear of it. Cruz and Ace had flown over the

Valley, but they'd been ordered not to approach me, so they watched me from their perch in the sky.

On the fifth night, I reached the plateau at the top. Pride enveloped me, and for a moment, I'd allowed myself a moment of respite under the ancient *panem* tree. I'd sat against its thick, twisted trunk, which was the color of wet clay, and nibbled its iridescent leaves. I remembered thinking they were the most delicious food I'd ever tasted. As juice ran down my chin, I took in the vast kingdom that my family had ruled over for generations. The mist almost kissed the ground, which made the view from atop startling. It also made adrenaline churn in the pit of my stomach, for to reach the palace, I had to cross the Hareni. Like all Seelies, I'd been taught Unseelies were the creatures of nightmares, more dangerous than *diles*, and *quila*, and *capra*.

I set out again, knowing that if I didn't reach the palace before sunup, it would be game over. The *lucionaga* would carry me back to the Valley, and I would have to begin again.

I skidded down the steep bank with caution but fell so many times I bled smoke like a faulty plane engine. The deep amethyst sky had lightened to a pearlescent lavender by the time I arrived at the edge of the Hareni. Keeping my gaze glued to the grotto-like entrance of the underground Unseelie prison, I raced through the coppery sand dunes.

The sun spiked over the horizon before I made it back home.

I was transported back to the Valley. It took me four more Neverrian nights to complete the treacherous pilgrimage. I reached the palace on the Night of Mist, Unseelie specters whirling around my battered body. Unlike most of the Seelies, Ace had waited for me outside the palace walls. He'd swung me around when I reached the floating garden, telling me how proud he was of me.

But my father, who hadn't come out to greet me, was ashamed. Never had it taken a Wood heir nine days to complete the hike! I was an embarrassment to the family, unfit to carry the name. Thank the skies, I would marry and take my husband's name someday, he'd proclaimed.

As I sat in the van, chains scorching my skin, I experienced deep gratitude for the man who'd nurtured me with cruelty and indifference. If I could survive in the Neverrian wilderness alone, I could survive whatever these two Daneelies had in store for me.

Unless they used their dust...

The car lurched to a stop. When the back doors grated open, I squinted to see into the darkness, but the dense rain screened off the world.

"I'm gonna carry you again, okay?" Cole said right before his hands scooped me off the floor of the van. He hopped out, then tossed me over his shoulder.

The chain skidded down my throat, searing the underside of my jaw. I bit down hard on my tongue to squelch a rising scream.

Mud slurped around the boy's bare feet, and his shorts and t-shirt were plastered to his skin. I wondered if he'd also been swimming or if the rain had soaked him.

The damp earth beneath his feet turned to concrete, and then we were out of the rain and inside a dark warehouse. Strings of Christmas tree lights were duct-taped to the ceiling and offered a faint glow. A brighter, almost green, light burned in the back of the warehouse. I squinted to make out what it was shining on. Dirty plastic tarp curtained off whatever occupied that space.

Thunder clapped through the dusky chamber, while rain pounded on the tin roof like mallets on a percussion.

Cole turned a corner, and then slid me off his brawny yet bony shoulder. The chains settled back on the strips of skin that had started healing, singeing them anew.

The air inside was almost as frigid as the air outside, but at least it was dry. In the semi-obscurity, I noticed Cole gather an armful of chain. I stared in horror at him, assuming he was about to cocoon me in iron, and shrank backward until my tailbone hit a wall.

"It's okay. I'm not going to hurt you."

Not going to hurt me? Did he not realize how much pain I was in?

He grabbed the piece of chain dangling from my shackles and

hooked it to the new portion with another padlock. Only then did I realize the new length of clinking links was bolted to the wall.

They'd chained me up like a rabid dog.

Steam puffed in the air between us, mixed with the smoke of my barbecued flesh.

"You really have fire in your veins." Cole gaped at the water evaporating from my clothes. "I heard you can fly. Why didn't you…when the boat sank?"

Because I'd been too paralyzed with shock. And then his sister— or was it he?—had grabbed me. I thought it had been to save me, but that hadn't been their intention. People who saved others didn't treat them like prisoners.

Footsteps resounded next to us. I peered past Cole and straight into a face with unseeing eyes that had somehow managed to see what I was.

16

THE INTERROGATION

"And so you have found us," Charlotte said. "How did you find us?"

"She can't talk, Ma," Cole said.

Ma? Cole was her son? I looked from mother to son but didn't see much of a resemblance. Where Charlotte's hair was a graying-black, Cole was as blond as his sister.

"I know she can't talk, Cole."

He blushed and mumbled, "Sorry."

Charlotte kept staring unnervingly at me.

"Where's Kiera?" Cole asked.

"With Quinn and the girl's friend. Trying to get some answers."

"Did he bring him to—"

Charlotte silenced him with a glare. I swear, if it weren't for the way her lids so rarely came down, I would never have guessed she was blind. "Would you like me to draw out a map so the girl can go to him?"

Cole tucked a piece of longish hair behind his ear and garbled another apology.

Little did they know I didn't need a map. All I needed was to concentrate on his location the next time my brand flared to life.

Charlotte took a step toward me. "Are more of you coming?"

I shook my head.

"Negative," Cole translated.

"What do you want with us?" Charlotte continued.

I stood there unmoving, facing mother and son, all at once dripping water onto the dusty floor and steaming. How was I supposed to answer them without the use of my hands?

"Ma, she can't talk," Cole said sheepishly.

"Get her a pen and a paper."

I didn't dare hope the pen and paper would lead to the removal of my iron cuffs.

Cole's quick footsteps resonated in the low-ceilinged complex. The wall next to Charlotte was red and the one behind me was yellow. We were in the shipping-crate building. Not that it would help me escape, but it comforted me to know where I was.

Cole returned with a pad of lined yellow paper and a ballpoint pen. He extended them to me. I tipped my chin to my shackles.

"Ma, she'll need her hands to write. Should I take off the chains?"

"Not yet. I don't trust her not to use her dust on us." She circled around me, giving me a wide berth. "Your friend doesn't react to iron, but one of his hands glows with dust, and he can control minds with sight and voice? Is he a new breed of faerie?"

"Ma—"

"I know she can't talk, Cole. I'm just thinking out loud."

She drummed her fingers against her calf-length, khaki skirt. It was snagged in places and bleached an ochre color on the hem. Not that I think she minded. One, she couldn't see, and two, this community lived simply.

Loud, rushed footsteps beat the cement floor.

Charlotte stopped pacing and turned toward the noise. It was coming from the opposite end of the crate complex.

I inhaled a sharp breath. Was Kajika coming?

No such luck. It was Quinn.

"The son of a bitch tried to strangle me with his chains." Quinn was puffing hard, his face as red as cherry juice. "He's fucking strong, too." He stopped a few feet in front of me, and his upper lip hiked up. "What the fuck is he?"

"I don't know yet," Charlotte replied calmly. "Perhaps a mix of human and faerie. Did you blindfold him?"

"I did better than that...I duct-taped his fucking eyes shut," Quinn snarled. "*And* his mouth."

Quinn had a death wish. Once Kajika broke free—because there was no doubt in my mind he would—he would kill Quinn.

"I didn't appreciate being turned into a puppet." Spittle flew from his mouth and glimmered in the air.

"Did you leave Kiera alone with him?"

"No. Pete and Tamara are there too," Quinn said.

"Did you secure the perimeter?"

"Yes."

Securing it so we couldn't break out, or so that if anyone came looking for us, they wouldn't be able to get in? How I hoped someone would be coming for us. Preferably Cat. She was like them. They'd listen to her. They'd release us and see we weren't their enemy. I sent a silent—surely useless—prayer up into the sky.

"Ma, get back. Her palm's glowing." Cole reached for his mother's arm and pulled her back. He raised the dive mask that was dangling around his neck back onto his face.

"I thought you said iron would nullify her dust," Kiera said, suddenly there again.

"Apparently we thought wrong," Quinn said.

I curled my fingers into a tight fist. The iron had numbed all the area surrounding the chain, so I couldn't feel the bond, but the sight of it almost made me weep. I tried to concentrate on his location, but all I got from our link was that he was close.

"If you attack us, we will kill your friend," Charlotte said calmly. "And we will make you watch."

I must've gotten noticeably paler, because Kiera smirked. "So he can be killed..."

Had she deduced this from my complexion? At least she didn't know how, or she wouldn't have looked for validation in my expression. She would've known she could use her dust... unless she didn't have any? Maybe Earthly Daneelies didn't possess dust.

How I prayed I was right.

Thunder cracked like a whip outside.

Charlotte tilted her head toward the ceiling. "Shut off the storm, children. I cannot hear myself think."

Kiera and Cole exchanged a look, and then both of them shut their eyes. Their chests rose with steady breaths and then became immobile. Blue sparks flickered around their hands, which they stretched heavenward. When their lips fluttered for air, the rain stopped pelting the tin roof, dousing the blue magic in their hands.

"Thank you," Charlotte said.

A realization hit me dead center. They'd created the storm to trap us!

I finally understood why Daneelies had been banished from Neverra. They were dangerous.

Kiera twirled a pencil between her fingers—not a pencil. I squinted until I made out what it was. A diminutive rowan wood arrow. Kajika never left home without his faerie-killing arsenal.

I tried not to flinch when she approached me with it.

"I found a couple of these in his pocket. What are they?" she asked, just as her brother grabbed her hood and yanked her back.

"Kiera, her palm! She could kill you," Cole said.

"She kills me, and we kill him. From what I saw, that would make her really sad..." She tracked the arrow down one side of my face. A path of fire erupted underneath its tip. Her breath hitched as she took in my graying skin. I didn't dare move for fear that she would stick the arrow through my flesh to test how it affected my internal organs.

Without hunter blood, it couldn't kill me, but damn, it would hurt.

"Ha." Kiera finally said, a smile blooming on her lips.

"What?" Charlotte asked.

"Her skin reacts to the piece of wood. Uncle Quinn"—Kiera

fished another stick from her hoodie pocket—"go test it on the other one's skin."

Eyes flashing with pure hatred, Quinn took the arrow from his niece's hand. Right before leaving, he spit at my feet. I held still as he retreated.

Charlotte called her twins away. In hushed voices, they discussed me. I inferred this from the way their eyes kept darting toward me.

Several minutes later, Quinn was back, clomping through the warehouse.

"It doesn't so much as leave a mark on his skin. I even prodded him with it, broke his skin. Nothing."

My gaze centered on the reddened tip, stained with Kajika's blood. A wave of nausea rose, and even though I no longer had anything in my stomach, I bent at the waist and threw up bile.

"Does blood make you queasy, Alice?" Quinn sounded like he was standing in a tunnel.

It wasn't until Kiera yelled, "Alice!" that I jerked my gaze up. "What happens if we poke *you*?"

She took the arrow from Quinn and walked it over to me. I clamped down hard on my lip so she couldn't see how wildly it wobbled. Death was in my future, but it wouldn't be at her hands. I tried to feel for my dust, and my fingers tingled.

It was there.

In spite of the iron, it was there.

Somewhere.

I jolted my hands up, not to form a weapon, but a word: STOP. I fashioned the letters with ribbons of dust.

Kiera froze.

She could see it!

She could see my word!

I wanted to leap from joy that I'd found a way to communicate.

"How did you do that?"

"What did she do, Kiera?" Charlotte asked.

"She made a word appear out of thin air."

"Get back!" Charlotte's voice whipped through the darkness. "She's using her dust."

Kiera scrambled back. "Why should we *stop*?"

I created another word: FRIEND.

"Friend?" Kiera snorted. "As if. You're a faerie. Faeries are *not* our friends."

Cole studied the air shimmering over my palm. "You do realize this means she could've used it on us before but didn't."

I could've hugged him for stating the obvious. Granted, I hadn't known I had access to my dust before.

"She is still the enemy, Cole," Charlotte said.

I shook my head as I gathered my dust back into my palms. I wasn't the enemy.

"Do you take us for fools?" Charlotte shrilled. "We know what your people did to ours back in Neverra. You are our *greatest* enemy."

Quinn's head jerked back a little. "Something just came to me. The boy...he's Native. Catori Price, too. They're related, aren't they? That's how you found us."

My first impulse was to shake my head. Just because Kajika was Native didn't mean he was related to all the other natives out there.

"Who is *Catori Price*?" Cole asked.

"The descendent of the wretch who got Quinn's grandpa to print the blasphemous book," Charlotte said. "Supposedly it was a work of fiction, legends of natives and faeries, but it was too close to the truth to be a work of fiction. It even mentioned us. The woman who wrote it used another word for us, though—*Mishipeshu*—and spoke of us as copper monsters, but she gave away our whereabouts."

"Why would your grandpa do that, Quinn?" Kiera asked.

"Ley seduced him with *magic*," he said.

Charlotte shifted her gaze in my direction. I knew she couldn't see me, and yet I recoiled.

"Faeries can do that?" Kiera asked, her voice breathy with disbelief.

Quinn glared at me as though *I* were Ley, as though I'd used *captis* on his grandfather. "Better not try that on us."

I'd never used *captis* on anyone. The only boy I'd loved was a faerie, and *captis* didn't work on faeries. From what I'd learned back in school, it also didn't work on Daneelies. But perhaps mixing with humans had watered down their magic.

"Quinn's father confessed his affair on his deathbed," Charlotte continued. "For years, we didn't even know there was a book out there that mentioned us. We thought we were safe, but we hadn't been safe for a long time. As soon as we found out, we confronted Ley Lakeewa, and she swore the only edition was still at Forest Press, so I flooded the archives. Shouldn't have taken the word of a faerie." She snorted. "First Catori Price and a little faerie friend of hers visited Quinn a couple months back to have a new book printed with strange ink. And then you, Alice, pay us a visit." Charlotte rubbed her hands together as though to rid them of dirt.

"How many more people know about the book?" Kiera asked.

"That's what we need to find out," Charlotte said.

"One more for sure. Catori Price came with that Wood boy... what's his name?" Quinn rubbed his temple with two fingers. "You know, the grandson of the faerie who killed off all our people?"

Air scraped down the sides of my throat.

"Ace Wood?" Kiera exclaimed.

"That's the one."

"You shared the same air as a Wood?" Kiera asked, horrified.

I dipped my chin down, making my hair cascade around my face, hoping it could somehow protect me from being recognized. If they knew I was Ace's sister— I couldn't finish that terrible thought.

"Why didn't you kill him?" she asked.

Oh, skies... They knew how to kill us? My lungs squeezed as tight as when she'd dragged me through the lake.

"Your mother told me it would bring attention to us. Besides, he is a Wood... Apparently they're harder to kill than normal faeries."

I tensed.

"He sent his guards the next day. I'm not sure if they knew what was inside the book—"

I shook my head.

"Alice seems to think they didn't…" Cole interjected.

I looked up and nodded.

"Like we can trust her…" Quinn let out a rough snort. "Since her friend can't compel you, Charlotte, you should go talk to him."

She considered this before nodding and heading toward the entrance of the crate-building.

"Tell him I'll prod his girlfriend with his little arrow until her fire leaks out." He smiled harshly, and it made his hazel eyes scintillate as though his irises were coated in tiny copper scales. "Better hope he talks."

My heart banged in time with the door Charlotte went through.

"That scares you, huh?" Quinn said, retrieving the arrow from Kiera. "Should've evaluated the consequences of looking for people your kind tried to eliminate."

I am not my grandfather, I wanted to scream. *The genocide was atrocious, the worst part of our history, but I didn't kill anyone. I wasn't even born. Times have changed. Our queen is one of you! You've even met her!*

I was tempted to raise these words from the palm of my hand, but like my stomach, my dust had shriveled into a tight knot.

Quinn approached me, and I pressed my spine and cheek against the cool wall, wishing I could vanish through it, but I wasn't a ghost.

Not yet…

"On what part of your body should we start?"

I raised my hands to protect my face. The iron cuffs slid over my leather sleeves, offering my wrists some reprieve.

Quinn was so close I could smell the mix of perspiration and lake water coming off his looming body.

I braced myself for the impact of the tiny stake, but the only thing that came was a crashing sound, followed by a shrill growl.

17

COLD NIGHT

I peeked through my fingers. And then I blinked, thinking I was hallucinating. But I wasn't.

Mummified in rope and chains, Kajika stood before me, breathing hard. His eyes were crazed, made even more so by the absence of eyebrows and the presence of angry welts on his forehead and cheeks. What had they done to him?

I lurched toward him, but the chain bolted to the wall yanked me back like a yo-yo. I came crashing down so hard I thought I heard my tailbone crack. It was probably Quinn's skull that cracked though, as a small table soared through the air and smashed into his forehead. He teetered, and the arrow fell from his fingers, but he somehow managed to stay upright. A string of lights unglued itself from the ceiling and drifted like an electric eel toward Quinn, who blinked at it. Kiera and Cole shrank back, perplexed by the object soaring through the air. When it wrapped around Quinn's neck, all three sets of eyes bulged. I'd seen Kajika move things with his mind, but it still dazzled me.

The hunter lunged toward me and started tugging on the padlock. Blood oozed from his nailbeds and dripped from his chin, falling onto the knuckles of my pale hands. When a crimson drop snaked into my cracked, singed skin, turning the spot the color of charcoal, Kajika dropped the lock as though it had electrocuted him.

Fear replaced the wildness. "Lily…" he whispered my name.

I'm okay. It won't kill me.

The second of hesitation cost us much. When Kajika spun to locate the key or to compel Cole to give it to him, a man I hadn't seen enter the building swung a saturated towel over the hunter's face that settled over his mouth and nose like wet plaster. He tightened it so hard that Kajika lost his balance and flailed backward.

Kajika! I shrieked into his mind. I pulled with all my strength on my shackles. The iron charred my skin to the bone and still I kept pulling.

When his body stilled, when his hands flopped onto the cement floor, I gasped. Someone yanked on my chain, and I slammed into the wall. The man who'd managed to make Kajika pass out swung the hunter over his shoulder and carried his limp body back out.

No! Kajika! NO! Please hear my voice. Please wake up.

"What. The fuck. Is he?" Quinn screeched.

I glared at him, at the rivulets of blood and sweat streaming down his face. Although I'd never asphyxiated a person, the desire to inflict more than pain made ribbons of dust spring out of my palms. The ribbons grazed his nose but plummeted, the iron limiting my control over them.

Quinn sniffed the air. "What are you? A skunk? What's that smell?"

I waited for him to come closer.

Closer.

Closer.

I pumped my fingers again, and again the dust lurched out—this time, it hit Quinn. It snaked into his flaring nostrils, into his narrowed eyes, into his parted lips.

He went as pale as cake flour. Kiera screamed. She ran to her uncle and grabbed him around the waist just before he fell. The momentum and weight of his body drove them both to the floor.

"What have you done?"

My pulse seized. What *had* I done?

The fire draining from my face, I reached out and spread my fingers wide, desperately recalling my dust before it extinguished the Daneelie's life, beseeching the skies it wasn't too late. However deep my hatred for this man, for these people, killing one of them would only make everything worse for Kajika.

The iron chains jangled against my skin and sent bolts of pain up my forearms. My wrists throbbed and my fingers stung.

"Cole, put your fucking mask on and grab her hands before she tries to kill more of us!" Kiera shrieked.

Cole dropkicked my outstretched arms. I gasped from the unexpected blow, my elbows buckling in time with my knees. The shock of falling vibrated through my bones. When he kneed my back, I collapsed onto my stomach, the air whooshing out of my lungs.

My ears rang from the impact, and my vision grayed like Quinn's body.

"What happened?" It was Charlotte who spoke.

She was back, nursing a bloodied bruise at her temple. Kajika must've knocked her out on his way to me. I cringed at the hatred puffing off of her.

"Quinn still has a pulse," Kiera said after what felt like an endless stretch of time.

The relief that I wasn't a murderer was short-lived.

"She tried to kill Quinn?" Charlotte's shock echoed against the crates. "You leave us no choice. Cole, truss her up in iron chains. Her entire body this time."

No, please. Please, I begged. Face still pressed against the grimy cement floor, I let out a muffled sob.

I hated being so weak.

Cole latched onto my shoulders and heaved me back onto my knees. He was firm but not rough anymore. After he let go, I sagged forward, chin tucked against my neck, shoulders shaking with more muted sobs.

Groans rose from where Kiera held Quinn, and then a coughing fit ensued.

He'd awakened. It would take him a while to shake off the noxious particles of dust, but in time, his lungs would clear and his mouth would stop tasting sour.

In time, he would heal while I hurt.

Metal clinked, and then footsteps approached. Cole's bare, dirty feet rounded my hunched figure. The chain around my neck rattled as he spun it, then the lock clicked open, and the chain fell away from my body, settling on the floor next to my knees like a limp snake. Bits of my blackened skin clung to the links.

Skies, what did my neck look like?

A new chain wrapped around me, but this time, my neck was spared. Cole wrapped the chain around my chest methodically, carefully, almost like he feared my reaction if his movements were too sudden. The only metal that touched my skin were the shackles around my wrist. The rest of my chain rested against fabric. I wondered if he'd done this on purpose, to spare me some pain.

Unlikely, but I dared hope the Daneelies weren't *all* cruel.

The will to fight back flickered and then snuffed out like a wet wick. Unlike them, I didn't want to inflict pain. I thought of Kajika as the chains tightened around my dried, water-hardened clothing. I gritted my teeth as Cole pushed me back onto the ground and lifted my legs, coiling the endless chain around them. My skin prickled from the proximity to the metal, but at least I didn't start crackling like a steak over a grill.

Once he'd clicked the padlock into place around my ankles, he rolled me onto my back. Slowly, I raised my gaze to his face. He was biting his lip, gnawing on it, as though he felt bad about what he'd had to do. Or maybe I was seeing what I wanted to see.

Quinn grumbled unintelligible words. Leaning on Kiera, he hobbled over to me. My pulse spiked when his searing gaze landed on my face. He cracked the knuckles of the hand that hung limply by his side and then crouched, picked up the discarded piece of chain, and coiled it around his fingers.

"If it was up to me, I'd kill you." He let his fist fly into my cheek, searing off a layer of skin.

Tears dripped along my temples, dissolved into my hair.

He hit me again.

And again.

Stars sparked in the corner of my vision, and then they flickered and darkness flowed over me like ink, blotting away the room, the people, the pain.

I CAME to the same way I'd entered this world...in silence.

I didn't dare shift a muscle as I took inventory of my body. My cheek no longer smarted and my wrists no longer throbbed. The back of my head rested on something soft.

Had I been freed?

Saved?

Through swollen lids, I peered around me. Rays of dusty light slanted through a makeshift window, streaking the cavernous space. I was still in the crate-building. Cole was slumped in a chair a couple feet away from me, sleeping. A chipped plate rested on a little table next to him, the porcelain piled high with cheese rinds and discarded bread crust. My stomach growled. I shut my eyes, praying the sound hadn't woken Cole. When I didn't hear him stir, I opened my eyes again. I spied a half-drunk glass of water, and my parched throat contracted. What I wouldn't give for a sip...

Next to the glass were the small keys to the padlocks holding my chain in place. I'd never wished to be Unseelie before, but at that moment, I wished I had some of their magic.

Sprinklers went off. I braced for a spray of cold water but none hit me. I craned my neck, my head slipping off the lumpy thing underneath my head—a sweatshirt that smelled of soap, boy, and motor oil. I imagined it was Cole's.

The patter of water had me twisting further. The chains were too tightly wound to clink. I finally found the source of the sound. Droplets of water splashed the plastic tarp that walled off a brightly lit, green area.

I first thought it was a hothouse for growing vegetables and fruits until I remembered the drugs they'd sold us. I'd have bet anything that the blotchy plastic curtain hid a thriving patch of weed. The door of the makeshift building creaked open, jolting Cole to his feet. He rubbed his eyes before flinging his hands off his face and jerking his gaze toward me as though worried I'd somehow managed to escape.

When he saw me, he exhaled a breath, but then his eyes moved to my head, and he lurched to his feet. In three quick strides, he stood over me, then crouched and swept up the wadded sweatshirt.

"Heya, Cole," came a chirpy voice, one I hadn't heard yet.

A girl with long brown dreads walked over to us. She crossed her arms as she peered down at me. A ray of sunlight caught on her skin that was freckled and had the copper sheen of someone who spent their days outdoors.

"Hi, Sam," Cole said, fingers scrabbling over the chains wrapped around my legs. I couldn't tell if he was pretending to adjust them or really adjusting them.

"I never thought I'd get to see a real faerie." Sam's gaze roamed over me. There was more curiosity than animosity, but still, my muscles flexed.

"Step back. She's dangerous," Cole snapped.

Did he really think this, or did he sense my fear?

Her forehead puckered. "She doesn't look dangerous."

"Don't you know faeries' looks are deceiving? They're like swans...attractive but vicious as hell." His eyes flashed down to me, as blue and deep as the lake. "Didn't you hear she almost killed Quinn last night?"

Sam smirked. "He probably deserved it. He's like one of those born-again religious people—more devout than God himself." Even though Cole had told her to stay away, she walked around me like a fisherman inspecting his catch.

"Sam, seriously, keep your distance."

"You're not keeping *your* distance," she remarked.

Cole's cheeks reddened. "I was just making sure the chain hadn't loosened during the night." He unfurled his skinny but athletic body. "Better not try anything, Alice," he grumbled. If he was trying to sound menacing, he was doing a poor job of it.

Sam's eyebrows writhed over her eyes. "Why did you call her Alice?"

"That's her name."

"No it's not."

"What do you mean, it's not?"

Goose bumps scampered over my skin.

"Are you serious right now? You don't know who you caught? Shit, Cole, don't you ever read magazines?"

"No," Cole answered sheepishly. "Besides, it was dark last night."

"Kiera wasn't with you?"

"She was."

"And *she* didn't recognize her?"

"You know all my sister ever reads are surfing magazines." His cheeks had become as colorful as the crate wall. "Can you just spit it out already? If she isn't Alice, then who is she?"

Sam sucked in a long, drawn-out breath, as though to heighten the suspense. Or maybe it was just to irritate Cole.

"Sam—"

She smiled. "The girl you have there"—she tipped her chin toward me—"that's Lily Wood."

"Lily Woo—" The last letter of my name never made it out of his gaping mouth. Cole backed up as though I'd turned into a *dile*. "No…"

"Shit, you really didn't know?"

Cole raked his hand through his pale hair so roughly he pulled out a couple strands. They fell, glittering like gold thread in the lines of sunlight striating the chilly, wet air. I didn't think he'd liked me much, but I also hadn't thought he hated me. From the dread staining his expression, I sensed that whatever pity he'd felt for me was gone. I'd deceived him, and deception was terrible. I lowered my gaze from his, hating the gathering revulsion twisting his features.

"Is it true? Is your name Lily?"

"What? You don't believe me?" Sam stuck out her lower lip in a pout.

There was no point in pretending I wasn't—there were pictures of me all over the internet—so I nodded.

"Told ya." Sam's voice lilted with pride. "You should probably go inform your mother. Unless you want me to go do it?"

"I've been tasked to stay with her." His tone was so, *so* low. "You go."

Guilt ravaged me, worse than after I'd accidentally gassed Quinn. It was odd to feel guilt for something as trivial as a mistaken identity. I supposed the feeling stemmed from the hurt contorting Cole's face. I reasoned with myself that he'd trussed me up in iron chains. He didn't deserve my guilt, but then I thought of the balled sweatshirt and the absence of my collar, and the will to despise him as much as I despised the others dwindled.

I twisted my head to mouth, *I'm sorry*, but he blurted, "Did you come here to finish what your grandfather started?"

This time *I* was hurt. I looked away, shaking my head from side to side, my hair picking up dust from the floor, against which I still lay like a worm.

He snorted. And then he just stood there, glowering down at me.

A deep, loud growl erupted from somewhere and shook the earth. I spun my head toward the makeshift window. I would know that sound from anywhere. *Kajika.* What were they doing to him? I writhed, the chains rattling around me as I tried to wriggle out of them.

Another loud keening sound rose.

I managed to roll onto my side. I needed to get to him.

Hands pinned me down. Cole's eyes settled on my hand that flared with Kajika's elevated pulse.

"Why does only one of your palms light up?"

Another bone-rattling growl reached me.

Kajika, if you can hear me, scream yes!

I waited and waited but he never yelled yes. There was one more sharp cry, and then silence. The worst kind of silence. My palm had stopped flaring. I fought the chains, but they didn't magically skid off my body. I was trapped.

Please be alive.

"It's not dust, is it? It's some sort of connection to your boyfriend."

I cursed my impotent vocal folds as I turned beseeching eyes toward Cole, pleading him to go check on Kajika.

Yellow rubber Crocs squeaked, coming to a standstill inches from my own feet. "What's not dust?"

Kiera was back. A spray of red adorned the front of her lavender t-shirt. *Please let it not be Kajika's blood.* But who else's would it be? Unless Kajika had managed to injure one of his captors...

I raised murderous eyes to her face.

"Morning, *Lily*." She insisted on my name, seemingly bitter she'd gotten it wrong.

"When he screamed, one of her hands lit up," Cole explained, getting back to his feet. "I think she's somehow connected to the other faerie."

Kiera frowned. "I remember Nana telling me about these magical bonds faeries could establish, but it wasn't with other faeries. I think it was with humans. As a way to keep an eye on them to better kill them." Her tanned forehead creased a little more.

I noticed a spot of blood at the edge of her hairline. A violent chill raked through me. Where had all this blood come from?

"I need to double-check with Mom. She'd know."

"What do you need to double-check with me?" Charlotte was back too.

I half expected Quinn to enter after her, but the door didn't reopen.

"Cole suspects she's linked to the man," Kiera said.

"You mean, a tracking bond?"

"Yeah. That's the one Nana referred to."

"Kiera's right. Faeries like to mark their prey," Charlotte said. "But the mark only takes to human skin."

"Which would mean the man is human," Cole said.

"He heals each time we cut him."

My stomach twisted. They were cutting him?

"He's way too strong to be human. You should see what he did to—" Kiera stopped midsentence and brushed the back of her hand against her forehead as though trying to wipe away phantom blood.

Maybe it wasn't Kajika's.

How I hoped it wasn't.

"He might be strong, Kiera, but he didn't react to iron," Cole said.

"Like Mom says, he's probably a human-faerie mix."

"Mark my words, I'll find out today what he is." Charlotte's pale, unblinking eyes swept over where I lay. "Cole, baby, go rest. Kiera will take your place. I'm going to see if Pete's managed to make the boy more responsive."

"You might have to wait a couple hours. Pete got a bit carried away after…the attack."

I felt my lashes hit my brow bone. At that moment I didn't even care that I still had lashes. All I cared about was what this man—Pete—did to Kajika.

I was done being useless. Skies be damned, I was a faerie, not a worm. I had dust. Dust they couldn't seize.

As Charlotte gave Kiera pointers about what to do with me, Cole waited by the door.

"No one comes through here until we understand why they've come," Charlotte was saying. "Until we understand all they're capable of, okay? If you need help, raise a roll of thunder, and I'll come."

What a convenient means of communication…

As I looked at Kiera, an idea materialized. I studied the shape of her jaw and eyes—both a little rounder than her brother's—and memorized the slight prominence of her ears, which stuck out of her curtain of uncombed, white-blonde hair.

Now I needed to figure out if, wrapped in all this iron, I still had control of my dust. I fisted my hands, trying to sense the pulse of magic, but located nothing. There was too much metal around me.

I'd done it last night. Granted I hadn't been encased in *this* much iron. I waited for the door to bang shut behind mother and son to try harder.

Come on…

I closed my eyes and tried again, focusing inward. The fire in my veins seemed to burn hotter as though it too were whooshing through my body in search of my hiding dust. Sweat beaded on the nape of my neck, and still, I'd achieved nothing.

I tried again. I would try as many times as I needed to.

A slight tingle pricked my fingertips.

I sucked in air, and the movement jostled the chain around my wrists, smothering the prickle and searing a patch of already-sensitive skin.

A foot pressed against my writhing hands, gave a slight shove.

My lids flew open.

"Don't try anything." Kiera twirled the slender arrow coated in dry blood and stuck it behind her ear as though it were a pencil.

I lay statue still, feeling for my dust again. This time it came more swiftly, or perhaps I recognized it quicker.

They'd said the Woods were harder to kill, and in a way they'd been right. We were bred and raised to wield *wita* like humans wielded guns. And since Negongwa had lifted the limitation he'd placed on our dust, my stock was bottomless. Which was good, because I would need a lot of it to put my plan to execution.

I reached for my dust again as I concentrated on the plan sharpening in my mind.

18

THE ILLUSION

*A*n hour into Kiera's watch, the girl with the dreads came back.

Kiera laid the boating magazine she was reading down on her lap. "Mom said no one should come through here until we know what the faeries want."

"She sent me to collect some of the good stuff. Apparently, they've run out." Sam waggled her brows and tipped her head toward the makeshift hothouse.

"Already?" A frown gusted over her face. "That was quick."

Sam glanced at me as she pushed back the heavy plastic curtain. The scent of warm soil and dewy leaves snaked through the warehouse. Did they know about their ancestors' scales? I imagined they did, because they seemed well versed in faerie history. Then again, they didn't know about hunters, so maybe I gave them too much credit.

A short moment later, Sam emerged from the indoor greenhouse. "All done." Instead of leaving, she approached us. "Do you really think more of them are coming like her friend said?"

"He also said that Catori girl was one of us, but that's clearly a lie. She's marrying that one's"—she tipped her chin toward me— "brother. No Daneelie would *ever* get with a descendent of Maximus

Wood, no matter how rich or powerful he might be. It would be like a Jew marrying a descendant of Hitler. Wrong. Wrong. Wrong."

"Maybe he's forcing her to marry him? Lily, is your brother—"

Kiera slammed her magazine shut. "You got to be kidding me, Sam! You think she'd tell us the truth? She'll just shake her head. Besides, Catori *isn't* one of us. Quinn met her. She's not."

"Quinn could be wrong—"

"Sam!" Kiera exclaimed.

Sam raised her palms in the air. "Fine. I'll shut up." Her dreads swung around her face as she turned and finally walked out.

After she left, I strained to hear more incoming footsteps, but the only noise was that of a car rumbling by. It soon faded.

Deciding the time had come, I took a breath and forced myself to tremble. It wasn't hard to fake. Unlike Kiera, who wore a puffer vest over her hoodie and a pair of roomy sweatpants, my jeans did little to ward off the chill in the air.

The chains around my body rattled, which made the Daneelie spring to her feet. The magazine hurtled to the floor, flopping like a dead fish.

Kiera's navy eyes narrowed on me. Her hair, which was as white as *lupa* fur, hung like window sheers around her dipped head. I increased my shaking, gritting my teeth as the chain on my wrists jiggled and sloughed off skin.

"What's wrong with you?" she asked roughly.

I let my eyes roll to the back of my head and saliva dribble from the corners of my mouth.

I must've put on a convincing show, because she muttered, "Shit."

I waited for her to sound her thunder before moving on to the second step of my plan.

She made me wait a long time, but in the end, she indulged me. Her hands filled with blue sparks. The sky darkened and then thunder cracked.

I shook harder, and she crouched, grabbing onto my flailing shoulders, trying to pin me down. I concentrated on filling my hands with dust. Once I was certain I had enough, I flung my fingers wide, dispersing my dust into the air like confetti.

Kiera blinked as though she could feel it settle over her face, and maybe she could. When I was young, I'd done it to Dawson to play a trick on Veroli...I'd disguised him as my father. In retrospect, it had been a cruel joke to make poor Veroli believe my father had come to visit. My father wasn't the type to "hang out," at least not with us. He was way too busy visiting all of his concubines. Anyway, after Veroli had stopped hyperventilating, Dawson had commented that my dust felt like cobwebs.

Car doors slammed outside. More than one person was coming. Kiera whipped her face toward the door. The second it opened, I activated step three. I threw my glowing fingers wide again.

Dawson was right; dust *did* feel like spiderwebs.

Kiera turned back toward me. "What the—"

Her eyes—now gray—went as round as bowling balls. I understood her shock. It was strange watching your own face stare back at you.

Several people rushed toward us.

And now, onto step four. I dispelled just a sprinkle more of dust into Kiera's gaping mouth. She coughed. It would burn the lining of her throat just enough to make it impossible for her to talk. I couldn't have her looking like me but speaking. It would ruin my—hopefully—clever ploy.

Loud voices resonated around the building's low ceiling and metallic walls, and then arms hooked under Kiera's and yanked her off me. She was coughing so hard I half expected her to throw up a lung. A man with bulging, blood-splattered arms and a bloody plaster over his cheek grabbed the chair and smashed it into Kiera's face.

The sight of my face getting smacked made me flinch.

"I got the key!" a woman with boy-cut, red hair shouted. She dropped to her knees and fit it into the lock at my ankles. Her movements were brusque, choppy, but fast. In seconds, the length of chain had been unwound from my body. I held out my wrists. She fumbled with the keys.

Come on. Come on.

I looked at Kiera, around whom they wound the chain. The iron links skimmed a patch of bare skin on her collarbone. It didn't catch fire like mine. Thankfully, the man wrapping her up didn't seem to notice.

The woman dropped the keys just as Cole burst into the building. His eyes zeroed in on fake me and then on real me. He seemed to hesitate a millisecond before running toward real me.

He pushed the short-haired woman aside and swept the keys off the floor. "What happened, Kiera?"

I worried my lip so I wouldn't have to talk.

He fit the right key into the lock and was about to twist it when he caught sight of tendrils of smoke rising from the chain.

Shoot. Shoot. Shoot.

His wide eyes narrowed to slits, and he removed the key.

I shut my eyes and squeezed them tight. If I could've banged my head against the concrete floor, I would've. I'd been *so* close.

So freaking close…

When I opened my eyes, he was still staring down at me.

"What are you waiting for?" the woman yelled at him, trying to steal the keys from his clenched fist.

"That's not Kiera."

"What do you mean that's not Kiera?"

"I mean. It's. Not. My. Sister," he said through clenched teeth.

The woman frowned at him, then at me. "What the hell are you talking about, Cole? It's Kiera! Get that chain off her."

She tried to wrestle the keys from him and then he got to his feet. "STOP! Everyone stop! The faerie played a trick on us!"

Silence filled the tumultuous room.

"What trick?" the man with the stained gauze on his cheek asked.

"What's happening, Cole?" his mother asked, moving carefully toward him.

"Lily's somehow making us think Kiera is her and that she's Kiera."

Gasps and *whats* ping-ponged around the building.

Cole stalked toward his sister and pressed a piece of chain against her chin. When no flames erupted, the man securing the chain released her. Cole returned to me and rattled the chain on my wrists. Sure enough, my skin bubbled and smoked, dispersing the scent of charred flesh.

"Faeries can create illusions, can't they, Mom?" he asked.

Sure enough, she confirmed it.

The volume of Cole's voice dropped. "Neat little trick, Lily."

Someone clapped, but my eyesight was too blurry to make out who was making fun of me.

"I'd say it was more than *neat* and *little*."

I blinked at the voice I'd know *anywhere*.

Every single person whirled toward the front door of the building.

My brother winked at me just as the man who'd been holding Kiera jumped to his feet and lurched toward him.

He cracked his neck from side to side and then extended a hand. "Unless you want to blend into your filthy home, I'd stop trotting."

The man skidded to a halt inches away from Ace's raised palm. Ribbons of dust leaped off my brother's palm.

"Release my sister before I get angrier than I already am," Ace said, his voice sharper than all of Kajika's arrows. "You *really* don't want to see me angry."

No one spoke. No one moved. Except for Kiera. She started coming to. When her eyes—that were hers again—landed on Ace, she balked, and then she stared around, her pale hair swishing from the momentum.

"Mom?" Cole asked.

Although all I could see of Charlotte was her back, from the ramrod straightness of her spine, I could tell she was on her guard. "Release the girl."

Without meeting my eyes, Cole did as he was told, and the chain fell off my wrists.

He rose and stepped back, bearing the look of a wounded animal.

On feet that felt gummy, I stumbled toward Ace. Only after he'd looped an arm around me did I let myself sag.

"I'm going to kill Kajika," he hissed into my ear.

I pressed away from him, shaking my head. I fisted my fingers and pumped them once against my chest. *Mine.* And then I flicked my little finger up and touched it to my forehead. *Idea.*

I needed to get to Kajika. I tried to break free from Ace, but he held onto me.

"You're not going anywhere anymore. Not without a fucking army surrounding you."

I sucked in a breath that whistled through the tiny gap in my front teeth.

"Mr. Wood?" Charlotte's voice sliced through the tense atmosphere.

"What?" He shifted his incendiary gaze to her.

Unlike most people, she didn't shrink back. "Never come back here."

He smirked. "If it were up to me, after how you treated my sister, I'd do one of two things. I'd either leave and forget all about you people, or I would torch your compound and make your life a living hell. But I'm a married man now, so it's no longer up to me. It's up to my wife, and my wife isn't going to want to leave the lot of you alone. Trust me, she's stubborn as hell."

Just as he said it, Cat shoved past him, giving him a playful smack on the arm before gathering me in her arms and hugging me to her so tight, she robbed me of breath.

"I'm not *that* stubborn," she muttered into my hair.

I smiled.

It felt *so* incredibly good to smile.

When she released me, her gaze swept over my body, stilling on my charred but already healing wrists. "You look better than Kajika. Are you okay, though?"

I was about to nod when I caught sight of the hunter standing on the muddy clearing outside the crate-building. His torso was bare, streaked with blood, and two of his tattoos had vanished from underneath his skin. The Daneelies must've carved them out when they'd tortured him.

I pressed past Cat. Ace tried to snag my arm, but Cat chided him. On wobbly legs, I walked slowly toward Kajika, afraid that if I went any faster, he would run from me...the girl who'd caused him to bleed and scream.

He didn't run.

He waited.

I felt my brother's gaze burn a hole in my back.

As though I'd smacked into an invisible wall, I came to a stop a couple feet away from the hunter. The scent of rotten food had my stomach clenching. I looked down, wondering if I'd stepped in something.

I lifted my gaze back up and took a step forward. The stench worsened.

Kajika scanned me up and down...up and down.

I stopped again, inspected his neck. The leather cord holding his opal was gone. The smell was coming from him.

His already stiff posture hardened as he understood what held me back.

I parted my lips and concentrated on breathing in only through my mouth.

My eyes prickled from the scent, but also from my body's physiological reaction to the hunter. We were made to repel each other. I didn't want to be repelled by him. My stomach lurched into my throat. I halted again, breathing so hard through my mouth I was almost panting.

Kajika's lids lowered over his dark eyes.

I'm sorry, I told him through our bond. Sorry for what had happened and for what was happening.

He crossed his corded arms and stepped back. The air became slightly more tolerable. "I tried to get to you, but they drugged me." His tone was clinical. "I could not get my limbs to move. I could not get my mind to clear." His mouth pinched shut for a long moment.

I took a step toward him, trying my damndest not to let his smell hold me back, but my stomach contracted again and made me stumble. Kajika whizzed toward me and caught my arm before I could topple into the mud.

Thank you. My nostrils flared, and again a wave of sick swelled through me. I pressed the back of my hand against my mouth.

His amber eyes filled with shadows. "You cannot stand the smell of me."

Because they took away your opal.

He released my arm and backed away so fast, his figure blurred.

I'm just not used to your smell.

His jaw was so tight that if it were made of rubber it would snap. He backed away from me.

Don't leave.

He shot me a long, pained look, so unlike any expression I'd ever seen on his face. Perhaps it was the absence of his eyebrows that made this expression so unfamiliar. Or maybe it was the desperation rising within me that colored my last image of him.

He turned and raced away, blending with the wind.

The sting of my iron shackles paled in comparison to the ache blooming in my chest at Kajika's abandonment.

I didn't cry, though.

I was all out of tears.

19

THE MEAL

I wanted to leave right away, but Cat made us stay a couple more hours. After talking extensively back in the crate-building, Charlotte, who'd been so adamant about never seeing us again, suggested dinner.

I thought it was a trap and signed it to Cat, who insisted it wasn't. Ace voiced my concerns out loud, reminding everyone that he had *lucionaga* circling the vicinity and an unparalleled technique of saturating soft tissue with dust. That made more than a few squirm. Charlotte promised it wasn't a trap.

She said it was an apology.

How she apologized to me.

I didn't forgive her.

I would never forgive her.

I didn't want to share a meal with the people who'd kidnapped and drugged and tortured us. From Quinn and Kiera's glares, I believed the sentiment was shared.

And yet, we stayed for dinner.

Charlotte showed us to her converted RV, so I could "freshen up." Ace had one of his *lucionaga* pick up some clothes from Cat's house and bring them over to the compound. Although thankful for the change of clothes, I didn't want to take a shower in Charlotte's RV. I didn't want to dry myself with her towels. I didn't want to be in this place that reminded me of singed flesh and iron chains. What I wanted was to crawl into my bed and never get out of it.

"Which ones hurt you, Lily?" Ace asked me as soon as it was just us.

I signed, *Quinn, the white-haired girl, Kiera, and the one who tried to attack you.*

"What about the blond boy?" he asked.

Cole had followed orders, but he'd done so with reticence. I showed the kid the mercy I wasn't afforded. **No.**

"And their leader? Charlotte?" he murmured.

She gave the orders but she didn't touch me.

"Cat, I know you think they're family," Ace said, his voice quiet as a stab, "but they're uncivilized and contentious. Look at what they did to Lily. To Kajika. I don't trust them."

"You also don't trust Gregor, and he's your right-hand man."

"That's not the same. I know Gregor. I know his motivations and his desires. I don't know what these"—he waved his hand in the air —"crazies want."

She pecked his cheek. "That's why we're staying for dinner. Keep your friends close and your enemies closer."

He grunted something I didn't hear. When he pulled Cat onto his lap, I went in search of the shower. It took me half a second to locate it, considering the size of Charlotte's home.

I took the shower I didn't want to take.

I used the towel I didn't want to use.

I got dressed and finger-combed my hair to make myself presentable, like the good little princess I was.

When I got out of the closet-sized bathroom, Cat and Ace were no longer all over each other...they were arguing. It was a quiet fight, but it startled me nonetheless. I waited in the shadow of Charlotte's room, studying the one-eye stuffed dolphin on the bed— probably her youngest son's.

"You shouldn't have told him you'd slice him up into tiny pieces and feed him to the fish," she whispered to him.

"Were you expecting me to congratulate him on helping my sister get imprisoned by Daneelies? He was supposed to protect her. That's the only reason I agreed to let them spend time together *unchaperoned*."

"Ace—"

"She's my baby sister, Cat. I'm supposed to protect her—" My brother's voice broke. It never broke. It deepened or lightened depending on his mood. Melancholic breaks weren't part of my brother's repertoire.

Cat snaked an arm around his shoulder and pulled him to her. She spoke softly against his temple. "I know, but she's also a big girl, Ace. She's lived half-a-century more than me, and yet you still treat her like she's barely a teenager."

My brother's shoulders shook. Was he crying? That dragged me out of my hiding place. I reopened the bathroom door and re-shoved it shut to alert them. And then I walked through the narrow corridor that led to the sitting area made of two rust-colored vinyl chairs and the beer-bottle green couch on which sat my brother.

Cat vaulted off Ace's lap. "How are you feeling?"

I watched my brother, who still had his back to me. I gave Cat a tight-lipped look that I hope conveyed my unhappiness.

"Can you tell me how you found them?" she asked.

I sighed. I pointed to her and then pressed my palms together and opened them like the word the gesture stood for.

"My book? You mean, The Wytchen Tree? You read it? The location of this encampment was inside?"

I shook my head and grabbed the block of lined paper and pen on the kitchenette counter. I wrote out how the idea came to me when we were waiting for Remo to be born. Cat read my account over my shoulder. When I was done, she gaped at me.

I snuck a peek at my brother, who was spinning one of his sapphire cufflinks. I wasn't sure where he'd come from, but obviously the search-and-rescue had interrupted some fancy affair. Cat, though, wasn't in any fancy dress. She wore her favorite leather leggings and a simple black sweater that matched her eyes, her hair, and my mood.

"Why didn't you tell us? Or Cruz? He told me you were on a road trip..."

I wrote, **I was afraid to get your hopes up for nothing.**

"Oh, Lily," she croaked, picking up one of my hands and squeezing it tight. Her gaze fell to our hands.

I knew what she was thinking. I heard it in her swift inhale.

My skin was cold. Colder than hers. Almost as cold as the air in the trailer, in spite of the electric radiator pumping heat.

Her mouth pressed into a thin line that matched my brother's grim expression.

I removed my fingers from hers just as a knock resounded on the door. While Cat went to open it, I turned to my brother. Our gazes held for a long, long moment. So much traveled between us. So many unspoken words. I hadn't had a loving father, and my mother was too ditzy to care much for me, but my brother...he'd made up for all the lost affection.

Cat cleared her throat. Ace looked away first. He sighed and walked toward his wife. I trailed them out. It wasn't Charlotte who'd come to fetch us, but Cole. He'd showered, changed, and slicked his hair back. Perhaps because I'd never stood beside him, I hadn't realized how tall he was. As we walked toward another part of the compound I hadn't seen yet, I had to crane my neck to look at him.

He wasn't as tall as Kajika though...

The hunter's absence was a punch to the heart.

Cole blushed, probably embarrassed about having partaken in the torture of a person who hadn't meant them harm. "I'm sorry, Lily. I hate myself so much for what we—what I did."

I nodded. I bet he was. I also bet he was one of the only ones who regretted hurting me.

After a long moment, I touched his arm to show him I accepted his apology. His entire face colored then.

"You're the prettiest girl I've ever seen," he blurted right before we caught up with Charlotte, Cat, and Ace.

The latter turned to glare at Cole.

Cole paled, and then he concentrated on kicking a little stone the rest of the way.

Cole had the potential to be a good man. For now, he was sweet in the way a puppy was sweet. He had yet to grow into a man. Not that it would make me like him more.

I liked one man.

One I wasn't supposed to like according to my brother and to Mother Nature. But brothers and Mother Natures didn't get to decide who my heart beat for. Only *I* got to choose that. And I'd chosen.

And for a moment, Kajika had chosen me back.

After today, though, he would never choose me again.

"Can you forget I said that?" Cole asked finally, brow scrunching.

I started to move my hands around but remembered he didn't understand sign language. I thought about my little trick with the dust earlier. I made two letters materialize from my upturned palms: **OK.**

He blinked at my dust, then after a stretch of silence, he asked, "Where did your boyfriend go?"

I closed my fingers and made a new word reappear. **Home.**

"Why did he leave without you?"

I didn't want to answer this because I was ashamed. Finally, I settled on **I hurt him.**

"Are you using your dust to speak?" Ace asked, falling into step with us.

I nodded.

"Clever."

I beamed at my brother's compliment. He draped an arm around my shoulder.

"That trick you pulled earlier, the switch with my sister, well now that we're...*not* enemies"—Cole spoke this like a question—"it was really neat."

And yet he'd caught me, so it wasn't as well thought out as I'd planned. I made four more words. **Does Kiera hate me?**

He raked his hair back and wrinkled his nose. "Yeah. She sort of does."

"As long as she doesn't try anything—" Ace started, but Cole interrupted him.

"She won't."

"Uh-huh." My brother didn't seem convinced.

"So...*what*...is your boyfriend?"

"A pain in my ass," Ace muttered. "And he's not her boyfriend. Right, Lil'?"

I stared at the rock Cole was still kicking. I felt the kicks inside my chest.

"Is he?" Ace asked again.

I shook my head abruptly.

After a moment, Ace answered Cole. "Kajika's a hunter. An Unseelie with a body. You know what an Unseelie is?"

"The spectral faeries?"

"Bingo. Glad to see you were taught something besides growing illegal substances."

Cole drew back. "We sell drugs to survive. Just like our ancestors did. We're not hicks, Mr. Wood."

"Not a fan of mister. You can just call me king or sire or the Neverrian term for sire, *massin*."

Cole jerked his head back. "I'm not your subject."

"Technically, you are. But if you don't like any of those, then at least call me Ace. Or *the brother*. But say it with gusto. *The brother*." Ace spoke the term as though he were some Russian kingpin, letting the *r*s roll off his tongue.

In spite of my sour mood, I smiled, which made Cole relax. He also smiled, but swiftly wiped it away, because we'd arrived in front of a white tent that looked like something a circus would've left behind. Next to the entrance stood Quinn, and next to him Kiera. On his other side stood the man who'd been streaked in blood, the one with the crimson patch on his cheek. The gauze had been removed, but it bore what looked like teeth marks. Had he been bitten?

Oh, skies, had Kajika bitten him?

I knew the answer was yes. I was almost certain this man had been the one to torture him. He'd been covered in so much blood earlier. I hated him instantly and regretted Kajika had sunk his teeth into his cheek instead of into his jugular.

Everyone had changed into, most probably, their fanciest attire. What they hadn't changed was their bitter mood. Kiera, Quinn, and the bitten man were the worst. They scowled as we walked past them.

I must've stiffened because Ace said in Faeli, "I'll turn them to ash if they so much as breathe your way."

I reached for my brother's hand that rested on my shoulder and clasped it.

Inside the tent, a long communal table had been set up with benches and heaps of food. Strings of twinkling lights had been wrapped around the metal structure. Platters full of food had been laid out.

"They better not have poisoned the food with iron," Ace muttered, again in Faeli.

Charlotte turned her pale eyes on Ace and replied in perfect Faeli, "We wouldn't do such a thing."

Stunned by her command of our language, Ace stopped in his tracks, and his arm fell away from my shoulders. "You understand Faeli?"

"Yes."

"Even though you never intended to come out of hiding?"

"It's still our mother tongue, Mr. Wood."

Ace didn't tell her to call him something else. He was probably mulling this information over. I wasn't as surprised as my brother. Why wouldn't they know their ancestors' tongue?

What I was more curious about was their dust, and I signed this to my brother.

Cat intercepted my message. "Lily asks if you have dust like your ancestors?"

Charlotte turned her head my way. I wasn't sure how she even knew where I was, considering I hadn't spoken. Unless she could sense me. That would be creepy…

"Like our scales, our dust has vanished. Only the first generation had both."

They still shine, I signed.

Cat nodded.

"If you went to Neverra, you'd probably get both back," Cat said.

How could she entertain such a preposterous idea?

"But they're not coming to Neverra…" Ace pivoted to take them all in. Even the youngest Daneelies had been convened to dinner. Maybe the adults were afraid to leave them alone with *lucionaga* swarming the area.

The children's eyes glittered at the mention of Neverra. I couldn't tell if it was in fear or in excitement.

"Going to our homeland was never a possibility before," Charlotte said slowly. "Is it a possibility now?" Ace was silent for so long Charlotte's mouth puckered. "We are not welcomed, are we?"

"You might be," Cat said suddenly. She'd waited for my brother to speak, but when his mouth didn't even shift, she took the decision upon herself.

A vein throbbed at my brother's temple. He didn't want them to return. The Daneelies sensed my brother's reticence because scowls were stamped on many a face.

"But you would have to prove yourself first," she added.

"Prove ourselves?"

"Your loyalty. This is no longer your ancestors' Neverra. This is a new Neverra," Cat said. She grabbed Ace's white-knuckled hand. "There is no more mist, no more palace, no more *cupola*, no more tithes."

"But there is still a king," the man with the teeth mark said.

Ace whipped around toward the Daneelie. "Just like there's a President in this country. My title is honorary and gives me the power to keep the peace."

"Is there still a *draca* and a *wariff*?" the red-haired woman who'd freed me earlier asked.

"The political system is still in place, but I've also created a new council where sit an Unseelie, a hunter, a Seelie, and a Daneelie."

"Let me guess, your wife is the Daneelie representing us?" Quinn said.

"You have a problem with that?" Ace snapped.

Some people muttered.

"I'd gladly offer my seat to a more deserving Daneelie"—Cat glowered at the ones who'd muttered—"but you'd have to prove your loyalty."

"Like you proved yours? By sleeping with a Wood?" Quinn hissed.

Cat flinched. Ace lurched into the air and landed at Quinn's feet so fast it stupefied the bald man. He then gripped Quinn's throat. "Loyalty starts with respect. If you *ever* imply that my wife whored herself again, I will kill you."

Tension thinned the oxygen.

Quinn's face turned as purple as a beet.

Ace still didn't let go. "I recognize you...where do I know you from?"

Quinn could obviously not answer.

Ace tipped his head and studied the puffing man. Suddenly my brother's head snapped up straight. "You're the owner of Forest Press."

Cat gasped, but covered up her gasp with her palm.

Quinn clawed at my brother's hand, but Ace didn't release him, and no one interceded, not even Kiera, who looked ready to leap to his rescue.

Finally, Ace uncinched his fingers and shoved Quinn so hard he stumbled and fell. Sputtering, he pressed himself back up, hazel eyes flaring with contempt. I wasn't sure who he was angrier at, though—Ace, who'd made a fool of him, or Charlotte, who hadn't defended him.

"You're the one who destroyed my book plates!" Cat exclaimed.

"They weren't yours," he muttered.

"Well they weren't yours either!"

"I'm the one who told him to get rid of them," Charlotte said. "I was afraid it would lead faeries to us." She'd been right to fear this. "Shall we sit? The food is getting cold." She gestured to the table.

No one looked in the mood to eat, but in waves, we took our seats. I sat in front of Ace and Cat. Charlotte slid in next to Ace, and Sam to my right. Cole dropped down to my left.

"Is it okay if I sit here?" he asked, straddling the bench as though about to spring up.

I nodded, and he pulled his leg over. Kiera and Quinn sat on one end of the table, as far away as possible from us. I only noticed then the large lump on Kiera's forehead. She'd been whacked hard, which surely contributed to her utter dislike of us.

Charlotte tipped her head down. The others followed suit. She said the Daneelie version of grace, thanking the water for their food. Once she was done, everyone but Ace and I dug into the food— piles of steamed vegetables, platters of grilled fish, and wooden boards topped with pinwheels of creamy cheese.

"Are there more Daneelies out there?" Cat asked Charlotte, taking a tiny bite of food as though testing it for poison.

"Only my husband and Quinn's family left the compound. When our great grandparents ran out of scales, Quinn's grandfather decided to go into another business. All the other families stayed. As you can see, though, not many of us survived the massacre."

I flinched at the mention of massacre, which was surely Charlotte's intent considering the weight of her empty stare.

"How many of you would come back to Neverra if the offer were on the table?" Cat asked.

"Is it not on the table already?" Charlotte asked.

Cat placed her elbows on the table and linked her hands together. "Would you immediately agree to Seelies moving onto your compound, Charlotte?"

Charlotte considered Cat's words. "I suppose we wouldn't."

"So how many of you would want to live there instead of here?"

Joshua was the first to raise his little hand. When no one followed suit, he whipped it down. But Cole, who was sitting next to his little brother, reached for Josh's arm and pulled it up, and then he raised his own hand. Josh beamed to have his brother's support. "Josh and I, Mom."

Kiera glared at her brothers. More hands came up and *me*s were spoken—for Charlotte's benefit. Kiera glared at all of them. Neither she, nor Quinn, nor the man who'd slammed the chair into her face when he'd thought it was me, raised their hands.

Finally, I gave in to the food, ladled steamed vegetables onto my plate, and speared a broccoli with more force than necessary, the tines of my fork scraping against the hard plastic plate. They would all be able to go there, unlike me...

"Would we be free to come and go as we pleased?" Charlotte asked.

"Yes," Cat said, "but you'd have to abide by the same rules as everyone else."

"Of course." Charlotte chewed a piece of sweet potato thoughtfully. "And how will you have us prove our loyalty?"

"We'll think of something," Ace said.

"You can attend our wedding on Beaver Island for starters," Cat said.

What was she playing at? Did she figure it would be condescending for them to attend a Wood function?

"Yes!" Sam said so excitedly her dreads pulsed around her face. "I mean"—she shrugged—"sure. Whatever."

Her attempt at tamping down her elation made some of my bad mood recede.

"Behave civilly and mingle with the other faeries who will fly in for the occasion, and you might earn a ticket into Neverra," Ace said glumly.

Cat wrapped her hands around Ace's arm, her touch softening his grouchy mood.

"Understood," Charlotte said.

"So those of us who don't feel like sucking up to you don't get to go to Neverra?" Kiera asked.

"Kiera!" Charlotte said sharply.

Ace leaned over Cat to have a clearer view of Cole's twin. "I'm sorry. Did you have your hand up earlier? Because if you did, I missed it."

She grumbled something under her breath.

"Oh. I forgot to mention something." His voice boomed in the tent. "Those who inflicted bodily harm to my sister and the hunter won't be allowed into Neverra. So that spares you the pain of *sucking up*, Kiera."

Charlotte blanched, and Cole stiffened.

"The other two people on the no-fly list are the two men sitting beside you, Kiera," Ace continued.

"This is bullshit!" Kiera muttered. "They came onto our land. They attacked us first!"

Attacked? All we'd done was buy weed from them. How was that an attack?

"Did anyone else partake in the torture?" Ace asked.

Cole's lids slid shut, and then his hand darted up.

Ace looked at me for confirmation, and I shook my head.

"My sister doesn't hold you accountable, so put your hand down. Anyone else?"

"I gave the orders to create the storm so we could trap them and glean what they knew. If anyone should be held accountable, it should be me."

"Mom!" Cole exclaimed.

"We may have acted out of fear, but we could've handled it differently. Actions have consequences. I'm sorry, Lily. It won't erase what we did, but know that I regret it."

"I don't regret it," Kiera sneered. "Did you see what the savage did to Pete's cheek? He bit him! And then *she* tried to gas Quinn. No. I don't regret anything we did."

Without turning her face toward Kiera, Charlotte said, "If this is truly how you feel, daughter, then pack your bags and leave."

"What? You're kicking *me* out?"

"Yes."

Kiera jumped off the bench, shaking her head so hard her hair danced around her face. "Dad was right to leave you. I wish I could've gone with him."

Charlotte closed her lids. I'd never even see her blink, and there she was shutting her eyes. Whoever this man was, I suspected there was blood in the water. "Now's your chance to find him, Kiera."

Kiera stalked around the table. She stopped right behind Cole. "Come on, Cole."

His Adam's apple bobbed in his thin throat.

"Cole?"

"I'm staying."

"Staying?" Kiera's dark eyes shot to me. "You are such a fool."

"Wait." Quinn stood. He tossed his napkin on his plate. "I'm coming. Pete?"

The man with the bite marks stared so hard at his plastic plate that I half expected it to melt. And then the red-haired woman beside him gripped his wrist and shook her head.

Finally, he whispered, "I'm staying," as though it were more painful than the bite marks on his cheek.

Quinn snorted, and then he walked toward the tent flaps where Kiera was waiting, and together they shoved past the two *lucionaga* manning the entrance. My brother gave a small nod and one of the guards walked out after them.

"My man will escort them off the premises," Ace said. "He will not harm them."

Charlotte was too sullen to answer. She wiped the heel of her hand over her cheek. Joshua slid under the table and then reappeared on his mother's lap. He locked his arms around her neck and nestled his little face against her neck.

"I won't leave you, Mommy."

She hugged him hard.

Silence garlanded the tent, punctuated by Charlotte's ragged breaths. Remorse swept back some of my hatred for her. By seeking her out, I'd destroyed her family.

A gust of cold air snuck through the tent, disturbing the quiet stillness. "Ace!"

Everyone turned to look at the newcomer. Even me.

Cruz was flushed and his eyes shone. He levitated, soared over the table, and landed at Ace's side.

Sam whispered, "Who is *that*?"

I crafted his name out of my dust.

"Hot name. Is he single?" Sam murmured.

Whatever Cruz had murmured in his ear made my brother lurch to his feet.

What now?

Cat's pulse must've spiked because Ace's palm glowed.

Cole leaned toward me. "Your brother and Catori are linked?"

I nodded, even though I was desperately trying to decipher from my brother's features if Cruz's news was good or bad.

"Does that mean she's his prey? Or is it a romantic bond?" Cole asked.

Cruz's green gaze slid to me. He smiled, and my heart held very, *very* still.

"We found the lock," he said. "And Gregor thinks he could match it to your stamp."

Erratic waves of heat and coldness slammed into me.

Cat shot to her feet and blurred around the table, her breathtaking speed kicking up hair ends and eliciting gasps from the Daneelies she passed. She stopped next to me, her feet bunching the turquoise fabric strewn over the bare earth.

"Lock? Stamp?" Sam sounded like she was on the other side of a portal. "What are they talking about?"

Cat placed her palms on my shoulders. Her fingers were shaking, or maybe I was shaking, or maybe we were both shaking.

"We're going to have to cut our visit short," Cat said. "Thank you for the feast you offered us. An invitation to our wedding will be delivered to you shortly. I hope to see many of you there." She squeezed my shoulders, and I stood.

I didn't thank anyone. What would I thank them for? Keeping me hostage? Injuring Kajika? I turned and walked out of the tent ahead of Cat.

It had started snowing. I lifted my face. Thick, downy pellets steamed off my face, using up more of my fire, but I suddenly didn't care.

I would have more fire soon.

I would have all of my fire.

"Let's go home," Cat said.

I assumed she meant Rowan, but perhaps she meant Neverra.

Both felt like home now.

I started levitating, when Ace's voice cut through the cold darkness. "Cruz, fly Lily over. I don't want her using up her reserve."

His comment brought me back down to Earth, literally and metaphorically. My boots and my confidence both sank into the thin white carpet. I closed my eyes to get my emotions under control.

"You will see the isle again, Lily. I promise you." The proximity of Cruz's voice made my eyes reopen. He scooped me up, and I burrowed against him, his fire warding off the chill my brother's words and the weather had set in my bones.

As we drifted upward, I caught sight of a body on the outskirts of the compound. At first, I thought it was Kiera or Quinn, but then the person's hand started glowing, along with my palm.

Kajika had returned.

I tried to signal for Cruz to fly me down, but he was concentrated on our upward trajectory. I let go of him to fly myself down.

I fell. Slowly, but still I fell.

Cruz dove down and bundled me back into his arms.

"What the hell, Lily? Hold on, okay?"

Cruz gripped me so tightly, even if I tried letting go, I couldn't.

Rowan. Meet me in Rowan, I whispered through our bond, hoping that in spite of the acre of frosty night that separated us, Kajika would hear me.

20

THE LOCK

*W*e went straight to the boathouse.

It was dark and bone-chillingly cold, made even colder by my exhaustion. The second Cat had closed the door, Cruz took a pen out of his pocket while Ace summoned flames on his palms to illuminate the obscurity. I touched the back of locker number four, and my portal stamp flared.

Cruz snapped a picture of it on his phone, and then he retraced each line on his own arm because cell phone screens scrambled in Neverra. He made me touch the portal again to light up my stamp. He checked his copy, green gaze swishing between our arms.

"Send me the picture," Cat said. "I'll go print out a copy in case your sketch isn't accurate enough."

Cruz emailed her, and then tucked a lock of hair behind my ear. "I'll be right back."

I nodded. He pressed his palm against the portal, and the perfect circle slashed by five irregular lines flared, unlocking the door between the worlds.

Cat ran out the minute Cruz was gone, leaving me alone with my brother.

I took a seat on the worn wooden bench. Ace dropped down next to me.

I signed, *The hunters will come home now?*

"I'm sure some of them will."

Kajika will be happy.

My brother's jaw clenched.

Did you really threaten to chop him up?

"Maybe." My brother wet his lips. "Don't *ever* disappear like that on me again."

I linked my fingers together and laid them on my lap, studying the chipped pink varnish I'd applied before my trip.

"I don't want you hanging out with him. Not until we've fixed your fire. He's dangerous and unfit to care for you. You will not talk to him. You will not breathe the same air as him. And if you so much as try to get close to him, so help me skies, I will ship the hunter on a one-way trip to Neverra."

I sucked in air so fast I wheezed, and then I unbound my hands and swished them through the air. *You don't get to decide who I see, Ace.*

"The Daneelies imprisoned you, Lily. That would've never happened if I had been with you." He fisted the fingers of his right hand, extinguishing the flames he'd conjured up to brighten the boathouse.

Kiera had been so quick that there was no way to know if Ace could've intercepted me. Anyway, I didn't want to dwell on *what ifs*. I had enough *what ifs* in my life.

It's not his fault.

"I'm not discussing this anymore. My decision's final. When you're healthy again, we can broach the subject—"

I shook my head, tears dampening my cheeks. *I never told you not to be with the person you loved.*

Ace's shoulder-blades strained his white dress shirt. "*Love?* Come on, Lily, you barely know him. Besides, you're a romantic. You fall in love as fast as hunters run."

A punch in the throat would've hurt less.

"A few months ago, you were madly in love with Cruz, and now it's Kajika."

I was so angry that I got off the bench and went to stand as far away as possible from Ace. If I hadn't been waiting for Gregor to tweak the damn lock, I would've fled.

"Have you considered that you might be attracted to him because of all the time you've been spending together?"

I was horrified by what my brother thought of me.

Cat burst back into the boathouse then, a piece of folded paper flapping in her hand. One glance between Ace and me had her eyes narrowing. "What just happened in here?"

"Nothing," Ace grumbled, scraping a hand over his hair that he kept shorn close to his scalp.

"Uh-huh." She splayed the hand not clutching the paper on her hip. "Spill. Now."

"Cat, it's between Lily and me." He grabbed the paper from her.

"It's about Kajika isn't it?"

Ace's sulky silence confirmed it loudly.

Cat sighed, her hand slipping off her jutting hip. "Ace, relationships are between two people, not three, not four. Lily's never gotten involved in ours. We owe her the same respect. Kajika is loyal and strong, and cares for her and—"

Ace got to his feet and punched a locker, denting the metal.

"Ace!" Cat chided him.

"He is irresponsible and dangerous. Have you ever seen him without his fucking rowan wood arrows? If he cared for Lily, he'd fucking trust her enough not to carry weapons that could kill her."

"He doesn't carry them to use them on her."

My brother's blue eyes flared with heat. Heat and anger. So much anger. Cat didn't deserve to be on the end of that look. He was being unfair. That look knocked him off the pedestal I'd always placed him on.

Instead of backing down, Cat's voice turned icy. "You're scared for her life and under a lot of stress, and you want to protect her. But keeping her away from someone she wants to be with—someone who wants to be with her—that's just selfish, Ace. Selfish and… Not. Your. Decision."

Ace laughed, a brittle laugh that scattered goose bumps over my arms and made Cat's eyes slant further. "Whatever. It's not like women are known for being reasonable. You just invited a band of fucking delinquents to visit us in Neverra."

Cat whipped her head back. "Because telling them they can never go would do our relations so much good?" she snapped. "Go home, Ace. Go home, and calm down, and when you're ready to apologize for being a jerk, you can come back here."

Ace stood so straight it looked like he'd grown a few inches. He turned toward the portal and pressed his palm against it. His stamp flashed, and then his body was sopped up by the magical door.

The fight had thinned the oxygen from the air. Every breath I pulled did little to expand my shrunken lungs. Cat's black eyes shimmered like the top of the lake crashing outside the boathouse. I walked up to her and hugged her. Her body stayed stiff, and for a moment, I was terrified that she was angry with me, but then she snorted.

"Unreasonable?" Her gush of breath tickled my earlobe. "Men."

After I pulled away from her, I signed, *You'll forgive him, right?*

She wiped her eyes on her sleeve and smiled. "This isn't our first fight, Lily, and it won't be our last." She bit her curved lip. "But he's going to have to grovel a hell of a lot to get out of this one. *Unreasonable?*" she said again, shaking her head.

The lightness of her tone perked up my sullen mood. *Sorry.*

"For what?"

For causing your fight.

"Are you kidding? You have nothing to be sorry about. Ace is worried out of his mind, and that's going to color everything that concerns you. But that's because he adores you. Remember that if he ever tries to tell you what to do."

She was right, and yet the pain of Ace's ban remained as fresh and raw as the new skin girdling my wrists.

Gold light erupted from the locker. Cat and I held our breaths, waiting for a body to emerge, but none appeared.

Minutes passed and still no one came back out. The air turned so frigid that I began to shiver. Cat rubbed my arms, and then she stood and walked over to the portal.

"If this is going to take much longer, then we should wait at home. You're freezing and probably tired as hell." She placed her hand on the locker, and her stamp flared. "I'll go see what's the hold-up and come right back, okay?"

I nodded.

She laid her palm flat against the portal, but it didn't swallow her up. Frowning, she lifted her hand and pressed it again. Nothing.

"It's...it's not working." As she pulled her hand back, horror painted her face a spectral shade of white. "They must've changed the lock."

She spun toward me, the W on the top of her hand glowing as wildly as her unusable portal stamp, and even though she remained uncharacteristically pale, her dread faded. She pulled me off the bench and all but squashed my fingers against the portal.

My stamp lit up. Heart walloping my ribs, I inhaled and waited for the familiar tug.

But there was no tug.

The portal remained as hard as a mirror.

They'd locked us both out and locked themselves inside.

"*W*e're not freaking out," Cat said, but anxiety coated her tone. "They're probably just tinkering with the combination, trying to align it with your mark."

My body felt filled with drugs—weightless, numb, and yet so incredibly heavy. I tried moving, but I couldn't even lift the soles of my boots.

What if they'd locked the portals forever because of my stupid, warped stamp? My brother needed Cat; she needed *him*. As though her heart were suspended outside her body, I heard it tear. She tried to appear strong for a couple more seconds, rambling on about how this was just a hiccup, but then she stopped talking and stared at the unyielding portal the same way she'd gawked at Kajika's body rising from his rose petal grave.

In absolute terror.

I'd been there; I remembered. I'd seen other hunters rise from their magical slumber since, and yet Kajika's awakening had remained the most vivid and momentous. Perhaps because it was the first I'd witnessed. Or perhaps because I'd been frightened by the magic that had come into play, but also awed by it...by *him*, the warrior with whorls of captive dust.

"I'm sure it's going to be okay," Cat said. She removed the hand she'd kept on my wrist and rubbed her clammy palm against her sweater. "They'll be back in the morning."

But what if they weren't? What if it took months for them to reconfigure the lock? What if Gregor had done this on purpose? What if the acorn—

"I'll run us home. Get on my back."

Although I wanted to object, tell her I'd rather walk or fly, I didn't put up a fight. I climbed onto her back, and she rushed through the gray, snowy darkness toward the cemetery. Once we arrived, she set me down. My legs were so numb they barely carried me up the porch and through the door.

The lights were off, but the TV was on. Cat's dad was lying on the couch, moving images splashing light over his face.

When he saw us, he jumped to his feet. "Lily, you're home!"

He hugged me, but I stayed so rigid, he stepped back and took me in, and then he took in his daughter. "Why do you girls look like someone died?"

"What?" Cat's voice was so strident it made both of Derek's eyebrows jot up.

"*Did* someone die?"

Cat swallowed. "No. No." She was still squeaking.

"Then what's wrong? Because something's wrong…"

"My dress might not be ready in time for the wedding," Cat blurted out.

"*That's* what's troubling you? It's only a dress. We can go tomorrow to the mall and buy you a new dress. Or to Detroit. Or wherever you buy fancy wedding gowns."

Cat kept up the charade. "But I wanted that one." Either she was protecting Derek, or thinking about the wedding and the dress kept her from breaking apart.

Derek smiled and shook his head. "You shouldn't lend such importance to a dress, honey. I know it's your big day and every-thing, and I remember how important it was for your mother. But take it from someone who's been there, done that…it'll be perfect. Because a wedding isn't about wearing a beautiful dress, it's about marrying the right person, and you've got the right person."

Tears streamed down Cat's cheeks as the full force of what had happened hit her. Derek tucked her into his arms. I gulped down the giant lump that had started forming in my throat in the boathouse and stepped around them toward my bedroom.

"Oh, Lily, Kajika stopped by earlier to drop off your suitcase," Derek said over the top of Cat's head. "Did you have a fun trip?"

I stared at him as though he'd asked if I were having my period. When his forehead scrunched, I gave him a paltry thumbs-up and entered my bedroom, closing the door gently behind me. For a long moment, I didn't move. I just stared at my suitcase, the last forty-eight hours spooling through my mind.

The golden flare of the portal haunted me. I walked over to the suitcase. As I unzipped it, I thought of the man whose boat sank.

I had to pay him back.

I removed my clothes from the suitcase and put the clean ones back into my closet and the dirty ones into my hamper, and then I stored my suitcase inside the little walk-in closet in the corner. I was about to crawl into bed when I noticed a little shopping bag on my nightstand. I picked it up and fished out a box. A new cell phone and a new chip.

Had Kajika gotten me a new phone?

I walked toward my window and looked out. Snow fell but more softly, like powdered sugar through a sieve. I scanned the woods, looking for the hunter, but he wasn't there. He was probably at home. I pressed my palm against the glass pane and watched as fog formed around my fingers.

I went through the motions after that—brushed my teeth, pulled on leggings and a long-sleeved t-shirt, then slid the chip into my new phone. I was about to send Kajika a message to thank him, when I realized he must have a new phone number, too.

Tomorrow.

I'd go see him tomorrow.

My lids shut, but sleep didn't come. I couldn't turn off the reel of nightmarish memories. They played out over and over. I wondered if other faeries had been locked out. How terrified they would be when their portal stamps didn't take them home.

My door squeaked open. I hadn't drawn the drapes closed, so moonlight fell over my visitor, illuminating her puffy eyes and pallor.

"I can't sleep," Cat croaked.

I patted my bed, and she slid beneath the comforter.

"What if they don't come back?"

I slotted my fingers through hers and squeezed.

"I made him leave."

Silence settled over us like drifting snow.

"What if those were my last words to him?"

Another long stretch of silence.

At some point I must've fallen asleep because when I awoke, the pillow Cat had slept on was cold. Bleak light stretched over my bedroom. I got up and padded to the kitchen. It was empty. I went upstairs, the steps squeaking beneath my bare feet. Cat's door was open and her bed made. She was gone. I suspected I knew where she'd gone—back to the boathouse.

I returned to my bedroom and got dressed. My shearling boots were gone and so was my favorite leather jacket, both ruined by the lake, but thankfully I had other boots and other coats. I belted my oatmeal cashmere jacket, slipped my new phone into my pocket, and then left.

Cat's car was parked in front of the house, but her footsteps were stamped in the snow. At some point, the trail thinned—the imprints of her boots too few and far between to follow. She must've been sprinting. It took me twenty minutes to reach the boathouse. She wasn't there, but fresh snow littered the floor so she must've come, unless another faerie had come through here.

I pressed my hand against the back of locker number four, and my stamp flared, but the portal stayed hard and unyielding.

I retraced my footsteps, about to head into the forest toward Kajika's house, when I spotted movement in Astra's. I went there.

Cat wasn't sitting at one of the communal tables.

"Lily!" Cassidy squealed. "Where did you disappear to? I tried calling you, like, a million times."

I signed, *Lost my phone.*

"Oh, no! How? Where?"

I pointed to the lake.

"That sucks."

I took out my new one and sent her a message from my retrieved contacts. **Lily's new number.** And then I typed: **Did Cat come by this morning?**

"Nope. You're my very first customer. You want anything to drink?"

I nodded.

"Your usual?"

I nodded. As she steamed soy milk, I took a seat at a table and phoned Cat. It went to voicemail. I sent her a message mentioning this was my new number and to call me back. Since no one else came in, Cass sat with me and filled me in on Faith and baby Remo, showing me a thousand pictures of Remo from every angle imaginable. At some point, Faith came in, pushing a bulky stroller. My heart, which had felt as clunky as a piece of corroded steel, lightened.

I lifted Remo from the stroller and clutched him possessively against my chest. My anxiety faded as I watched his tiny lips stretch into a yawn that turned into the sweetest whimper. Although I didn't want to hand him over to his mother, I did. She tucked him under her sweater, where he squirmed before becoming blissfully still. When he was done suckling and had passed out into a milk-induced coma, she handed him over. I held him all morning, marveling at how absolutely exquisite he was.

"Lily, is it me or is your palm glowing?" Faith asked after she'd deposited a cinnamon bun in front of a customer.

I sucked in a breath and tucked Remo closer, but Faith leaned over to have a better view of my hand, her auburn eyebrows mashing up over her eyes. I didn't think she could see faerie light, but her father was Gregor—a pure fae—and her mother had been half-fae. I cast my gaze toward Cassidy, who was laughing at something a customer had said. Could she also see faerie light?

Faith plucked my index finger off the baby blanket. Thankfully my hand had stopped glowing.

"I seriously need more sleep." She yawned and returned to the counter to help Cass out with the lunch crowd—mostly high school students who'd come for a sandwich or a slice of homemade quiche.

Remo opened his little eyes and fixed them on me. They were as penetrating as his grandfather's. His grandfather who wanted to bring his family to Neverra. Last night, I'd accused him of messing with the lock. Only now, gazing into his grandson's face, did I realize how unfair that was.

Remo closed his eyes, oblivious to the entire world. How I envied his peacefulness, his lack of worries, his absence of fear. As I slicked a silken cowlick down, my palm glowed again. What was Kajika doing? Working out? Had he heard about the portals? Had Cat called him? I checked my phone, expecting an answer to my text message, but Cat hadn't answered me. Had she even seen my message?

The light in my palm extinguished before returning and then shutting off again, the sequence as quick as hummingbird wings. I stood up so abruptly, a cry burst from Remo's mouth. Placing an apologetic kiss against his wrinkled forehead, I set him down in the stroller.

Faith was already coming toward us, wiping her hands on her apron. "What happened?"

I speared my glowing hand through my coat to conceal the glow. With my other hand, I grabbed my phone and typed: **I promised Derek I would go grocery shopping with him.**

She bent over the stroller and shushed her little boy by drawing circles over his brow. "Will you come back later?"

I nodded.

"Or you and Cat can come over tonight, and we can do a girl's dinner." Faith bit her lip. "Unless you have other plans."

I'd love to come. Let me check with Cat once she gets home. I'll text you.

Even though my hand was still ensconced in my coat jacket, heat prickled my skin, followed by the most chilling cold. I concentrated on Kajika's location.

The cauliflower lake.

The small house.

He was home.

Then why was he in mortal danger?

As soon as I penetrated the outskirt of the forest, I soared off the spongy layer of pine cones and deadened twigs. In my haste, I'd forgotten about my pitiful attempt to tread air the night before. Just as it happened when I'd torn myself out of Cruz's arms, gravity tugged at my heels and flung me to the ground.

Snow hadn't penetrated the dense foliage, and I hit the earth with a dull thud. I sprang to my feet and dusted myself off, taking off at a rapid run down the trail that led away from the beach toward Kajika's house. I focused wholly on not tripping so as not to dwell on my inability to fly.

On what it meant...

My palm flickered, stealing my attention away from my trajectory. A branch slapped my cheek so hard it startled me to a stop. I nursed my throbbing cheek, but then I thought of Kajika and took off again. More branches whipped me, and I winced from their assault, but I didn't slow, not even when my lungs felt close to collapsing.

I was used to walking. I wasn't one of those faeries who kept their feet bare of shoes because they didn't want to tread the same ground as the *calidum*, but I wasn't used to the strain of running.

It took me almost fifteen minutes to reach Kajika's house. In the silver gloom of the afternoon, it seemed empty of life, and yet there was life somewhere in there. A heart beating too fast or too slowly.

I knocked on the front door, tossing my silent voice to warn him of my presence. I waited for an answer, but one never came. Hesitantly I walked toward his bedroom window, keeping my eyes lowered in case—

I swallowed, the memory thickening my saliva.

I knuckled the window, still not daring to look in. *Kajika, if you want me to leave, just grunt.*

Besides the rustling of nearby leaves, there was no sound. Finally, I lifted my gaze. What I saw through that windowpane iced the fire in my veins.

THE STONE

I clawed at the window, banged on it, trying to get the hunter to startle awake. He was wearing jeans and nothing else. His skin, usually dark, was the hue of molten wax. What the hell had happened to him?

Kajika! I screamed into our bond. *Kajika!*

The hunter was sprawled on stained, crumpled bedsheets. Hunters bled like humans but healed like faeries. His pallor told me he wasn't healing from whatever wound he'd incurred. Had he been attacked? Had one of the Daneelies returned to finish him off? Pete or Quinn, maybe? I stopped banging on the glass, stopped breathing, and listened for another presence.

If someone was here, they were being exceptionally quiet. I pumped my fingers to fill them with dust and then stared around me for a rock to crack the glass, but then thought better than to shatter a window and invite the brutal chill of autumn.

I loped around the house to the front door and twisted the knob. When it didn't give, I summoned my fire and heated the lock until it melted, pooling along the grains of wood. I drew the door wide and stepped in, scanning the dark foyer for a sign of life. When no one leaped at me, I headed toward the gaping bedroom door. My boot skidded over the hardwood floor, and I windmilled my arms, catching myself on a chest of drawers that was so rough, a splinter snaked underneath my skin. Smoke leaked from the puncture wound. I hissed as I pinched the tiny stick and flicked it onto the floor where it landed in what had made me slip.

I crouched and sniffed. Blood.

I rushed to Kajika's side.

Kajika? I palmed his face.

He was as hot as a skillet. Even though the W on the top of his hand still flickered—a sign of life—I hunted his wrist for a pulse. It tickled the tips of my fingertips, but the beats were so sluggish it did little to appease me. Carefully, I probed his chest for the source of blood.

Although his waist was reddened, there was no cut. At least none that I could see. I tried to roll him onto his stomach to have a view of his back when my thumb grazed a lump on the inside of his forearm. A lump that had been patched with thick stitches. Rivulets of blood thinned by a yellowish liquid oozed around the thread, widening the puddle beneath the hunter.

I was no doctor, but whatever had been sewn beneath his skin was infecting his body. I was about to pad out to the kitchen when I spotted a pair of nail clippers on his nightstand, along with the needle and thread that had been used. Anger rammed into me like the dust bull a jouster had long ago created during a Middle-Month celebration.

I would gas whoever did this. *Wita* pricked my fingertips. I pushed it back as I snatched the nail clippers. Carefully, I snipped the thread and tugged it out. The wound gaped like an open mouth, and blood gushed out, splashing over my hands and splattering my coat, ejecting the trapped lump. I prodded the skin around the torn flesh for more lumps, but was met only with taut sinews and elastic muscle.

Before my very eyes, Kajika's skin zippered shut, confirming that what had poisoned him was gone, that his body could now start healing. Even though Seelies and Unseelies weren't "allergic" to the same things, I didn't dare touch the blood-slickened clump with my bare fingers. I created a net with dust and then scooped up the thing and carried it into the bathroom. I dumped it into the sink, where it clattered like a rock. My dust funneled back into my palm as I twisted the faucet handle. Water streamed out and rinsed away the blood, revealing a cloudy-white surface veined with neon oranges and electric blues.

Confusion tamped down my earlier anger as I took in what that had poisoned the hunter—opal. I waited until the water ran clear before reaching down and picking it up. How had it gotten under his skin? Had someone—a vengeful Seelie or a bitter Daneelie—figured out that opal had a hostile effect beneath flesh? I didn't even know this, and I'd been versed in all thing Unseelie and hunter-related.

A gust of something foul stained the air and turned my stomach. I held the opal farther from my nose, thinking it to be the source, but it didn't lessen the smell. I jolted my gaze toward the doorway beyond which the hunter lay. I parted my lips and breathed in only through my mouth as I returned to the room.

I pressed a fist against my mouth as I approached his motionless figure. I placed the stone in the waistband of his briefs so it came into contact with his skin, and as suddenly as it had breezed through the house, the smell dissipated.

I straightened up and gazed down upon Kajika, hating that a stone had to come between us, and yet thankful for its existence. I sighed as I went about cleaning up the mess. I started with burning the blood underneath the sole of my shoes so I wouldn't leave gory footprints in my wake, and then I explored the house, opening doors and cupboards until I located what I was looking for—a mop and a bucket. I filled the bucket with water, squirted soap into it, and then grabbed the mop. I returned to the bedroom and mopped, the coarse strings of yarn squishing wetly as they soaked up the hunter's blood. I rinsed and repeated the motion throughout his entire bedroom, and then I retraced my steps into the bathroom, swirling the mop.

When the water dried, curly white streaks remained. Had I

mopped wrong? Was I not supposed to put water on wood? Or was it the soap I'd used? I'd never mopped anything in my life…had never ironed or dusted. Everything had been done for me when I lived in Neverra, and since I'd moved to Rowan, I'd used fire.

If I'd managed to fly earlier, I would've conjured up flames to clean Kajika's house, but I hadn't managed to fly. I was running out of time. And now with the portals closed—

I shook my head to dispel the macabre thoughts.

I emptied the pink water into the toilet and then returned both the mop and bucket to the closet. I grabbed a dishtowel and saturated it with water and soap, and then I stole a dry one from the pile in the closet and treaded back to Kajika. I gently rubbed his skin, smearing the blood at first, but then the wet cotton absorbed the red smudges. I patted him dry, then rested my palm against his forehead.

The fever had dropped. I pressed my palm against his bare chest, and the steady vibrations of his heart drummed into my hand. My fingertips met the edge of one of his tattoos. I traced the pattern with my index, sensing the captive *wita* palpitate. Was it my mother's, or had my mother's been one of the ones released in the Daneelie camp?

Sensing Kajika wouldn't appreciate my exploration, I pulled my hand away and went to deposit the soiled dishtowels in a corner of his bathroom. In the mirror over the sink, I caught sight of my coat. I conjured up a minute amount of fire and burned away the blood splatter.

And now on to the bed…

I heaved open the dresser drawers. They squeaked as they slid out. In the first two, underwear, socks, and t-shirts were arranged in neat, monochromatic rows. There wasn't a hint of color in the hunter's wardrobe.

The last drawer enclosed what I was looking for—fresh sheets. I removed a stack and set it on top, then untucked the sheet underneath Kajika and struggled to roll him over, but it was like trying to dislodge a boulder wedged in sand. I tried to shimmy the sheets from underneath the hunter, but the attempt was useless. All I managed was to crease the soiled sheets.

I walked to the other side of the bed and crawled, kneeling beside him, hoping the new angle would give me more leverage over his body. I slid my hands underneath his waist, attempting to roll him over again, but my second try was just as pathetic as the first. I didn't even manage to lift his body an inch.

Warmed by the effort, I took off my coat and flung it at the desk chair. Even though I could hear my brother yelling at me not to waste my fire, I summoned it into my fingers and directed it onto the spillage. The red stain lifted from the stone-colored sheets like a wave retracting from sand.

So much blood had leaked from the hunter's arm that it took almost a minute to burn it all away. I curled my fingers and turned to get off the bed, but my vision dotted and then the room swam out of focus.

When I opened my eyes next, I was staring at the low timber rafters of Kajika's ceiling. Darkness lapped at the corners of my eyes and then swept me under again.

23

FIXED

*F*ive points of heat radiated around my navel. I dipped my head down to see what was causing this sensation and froze when I saw a large, dark hand resting lightly on my stomach. I jerked my gaze around the room, trying to remember where I was. A sliver of moonlight shone on a small desk and a wooden dresser. Above my head, a motionless fan was nailed to timber rafters.

Oh, skies, I was in Kajika's room...in his bed. What he must think...

I tried to roll away from the hunter, but the hand flattened against my skin and rolled me toward him instead.

His dark eyes were wide open, and they were staring straight at me.

My breathing hitched. *I'm—I'm sorry. I didn't mean to fall asleep in your bed. Your brand flickered.*

His thumb stroked my spine and raised goose bumps.

Kajika, someone tried to poison you!

His thumb stilled.

They sewed opal beneath your skin, and...and it was infecting you. I—I took it out.

He removed his hand from my skin and touched the spot on his forearm that was completely healed. "Where is it?" His voice sounded hoarse, as though it too had been affected by the opal.

In your waistband.

He fished it out and clutched it so tight I expected it to drip through his white-knuckled fingers like grains of sand.

I sat up and pulled my knees against myself to reduce the space my body illicitly occupied. *Did you see who did it?*

The muscles in his broad shoulders twitched, and then his eyes slid shut, the few black lashes spared by the duct tape grazing his cheek. He, too, rolled up, each abdominal muscle shifting beneath his dark skin. He flung his long legs off the bed and sat there with his curved back to me.

"No." His whispered word skated over my skin.

I reached out to touch his hunched shoulder. When my palm connected with his warm skin, he turned as stiff as one of the quartz spheres that used to adorn the palace turrets. *We'll find who did this to you, and we'll make them pay.*

He hung his head.

For a moment, we sat there bathed in dusk and silence, but then an insistent vibration cut through the stillness.

Realizing where the sound was coming from, I crawled off the bed and hurried to my coat for my phone. Sure enough, the screen was lit with a dozen messages. Two from Faith, all the others from Cat.

Where are you? The last one read, **I'm worried.**

I texted her immediately to ask about the lock, leaving out the answer to where I was.

"Is everything all right?"

I snapped my head up toward the hunter, and my forehead bumped into his collarbone. I jerked back, surprised by his proximity. I hadn't even heard him approach. My senses were so dull I wanted to scream.

"Is everything all right?" he repeated hoarsely.

I shook my head. At least it hadn't been. Maybe it was now. Maybe—

My phone pulsated, and I jolted my gaze to the lit screen, to Cat's two-letter answer: **No.**

A chill steeped my body.

"What is wrong?"

Where are you? I texted.

Home.

On my way.

The hard lines of the hunter's face fragmented before piecing together again. *They found the lock to the portals yesterday.* Was it yesterday or had more time elapsed?

His pupils churned. "They found it?"

I bit my lip and nodded. And if it hadn't been for me, his family could've been given stamps; they could've come back to him.

I wasn't sure if he heard my thoughts, but a muscle pinched in his broad shoulders.

"And?"

I stared down at my thick black socks. *And they tried to change the lock to match my stamp.* A tear tracked down my cheek. I scrubbed it off.

"It did not work?"

I hoped he didn't think that was the reason for my crying. I listened to his steady heartbeats, to the slow chug-chug of blood through his veins. I was probably imagining it. You can't hear blood move.

How I wished I could have blood, too. If only my mother had thought to deliver me on Earth... I grew angry at her.

Kajika gripped my chin and forced me to look at him. "What happened, Lily?"

It didn't allow me in, and now it's locked. My lungs shuddered. *Cat tried to get in, but it wouldn't let her in either. And Ace...he's... And your family...* I was unable to finish a single thought.

Even though his face was distorted by my falling tears, his gaze wasn't. There was so much anger in his eyes, and it was all my damn fault. I ripped my chin from his grasp and grabbed my coat, poking my arms through the holes blindly. And then I sought out my boots and slipped them on too, stumbling.

I should've just killed myself, because now my slow death was hurting people.

Kajika wound his fingers around my bicep and twirled me toward him. "Where are you going?"

To see Cat. She needs me.

Did she need me? What she probably needed was for me to go away for good...

"Lily, this is not your fault. They would have had to alter the lock to let my family back through those portals."

No they wouldn't! They just needed to find the lock to apply the stamp to your people's skin because Gregor couldn't engrave it like he can to Seelie skin. Besides, Ace wouldn't have gone back to Neverra without Cat if it wasn't for me. They wouldn't have fought if it wasn't for me.

"Why did they fight?"

My cheeks flamed. *I have to go.*

"Why did they fight?"

I don't want to talk about it.

"Lily..."

It's pointless. I snatched my arm out of his hand and stalked outside. The brisk air was a welcome balm against my overheated face. I began the long walk back toward Cat's house. I didn't even attempt to fly.

A branch snapped behind me. I whirled and scanned the darkness, my dust at the ready.

A shape as dark as the night itself detached itself from the obscurity. "It is just me."

I curled my fingers into my palms, my nails imprinting crescents into my skin. *Kajika, please...I want to be alone right now.*

He stopped. A gentle wind blew his black bangs into his eyes. "I will leave you alone once you are safe with Catori."

I'd scaled cliffs and traversed a desert alone; I'd double-crossed my father and Gregor; I'd shattered a bond to bring change into my world, but I'd done these things when I believed myself invincible.

I no longer possessed the luxury to think like this, so I let him follow me all the way back to the graveyard.

24

NAILS

*W*ithout glancing at Kajika, afraid of what I would see on his face—the disappointment of not getting his family back—I entered the glowing house, unzipped my boots, and hung up my coat.

Cat and Derek were sitting in the kitchen at a table set for three. Only Derek was eating. Cat had a plate full of macaroni and cheese in front of her. Although she held her fork, she didn't scrape any food off her plate. She simply stared at the mound of pasta, her eyes swollen and rimmed with emotion. I wondered if Derek still thought her tears were due to a dress.

My stomach felt like an elaborate origami, all twisted and bent, yet the creamy scent of cheese made it growl. After I took a seat, Derek touched the back of my hand.

"You had a good day, honey?"

I pressed my lips into a smile, not wanting to burden this incredibly kind man with my intractable heartache.

"Where were you?" Cat asked, her voice as raw as her expression.

I signed, *At the bakery.*

"With Faith? How's little Remo?" Derek asked.

Both Cat and her father had become so fluent in my silent language that it made my heart squeeze.

Great, I signed, then pointed to Cat. ***Did you see him?***

She shook her head.

"Cat was with her wedding planner all day," Derek said.

She studied her distorted reflection in her fork.

"I was just telling her that if the wedding's going to cause her so much stress, she should postpone it."

"I might have to," she whispered, spearing a lone macaroni and pushing it between her lips.

"Where's Ace anyway? Shouldn't he be going to all these meetings with you?"

She choked on her measly mouthful. After gulping down water, she croaked, "He's busy with work."

Derek cocked an eyebrow. "Well, tell him to take time off work. Better yet"—he slid his napkin on the table and rose—"I'll call him." He took his phone from the kitchen counter and dialed Ace's number.

Both Cat and I knew he'd be met with an answering machine because phones didn't work in Neverra.

"Ace? Hey, it's Derek."

Cat's fork clattered against the plate, and her gaze whipped toward me, pulsing with so much hope that I prayed Derek wasn't in the middle of leaving a message.

"She's under a lot of stress...yes. Exactly." Derek was nodding. "It should be unlocked, son."

The front door snicked open. Cat shot up so fast her chair skidded backward, tipping and clattering against the tiles.

"Cat? Lily?"

Like oxygen, my brother's voice inflated my body. I pressed my palms into the table and rose onto unsteady feet.

Cat dashed toward the living room so fast that her form blurred. Derek blinked before looking at his empty bottle of beer. His rational mind was probably telling him alcohol was playing tricks on his eyesight.

Soft sobbing echoed from the living room.

Derek let out a long sigh as he righted Cat's chair. "Now I get it." He looked my way, a knowing smile curving his lips. "Those two had a fight, didn't they? That's why she was acting so strange."

It wasn't the entire truth, but it was close enough. Keeping one hand on the wall, I nodded, then inched toward the doorway that separated the kitchen from the living room. Cat had her legs wrapped around my brother's waist, and her face buried in his neck, and Ace was speaking to her softly. When he saw me, he smiled. I clutched the doorframe, afraid that if I let go, I might collapse with relief.

He set Cat down gently and then advanced toward me. I was still holding on to the doorframe when he locked his arms around my neck and pulled me against him.

He didn't say a word to me, but his hands and the stiffness of his fingers told me everything I needed to know. That he was happy to see me again but sorry it hadn't worked.

As though fearing he might blink out of existence, Cat stayed close to Ace. After he released me, he slotted his hand through hers and didn't let go once. Not when he greeted Derek. Not when he ate. Not when dinner was over, and Derek left to meet Milly. I didn't think Ace would ever let go of Cat again.

"Gwen and Menawa came back with me," he said, as we sat on the couch, sipping warm tea.

"The portal stamps took to their skin?" Cat exclaimed.

Ace studied the steam that curled off the filmy surface of his beverage. "Yes. The lock made the new stamp stick." Ace traced the circle slashed with five lines that adorned her arm. "We're going to have to get yours altered next time you're in Neverra."

He displayed the new one. It didn't glow, but the pale trace of it was etched on his skin.

"How will I get back in? I'm not Seelie," Cat said. "Or does this new combination allow all faeries to enter Neverra?"

Ace's finger froze. Had he not considered this? "The portal is Seelie-made."

"Which means I can't—I can't come back…" Cat whispered.

I scooted to the edge of the armchair, then gripped my phone and typed: **Unless they put the combination back to what it was.**

"It's more complicated than it appears." Ace scrubbed his hand over his face. "That's why we got stuck."

Maybe the book pages magically updated.

Cat sprang off the couch and raced up to her bedroom where she'd stashed a few pages. She tore back down before I'd even exhaled the breath I'd taken. The thin, yellowed vellum she held shivered in her hands.

Ace glanced at the page, but the ink was invisible to us. One look at her taut expression confirmed the symbol hadn't morphed.

"Shit," Ace muttered. He tugged on Cat's hand and she fell into his lap. He kissed her temple. "We'll find a way. I promise."

I hated to think what would happen if they didn't. Cat and Ace would have to live apart…She'd age. He wouldn't, because it wasn't as though he could move here. At least, not without facing my predicament. As he spoke to her softly, I thought of Kajika. He, too, wouldn't be able to enter Neverra.

I picked at my chipping pink polish.

Maybe it wouldn't matter to him, though. He said he'd stayed here for me, but perhaps he'd stayed because he simply didn't want to go to Neverra, and drugs had loosened his tongue and made him say things he didn't mean. Under the influence, people said lots of things they didn't mean.

I wondered if he'd be disappointed. At least worrying about this momentarily distracted me from the question mark of my own fate.

I turned my gaze down to my ring finger. I peeled a long strip of polish off the nail. As it fell onto the carpet, I froze. My nails, usually a paler shade of peach than my skin, had turned the gray-purple of a raincloud. I gasped.

Ace swept a fretful gaze over me. "Everything all right, Lil'?"

I shot up to my feet, ears buzzing. I conjured up a small smile that jumped off my lips almost as swiftly as it had hopped on.

Tired, I signed, before remembering what had prompted me to stand. I balled my fingers and kept them clenched at my sides as I disappeared into my bedroom.

"Night, little sister." I heard Ace say through the door.

I headed to the bathroom and saturated a cotton disc with acetone, then scrubbed my nails energetically, hoping the purple shade would rub off along with the remnant of polish.

It didn't come off.

I touched my eyelashes, pinched one, and tugged gently. It didn't fall away, which momentarily reassured me, but my nails were purple, and I could no longer fly. It wouldn't be much longer now. I clutched the edges of the sink and leaned against it, eyes closed, chest heaving with a mixture of slow breaths and rapid heartbeats.

I had to leave Rowan fast—this time unaccompanied and untracked—because if Cruz caught wind of my failing body, skies only knew what he'd be capable of doing.

25

GOODBYES

*a*fter reapplying a new coat of polish to hide my decay, I curled onto my bed and fought off sleep, fearing more than ever that I wouldn't wake up. I thought of all the things I still longed to do, but that made me wistful, so instead I thought of all the things I'd gotten a chance to do.

In the twilight of my bedroom, I ran through the short list of people I'd been grateful to meet in the last year. Cat, Kajika, Derek, Cass, Faith… The Prices had become family. *My* family.

How do you thank someone for brightening your existence? How do you thank them for having made you feel loved and safe?

Derek's gift came to me swiftly. He loved sailing, so a lake boat would probably make him happy. I contacted my family's assistant. Even though it was the middle of the night, she answered my text messages immediately—which was one of the reasons she'd stayed in my family's employ for decades. The other reason was that she was part faerie. She asked me what her budget was, and I told her to get him the best boat on the market along with prepaid, lifelong maintenance. And then I asked her to book one of our private jets for a friend of mine and have it ready at lunchtime at the closest airstrip.

After she confirmed all would be ready, I tapped my phone

gently against the comforter. I couldn't just leave without saying goodbye to the people who'd been kind to me, who'd been true friends, so I got out of bed, added a thick sweater over my nightie and then tiptoed into the living room and pulled on my boots, coat, and grabbed Cat's car keys from the hook beside the door. Hoping that revving up the car wouldn't wake anyone, I slid behind the wheel and turned the key in the ignition.

I had never driven a car before and realized I was sort of excited to be sitting behind a wheel. For the first time in my life, I felt like I was steering my own life. The snow had thankfully not turned to ice, but it did make the tires slip a little. I could get used to driving...not that I would need to, but at least I understood why a lot of faeries enjoyed it. I thought this until the car skidded and almost ended up sidling against a tree.

My near-collision reminded me of the Eagle River fisherman whose boat now sat at the bottom of Lake Superior. When I arrived at my destination, I plucked my phone out of the cupholder and emailed my assistant to find out the identity of the owner so I could compensate him, and then I unstrapped my seat belt—a useless and so very human habit...a piece of tight fabric could unfortunately not save my life—and stepped out of the car.

I rang Faith's doorbell. A minute later, she drew her front door open. "Lily?" Her puffy eyes dragged over the darkened street behind me. "Is everything all right?"

I nodded and held out my arms for the screeching, bundled package in her arms.

"You came to babysit?" She snorted softly then gestured for me to enter before placing her son in my arms. "You do know he's not sleeping through the night?"

I nodded and mouthed, *Go.*

"You're sure you're—"

I smiled wide.

"Okay. If he gets hungry, just come and wake me. And his diapers and pacifier are..."

I nodded at everything she was saying, even though I was

entirely focused on Remo, who blinked eyes larger than his face at me.

When Faith returned to her bedroom, her son had stopped fussing. I rubbed my lips along his peach-fuzz cheek, then kissed the birthmark at his temple, taking in the milky, warm scent of him deep into my lungs.

My visit wasn't completely selfless...wasn't selfless at all, actually. My reasons for coming over were completely and utterly selfish.

Once Remo had fallen asleep, I padded over to the kitchen counter upon which Faith had dropped her handbag. I checked that her bedroom door was closed, then rummaged inside until my fingers closed over her wallet. I extricated it, then unzipped it with my teeth and pulled out her platinum Amex.

I snapped a picture of it, back and front, then returned the card to the wallet and the wallet to the bag. I sat on the couch, nestling Remo closer to my chest, and booked my hotel suite using the credit card information. Then I sent one last email to our assistant, asking her to open a bank account for Remo Sakar and to transfer five hundred thousand dollars from my account into it. The sum would cover what I'd borrowed from Faith and so much more.

Finally, I set my phone down and focused wholly on the little guy.

REMO SLEPT five hours against my chest, keeping me delightfully warm.

While he dozed, I caught up on all the social happenings in the world. Faith had a collection of tabloids that exceeded the CVS selection. Ace and Cat's nuptials graced the front page of many a magazine, but I skimmed those articles, already privy to all the details.

The only article I read was the one about me and my "bodyguard." The reporter had clipped a picture from the gas station video and added it beneath the headline: Mystery Bodyguard Unmasked. Although the picture of Kajika and me was fuzzy, the shot they'd added at the end of the article wasn't. It was a picture taken during one of his fights, in an arena that wasn't the barn. Row upon row of seated spectators graced the background. *Native American ultimate fighting champion signs record deal.*

Kajika had signed a contract to fight? When had that happened?

The article went on about his brisk rise to stardom and the speculation that it had to do with being in my employ. And of course, that bit was followed by hearsay that we were secretly dating. I closed the magazine and picked up my phone.

When did you become a professional fighter? I texted him.

Even though the sun had barely peeked over the horizon, my phone lit up with an answer. **A few weeks ago.**

Why didn't you tell me?

Because it does not matter.

It does. It's huge news. Congrats!

Thank you, Lily.

Question: do you remember the name of the boat we were on? The one that sank?

Why?

Because I feel bad and want to replace it.

I have already taken care of it.

Kajika.

Lily.

Let me at least pay you back.

No.

For a brief moment, I thought of insisting. Boats cost a lot of money. Money he probably didn't have, even though he'd signed a contract, whereas I had so much and not a lot of use for it. In the end, I let it go.

My brother and Gwenelda are back.

I heard. How are they?

Well.

Happy to be home?

The dot-dots lit up for so long that I expected an exhaustive answer. All I got was: **Why are you up so early?**

I didn't sleep.

Is something wrong?

I was incredibly thankful he couldn't read my mind through the device. **No. Everything's great.** I added a smiley face. **Why are you up so early?**

I was catching up with Menawa.

So did he hate Neverra?

There was a long pause. **You know the answer to that.**

AHA.

He told me they failed to match your stamp.

I shrugged, which made little Remo squirm. I waited until he settled down before answering, **I didn't expect anything different.**

What happens now?

I leave. That was what would happen now. **They're working on a new solution.** I rubbed the tip of my index finger over my thumb-nail as though I could feel the purple color of it beneath the three coats of red varnish.

Where are you?

My heart spiked. **Why?**

Because you are not home.

I am at a friend's house.

Which friend?

A friend.

Why do you not want to tell me which friend?

Because I don't want you to come and pluck thoughts from my mind and foil my careful planning. I stared down at Remo. **A male friend.** Kajika would interpret my words very differently. I hated to make him believe I was with a grown man, but realized it would keep him away. **I should get off the phone. He's waking up.**

The hunter didn't answer me. I wondered if he would ever answer me again or if this would be our last conversation. My throat felt thick with things remaining to tell him. I swallowed but it didn't help loosen the lump. I kissed little Remo, and like in Sleeping

Beauty, my kiss awakened him. The pacifier tumbled out of his mouth, and then the shrillest cry tore out of his lungs.

A second later, Faith barreled into the living room, red hair crimped in wild waves. "Oh, God, I didn't even realize the time! He must be starving."

I smiled, hugged him to me one last time, then released him into the cradle of his mother's arms.

Faith slid him against her breast to nurse him while I rose from the couch. I watched them a moment, my chest clenching at the idea that this was goodbye. I touched Faith's shoulder and smiled down at her.

"Lily, I don't know how to thank you for tonight. I—" She glanced up at me then. "Are you crying?"

I rubbed my eyes. Sure enough, my skin came back slick with tears. I mimed being sleepy, and that seemed to reassure Faith. I caressed the top of Remo's head one last time, then turned away before I became a weepy mess.

I sat in the car a long time before turning the key in the ignition. I needed to get my emotions under control before I headed home. When the sun rose, I drove over to Astra's, where Cass was already setting up. I feigned having been sent to pick up muffins. While they finished baking, she told me she wanted to organize a bachelorette party for Cat. As much as I longed to be part of it, my staying would darken the coming days. I hugged Cassidy tight before picking up the cardboard box filled with sweet-smelling, gooey muffins.

After I reached the cemetery, I walked around the jungle of headstones, reading each and every inscription, until I stopped by Ley's grave. My name would never be immortalized in stone, but a flower would rise from my ashes the same way a liana of sparkling roses had emerged from hers.

I hoped it would be a startlingly beautiful flower.

THE PASSENGERS

"*W*here were you?"

I spun to find my brother leaning against the porch railing.

I signed Faith's name, before he could jump to another conclusion.

"Uh-huh." He pushed off the balustrade and walked down to where I stood.

It's true, I signed.

"I believe you."

You don't look like you believe me.

He cocked his head to the side, staring deep into my eyes. "How did you get to her place?"

I pointed to Cat's car—the only car parked in front of the house. Derek must've left early, or maybe he hadn't come home.

"You drove?"

I nodded, proud.

"How many pedestrians are going to be suing us for severed limbs?"

I rolled my eyes but smiled.

His stance loosened then. He peered past me, at the circle of graves enclosed by the leafless Rowan trees. The memory of the hunters awakening still haunted me. It hadn't been the stuff of nightmares—Kajika and Gwen had ended up using warm corpses to awaken their dead relatives—but still, I'd found the process unnerving.

The idea had been Cruz's. He'd retrieved one of the two corpses in the metal fridge from Cat's basement. The spirit still lingered in spite of the fact that the man had died several hours earlier. He'd tossed the corpse at Gwen's feet, suggesting they use it. Kajika had refused to risk the life of one of his tribespeople.

What about an animal's spirit? I'd asked him through our bond.

He'd stared at the casket he'd unearthed but which still lay sealed. *I do not think it will work, Lily.*

Better hurry. The man's spirit will detach itself soon, Cruz had said.

Sure enough, like a spiderweb, the spirit was already ripping.

Gwen had laid a hand on Kajika's forearm. *Let us try.*

What if the body of Menawa rests in this grave?

That had made Gwen pull her shoulders back into a line as tight as a bow string.

There is a man who sleeps by Bee's Place and who reeks of alcohol, Kajika had told Cruz. *Fetch him. If your idea disappoints, all will not be lost.*

Cruz had gone to find the man. Grimacing from the stench of the man's unwashed body, which was almost as noxious as a hunter devoid of opal, Cruz had dropped him on the transparent divide between the graveyard and the ancient circle.

Gwenelda, who'd already set the corpse next to the grave, pulled the homeless man into the circle of rowan trees. He didn't put up a fight, too busy gawping between the sky and Cruz.

When Kajika lifted the casket's lid, I'd pressed up on my tippy toes to peer at the body inside, but could only see the layer of spelled rose petals and legs that seemed too feminine to belong to Menawa. From the few stories Kajika had shared with me, I'd deduced the brother who'd carried him to safety when Kajika was just a boy would be tall and lithe too.

Of course I could've been wrong, but one look at Kajika's face told me the person in the grave wasn't his brother. Gwenelda read the Gottwa inscription while offering up the corpse, whose spirit hung by a thread as thin as the one that had hemmed the cloud-blue silk dress I'd worn that day.

The spirit detached itself, as though blown by a gust of wind, but instead of rising into the sky, it slipped inside the open grave.

Magena, Gwenelda had whispered as a girl with short black hair sat up, stirring rose petals as she stretched thin arms over her head.

Without uttering a single word, Kajika had stared and stared at Ishtu's sister. I watched him watch her. When his dark eyes gleamed with tears that never fell, something disconcerting had stirred deep within me.

His eyes had cut straight to me, and I'd blushed, but I hadn't turned away or fled. I'd stayed rooted to the edge of the rowan circle until the other hunters awakened with more fresh corpses Cruz and two *lucionaga* had flown in from mortuaries. I watched Menawa come back to life and embrace Gwenelda, adoration crackling between them, then cinch his brother in a bone-crushing hug.

Only after they'd all risen did I leave. I'd gone to walk on the beach, which was where Cruz had found me hours later.

He'd been the only one to come looking for me.

"If faerie petals kept the hunters alive, then maybe they could keep you alive, Lily." My brother's voice broke me out of my reverie.

I stared at him in horror. Had he just suggested interring me?

"It would only be until we figured out a way to get you home."

I shook my head so vehemently that my ponytail whipped my cheeks.

Ace's Adam's apple worked in his unshaven throat. He reached out and plucked one of my hands, squeezing it between his own. "Your skin is ice-cold."

I snatched it away then pointed to the gray sky.

His blue eyes narrowed. "You can lie to many people, but not to me. Never to me."

Not a lie.

He snorted.

Is Cat still sleeping?

The assistant had sent me a message while I was at Astra's that my ride out of Rowan was sitting on the airstrip, waiting for me. Even though the pilots were at my beck and call and would wait for me, however long it took, I needed to leave before my plan was unearthed like the Gottwas's caskets.

I started toward the house when Ace called me back. "What are your plans for today?"

I froze. Was this a test? Had the assistant or one of the pilots betrayed me? Making sure my face was blank, I turned toward him. *Sleep. I didn't sleep last night.*

I didn't wait around to see if he believed me. Once I reached my destination, I would leave him a letter. Oh, skies, the next few days would be so difficult. I gulped but the lump stuck to my throat.

Inside the house, Derek was having coffee with Milly, who was already dressed in her purple scrubs.

"Hey, sweetie, how did you sleep?" Derek asked.

I gave him a thumbs-up.

"Want some coffee?" Milly asked me.

I shook my head but grabbed a bottle of water from the fridge before climbing the stairs toward Cat's bedroom. I knocked.

"Come in."

I let myself into the still-dark room. Cat was in bed with the covers up to her chin. When she saw me, she stretched her arms and smiled slowly. "Where did you spend the night?"

I frowned.

She turned onto her side. "I know you didn't sleep here. Ace went to check on you, and you weren't in bed."

I signed that I was with Remo, which made her already slanted eyes slant some more.

"Really?"

I nodded.

"I thought you would've been with—"

I shook my head before she could utter Kajika's name because footsteps resounded on the stairs.

My brother burst into the bedroom. "Cat, we need to get going, so get dressed."

A frown gusted over Cat's face. "Where is it that we're going?"

"To Holly's farm."

Cat sat up. "Holly's farm? Why?"

"'Cause there's a fucking new hunter in town."

"What?" She flung the covers off her legs and stood. "Who made a new hunter?"

Ace's gaze slanted toward me. "Kajika."

My heart banged, and I felt its echo against each one of my ribs.

Cat furrowed her brow. "*Kajika* made a new hunter? When?"

"Remember that guy who Kajika went Hannibal Lecter on? Well apparently he wasn't Daneelie; he was just married to one."

Cat's lips formed a perfect O while mine parted to release a relieved breath. Not because a new hunter had risen—that was terrible news considering the human he'd been—but because Kajika hadn't done it on purpose. Ace had no reason to hold it against him.

"Gwen just stopped by to tell me all about the new recruit. Today just keeps getting better and better." He glanced at me as he said this, which of course made my cheeks tingle with guilt.

He doesn't know what I have planned, I reassured myself.

"He's here in Rowan?" Cat yanked clothes off hangers, then vanished into the bathroom to get dressed.

Ace's gaze finally unfastened from mine. "Yes," he answered loud enough for her to hear through the door, which opened, letting out a sweet lavender stream that trailed Cat as she blurred around the room, grabbing phone, keys, and a couple of folded twenties.

Cat's hazy form sharpened as she finally stopped moving to stuff everything in the pocket of her skinny gray jeans. "Are others with him?"

"Charlotte, her eldest son, and the guy's wife came along for the ride too."

What's going to happen to the man? I signed.

"What do you mean, what's going to happen to him?" Ace asked.

Will they kill him?

"Kill him? Why, Lily, hunters aren't murderers...*right*?" Sarcasm dripped from Ace's tone. Anger didn't bring out the best in people, but in my brother, it brought out the absolute worst.

I didn't want to remember him like this. Cat must've been really preoccupied by Ace's news because she didn't comment on his surly remark.

She tugged open her window. "Lily, are you coming with us?"

"Lily's going to take a nap."

"Why don't you take a nap later?" she asked me.

"Because her night was too exhausting."

It hit me then that my brother truly didn't believe I'd been with Faith and Remo.

Making sure Derek wasn't out and about in the graveyard, he grabbed Cat, hoisting her into his arms. She hooked her arms around his neck. Before taking flight, he tossed out, "Have a nice nap, sis. Oh, and I stationed a guard by the house, so don't try anything stupid." And then he leaped out the window and took to the mottled gray sky.

Crap. Now I had a *lucionaga* to get rid of?

After they shot through the clouds, I returned to my bedroom. I'd been about to unplug my charger and roll it up when I remembered I'd need to get rid of my phone to stay untraceable. Besides the cash I kept in a hatbox in the closet, nothing was coming with me.

I called a cab, then hesitated to send Kajika one last message, but instead I powered off my phone and stashed it inside a fur-lined boot. I wouldn't be needing it where I was going. I looked up at the light fixture illuminating my closet and an idea came to me. Not a great one, but it would have to do.

I went out into the graveyard and squinted around the white landscape for the black-clad guard, but saw none. Maybe he'd followed Ace. Maybe—

A firefly buzzed by the porch railing.

I gestured to the luminescent creature, and it grew into a large, black-clothed, golden-eyed man.

"What is it, Princess?" he asked in Faeli.

I tipped my head to the house.

Reluctantly, he followed me inside.

I pointed to my walk-in closet. I flicked the light switch insistently to make him understand the lightbulb was shot. Even though his dark blond eyebrows knit together, he didn't suspect me of foul play. He stepped inside the closet and reached up. I whipped my hands, and ribbons of *wita* braided between the doorframe into a net from which not even a firefly could emerge.

I'm sorry, I mouthed and shut the door.

The guard banged and banged against the walls of the closet, and then he began to yell. Considering Derek wasn't home, I wasn't too worried about anyone rescuing him before I could escape. I passed my palms over my face next, using more of my dust, and then left the house.

The taxi was just rolling into the driveway when I stepped out. Without looking back, I climbed into the backseat and showed him the paper on which I'd written the address to the private airstrip.

The driver kept darting glances at me in his rear-view mirror as he drove. Finally, he asked the question that must've been burning on his lips since he'd pulled up to the graveyard.

"You friends with that celebrity…Lily Wood? I heard she was shacking up with the Prices."

I shook my head and drummed my nails against the armrest. Dust could change my appearance, but it couldn't mask my muteness.

"Buried a loved one then?"

I nodded.

For a while, he was silent. And then, "That Derek Price. He's such a good guy. Good coroner too, or so I've been told. Touch wood, I've never lost no one yet." When I didn't answer, he went on, "Many people are starting to arrive for the wedding. I heard they were going to have drones and circus entertainers and fireworks. You invited?"

I shook my head, then closed my eyes and pretended to sleep so he would stop firing questions at me. Even though I'd camouflaged my true face, I didn't want him to remember driving a mute girl. I wanted him to remember a grieved, gray-haired widow who'd visited her late husband's corpse in a graveyard, or to forget me altogether.

I wanted *everyone* to forget me.

Skies, how did terminally ill people endure this limbo? I almost regretted not staking myself with one of Kajika's rowan wood arrows. Not that he would've willingly imbued it with his blood, but surely another hunter would've done me the honor. I thought of the new hunter then—his name came back to me...*Pete.* I was sure he would've taken great pleasure in wetting an arrow with his poisonous blood.

Enough, I scolded myself, as the cab came to a stop in front of a gleaming silver jet ribboned with a navy W.

The pilot, who'd been standing by the plane's stairs, strode to my door and pulled it open. I didn't drop the disguise of severe updo and wrinkled skin. From his grooved brow, I guessed he'd been expecting the real me, or my brother.

"No luggage?" he asked, after he'd popped open the trunk of the cab and found it empty.

I shook my head and ascended the stairs of the jet, then took a seat. The air hostess tried to offer me coffee and finger sandwiches as we took off, but I closed my eyes and again pretended to sleep. When the tires lifted from the ground, I spread my fingers wide and concentrated on the dust I'd left behind, until it trickled back into my palm. I balled my fingers. The guard would now be free. It was a matter of seconds until he went to tell my brother that I'd escaped.

By the time they figured out I'd taken a plane—*if* they did—I'd be long gone. I thought of my destination, of how I would lose myself there, how easy it would be.

Las Vegas.

The city of anonymity and sin with desert temperatures.

Memories of the strip flashed through my mind. I'd been fifty-one—ten human years—when a portal was created to link Neverra to the Flamingo Casino (one of the first hotels on the strip). Faeries loved gambling, which had contributed to the astronomical growth of Sin City.

To that day, Vegas was a favorite Neverrian destination, which meant I would have to live cloaked. Perhaps I should've headed to the Caribbean—few faeries went there—but I didn't want to die alone in silence on a beach. I wanted a loud, lively ending to my life, a place where nothing ever closed, a city that didn't sleep, because I had no plans on wasting any more precious time sleeping.

MANY FACES

$\mathcal{F}$ire pulsing behind my eardrums, matching the frenetic loudness surrounding me, I crossed the teeming lobby of the hotel toward the bank of elevators.

The concierge escorted me himself to the rooftop suite I'd paid for with Faith's credit card. After taking in my sprawling living room, private swimming pool, wrap-around terrace, and four gigantic bedrooms decorated in every shade of beige imaginable, I handed the man a hundred dollars and closed the door behind him.

I was no mastermind, and yet I'd made it. Being a person who flew—more like walked now—under the radar had finally served its purpose.

Keeping two wads of cash, I laid out the rest in a drawer and cloaked the stacks in dust so that they resembled a row of socks. Until I died, my dust would adhere to the green bills. After that, it would be open season. I hoped that whoever found the cash would use it to noble ends.

I grabbed my keycard, then changed my appearance to a redhead with streaks of liquid liner along her green eyes and bright red lipstick on her mouth. I checked my appearance in the elevator mirror, added a beauty mark above my lip, and then strode out into the shopping maze that took up the first and second floors of the hotel.

I spent several hours and thousands of dollars creating my wardrobe. Of course, I could've made outfits out of dust, but there was always the risk it would fade in places or altogether. At least that was what happened before the regulation on our dust had been lifted by Negongwa. The habit of using it parsimoniously clung to me like *wita* on skin.

That night, I selected a tight, black sequined dress so unlike the loose pastel silks I favored. I kept the appearance of the redhead I'd adopted earlier, but darkened my eyes some more and added black diamond earrings that grazed my bare shoulders. Since I couldn't change my body shape or height with dust, I slid on a lacey push-up bra and platform heels that made me almost as tall as Cat.

The sudden thought of her pricked my chest like a thorn. How I wished she were there, getting ready alongside me. I itched to text her, but remembered I'd abandoned my phone.

I left my suite and descended to the casino floor. I took a seat at a poker table, next to a man who'd sweated through his pink button-down and a woman with purple pockets of exhaustion underneath her eyes. I handed the dealer a stack of hundreds, which he converted into chips without raising a brow. I was a high-roller tonight, which sent a tiny thrill through me. Never had Lily Wood acted so rashly.

The dealer slid me two cards face-down—queen of diamonds and eight of hearts. Pink-shirt checked, but the woman bid, and I followed, tossing my chips into the pot. Pink-shirt folded. The dealer aligned three cards on the table and flipped them over. I now had a pair of queens. Better than nothing, but not great either. The woman pushed a stack of chips toward the pot. I matched her stack, then, for the heck of it, added an extra chip.

She raised her eyes to mine, scrutinizing my expression. I crossed my arms and leaned back in wait. Finally, she matched my bet. The fourth card was dealt and turned. Another queen. Okay, now I *had* a solid hand. I sat up a little straighter and unwound my arms. Another round of betting thickened the pot, and then the last turn card was flipped.

An eight.

I had a full house.

I thought of what the woman could have that could best a full house. A royal flush? A straight flush? Four of a kind?

She pushed a stack of chips into the middle. Twice the amount she'd bet earlier. I matched her bet, because what did I have to lose besides money I would have no use for beyond the grave?

We showed our hands. She had one eight and the pair of queens on the table. Two pairs. I smirked as the dealer pushed the mountain of chips toward me. I arranged them in neat stacks. I won the next thirteen hands, bluffing my way to success six of those times. I hadn't played poker in ages but hadn't lost my touch.

Pink-shirt's armpits turned more transparent as sweat poured from his pores. He didn't win once and finally left, but was replaced by a new player.

This man's hair was combed back and looked so rigid he'd probably used an entire bottle of gel. "The floor manager mentioned this table has one hell of a lucky player. I like lucky players." His bright blue gaze brushed over my face and then lower.

Sleazeball.

He extracted a stack of chips from his fine wool jacket. Had he just come from a fancy dinner or did he dress up to gamble? Or maybe he worked here?

What had I been thinking? Winning attracted attention. I needed to leave, but leaving instantly was conspicuous. No, I would lose the next two hands and then leave. As the dealer slid us our cards, the newcomer shifted in his seat. He was so close that I could smell his aftershave.

"Huh," he said.

I glanced at my cards, then up at him.

He cocked his head to the side. "Small world."

I frowned, not understanding what he was insinuating. It wasn't like we'd met before. At least he wouldn't have met me in this form.

He sniffed the air, then leaned toward me and whispered, "Nice perfume. Eau de *wita*?"

THE STORM

I sucked in a breath. Dust had a particular odor, but only hunters and faeries could detect it. Which meant he was one of us. What crap luck…

I slid toward the edge of my chair, even though what I really wanted to do was haul ass out of the casino and barricade myself in my suite.

As the dealer arranged the flop, the fae asked softly in Faeli, "Do we know each other?"

I studied my chips, selecting the amount I wanted to bet. As I tossed them into the pot, I shook my head. From the corner of my eye, I saw him squint at my face. He could look as hard as he wanted, he wouldn't see through my dust. I was good at disguises.

"Cat got your tongue?" the fae tried again.

I glared at him, hoping he would just stop and leave me alone, then focused on my cards, reassuring myself he couldn't tell who I was. When he asked why I was hiding my true face, I folded and stood. Shooting my opponents a cordial albeit stiff nod, I scooped up my chips, tipped the dealer, then strode away.

The fae didn't follow me…at least not right away. After a minute, he got up and crossed the casino floor after me, eyes gleaming in the felted darkness. Keeping my pace steady, I walked into the ladies' room. I debated whether to change my appearance. In the end, I didn't. He'd smell my dust and just follow my new persona.

I spied a small window. After making sure the stalls were empty, I climbed atop the radiator and pushed on the handle. It took several attempts to get it to creak open. A coat of paint crackled around the frame as I pushed it out. Outside, voices approached. I hoisted myself through the opening and onto a narrow metal deck. I didn't have time to close the window, but doubted the two women would worry about an open window. They'd probably think the bathroom was being aired out.

I had no clue where I was but decided that my best option was to get back down to the street. Changing my face into a curly-haired brunette's, I jumped off the ledge to the street two stories below. I'd planned on floating down—even if it wasted fire—but failed miserably and landed so hard that my vision blackened.

Limbs sprawled like a starfish, I took inventory of my body. Some of my bones had most definitely shattered, but slowly, they mended. Soon, I was pushing myself upright. I felt my face to make sure my dust hadn't gusted away. My fingertips tingled from its presence. One of my heels had flown off, and I hurried to retrieve it. I raced down the dark alley toward the street soaked in bright neon lights. And then I reentered the lobby and steadied my pace to reach the elevator, my loot of chips swishing noisily inside my handbag. I scanned the lobby but no one looked my way. Keeping my arm tucked firmly around my bag, I pressed on the call button, and then once the door swept open, I pressed my card against the electronic security box at the bottom of the keypad and the top floor lit up. Praying the elevator wouldn't make any stops on the way up, I worked on lengthening my breaths.

I almost couldn't believe it when I reached my suite. My bag slid down my arm and dropped onto the marble floor. I leaned against the front door and laughed, my wound-up nerves finally releasing.

Tonight had been all at once tantalizing and terrifying, fun and perilous. I kicked off my heels and ransacked the mini bar for snacks and a drink. I tossed down a mini bottle of whiskey, savoring the trail of fire it left behind. Popping a bag of chips, I padded out to my private terrace and reclined on one of the moon-lit lounge chairs. The view of the city was almost as intoxicating as the whiskey. I ate the chips, and then I returned to the marble bar in the living room, grabbed a jar of smoked almonds, and ate those next.

I thought about returning to my terrace but worried about faeries sighting me, so I slid the patio door closed and retired to the bedroom. I watched hours of mindless TV, and even though I'd vowed not to fall asleep, I lost my battle.

I WOKE up to the brightest of sunshines. I sat up fast, blinking, half expecting yesterday to have been a dream, but the light beige walls around me were solid. The creak in my neck and the imprint of sequins on my thighs were also both very real.

I stretched, then tugged off my dress, slid my patio door open, and skipped over to the pool I'd requested jacuzzi-hot. The water coiled around my body, warming my submerged skin. I swam to the infinity edge and laid my chin on my crossed arms, trying to decide what to do with myself today. I'd never had so little yet *so much* time on my hands. Back in Rowan, there was always someone to see… something to do.

I pressed back my regret. I'd chosen this solitude for a reason.

After a long, quiet while, I got out of the pool, water beading from my black lace bra. I toweled off before my fire could counteract my skin's wetness. However quick I was about it, curls of steam rose off my body.

As I changed out of my wet undergarments, I turned on the TV to offset the silence and tuned into CNN. While I scanned the in-room dining menu, I listened to the human news.

Diplomatic tension with Russian officials.

Oil stocks plummeting.

A school bus full of children capsized in Ohio. Three casualties. Ten gravely injured.

As much as I didn't care for the two first subjects, the third heightened the pounding of my heart. Thank the skies my rapid heartbeat wouldn't register on Kajika's hand. I absent-mindedly stroked my palm that hadn't glowed since the day I'd found Kajika bleeding in his bed.

I hoped he'd found out who did it.

I shoved my stringy hair off my forehead and used the hotel-linked tablet on my nightstand to place my in-room dining order. I tried to rekindle the excitement I'd felt the previous evening, but loneliness consumed me.

I needed a distraction. I looked up the timetable of shows on the tablet, booked front row seats to two, and then worked on altering my appearance. I painted my eyes hazel and my blow-dried hair chocolate brown. It fell in lustrous waves over the spaghetti straps of my short, red jumpsuit.

As I slid my feet in tall wedges, I heard my last name on the news. I turned to the TV and listened as the reporter showed clips of Beaver Island, entirely decked out in white tents in preparation for the wedding.

"Catori Price and Ace Wood have pushed back the date of their nuptials because of a Nor'easter that is scheduled to hit Michigan this weekend," the reporter was saying. "Guests are extending their trips, which has benefited the hotels and restaurants in the region greatly. Here with us today is Beatrice Wells, owner of Bee's Place, Rowan's quaintest inn."

As I watched Bee's creased face, listened to her quiet voice, pang after pang of nostalgia hit me dead center. And then Cat's aunt Aylen popped onto the screen behind Bee. Once she realized she was on camera, she became all flustered, but soon, she was chatting avidly with the reporter about her niece's upcoming nuptials.

I watched her fuchsia-tinted lips move, but could hardly focus on what she was saying. Was a storm to blame for the postponement of the wedding, or was it simply a Daneelie-manufactured diversion? Were Cat and Ace looking for me? Had the *lucionaga* been tasked with locating the runaway princess? Had Kajika been alerted to my disappearance?

I turned off the TV and fled my suite, praying it was a real storm. That no one would come.

AFTER THE FIRST SHOW, I grabbed a burger and lunched alone at a little table set in the sun, then walked around another casino. I didn't dare sit and play, even though I itched to try my luck at blackjack. I did end up trying my luck at the slots. Each time I won, and the machine blared, my heart would snake up my throat and remain suspended there for long minutes. No one paid me any mind, so I finally began to relax.

Finally the time came for my second distraction of the day. I stuffed my new winnings into my bag and left to attend the concert. The show was mesmerizing and emptied my mind of thoughts, filling it entirely with music. I walked back to my hotel after that, heels clicking against the cooling asphalt. My mood had lifted, but the effect faded the moment my hotel came into view.

I blinked and blinked, and then I ducked my head and watched as Cruz Vega, flanked by Silas and two *lucionaga*, strode right through the main entrance of my hotel.

LOST AND FOUND

*H*eart pounding in my throat, I whirled around. Even though I didn't look like Lily Wood, I was afraid Cruz would see through the dust. I retreated the way I'd come, hands shoved deep in the pockets of my tan leather jacket. I wouldn't be able to return to my hotel. As much as the fae's presence the night before had to have been a coincidence, Cruz's arrival couldn't possibly be one.

Either the fae had gotten wind I was missing and mentioned he'd played poker with a cloaked faerie who refused to speak to him, or Ace found out about the jet that had left Rowan the morning of my disappearance, or Faith had noticed the Vegas charge.

I was walking too fast, drawing attention, so I slowed, hesitating to head into another hotel. Cruz and the guards couldn't canvass the entire city...could they?

I veered off the main road onto smaller ones, drifting through parts of the city that didn't glimmer and shine. I ended up in a shabby motel with none of the amenities of the luxurious resorts. Cruz wouldn't look for me here. I rifled through the zippered pocket of my handbag for my remaining cash. I came up with a wad of twenties—enough to get me a room in the establishment for a few nights.

I'd have to cash in the thousands of dollars' worth of chips, though, if I wanted to leave Vegas. I really didn't want to end my days here—in this yolk-yellow and brown-carpeted hole. The attendant handed me a clunky room key and collected three of my twenties. She gave me change and then led me to a room that reminded me acutely of the room I'd spent the night in back in Manistique.

Skies, that trip felt like eons ago.

I sat on the bed that was as hard as a slab of wood. The springs creaked under my slight weight. I didn't take a shower that night. I brushed my teeth with my finger, then surfed channels for hours on end, and then I slept.

Another wasted night.

THE FOLLOWING MORNING, I remained in bed until the growling in my stomach turned painful. I dusted myself, choosing a pink, pixie haircut and adding piercings through my nose and eyebrow that clashed violently with my red jumpsuit, but I was past caring.

Watching the sky more than the streets, I returned to the hotel in which I'd played the slots, to cash in my chips. The cashier in the cage tendered me the cash for those chips. However, when I pushed the chips from the other hotel his way, the man frowned as he tallied up the amount.

"That's a large sum, miss. Give me a minute. I got to ask my superior if I'm authorized to cash it for you."

When he reached for his phone, I spun and abandoned my thousands worth of chips. He would probably assume I'd stolen them and send guards to retrieve me. I hurried across the floor, wending my way through the already dense crowd, and discreetly pressed my palm against my hair to change my short pink do into a razor-sharp blonde bob. Security guards dashed past me, but neither glanced my way. Sure enough, they headed for the cashier cage I'd just run from.

I sped up, knocking into a cocktail waitress. She gasped as

drinks spilled all over her feathery outfit. I shoved a large bill onto her tray and took off again. My wedges didn't make any sound against the carpeted floor, yet in my head, they resonated, broadcasting my presence to everyone.

I needed to slow down and stop swiveling my head like a tracked criminal, so I concentrated on my feet.

No one is coming after me.

No one is coming after me.

Mud-splattered black boots stepped into my line of sight. I almost tripped over them but swung to the side, changing course to avoid the person. A hand shot out and gripped my arm, reeled me back.

Shit.

Noise faded as my gaze climbed up to my captor's face.

*K*ajika's eyelashes and eyebrows had grown back. That was the first thing that struck me. The second thing was the livid, red sheen of his dark eyes.

"Are you aware of how many people are out looking for you, Lily Wood?" he said through gritted teeth.

Again, I lowered my gaze to the wedges that pinched my feet. If only I'd worn flats... *I assume a lot.*

"You assume right. What were you thinking? What the hell were you trying to achieve?" Although it sounded like he was shouting, it was more of a growl.

I shrugged him off but made no attempt to run. It wasn't like I could outrun Kajika. *How did you find me?*

"A *lucionaga* showed up at Holly's farm, blubbering that you had vanished. Your brother was certain I was hiding you, but I told him he would have better luck finding you at the house of the man with whom you had spent the night."

He paused for so long that I looked back up at him. His eyes were so chillingly cold that I hugged myself.

"Cat said you had been with Faith and Remo, and then she called Faith, and Stella Sakar's daughter confirmed you had looked after her son the entire night." Again, he stopped talking.

"Is there a reason you left the age of your companion to my imagination?"

I didn't answer him. Instead I repeated, *How did you find me?*

"I have been viewing security footage for the last twenty-four hours." It explained the burst blood vessels. He scrutinized my face, which he could see perfectly through the layer of dust. "Why did you leave?"

I tipped my head to the side. *Why do you think?*

"I do not know what to think."

You can read my thoughts, Kajika. I left because you can read my thoughts.

He frowned, but then he didn't because he understood. "And you had something to hide…" he said in a low voice.

I squeezed my eyes shut and desperately tried to block out my secret, but his breathing hitched, and I knew he'd uncovered it. I pried my lids up, cursing the day I'd marked him.

His body had become one solid, pulsing muscle. A beat passed during which he tugged on a lock of my real hair. When it didn't detach from my scalp, the hard line of his shoulders became slightly less hard…which wasn't saying much.

"Since when?"

I bit my lip. The din of coins spewing from the neighboring row of slots angered the pounding at my temples. Or maybe it was having this conversation that was giving me a headache. *Since you were attacked with the opal.*

His Adam's apple moved underneath a couple days' worth of stubble. "Cruz is waiting for you."

Did you ever find out who did it?

"I have to get you to Cruz."

No, you don't need to get me to Cruz. I don't want to see him. Or anyone, for that matter. I ran away for a reason.

"And now that I know your reason, there is no way I am letting you out of my sight."

I inhaled sharply. *You can't tell Cruz my reason!*

"He needs to know so he can act accordingly."

He'll kill himself to save me.

"If he does not die, then you do, and I am not willing to let that happen."

You don't have a say in what I choose to do!

He narrowed his eyes and dipped his chin lower.

I'm serious. Don't you dare tell him. Or…or—

"Or you will run away again?" His lips arched in a dark smile.

I gulped. What was he going to do? Chain me to him?

"Possibly."

Stupid mind link. *If you tell him, I will* never *speak to you again.*

My threat made his smile falter. But only briefly. Soon it returned full force. "It is not as though you have ever spoken to me."

Was he really making light of this situation? I tossed my hands in the air. *I mean I will never communicate with you voluntarily or involuntarily ever again.*

"I will take my chances."

I'd expected him to back off, not to defy me. *It's my life. My choice!*

"Your life affects others."

My life is worth nothing in the grand scheme of things, but Cruz…he deserves to live. Look at what he's done for Neverra. For your tribe. Look at the changes he's brought about. What have I done, Kajika? Nothing! *I have done* nothing *to better any world.*

He shook his head, and his bangs shifted over his weary eyes. "You give yourself so little credit, Lily."

I huffed. *Name a single thing I made better.*

"You stole the book from Gregor and gave it to Gwenelda."

Cruz helped.

"*You* sacrificed yourself so Cruz could stay in Neverra and orchestrate the removal of the mist."

I snorted.

"You brought Derek, Faith, and Cassidy much joy."

Again, I snorted. *Those aren't accomplishments. They're just…*

"Just what?"

Normal things. Friendships.

"Why do you have such little regard for yourself?"

Because the things you are speaking about are trivial.

His jaw clenched. "You saved me. Do you consider that trivial?"

Saved you? From what? The piece of opal? I doubt it would've killed you.

"I was dead inside until you marked me."

What are you talking about?

He cocked his head to the side, observing me with the acuity of a *quila*. "What do you think I am talking about?"

My heart knocked against my spine, and fire rushed into my cheeks. *You can't save me because you like me better than you like Cruz. It wouldn't be fair.*

"Because watching you die would be?"

Kajika... I forced back my frustration. *I won't run away again, but don't tell Cruz about my fire.*

"I am sorry, Lily, but I will not watch you sacrifice yourself again."

When he slid his phone from the back pocket of his jeans, I backed away. He stepped forward, then cinched his arm around my waist. I tried to break free, but his grip was a vice.

"I have found her," he said into his phone.

No. You haven't found me. You've just lost me forever.

I felt his pulse quicken, saw the W flare against the dark hand pinning me against him.

I will never forgive you for this, Kajika.

DILES AND DECLARATIONS

$\mathcal{M}$y welcoming committee at the suite turned out to be larger than anticipated. Cruz and Silas were there, as well as Ace, Cat, and five *lucionaga*, stationed at each exit. I felt like an enemy of the state about to face a trial by fire.

"Lily!" Cat, whose face was as pale as it had been after the portal lock had been altered, launched herself off the couch and hugged me.

She was the only one who hugged me, though. All the others simply gazed up at me through lowered lashes. Glared more than gazed. Except Cruz. There was no bite to his look. If anything, his look was worse than the others because it mirrored mine...devastating apprehension.

"Drop the guise, Lily," Ace said.

Right. He couldn't see through my dust like Cat and Kajika could.

I ran my hands over my hair and face until my pale skin and limp blonde hair bled back to the surface.

Kajika, who'd released my arm only after crossing the threshold, had gone to stand by the bar, one boot up against the wall and forearms firmly crossed in front of his pecs.

"What the hell were you thinking?" Ace spat out.

My gaze snapped to his.

"You probably weren't thinking, were you? At least not about me or Cat or"—he threw his hands in the air—"about anyone but yourself!"

My spine snapped straight, and then I chopped the air with my hands. *You're right, I wasn't thinking about you or Cat, but I was thinking about Cruz.*

"You wouldn't have run away if you'd been thinking about me, Lily," Cruz said quietly.

I blinked at him.

"Lily, this was clear from the beginning…my mess. My fault. My clean-up. What's going to happen if your fire is as low as Kajika tells me, is not up for debate."

I speared the hunter with a look so cutting anyone else would've averted his gaze. But not him. Of course, not him.

I hate you, I whispered into his mind.

He didn't even flinch, but his gaze finally moved off me to settle on the flamboyant painting gracing the wall opposite him.

"How low is it?" Cruz asked.

I shrugged. I had no clue. It wasn't as though there was a thermometer that could measure it.

"You cannot fly at all?" he continued.

I was desperate to lie, but I had a human lie detector in the room. Besides, considering how pallid and sallow my skin had become, it was obvious I was running on fumes.

"How long?" My brother's question was like a stray bullet, whizzing through the room, searching for its mark.

Silas shifted on the beige leather armchair. "Impossible to say, but according to Gregor, once her hair falls out, we'll have a couple hours." As though talking about my hair reminded him of his own, he tightened the leather tie that bound his shoulder-length locks off his face. "All the bonds established between faeries vanish the second a faerie dies"—Silas eyed my brother—"so potentially we can wait until Lily loses her hair, but waiting comes with risks. If she loses her hair during the night and no one notices until the morning—"

"Lily will be under twenty-four-hour watch from now on," Ace said.

I gasped.

"Don't even try to object, Lily. I'm your brother *and* your king."

I glowered. *Way to lord over me, brother.*

"I'll watch you during the day. Cat will be with you at night."

Cat didn't nod. Obviously this had been discussed beforehand. She twined her fingers in her lap and shot me an apologetic look. She wasn't the one who had anything to apologize for.

My brother and Kajika on the other hand—

"Kajika, you may go," Ace said. "Thank you for...helping."

The hunter didn't budge. "I did not do this for you, Ace."

The five *lucionaga* tensed. All looked at Ace, awaiting an order from him. My brother didn't give any.

"I will stay," Kajika said.

Without looking his way, I spat through our bond, *I'd rather you leave.*

"I can hear her. If she is planning to escape, I will be able to tell you."

Silence swathed the room.

I scowled, which made one of Cat's eyebrows rise.

I won't run. I promise, I signed to my brother, hoping he could force the hunter to leave.

Kajika grunted. "No one gives me orders, Lily."

Ace studied the hunter, then he studied me. My stupid scowl seemed to sway his verdict. "Fine. You can stay."

"Don't you have a fight coming up, *ventor*?" one of the *lucionaga* said.

"You are aware of my work schedule?"

The *lucionaga*'s gold eyes flickered uncomfortably. "We keep track of every hunter's schedule and whereabouts."

"And here I believed we were no longer considered the enemy."

The guard readjusted his posture.

It was Silas who interjected, "What he means is that we keep track of all faeries when they are on Earth. Not just Unseelies."

"You did not keep track of Lily." Kajika's lips barely moved as he said this.

Silas became a block of granite. Only his eyes moved...straight to my brother.

I trapped the bodyguard. It's none of their faults.

"I thought you were no longer addressing me, Lily."

I balled my fingers into fists and squeezed hard, imagining they were clutching Kajika's throat.

The hunter smirked. He freaking smirked! Instead of acting like a grown-up, I marched out of the living room and into my bedroom, flinging the door shut behind me so hard the hinges shook, and then I dove onto my bed and buried my face in my pillow. I wanted to scream and to hit someone. Preferably Kajika.

A soft knock sounded on my door. "Lily, it's me," Cat said. "I'm coming in, okay?"

When the door snicked open, I flipped onto my back to make sure it was only her. I had no desire to see a single other person. Not even Cruz. Not yet anyway.

After closing the door, she came to sit beside me on the bed and captured one of my fists between her hands. She wrenched my fingers open, then slid hers through mine. She wasn't Seelie, yet her skin was as warm as the heated travertine floor in the ensuite bathroom.

"Don't be upset. We're all just trying to protect you."

I shook my head. *I never asked for protection,* I signed.

"That's not how family works. You never ask for protection. You just naturally receive it. It's part of the package."

Cruz is family too.

She must've bit the inside of her cheek, because it dimpled. "Cruz..." She paused. "It's not the same."

He can't die.

"And you can?"

I nodded.

Her black eyes turned as forbidding as two pieces of polished obsidian. "Don't you dare even think this."

Did any of them even care what *I* wanted?

"Besides, no one's...dying. We're not out of strategies."

I challenged her to tell me one solid idea.

She raked her fingers through her long black hair. The diamonds on her crown ring glittered fiercely, reflecting the sunlight pouring through the wall of glass doors. I felt the inclination to pull the drapes shut when I caught sight of a guard positioned against the terrace railing. He was looking out over the city, but clearly he was there to keep me from escaping.

When she didn't utter a single new strategy, I snatched my hand out of hers and curled onto my side. Exactly what I thought...they were all out of ideas.

"Lily—"

I eyed the fluffy white carpet that extended from one wall to the other. It was so freaking white. I looked for stains, because nothing was spotless.

For a long moment, she didn't talk. But then, even though she wasn't a person who needed to fill silences, she told me about Pete, about how angry he was to have been turned into a hunter, until Menawa showed him how to use his nascent powers.

Was that even a good idea? The man was unhinged...

"I think it'll work out. Everything ends up working out, doesn't it?"

No it doesn't, I wanted to tell her, but I kept my hands tucked underneath the pillow, kept my gaze fixed on the too-pristine carpet.

"Lily, please don't be mad at Ace or at Kajika for putting you under house arrest. They're both blinded by how much they care for you."

Whatever. It didn't change the fact they were taking the decision out of my hands, which wasn't fair *or* right.

"Is there a way to communicate with the Cauldron?"

I finally detached my gaze from the rug to frown at her.

"I know it's not a person, but it's magical, right? Is there no spell that can be cast to rid it of bonds?" She tucked a strand of hair behind her ear. A tiny white scar extended from the hole to her lobe. I didn't remember ever seeing it. "Like a *Cauldron for Dummies*?"

Cauldron for Dummies. Seriously…

"Don't make fun of me, but there must be a spell manual somewhere, right? How did your people learn to use it in the first place?"

I finally heaved my hands out from underneath the pillow.

They just learned. The same way humans learned to walk or build fire.

Cat pursed her lips. "One of the history teachers Gregor saddled me with said faeries taught humans all about fire."

I sat up then signed, **Give me your phone.**

She took it out of her wine-colored leather jacket and handed it to me.

I entered her password and typed, **The faeries who would've taught the first human about fire have been dead for a long time, so who knows? As for the Cauldron, all we know about it comes to us from the elders, and what they know came to them from their ancestors. Perhaps, once upon a time, there was a book of spells, but if it existed, it's been lost.**

"Maybe an elder remembers something?"

Didn't they already interrogate all the elders?

Cruz and Ace were thorough. I doubted they'd left one stone, or in this case, one elder unturned.

In my opinion, you'd be better off questioning *diles*.

She turned her entire body toward me, knocking her bent knee against mine. "We can communicate with them?"

I rolled my eyes. **Sarcasm, Cat. Sarcasm.**

She tsked. "We can communicate with *lupa*, so it wasn't such a stretch to assume we could communicate with other species…"

She said something else, but her voice faded as a thought overtook my entire brain as swiftly as the lake had overtaken the fishing boat.

As if she'd heard the mechanisms grinding inside my skull, she asked, "What?"

I clutched her phone long seconds before I could get my fingers to move and transcribe this...this potentially game-changing brainwave. *Dile* **poison can stop faerie hearts for a few minutes if used in the right quantity.** Too much would stop a heart forever, but I didn't write that, because that wasn't my solution. **What if—**

I was about to write more when Cat tore the phone from my fingers and sprang to her feet, dashing out of my bedroom. I didn't follow her out, still processing this very real solution.

A long moment later, a soft knock sounded at my door. I looked over to find Cruz standing on the threshold. "Can I come in, Lily?"

I nodded, then scooted back until my back was flush with the headboard's cream leather Chesterfield padding and gathered my legs against me, locking my arms around them.

He sat on the mattress. "I'll try it, but if it doesn't work, Lily—"

I shook my head to prevent him from saying more.

He shot me such a sad smile that it compressed my heart. "I don't know if you are aware of this, but Catori still owes me a favor, and I was going to claim some of her blood. The advantages of *dile* poison had slipped my mind. We have such an immortality complex, us fae." His sad smile turned crooked, as though he believed that what he was saying was funny.

There was no humor in talking about dying.

"It's actually one of the better deaths because it stops your heart instantly instead of charring your insides like *wita*. Then again, I wouldn't have asked to be gassed. I would've gone the way Borgo did. Suicide by hunter blood."

I was torn between slapping him and sobbing uncontrollably. How could he sit there and discuss the best way of erasing himself from the universe? I scowled, and his lips finally settled back into a grim line.

He placed one of his hands on my knees. "I'm not afraid, Lily. I just want you to know that. I've had a good life. I've done what I wanted to do. Of course, not all I wanted to do. I would've loved to have children."

A lump as hard and sharp as a shard of glass stoppered my throat.

"With you. I would've loved to have children with you," he whispered.

That cracked the dam I'd tried to build in my chest.

"You know what my only regret will be? That I took you for granted. I was so sure you'd be by my side forever. I was so certain I would have time to show you how much you meant to me." His fingers seized my cold hands. "I love you, Lily Wood."

Tears cascaded down my cheeks.

"I have always loved you. In a hundred different ways. I loved you as a friend. As a sister. And then, when the Cauldron separated us…when it was too late…I realized that I loved you so much more than that. I'm sorry I'm only telling you this now." His thumb stroked my knuckles. "It's not really fair of me to spring this on you now, is it?" His voice had become so hushed that I barely heard it over my sobbing. "Oh, Lily…" He kept stroking the top of my hand. "Please don't cry. Please…"

I'd waited decades for him to say all these things to me. My chest clenched so tightly it cheated me of breath. I curled over my knees and let my hair fall around my face. Without letting go of the hand still trapped in his, Cruz moved up on the bed and smoothed one of his palms down my curved spine, up and down, up and down. Veroli used to do that when I came home from school in tears because someone had been mean to me. She'd rub my back until I calmed down. Sometimes I even fell asleep that way. Instead of being soothing, Cruz's touch increased the tremors racking my body. At some point, he stopped and the mattress shifted and a new set of arms came around me, thin but hard, with skin that smelled like lavender.

Cat forced me to lie down, then curled around me and held me until I stopped shaking, until I stopped crying. She hummed a soft melody that sounded like a lullaby. Had her mother sung it to her when she was a child? Or was it Derek who'd sing her to sleep?

The melody twirled around me, filling the gargantuan chasm of Cruz's declaration. My gummy lids closed, and then I felt myself slip into the darkest of sleeps.

LAST DANCE

J woke up to a black sky and muted lights. Cat was no longer holding me, but she must've been close by, because her voice drifted toward me. I tried to get up, but the mattress dragged me down. I stayed pinned to my bed for a long time, just listening to the drone of her voice and to my brother's answering one.

I turned to my side and saw them through the slash window. They sat on two chairs set around a small granite table. My brother had a tumbler full of what I assumed was whiskey in front of him. Cat was drinking water, unless it was vodka, but I doubted it. She wasn't a heavy drinker. I searched the terrace for the others and caught a shadowy movement by the railing—a *lucionaga*. The sentry stood very still and very straight, golden eyes ceaselessly roving around the terrace as though on the lookout for a threat.

Were there threats? In the last few weeks, I'd been so focused on the drama of my own life that I'd forgotten my brother and Cat bore a title that came with danger. Sure, my brother was ten times the man my father was, but no one is universally loved.

Loved...

That made me think of Cruz. Which in turn made my stomach shrink and sink. Hadn't I grieved enough for one day? I sighed, then finally rolled up to sitting. The movement caught Cat's eye. She was already out of her chair and pushing the window further open to step inside my bedroom.

"Hey."

I swallowed. My throat felt like it had been scrubbed with sandpaper.

My brother turned his head to look at me, but he stayed sitting, one leg crossed over the other, index finger going round and round the rim of his glass. He was worried. I wasn't sure if it was about me or Cruz or the *dile* venom or something else entirely.

A piece of sky moved, and then a man landed in a crouch. Silas pushed himself up and advanced toward Ace. The pool lights flickered over his face, revealing tiny lines of tension. He stooped to speak to Ace.

Cat and I both watched them even though we couldn't hear what they were saying.

I touched Cat's shoulder, then signed, *You think they captured the* **dile**?

She let out a long, whistling breath. "I hope so. But who knows? There's always something happening in Neverra. On Earth too. The world never stops spinning."

For some people, it did.

"I was thinking...because whatever happens, it's not happening tonight—"

How do you know that?

"Ace said it takes a while to harvest poison from a *dile*."

True. I remembered my fauna teacher telling us that, although *diles* could eject poison as fast as a faerie could whip out dust, if the creature sensed danger, they hid their poison somewhere inside their bodies, and the only way to get to it was to pierce every inch of its scaly skin. If you killed it, the poison broke down instantly and became unharvestable.

Cat traced the whorls of ink on her forearm. A filament of confined dust tacked onto her fingertips and rose. She tore her hand away and it snapped off, just like Blake's spirit had torn away from his body to enter Kajika's last winter.

Kajika… Where was he?

What did I care where he was?

I didn't care.

Not in the least.

I jerked as a loud noise sounded in the foyer. A door slammed, heels clicked, high-pitched voices bellowed out *hellos*. Cat shot me a sheepish look.

"So I did something…or rather I got coerced into doing something…Cassidy can be really convincing…" The fact that she wasn't finishing a single sentence had me on edge.

What did you do?

"Um. Well." She raked her hair off her glowing cheeks. "Well, I had Cass on the phone earlier and, well, she wanted to organize my bachelorette…apparently she told you—" Cat gave me a pointed look, as though whatever she'd done was in part my fault. "Anyway, I thought that we could all use a night of fun, and well"—how many *wells* could one person place in a sentence?—"I sent them the jet."

Them?

"Cass and Faith."

They're here? I signed just as the door flew open.

"Hey, bitches!" Faith squealed.

That answered my question. Not only were they here, but they were wearing slinky dresses, sky-high stilettos, and accessories that didn't include a baby.

Where's Remo?

"Derek is babysitting him," Cassidy said, tackling me into a hug.

"I told you!" Faith fake pouted. "Lily only likes me because of my son."

I rolled my eyes at her, and then, miracle of miracles, I actually cracked a real-ass smile. **Not true,** I signed, right before Faith flung her arms around me and hugged me.

I wondered if she'd noticed the missing money in her account.

"Lily says that's not true," Cass translated.

I tipped my head from side to side in a maybe. I did love Remo completely. Then again, he was a baby and had no faults yet. I supposed I would love him, faults and all. There was something truly special about him. Suddenly, it hit me that I'd get to know him. I'd get to see him again. And the anvil that had been crushing me for days lifted.

"She totally likes him better than she likes any of us, but I'm good with it!" Faith said, dropping a kiss on Cat's cheek that left a red mark. "Thanks to her, he can now go to any Ivy league college he wants. What got into you to give him so much money, Lily? I mean, I so appreciate it, but...it's—it's too much."

I shook my head while Cat studied me with a raised eyebrow.

After Faith filled her in, she said, "So we're ready, but you two aren't." She clapped her hands as Cat rubbed at her cheek, trying to erase the lipstick stain. "Come on, come on. The bachelorette party has officially begun. Get up. Get dressed. Put on your makeup and your sluttiest clothes, and let's hit the town."

I whipped my face toward Cat. *Bachelorette party?* We were doing her bachelorette party right now? In the middle of all this...this madness? Going to a club, or whatever it was they had planned, was like eating chocolate mousse between your starter and main course.

We couldn't go party.

I looked over at my brother, who was still speaking with Silas. Although he wasn't watching us, a smile curved his lips. Was that smile due to the chaos that had just erupted inside my bedroom in the shape of two leggy, loud girls, or was it brought on by his discussion with the guard?

Is Ace okay with this? I asked Cat.

"It sort of...was his idea." My eyes must have gone really wide, because Cat added, "Oh, he'll be coming with us, along with all our bodyguards, but yeah. He's the one who said there would be no better night for this."

Faith tore my closet open, and Cassidy removed hangers, moaning as she looked at my new wardrobe.

"Can I move into your closet when we get back to Rowan?"

I laughed, and the sound softened the tightness of Cat's shoulders.

"This. You have to wear this, Lily!" Faith tossed a silver dress at me that was as tight as a band-aid.

Cat held it up and frowned at it. "*You* bought this?"

I nodded sheepishly. Her shock didn't surprise me. Tight dresses —tight anything—were not usually my style.

She dropped the dress when another whacked her in the face. "Ouch."

"Oh come on, Lara Croft," Faith said. "You can't tell me that wad of silk hurt you."

"No, but the hanger did." As she plucked the dress off the comforter to observe it, Cat fake-scowled at Faith, who grinned wide.

"Oh, and we brought you this." Cass took a plastic silver tiara attached to a short fluffy white veil out of her bag and tossed it on the bed.

"Nuh-huh."

"Yeah-huh," Faith said back, at the same time as Cassidy lobbed a pink sash printed with the words: Bride To Be.

"Because the veil isn't self-explanatory?" Cat grumbled.

"We all have a sash." Cassidy pulled three white ones from her bag with the word *bridesmaid* written in swirly pink letters.

She handed one to Faith, who hooked her arm through it and adjusted it until it lay diagonally over her A-line navy dress. "Aw, man, it totally hides my assets."

Cassidy snorted. "There is no possible way that *anything* hides your cleavage, woman. Each boob is like, the size of your son's head."

"My son has a tiny head." Faith was still toying with the satin, trying to inch it to the side to reveal more cleavage.

Cassidy laughed. Even Cat was smiling. And me? Well, I felt like someone had powered me back on.

Having dessert in the middle of the meal was unusual, but why the hell not? When had I ever turned down chocolate mousse?

Never.

33

JEALOUSY

$\mathcal{I}$ curled my fingers into a fist as we wended our way through the club. Kajika's stupid mark had begun to glow when we'd left the penthouse and it just wouldn't turn the fuck off.

"Don't worry. He's fine," Cat yelled into my ear.

Who? I signed.

Above us hung a sea of spinning disco balls that cast rainbow-colored tinsel over the lively crowd as though a child had tossed a handful of glitter over our heads.

"Kajika!" She spoke his name so loudly that my eardrum quaked.

I don't care.

Cat shot me a wary look. "You're still mad at him?"

I stopped walking. *Mad at him?* I was furious. Hurt. Annoyed. *He betrayed me!*

A frenzied dancer elbowed me in the ribs. One of the *lucionaga* shoved her back, then positioned himself between me and the crowd. Two more sentries stood around Cat, and the last two brought up the rear behind Cassidy and Faith. Ace and Silas had stepped away a moment to place phone calls. Or maybe they'd popped through the Flamingo's portal to get an update on the *dile* situation.

Even though the music roared, Cat lowered her voice. "He only told Cruz because he cares about you."

My lips thinned, and my hands came back up, weaving through the liquor-and-perspiration-scented air. *Doesn't make it okay.*

Cat sighed, and her pink sash lifted and fell over her chest. I couldn't believe my brother had dared leave his bride-to-be's side for even a second looking the way she did. Even though she was wearing a veil and was enclosed by bodyguards, she was garnering quite an audience. The white dress, which I'd bought for myself, fit her, albeit the hem hit so high on her thighs that my brother urged her to wear stockings. She'd laughed off his suggestion.

Smart phones flashed around us. The attention had one of our guards barking at the crowd, "No pictures."

Cat ducked her head, threaded her arm through mine, her tattoo pulsing against my skin, and pulled me forward toward a round booth on the VIP podium. It was supposed to afford us privacy but was in no way private. Sure we were a couple feet higher than the crowd, but we were basically on a stage next to six other round booths.

The DJ spun the latest hit, and the crowd went wild, momentarily forgetting about their celebrity sighting. But not everyone had stopped staring. At the table beside ours, the six college-aged boys sitting on the curved banquette were giving all of us a once-over. Gold watches glinted furiously on their beefy wrists. Trust-fund babies. They were too young to be businessmen.

As I pivoted away, one of them held my attention. His dark hair was artfully messy, as though he'd just rolled out of bed, and his white button-down shirt was open at the collar. I wasn't a flirt, but if I had been, I would've kept looking until he'd amassed the courage to walk my way. Since I didn't want to encourage him, I turned my back on him.

"Okay, this might be the second best night of my life!" Faith yelled into my ear.

What was your first? I typed on my phone.

"The night I met Remo, duh." She rolled her bright blue eyes at me. Even though she was still carrying extra weight from her pregnancy, Faith was dazzling, and carefree, and happy. How I envied her. "So tell me," she said-yelled into my ear, "is Silas single?"

Silas? I wouldn't have guessed he was Faith's type; then again I'd never really discussed boys with Faith. I'd tried a few times, but she clammed up on the subject. I suspected it had to do with the way Remo had been conceived.

I don't know if he's single, but he was last I heard a month back. What I can tell you is that he's a really good guy.

Speak of the devil. He and Ace were making their way up the steps toward us.

He's one of my brother's closest friends.

I left out the part that he worked for Faith's father and could turn into a dragon as fast as she could stick a pacifier in her son's mouth. I wondered if Ace had told Silas that Faith was Gregor's daughter. I assumed the *draca* had been informed of this.

"You think I have a chance?" she asked me.

I looked at Faith, then at Silas. At any other time, I would've written yes, followed by dozens of exclamation points, but considering all that was happening, I wasn't sure Silas would be game to flirt. At the same time, I didn't want to be a Debby Downer, so I typed, **Go talk to him.**

Faith, who was the most confident person I knew after my brother, grimaced. But then she adjusted her sash for the umpteenth time, ran her fingertips underneath her eyes to make sure her mascara hadn't smudged—it hadn't; she looked stunning—and advanced toward Silas.

She leaned toward him and spoke into his ear. He smiled. She told him something else, and he kept smiling. It tugged on my heartstrings to watch them. Faith deserved some happiness. Especially after her mother—

She still didn't know…

My gaze tripped over Cassidy, who was desperately trying to flirt with one of the *lucionaga* tasked with our security, toward Cat, who was sitting on my brother's lap. His hand kept running up and down her thighs. Would Faith understand? Could a person understand why someone had killed their parent?

I gnawed on my bottom lip, forgetting about the bright red lipstick Cassidy had applied when she'd done my makeup. I had surely ruined it. Because I was helplessly coquettish, I checked my reflection in my phone's camera. The lipstick was surprisingly still intact.

In my phone's screen, I caught movement behind me and then felt a hand touch my waist. I twirled and found myself almost face to face with the boy who'd been ogling me earlier. I was in part shocked and in part flattered by his ballsiness. I was also incredibly surprised that no *lucionaga* had ripped his arm from its socket yet.

"Can I get you a drink?"

I shook my head, darting a nervous glance toward my brother to see if he'd noticed the attention. His gaze was locked on the guy. Of course it hadn't escaped him. Cat, too, was staring. Astonishingly, though, neither gave the *lucionaga* orders to intervene, which had me wondering if Ace was condoning this.

I spun back toward the guy, but he'd vanished. I frowned, until I caught sight of him again a couple feet from where he'd stood a moment before. Kajika had him dangling in the air, one hand circling the boy's throat. The hunter muttered something to him, then tossed him onto the banquette occupied by his buddies. The boy's flailing hand knocked over a pitcher of cranberry juice that splattered like fresh blood over his pristine button-down.

I folded my arms in front of my chest. Kajika had no right to intrude in my life. A bouncer as large as an industrial fridge approached him and started admonishing him, but stopped so suddenly I presumed the hunter was influencing him. When the man whipped out his cell phone and held it at arm's length, my frown deepened. Kajika didn't smile for the bouncer's selfie, but he also didn't squash the phone. The enormous man all but bowed to the hunter as he retreated to his post next to the VIP stairs.

I'd told Kajika I was never speaking to him again, so I wasn't about to ask him what the whole fanboy moment had been about. The hunter unwrapped white tape from around his hands, and it struck me that he must've come back from a fight. Had it taken place in Las Vegas? Or had he run back from wherever he'd competed?

At least it explained the bouncer's peculiar behavior. He must've been an ultimate fighting enthusiast. I shook my head and turned away, and then I uncrossed my arms, grabbed the magnum of champagne that sat in an ice bucket on the table, and served myself a flute. I downed the bubbly in three swallows, then filled the glass back up. I didn't drink it as fast, even though I was incredibly tempted. Kajika had just single-handedly turned my mood from bright to bleak. *Ugh.*

I plopped down on the leather seat and crossed my legs.

A second later, the banquette shifted as Cat took a seat next to me. "How are you doing there?"

I sipped my champagne.

"I never thought a day would come when Kajika would become a celebrity."

Why was Cat so adamant on talking about *him*? I didn't want to talk about *him*. I never wanted to talk about *him* anymore. I took another long swallow of champagne.

"Matthias"—she tipped her chin toward the blond *lucionaga*—"was telling me that when Kajika called his manager to tell him he couldn't make his fight, the guy found him an impromptu gig in one of the casinos here. Apparently it's a super popular event."

I didn't ask if he'd won. It wasn't like he could lose. At least not to a human.

"Oh, Great Spirit, look at them." Cat scrunched up her nose.

Since she hadn't said him, I looked. Sadly the *them* were next to the *him*. Two girls who resembled showgirls in their butt-cheek-baring dresses and bruise-colored makeup had strutted up to Kajika. One of them even had her hand on his forearm. I couldn't believe he was letting her touch him. As though he'd heard me—which he probably had...I doubted the deafening music was impacting our link—he pulled his arm back and shifted his gaze to me.

I hiked up my lip in disgust and turned back toward my empty champagne flute. I went to fill it up, but Cat stopped me.

"You might want to pace yourself."

I shrugged Cat's hand off my wrist and refilled my glass. *Pace myself.* I snorted. What did she think I was? Human? Nope. Never would be. My tolerance for alcohol was remarkable. I could probably drink the entire contents of the mammoth bottle and be just fine. As I downed the next glass, I heard one of the girls next to Kajika squeal. He'd autographed her hand, and she was flapping it around ecstatically, cackling that she'd never shower again. *Classy.*

Having had enough, I typed, **Want to dance?**

"Sure." She stood and began to sway her hips.

Down there. I gestured to the teeming crowd below us.

"That's not a good idea, Lily."

What was the worst that could happen? Getting my feet trampled? Getting too much attention? It wasn't like anyone would ask me for an autograph. I didn't have groupies like the hunter. Besides, I was done sitting around, drinking my weight in alcohol. I reached over Cat and trapped Cassidy's wrist, then tipped my head toward the dance floor. She perked up instantly—she wasn't making much headway with Matthias.

"Lily, we shouldn't—" Cat tried to stop me, but I stepped out of her reach, Cassidy in tow. She grabbed onto Faith on the way and then we were all three brushing past Kajika's ginormous fanboy. He unhooked the velvet belt to let us through.

As we descended the stairs, the crowd hemming the dancefloor swiveled to watch us. Or maybe they were watching the two men decked out in all black with gleaming golden eyes tailing us.

Who cared?

I certainly didn't.

I just wanted to lose myself to the glittery darkness.

A new song spilled out of the loudspeakers, and I moved to match the tempo. Cass and Faith giggled as they twirled around me.

"We need to get Cat down here!" Cass yelled.

Fat chance my brother would let her onto the surging dance floor. That he'd let me come down here was shocking enough. He probably sensed I was in no mood to be told what to do.

I raised my arms over my head, feeling the bubbles of the champagne drift through my body, feeling the ends of my long hair brush my bare shoulder blades. I could no longer fly, but damn I could still dance.

I threw my head back and spun, letting the disco balls blind me with their dazzling pinpricks. One of the faceted spheres sank to a spot just above my head and rotated slowly. Gasping with amazement, I reached out to touch it. Instead of swinging, it dropped lower until it was nestled in my palm.

Cass shrieked next to me, which made my neck snap back straight. I thought it was the miniature disco ball that had made her squeal with delight, but it wasn't. Against all odds, Cat had joined the party.

Still clutching the mirrored orb, I looked toward the VIP area. Kajika stood at the railing next to my brother and Silas. He tipped his head, and I realized that *he'd* unhooked the disco ball and placed it into my fingers. I squeezed it and then, eyes narrowed in defiance, stretched my arm up high and spread my fingers wide.

The mirrored ball dropped at my feet.

Kajika could unhook the moon from the sky and gift it to me, and still, I wouldn't forgive him.

34

AFTER PARTY

*S*adly, no man tried to approach us on the dance floor. Even if they'd wanted to, there would've been no way for them to reach us. The chain-link fence of bodyguards had worked its magic—without any magic involved.

They'd kept us safe. Damn, I didn't want to be safe tonight. Hadn't I been playing it safe enough for the past four-and-a-half months? It almost felt like a punishment when Ace and Silas came down from the podium and signaled that we needed to head home. I didn't want to leave. I never wanted to leave.

Granted we'd stayed three hours, so it wasn't as though we'd just gotten there, but leaving was bittersweet anyway.

When we reached the penthouse suite, which thankfully had enough bedrooms to accommodate almost everyone, Cass exclaimed, "Pool party!"

And then she and Faith were racing toward the bedroom they'd decided to share to throw on bathing suits. I grabbed a bottle of water from the mini fridge while Cat sat on one of the barstools.

"I don't think I'll ever be able to walk anymore," she said, rubbing one of her feet.

My feet were also feeling pretty battered, but the blisters were proof I'd had fun, so I didn't mind.

"Can you hand me one?" Cat pointed to my bottle.

I pulled another from the fridge and slid it across the polished granite. Ace came up behind her and began massaging her shoulders.

"I heard something about a pool party," he said.

She looked up at him. "Are you joining?"

"Me? Swim? I don't swim. I leave that you." He winked at her. "But I'll gladly watch. I'll even help you into your swimsuit."

I couldn't help but roll my eyes for the hundredth time tonight. I signed, *Get a room.*

My brother smirked. "Oh, we already have one."

Cat blushed but smiled as she let him pull her off the stool toward the other master bedroom in the suite. I marched out onto the terrace for fresh air. Silas had left earlier with two of the guards. The other three had returned with us. One stood by the front door while the other two had retaken their spots on either end of the terrace. The only person who hadn't returned from the club was Kajika. He was probably too busy autographing some girl's ass.

After I'd left the VIP area, I hadn't sought him out, and since I couldn't hear *him*, out of sight, out of mind. I tossed my glass water bottle into the trash, then headed to my bedroom to change into my bathing suit—a black mesh one-piece that I'd purchased because it was hot, but hadn't expected to wear in front of anyone.

I slid my patio door open and walked out onto the terrace, but squeaked as I passed through my sash window. Kajika was sitting at the small table, drinking from a bottle of Coke, staring out into the night.

I hope you didn't bring home any of your new groupies.

He slanted his gaze toward me. "You're talking to me again."

I shoved back a growl and started toward the pool, but he caught my wrist and reeled me back. I slammed my palm against the table to avoid tipping over.

"Sit."

I snatched my hand back. *What part of I'm no longer talking to you did you not get?*

"Every part of it," he said in a low voice.

I narrowed my eyes.

"Please, sit."

I rubbed my wrist, still feeling the sting of his steely grip. His gaze dropped to the skin I was nursing, and a nerve ticked in his jaw.

"Did I hurt you?"

Yes.

"Let me see your wrist."

I'm not talking about my wrist.

He let out a deep sigh and scrubbed his palms against the sides of his face. And then he focused those dark, glinting eyes of his on me. "I will not say I am sorry, because it would be a lie, and I am not a liar."

I snorted.

He watched my nostrils flare, and then his gaze slid down my neck, over my collarbone, chest, waist, legs. Never had someone's attention made me feel so completely naked. I knotted my arms in front of my chest.

"You are right. I did lie about one thing."

He hunched over and rested his forearms on his knees that were spread apart. He fingered the multiple strands of brown leather wrapped around one of his wrists. Each string was threaded through with an opal. He spun one of the beads. Even in the darkness, the milky stone's neon veins flashed.

He peered up at me through his rebellious locks of black hair. "Do you want to know what I lied to you about?"

No.

To my left, Cass cannonballed into the pool, sloshing water everywhere. The few drops that landed on me steamed off slowly. Thankfully the patch of darkness in which I still stood—skies only knew why—veiled my body's reaction to the water.

"I lied about the opal. No one attacked me."

I frowned, but then smoothed out my features and turned my

head toward the pool just as Faith dove in. I didn't want to look interested in anything he was saying.

"I did it to myself."

Like an elastic, my gaze snapped back to his. *Why would you do that?*

"Why do you think?"

You were trying to kill yourself?

One side of his mouth kicked up, and he sat back. "*Gejaiwe*, I wish that had been my reason." He looked off to the side toward Matthias, who was standing a couple feet away, staring at the pool where Cass was trying to fix Faith's runny mascara.

Why did you do it then?

Slowly, Kajika turned his gaze back to mine. "So you would never again look upon me the way you did in the Daneelie camp."

A breath rushed up my throat.

"It is the only thing I have ever lied to you about though, Lily."

My heart felt as though it were being licked by the flames underneath my skin. It wasn't fair. He wasn't allowed to confess stuff like this to me. Not now. It toyed with my emotions, and he had no right to toy with me. He'd lost that right when he'd betrayed me.

Faith and Cass called out my name.

"You can push me away," Kajika's voice was so faint I thought I was imagining it, "but I will not leave until you are cured. After, if you still want nothing to do with me, I will step out of your life."

His words chafed my already aching heart. *Stay away from me,* I whispered, and then I raced to the pool and dove in to hide the tears already gathering in the corners of my eyes.

35

GLIMMER

*W*hen I burst out of the water, I remembered I was wearing human makeup and rubbed forcefully at my cheeks. Sure enough black streaks stuck to the pads of my fingers.

"Here, let me help," Cass said, scouring my skin with her thumbs. Then she pushed her wet bangs out of her eyes and tipped her head to the side. "Are you crying, hun?"

I shook my head.

"You are."

I ducked my head back under the water and stayed until the edges of my vision began to scramble like those boxy, human TVs from my youth. I needed to get my emotions under control. But how could I? I felt like one of the hunter's boxing opponents—cornered and beaten. Why did he have to deliver his stupid confession tonight?

Cruel.

It was cruel.

He was cruel.

And stupid.

Who tries to poison himself to change his nature?

A desperate man. That's who. Kajika was desperate, stupid, and cruel. Oh, and impolite. Skies, he was impolite. Who the hell stayed after they were shown the door? Only someone who hadn't been raised with *any* manners.

Air bubbles snaked out of my mouth. I heard Cass asking Faith if she should tug me up.

He'd had no right to slap me with his confession and make me look like the cruel, heartless one. Unlike him, *I* had a heart, and he'd squashed it.

Cass scooped me up. "Lily?" Her eyes flashed wildly over my face. "Are you training for some freediving competition?"

In my peripheral vision, I made out Kajika's form. He was still sitting at the table in front of my bedroom. He better not be thinking of sitting out there all night.

"Finally! The bride!" Faith whooped.

"Sorry, girls. I was just placing an order for mini burgers and milkshakes."

"Is that what we're calling it?"

Cat smiled and shook her head, her long locks brushing over the one-shouldered strap of her red bathing suit. It wasn't one of mine, so I assumed she'd somehow bought it at some twenty-four-seven swimwear shop.

Cass finally stopped looking at me like I was suffering from apnea-related symptoms. "Oh my God, I love you! I. Am. Starving."

"I, on the other hand, hate you," Faith said. "I'm supposed to be on a diet."

"You can diet tomorrow." Cat whipped her arms over her head and dove in. As she hit the water, I thought of her skin, how it would glimmer. Even though Cass's faerie sight was nil, I'd remarked that Faith could see things she shouldn't have been able to.

I turned toward my brother, who'd just come out onto the terrace. He hadn't changed out of his clothes, but his shirt was rumpled and his hair mussed up. I signed, *Her skin.*

He pursed his lips and waited for Cat to emerge. When she surfaced, and her gaze locked on his, understanding washed over her. She touched her cheeks. They definitely sparkled, but nothing she couldn't pass off as the effect of glittery, waterproof makeup, especially in the muted lighting.

I made the OK sign with my fingers, and she exhaled a breath that rippled the water.

"Can someone put some music on?" Cass asked.

Ace nodded to one of the guards and then strolled toward Kajika. Were they friends now? The irony of it made me grip the watery edge of the pool and squeeze it hard. When the speakers erupted with music, I shoved all thoughts of Kajika out of my skull.

"Are none of the guys coming in?" Cass asked, pouting.

"Maybe later," Cat lied.

They wouldn't be joining us. The guards were on duty. My brother, whose fire burned hot, would look like a steamer. And Kajika wasn't the type of person who enjoyed splashing around, unless there was a Daneelie to strangle or a misbehaving faerie to stake.

"I know what we need." Cass heaved herself out of the pool and dripped water through the glowing living room.

She came back with an armful of mini liquor bottles, several packs of candy, and the vase that had adorned the bar until moments ago. She dumped the bottles and candy packs by the edge of the pool, then walked toward the railing, set the vase down.

After she'd hopped back into the water, she divided the packs of candy between the four of us, then instructed us to open them. "No eating," she admonished Cat, who'd chucked an M&M inside her mouth. "So now, for the rules. Remember the fish bowl toss at the fair?"

"The one you won every summer?" Faith said.

Cass nodded enthusiastically. "Same thing, except if you miss, you take a sip. Easy-peasy."

"This cannot end well," Faith mumbled, but there was a definite lilt to her tone. "If Remo gets alcohol poisoning tomorrow, it's all on you, cuz."

Cassidy snickered. "Cat's the bride, so she gets to start."

"Lucky me." Cat tossed first. Her M&M hit the rim and pinged off the vase. She drank.

They made me go next. My shot went wide too. Cass got hers in. Faith did not. By round ten, I'd had ten sips of various alcohols. They were all starting to blur on my tongue, so skies only knew what I was ingesting. Faith had had eight. Cat six, and Cassidy was only on her third.

When Cassidy's jelly bean sank in for the eighth time, Faith shook her head. "I'm starting to think you secretly practice at the bakery instead of serving customers."

"How do you think I get cupcakes onto plates?" Cass laughed. "She tosses; she scores!"

Faith snickered. "Careful, the boss might just toss *you* out."

Cass pinched Faith's thigh and they both giggled.

Cat was up again. She got hers in. Mine did not go in. It didn't even hit the vase. It just arched right off the terrace railing.

"You girls better stop before my sister kills someone," Ace said.

"Imagine that." Faith smirked. "Death by M&M."

Sure, we were sixty floors up, but could a falling piece of candy really kill someone? It would probably hurt. Worried, I jumped out of the pool and traipsed toward the plexiglass railing. Thankfully, this side of the terrace gave onto a deserted courtyard, and no one was lying unconscious.

A towel settled over my shoulders. Then Ace leaned his hip against the railing and said in Faeli, "Even though it reassures me to see your fire at work, Faith's looking."

I peered over my shoulder and sure enough, Faith was staring at my hair, one tawny eyebrow hiked up. *She'll blame the alcohol for making her see things.*

"Perhaps. She'll find out soon enough, though. I promised Gregor he could speak to her at our wedding."

Oh. That would be soon. *I've been meaning to ask...the storm: Earth or Daneelie-made?*

Ace turned toward his wife, sticking his elbows on the thick plexiglass rim. "What do you think?"

I watched Cat sip a creamy white milkshake through a pink-striped paper straw, then laugh as Cassidy stuffed an entire burger inside her mouth.

I think you're lucky it's almost winter so people don't question the weather too much.

"Smart girl."

Of course, the storm made me think of the other one raging through my life. *Did they find the* **dile?**

Ace nodded. Even though he was still speaking Faeli, he lowered his voice, "Silas will return once they've harvested enough poison. Should be sometime today…tomorrow at the latest."

I suddenly abhorred my idea of using poison. What if they dosed it wrong? What if—

Sensing my inner turmoil, Ace laid a hand on my arm. "Don't start stressing. We'll have an entire team of people monitoring Cruz."

I gulped, but my saliva felt like it had turned to cement. I touched my throat. I was going to throw up. Cold sweat broke out over my upper lip. I dropped to my knees just as the first wave of vomit surged up my throat. I hunched over the vase. My thankfully still wet hair clung to my shoulders instead of tangling with the vomit.

Even though the mere thought of alcohol made me want to weep, I was glad I'd downed copious amounts. At least the girls would think my drinking was the reason for being sick.

I threw up for what felt like a Neverrian hour. It probably didn't last more than an Earthly minute. When I was done, I picked up the vase to go wash it out, but Ace said, "Leave it, Lily. Get yourself to bed."

The girls crowded me. Cat insisted on helping me walk back to my bedroom. Light-headed, I leaned on her. I was acutely aware of Kajika's watchful gaze. I bet he also thought I'd drunk too much.

The man was such a puritan. *Ugh.*

Whatever.

It wasn't as though I cared what he thought of me. It couldn't possibly be worse than what I thought of him. *Cruel, stupid, desperate, and ill-mannered man.* I stared at him while those words reeled through my mind, drilling each one of them through the dark air between us.

Cat forced me into a shower, then helped me strip off my bathing suit and squirted soap into my hands. I let the first handful slip between my fingers like sand. She didn't try to give me more soap. I turned my face toward the shower head and opened my mouth, letting the water whisk away the vile taste inside my mouth.

The water turned off suddenly, and I shivered. Cat wrapped a new towel around me and then she dropped a silk slip over my head and led me to bed.

"I'll get you some water," she said, tucking the duvet around my shoulders.

I watched her leave through my open patio door. She hadn't closed my curtains, so I could see Kajika's broad back, his stiff neck, his fluttering black hair.

Obstinate. I added that to the long list of terrible things he was. A tendon pinched in his neck.

I turned around and fixed my gaze on the beige wall. Shadows drifted over it. Slowly those shadows materialized into a person.

Cruz stood before me, his mouth pressed into a soft line, his green eyes gleaming like the emerald earrings my mother had given me for my fiftieth birthday.

I sprang out of bed and went to him.

36

MY BEAUTY

I reached up to touch his jaw. His bones seemed to grind underneath my palm, realigning into another jaw. Brown bled across the green of his irises, and tattoos rose to the surface of his skin.

"Goodbye, Lily."

A gust of wind blew around us, flicked Kajika's black hair, freed it from his scalp. I gasped and snatched my hand back. It was coated with bits of skin and stubble. I raised horrified eyes back to his face.

This isn't supposed to happen to you. You're not supposed to die.

"But you are?" Another gust of wind filed away his nose. He prodded the exposed bone.

I pressed my knuckles against my mouth. *NO! No. This can't be happening. This isn't real. Kajika, you can't die. You can't leave me.*

"Isn't that what you wanted?"

More skin peeled off his high cheekbones, and then he burst into black glitter. I gagged as it rained into my mouth.

No. No! NO! Kajika!

The floor swayed, then rushed up to meet my body. My cheek hit the soft carpet. I kept my lids shut as I lay there, absorbing the steady pulse of the floor.

Pulse? Carpets didn't have heartbeats.

My eyes jerked open, and I tried to move but the floor pinned me against it.

Not the floor.

Arms.

I squirmed to crane my neck. A face as dark as the air in my bedroom was angled toward mine.

"It was just a nightmare, Lily," Kajika's low voice rumbled through me. "I will not leave you."

The dream flickered through my mind, and a new wave of terror licked my spine. I shuddered, and then I pressed my palms into his chest and shoved. *I was dreaming of Cruz.*

The hunter's body tightened, and then he dipped his head and crossed his arms. "Then why did you scream *my* name?"

I didn't.

"You did."

Did not. I raked my hand through my hair. *Get over yourself, Kajika. It was just a stupid dream.*

A tendon shifted in the hunter's corded neck. "You really want me to leave then?"

I crossed my arms to stop them from trembling. *Like you'd actually do what I ask,* I muttered into his mind.

His nostrils pulsed, and then his long legs ate up the carpet toward the open glass doors.

He was leaving... Really leaving... The temperature dropped so suddenly that the tremors that had started in my arms spread to the rest of my body.

My knees gave way, and I dropped to the floor. I leaned against the leather-covered box spring, feeling the hard frame of it dig into my spine.

What had I done now?

My teeth chattered, and I hugged myself harder.

When the front door slammed shut, a sob escaped my trembling lips. I hunched over my knees and pressed my burning eyes into the sharp bones to stanch the flow of tears. I'd blamed and criticized the hunter, but it hadn't been his fault.

None of it had been his fault.

All mine.

I was the selfish one.

The cruel one.

The stupid one.

The air shifted, and then arms bundled me up and set me on the bed. I pried my lids up, expecting to see one of the faerie guards, or my brother.

But it wasn't a *lucionaga,* and it wasn't Ace.

Kajika stalked back toward the sash windows, and my heart throbbed. He'd come back.

You left.

"You told me to."

You listened.

"I tried." He punched the frame of the sash doors, and a dent appeared in the white-lacquered metal. "If you want me to leave, Lily, do not cry. I cannot stand to hear you cry." He gripped the frame, and the W etched on his hand lit up, burning like a beacon in the dark night.

My palm flared. Instead of crushing the glow, I let my fingers fall open like flower petals.

He hung his head, turning his eyes down to his black boots. "You are right. I am selfish."

My eyes snapped to his shadowy form.

"I want to keep you alive so damn much that I could kill Cruz with my bare hands."

My breaths stilled in my lungs.

"I do not know if he told you, but he asked me to end his life." His deep voice vibrated through the ripe air like a swarm of locusts. "I almost did. But I knew that if I fulfilled his request, I would lose you forever. I lost you anyway." He turned his head toward me, and his long bangs glided over his eyes. "If I leave this time, Lily, I will not come back. I cannot come back. Not from this." He pressed off the frame and straightened to his full, commanding height. "This is why I did not want to love again. Because love turns men into such fools."

His words sank into my chest like raindrops.

I pressed one hand into the mattress and then the other. And then I was sitting. And then I was crossing the room, my silk slip whispering across the raised goosebumps on my thighs. I rested my hands where his had been and slid the door shut. And then I turned toward him and raised a hand to his neck, curling my fingers around his warm skin.

A thousand words coalesced inside my mind, but two rang louder than all the others: *Don't leave.*

He pulled in air through his parted lips.

Don't—

He slammed those lips into mine, subduing my brain. And then his hands caught my thighs and hoisted me up so our faces were leveled and my legs were wrapped around his waist. Hooking his arms under me, he broke the kiss and narrowed his eyes at the window.

I spun my head, certain we'd been caught, but it wasn't the window Kajika was staring at. It was the curtain. The taupe crushed velvet swung closed. I turned back toward him.

Convenient little power of yours.

He grunted, then strode over to the bed, knocking his foot against the nightstand. Gottwa swear words erupted from his mouth.

I laughed.

He grimaced, but then a smile reached every corner of his face. I sobered up and gazed at the hunter.

I think this might be the first real smile I've witnessed.

He turned so serious again I wished the thought hadn't passed between us. But then his expression softened, and he laid me down on the bed. Like a mountain cat, he stretched out over me, bracketing my head between his forearms. His mouth was so close to mine that I could taste his breath.

"If someone had told me two centuries ago that there would

come a day when I would desire a faerie, I would have crushed their throat."

My gentle, poetic hunter.

His face warped with the appearance of yet a new smile. He looked younger, less encumbered by the crushing weight of his past. "I like those words better than the ones you attributed to me earlier."

I wrinkled my nose. *I was angry. I didn't mean them.*

He nudged my still scrunched nose with his. "You were not wrong, though. I am selfish. I am ill-mannered. I can be cruel, and I have been stupid." His lips touched mine with such tenderness that my pulse tripped. And then he was dragging his mouth down the side of my throat across my collarbone.

I'm sorry about the disco ball.

"You are forgiven."

I loved it.

"Could have fooled me." He propped himself up on one elbow. "I was expecting you to launch it at me."

I thought about it.

"I know."

Of course he knew. I was forever inside his head.

"You are inside my head," he murmured, "and underneath my skin."

I wish I could hear your thoughts.

Amusement flickered over his features. "You would get bored of my thoughts, Lily. They are always the same...always about you—about some part of your anatomy, your lips, your legs, your eyes, your hands." He towed his long fingers over the top of my hand, up my wrist, up my arm, then back down. "I think about how soft your skin is, and how you smell as sweet as sap. I think about what makes your eyes shift to silver, because when you are happy, they become silver. And the rare times I do not think about your body, I am thinking about ways to spend more time with you without appearing as desperate as a pup."

Emboldened by his confession, I reached for the hem of his t-shirt and rolled it up his back. He pressed himself to his knees and took it off. Muscles rippled underneath his burnished skin, and the whorls of trapped dust skittered in their tracks.

Seeing him bare-chested reminded of the day in the barn when Cat and I had interrupted his workout. How I'd gaped at that striking chest. And now I could touch it. I stroked his skin, felt the ridges of taut muscles, flattened my palms against his pecs. He didn't move, letting me explore him with my fingertips. His dark nipples tightened, and his glorious skin pebbled.

You really are an impressive specimen, Kajika.

A corner of his mouth lifted. "You only think this because you have never seen an Unseelie in skin."

I snapped my eyes back to his face.

"Is that not what I am, Lily? An Unseelie." He spoke the word slowly, the consonants rolling off his tongue. For the first time, there was no sour inflection to his pronunciation.

My lips must've parted from shock, because a cocky grin curved his mouth. How many smiles had he graced me with in one night?

His thumb grazed my chin, slid down the center of my throat, dipped in the hollow of my collarbone, and moved to my shoulder. He hooked it around the thin strap of my slip and glided it off, then bent and pressed a kiss to where it had lain. And then he trailed his bristly jaw across and tugged the other strap down with his teeth. I rolled my head back and closed my eyes, a moan slipping through my lips.

Slowly, he lowered himself over me until every inch of our bodies was connected. As he moved against me, my slip slid up my thighs, and I shivered.

Kajika, I've never... I stuttered as his jeans chafed my sensitive skin.

He pulled his mouth off mine and rolled onto his side, keeping his palm on the bunched silk. "You have never what?"

I felt near the point of combustion. *Um...done it.*

His brow furrowed. "Lain with a man?" He dragged his

calloused paw off the silk and down the length of my bare thigh. "Would you like me to stop?"

Heat surged into my cheeks, and lower. *No.* Losing my virginity had been high on my bucket list.

Still caressing my skin, he asked, "What is a bucket list?"

Things you want to do before dying.

His hand stopped moving. "You will not die."

Everyone dies sometime.

He rolled onto his back and stared up at the ceiling, breathing in the oxygen that seemed to have thinned.

I turned onto my side and placed an open palm on his navel. *Don't be angry with me, Kajika.*

He sighed, long and deep. Finally, he looked at me. "I know everyone has a beginning, a middle, and an end, Lily, but that does not mean I want to focus on the end." He wrapped his fingers around mine, but didn't move my hand off his stomach. "And I certainly do not want to make love to you because it is on some to-do list."

I bit my lip.

"Were you planning on lying with just *anyone*?"

I blushed. *Of course not.*

He sighed again, and then he tugged on my hand until I lost my balance and fell on top of him.

His breath skated over my nose and chin. "*Gejaiwe*, I have wanted you for so many moons, *ma mika*."

Mamika?

He gazed at me with the same wonder as a child beholding a night sky full of stars. "My beauty. *Ma. Mika*," he repeated slowly.

No one had ever called me my-anything before. My eyelashes fluttered.

He dragged my palm over his beating heart. "This belongs to you now. Do not break it."

Heat flared beneath my navel. *Never.*

He smiled.

Again.

And then he kissed me.
Again.
And then he made love to me.
Once.
And then again.

37

TERROR

J woke up to pounding against my bedroom door and then a booming voice, "Lily! Open up!" followed by another voice telling my brother to leave me alone.

I jerked into a sitting position, blinking against the bright light spilling past the gawping curtain. The night rammed back into me, and I spun toward the other side of the bed. The pillow was creased but cold.

When had Kajika left? Had he even slept?

I scraped a hand over my pounding forehead, but then dropped that hand to my stomach that was burning with a brand new fire. My legs almost gave out when my feet connected with the rug. I crouched to retrieve my slip, and a string of curses spooled through my mind. Kajika had said it would hurt, and skies was he right. I pulled on the piece of black silk and limped toward my door. I unlocked it and drew it open a crack.

Ace craned his neck to look behind me. "The jet's ready. We're leaving."

I sucked in a breath because I hadn't checked the room for incriminating evidence of the night before. Thankfully, when I did turn, I didn't find any stray sock or boxers.

"Did you have a wrestling match with your bedsheets?" he asked.

Cat's fingers closed around her husband's bicep. "Ace, let her get dressed," she admonished him, but a smile tipped the corners of her mouth.

She knew.

If she knew, then my brother knew. A *lucionaga* must have seen him enter my room and report it.

Crap. Crap. Crap.

I didn't sleep well, I signed, trying to make it look like I'd had a fitful night.

Ace shot me a look that set my entire face aglow. "Where's the hunter?"

I flushed hotter.

"Obviously, he's not here," Cat said, trying to pull him away.

"He better not be." Ace pulled his arm out of Cat's grasp. "He's not here, right, Lily?"

I shook my head, but wondered if he would believe me considering how red I'd become.

The front door clanked shut.

"I brought breakfast." Kajika's voice echoed down the short hallway.

"You see? I told you he wasn't there," Cat said.

My brother harrumphed. "Ever heard of room service, Kajika? Probably not."

I didn't get it...get him. Yesterday he and the hunter were all tight, and now he was out for blood.

"I went for a run and came upon a bakery that smelled pleasant." Kajika appeared at the end of the hallway, a brown paper bag swinging from his fingers.

His expression was so perfectly blank that for a second I wondered if I'd imagined last night...or worse, if he was pretending like it had never happened.

His eyes flashed to mine, and for a moment I forgot about the throbbing between my legs. But then his gaze dropped to that place, and it became the only spot on my body I could feel.

"No, and no," he said, and his words stilled my insecurities.

"No and no what?" Ace retorted.

"Lily asked if I had slept," Kajika explained, his gaze drifting back to my face. "Is everything all right, Ace?"

My brother's gaze slalomed between the hunter's face and mine a couple times more. "Silas stopped by a half hour ago. They're ready. We leave for Rowan as soon as Lily's dressed."

My heart came to a full stop.

The same way Cruz's would soon.

The hunter's Adam's apple jostled in his throat. "A portal exists here? Why not head to that one?"

"The portal's inside a slot machine. Not the most convenient place to hang around, especially at lunchtime on a weekend. I favor the boathouse. It'll be empty."

My hands started shaking. I pulled them through my hair but my fingers got trapped in the snarls. I forced them through. Instead of untangling anything, I ripped out a thick lock. I brought my fingers in front of my eyes and gaped at the number of golden strands coiled around. Silence clogged the hallway.

I combed my other hand through my hair, gently this time, barely tugging, and yet my fingers came back wrapped in more limp hair. The tremors raking my body grew so rough that I teetered on my feet. The room darkened then brightened then darkened. Kajika dropped the bakery bag and caught me before I collapsed from shock.

Ace yelled for the blond *lucionaga*. "Change of plans!" he barked in Faeli. "It'll happen at the Flamingo. Get Lynn to clear the casino floor."

"Lynn Vargas?" Matthias asked.

"No, Lynn Smith," my brother roared. "Of course, Lynn Vargas." Matthias's gold eyes went wide.

"Get to her office. It's at the top of the Flamingo." When the guard still hadn't moved, Ace yelled, "Now!"

Matthias passed by me, but stopped halfway through my bedroom. "And if she isn't there?"

My brother tugged at his own hair. Unlike me, none fell from his scalp. "If she's not there, you figure out another way to clear the casino floor. Pull the fucking fire alarm, for all I care! And then tell Silas there's been a change of plans. Tell him we'll be ready in ten minutes."

Matthias raced to the terrace, then shot into the sky.

Kajika smoothed my hair back. Or what was left of it anyway. I shuddered as I felt an air-conditioned breeze touch my exposed scalp.

I was scared.

Scared that I would begin to gray.

And scared of how the sight of me must disgust him.

"*Ma mika.*" His voice was so very soft.

Tears pooled in the corners of my eyes, and I turned my head, burrowing my face against his chest. I heard Cat speak quietly, her voice edged in panic. She mentioned Faith and Cass, surely trying to figure out what to do with them...how to explain the change of plans.

Don't let them see me like this, I whispered into Kajika's mind.

He tucked me harder against him. "I will keep you safe."

From prying eyes, yes, but he couldn't keep me safe from anything else.

His mouth dropped to my ear. "You promised not to break my heart," he murmured. "I hold you to that promise."

Even though my world was falling apart, I smiled thinly.

Ace insisted on flying me down to the Flamingo, but Kajika tightened his hold on me. I locked my arms around the hunter's neck as he tore out of the apartment.

The world blurred around us, and air blew against my bare legs and arms. Cat ran beside us while my brother flew, casting illusion upon illusion, so no one would notice our mad dash through the human world.

DILE POISON

*T*he casino had been cleared and the lights had been shut off, or maybe my sight was going. I inched my face off Kajika's chest so I could look around. The effort angered the pounding that had started in my head when I'd woken up. It was as though my fire were flickering, its flames pulse-pulsing against my skull.

The only sources of light in the casino were the green glow of emergency lights and the conical beam that spilled from the ceiling and glinted off shiny chrome—the portal.

Kajika was walking now, carefully maneuvering around the blackjack tables toward the beam. Back in the day, the slot machine had been one of many, but times had changed, and the machines had all been updated with computer screens.

Except this one.

Management had tried to remove it but found they couldn't. When they attempted to destroy it with explosives, and the portal shook in Neverra, faeries were sent to Vegas. The Flamingo changed ownership then—a faerie, Mart Vargas, bought it back for a monstrous sum of money, then Mart bequeathed it to her half-human, half-fae daughter, Lynn.

Lynn was the one who came up with the idea of framing the slot machine with velvet ropes and crafting a legend around it that humans lapped up...something about it being akin to a genie lamp. If you inserted a dime, then pulled the lever, and three bells lined up on the reel, your wish would come true. Humans fed the machine so many dimes it had jammed up more than once.

If only Lynn's legend were real...

Matthias and Silas were standing next to a woman with cropped white hair—Lynn. I hadn't seen her in ages. She wasn't a fan of my father's regime, so she had spent much of her adult life outside of Neverra. To think she had been just a couple years older than my brother. Earthly time had taken its toll on the faerie.

"*Massin*." She bowed her head to my brother.

He nodded at her. "Lynn." Then he turned toward Silas. "Is Cruz ready?"

"Yes," he said.

"Tell him we're in place. And come back once the venom takes effect."

In other words, when Cruz's heart stopped beating...

Silas gripped the lever of the slot machine firmly. His stamp flared, and then his body shrank and vanished through the cashback slot.

We waited in terrible silence for Silas to return. Lynn was trying to converse with my brother, but Ace kept palming his hair and saying, *excuse me, what?* At some point, Lynn stopped trying to make small talk.

He walked over to me and plucked one of my arms, prying it away from the hunter's neck to inspect the warped pattern. I nestled closer to Kajika, absorbing the warmth of his skin, the steady beat of his heart. The sound vibrated across my cheek, echoed in my ears that were buzzing with white noise.

Ace released my wrist. "Kajika, get her closer. I want her to be ready when"—his Adam's apple bobbed—"when it's time."

Kajika didn't need to be told twice. He strode right up to the slot machine, and Ace placed my hand on the lever, cementing my fingers underneath his.

My portal stamp flared, the peculiar symbol a bitter reminder that I was no longer welcome in my home.

The air shifted then, and Silas materialized. "It has begun."

"How much time...will his heart stay stopped?" Cat asked.

Dread was stamped on Silas's face. "According to Gregor, three minutes."

Cat cleared her throat. "Three human minutes or—"

"Neverrian."

"That's good." She licked her lips as though they were chapped. "That's fifteen minutes. That's good." She wet her lips again. And again.

A chill enveloped me, and I shivered. I couldn't see how it was good. Cruz's heart was no longer beating.

Kajika rubbed my extended arm, attempting to drive heat into skin that felt rubbery and numb.

Thank you for giving me last night.

He lowered his gaze to the navy carpet beneath his feet, tracing the geometric pattern with his eyes, his hand still skating over my skin.

I loved last night. It was...magical.

"It will work," he said so roughly that his voice scoured my skin like a Brillo pad.

Don't lock up your heart, Kajika. Dare to give it away again. After me.

He jerked his eyes off the carpet and set them on me. "It will work!"

Kajika... I tried to prepare him.

"No."

I tried to offer him a comforting smile, but my weak lips wouldn't bend.

Couldn't bend.

My wrist started flickering, my stamp's botched lines and curves shifting.

Cat and Silas crowded around us.

"Her stamp won't be able to let her through," Cat was saying softly. "Someone's going to have to go with her, Ace."

"It's already been decided." My brother removed his hand from atop mine. He wouldn't be the one to take me.

It wasn't a surprise. Until the lock was altered to let Cat back in, my brother wouldn't risk leaving her behind on Earth. Not even for a second. Not even if it meant he incurred the same fight as mine.

As though someone had pulled a lever on my wrist, my stamp reeled and reeled, warping at lightning speed. Dread and hope dripped into me, seeping into my bones, down to the marrow. I averted my gaze, not daring to watch anymore, not daring to hope.

Hope was too dangerous an emotion.

My mind wandered to Cruz. Was he scared? Was he comfortable? Was he lying in his bed? Was Veroli fussing over him? I hoped so. I tried to picture him. Not with a stilled heart, but with a lively one.

A long-ago memory washed over me. It was the year of flight. I was five—twenty-five human years, a mere child still. It was the year we learned to use our fire. Once we achieved this, we evidenced the accomplishment by removing our shoes. Every day, one of my friends either came to school barefoot or took off their slippers before the end of the school day. I was almost six, and I still wore my soft-soled shoes. Ace tried to reassure me that there existed no Seelie unable to fly, so I would eventually *get it.* It hadn't reassured me.

One morning, after yet another miserable attempt at flying that had rendered my uniform mucky, Cruz barged into my classroom on the first floor of the school *calimbor.*

I have orders to collect Lily.

My teacher had frowned, but everyone knew Cruz was almost a member of the royal family, so she'd let me go off with him.

Did something happen to Ace? My brother was always first and foremost on my mind. *Or is it Veroli?*

A smile had danced over Cruz's face. *Everyone's fine. Hop on my back.*

I climbed onto his back and clutched his neck as he soared upward and out toward the cliff that overlooked the Hareni. Not many faeries went there, either afraid of the wild animals that crowded the cliffs and valley behind it, or afraid that an Unseelie would somehow sneak out of their underground prison.

I heard you wanted to learn to fly, he said once we'd landed and he'd put me down.

I grimaced.

So I'm going to teach you.

I started to tell him that I was a disaster. That perhaps not all Seelies could fly. That maybe I was defective. The same way I couldn't talk, maybe I couldn't fly either.

He placed his hands on my shoulders. *Lily, mark my words. By the end of today, you will be flying.*

He ran me past the fundamentals again, and then he made me work on pushing my fire into my legs and feet, which was the key to taking off. Once piping hot, your feet lifted off the ground. This was called hovering. To fly, though you had to redistribute your fire into your body. Easier said than done. I desperately tried repositioning my fire, but it was useless.

I was useless.

I hopped and fell, and hopped and fell, my slippered feet inevitably smacking against the rocky ledge.

Twelve-year-old Cruz crouched to my height. *Lily, it'll happen. It'll happen.*

Embarrassed, I wept.

You can do this. He'd rubbed my legs to get the dirt off my tunic pants, then rested his palms on my feet.

His hands were so warm, and my feet so cold. The heat felt good. It made my numb toes prickle. The soggy insoles of my slippers made the balls and heels of my feet ache, and my arch tingle. My shoes felt too small, too tight. I was desperate to kick them off and scratch my skin until it bled smoke, but I didn't want to push away Cruz's hands. I wanted him to keep them there forever.

Hey, Lily. He glanced up at me, a devastating smile arcing his lips. *Look.*

And I had looked.

He rose, and so did I. My feet hovered next to his chest, still caged in by his fingers.

I'd held my breath. *You're doing that.*

He released me gently, and my body dipped but then shot back up, pitching sideways. I was the only person who could stumble on air. Cruz had leaped off the ground and grabbed my hands. At first, it was to steady me, but then it was to spin me around...and around...and around.

Oh, Cruz...

I felt my brother peel my fingers off the lever. "Fuck," he roared. "Matthias, go to Neverra. Get an update. Quick."

My stamp had stopped flashing.

It hadn't worked. And now there was no more time for other experiments. I wouldn't be buried in magical rose petals. I wouldn't see Neverra without its cloak of mist. I wouldn't get to laugh again, or be kissed again.

I would miss that most.

Skies, I would miss so many things.

My gaze bumped into Kajika's. The whites of his eyes were marbled with burst blood vessels. I tried to touch his jaw with the hand clutching his neck, but I couldn't inch my fingers down. It was as though the spindly bones had fused together.

I tried to rotate my head, but like my fingers, my neck wouldn't obey. My body was shutting down. I peered at my legs, made sure they hadn't grayed and flaked off. Even though I couldn't move them, they were still there, still draped over Kajika's taut forearm.

I stared back up at him, watched the reflection of my own face in his dark irises, my anger and desperation boiling down to the quietest stillness.

All of me became quiet.

"Lily…" Kajika croaked.

"Wait!" Cat all but shrieked.

I didn't think I could wait any longer.

Something tugged at me.

Death.

My body rocked, and the faces of the people I loved blurred. Soon, the world turned into an endless sea of ink and silence.

THE PINK SEA

*T*he afterlife was bright. The palest of whites.

And noisy. Waves crashing, birds cawing.

And odorous. Briny and metallic.

I inhaled deeply. Listened carefully. I'd imagined ghosts couldn't smell, but perhaps I'd been wrong?

Something brushed over my legs.

I still had legs?

I could still feel?

I blinked, and my lids came upon. Like a developing negative, an image ripened before me. First, pale with the faintest of gray lines, but then color tinged the whites and grays—a blue-thatched roof, a glittery lavender expanse of water, sheer white fabric fluttering around a canopy bed.

Truthfully I hadn't believed in the afterlife, so I hadn't given it much thought. But, skies, it was beautiful.

I pulled off the feather-light sheets stretched over my body, then combed away the fine netting ensconcing my bed and placed the pads of my feet on cold, smooth stone. My body was so delightfully warm that I welcomed the nippiness. Carefully, feeling out my limbs, I padded out onto a small deck made of yellow wood.

All around me, water frolicked. I knelt and peered underneath the edge of the deck. My hut was suspended in the air over this strange ocean. It reminded me of the palace of my youth.

No mist here, though. I turned my face toward the pale lilac sky and closed my eyes against the relentless sunshine. But then I jerked my eyes open.

Lilac?

I got to my feet and walked around the wrap-around deck of my new house. No castle rested on a ribbon of mist, but the sea lapped at a towering cliff crowned with a sprawling tree. Its iridescent blue leaves swayed and glinted like diminutive peacock feathers. I swallowed, and my saliva slunk painfully around an expanding lump in my throat.

I knew that tree.

I knew that cliff.

A black form cut across the sky, growing larger as it soared toward me.

I backed up.

I knew that shape.

I was in Neverra.

Which meant—

I winced, unwilling to think of what it meant.

The *draca* landed, tucking its leathery wings along its frightful bulk. Green eyes gleamed at me. Of course Lyoh Vega would be the one to welcome me back. Maybe this small hut was a new type of prison.

The air shimmered as the black creature morphed into a human.

A man.

Not a woman.

Silas.

Of course…Silas was the new *draca*.

An elusive smile touched his lips. There one second, gone the next. "You're awake."

Awake.

Alive…

I'd made it through the portal. I passed a hand against the top of my head. Short, bristly strands tickled my palm.

"Veroli sheared off your hair."

What was left of it, he meant.

"I sense it will become all the rage with the courtiers once they see you."

Courtiers… I was really, truly back.

I stared at Silas, then signed Cruz's name, but Silas didn't understand sign language. Somehow, though, he must've understood what I was asking.

He lowered his eyes to the shivering, shimmery waves.

"He…when…" Silas rubbed the back of his neck. "He made Gregor inject all the venom in the syringe."

My chest swelled and burned as though my raging fire had gathered there…charring the organ that had kept me alive…that had failed to keep Cruz alive.

"Lily, I owed him a *gajoï*. So did Catori. If it hadn't been *dile* venom, he would've asked me to do the unthinkable. By suggesting the venom, you spared us." Silas's voice broke, and he pressed his lips together.

I raised my face toward the sun and closed my eyes, willing the slippery heat of my tears to evaporate from my lashes. When I felt like I had gotten myself under control, I looked back at Silas, whose face was scrunched with pain. Cruz had been a dear friend.

"How are you feeling?" he asked, his voice inflected with the slightest quiver.

How was I supposed to answer that?

Alive and dead. That's how I felt.

Instead of attempting to make words out of air, words that wouldn't register with the *draca*, I stared beyond him.

"It's been named the Pink Sea even though Ace wanted to baptize it Catori's Sea."

Of course Cat would refuse to have something named after her.

"Gregor would like you to go to him."

I shook my head. I wasn't ready to see Gregor.

"It's to fi—"

"Lily! My Lily!" A *runa* swayed in the pastel sky. Veroli was frantically agitating her hands, and then she carped to her driver to hurry.

It took me a moment to realize that the fae carrying the *volitor* basket was Dawson. The sight scraped off a sliver of grief.

The basket bumped onto the deck, and then Veroli stumbled out and rushed toward me, squashing my body with her arms. She snuffled loudly against my shoulder, tears wetting the thin white muslin that encased my body like a shroud. I held her tight.

"Welcome home, Lily," Dawson said shyly, unhooking himself from the basket.

I removed my hands from around Veroli to formulate a question.

How long have I been here?

"You've been asleep for three days, deary."

Three days… Just over two human weeks.

I signed my brother's name next.

Veroli glanced sideways at Silas. "He hasn't returned yet."

I frowned.

Silas's eyes shot to my wrist, to the faint circle slashed by five irregular lines. "He's waiting for Gregor to fix the lock. That's why" —he cleared his throat—"that's why the *wariff* would like to see you. We need you to touch a portal for it to glow."

Take me to him, I motioned to Dawson, who'd learned to sign before he'd learned to fly.

I started walking toward the *runa* when Dawson's eyebrows shot up. "You want me to carry you? I mean, I'd be honored, but I thought you weren't a fan of *runas*."

I wasn't, but what alternative did I have? Climb onto Silas's back? It wasn't as though I could fl—

I froze, stared down at my feet. Like Cruz had taught me many decades ago, I willed my fire downward. Slowly, my feet lifted off the yellow deck.

And then I soared higher.

I can fly again.

Like during my very first flight, happiness curled through me, and I smiled. But then I thought of Cruz, and my smile wilted. I hovered in the air above the submerged Hareni and took in my brother's kingdom. The cliffs sparkled with sunshine, the immense liquid expanse glimmered like cut quartz, and the air was rife with the scent of sunbaked moss and tinny soil. The *calimbors* in the distance stood like ageless sentinels over the land.

I remembered Cruz telling me how he'd always dreamed of seeing Neverra without its cloak of mist. His dream had come true, but at what cost?

I refused to cry as I twirled, filling myself with my home.

Home? Was this even still my home? Who did the hut I'd woken up in belong to? And the larger one bobbing next to it?

Without turning into his dragon form, Silas took flight and joined me in the air. "It has changed, hasn't it?"

I nodded.

"I... In case you wanted to visit Cruz"—the name soared from his lips as silently as one of Kajika's arrows—"we placed his ashes... he asked me...said it was—"

To spare him the pain of explaining, I raised a palm. I knew exactly where Cruz would've wanted to rest for eternity. I dove into the air toward the cliff and landed beside the *panem* tree. A soft breeze blew through the branches, the wood tinkling like Catori's windchime. The palm-shaped blue leaves frisked, dispersing the scent of warm, buttery bread.

I gazed around me until I saw it.

A carpet of orange dandelion clovers stretched over the chalky stone. The fluffy bush was slowly overtaking the rock, growing through each crack and crevice. I crouched and stroked the cottony stalks, and then I plucked one up and twirled it between my fingers. Unlike Earthly dandelions, the tiny blooms that made up the three flower heads didn't blow away, and as I spun them, they changed color—from orange to yellow to pink, then back to orange.

For a long time, Cruz had hated these flowers because his father had also turned into them upon his death, and everyone had convinced Cruz that his father had been evil. Yet upon opening one of my ex-fiancé's many books, I'd found a flattened dandelion clover. It was then that I realized Cruz had forgiven his father.

Under Silas's watchful gaze, I tucked the stalk behind my ear, rose back to my feet, and then sprang into the air.

"Should I take you to Gregor now?"

I nodded and trailed after him, flattening one palm against my ear to keep Cruz's flower from falling away from me.

40

THE ACORN

*T*he palace no longer existed.

The mist, too, was gone.

These were the two strangest parts of this new Neverra.

Where did Ace and Cat reside now? Where did Ace hold meetings with his fae ministers, with his *wariff*? Where did the *draca* and the *lucionaga* convene?

My fingers itched for a phone on which to type all these questions, but phones didn't work in Neverra. I needed a pen and paper. Or Veroli and Dawson. I glanced over my shoulder at the small hut that was no larger than a poppy seed from my vantage point. I couldn't tell if the *runa* was still parked on the deck.

The deck which must have been made of *volitor* fronds.

Whose bed had I been slumbering in?

A sudden influx of gasps resonated around me. I froze, jerking my attention to the space in front of me instead of the one below.

Hundreds of faeries had approached. Whispers went through the crowd like wildfire. Two girls detached themselves from the crowd and flew toward me—Nadia and Eleanor. The girls I'd considered my closest friends until I'd made real friends. They squealed and encircled me with their arms. I let them gush into my ear about how happy they were to see me again—they hadn't come to visit me once since I was tossed out of Neverra—before pressing them away and returning to Silas's side.

The shy princess I used to be would've blushed from the attention of all the *caligosupra*—no…that term had been abolished…what were they called now?—but the Lily who'd stared death in the face only felt annoyed.

I gave Silas a short nod, which he rightly interpreted by flying off. We bypassed the clusters of portals that gleamed like upturned compact discs, reflecting the different locations they led to, then dipped toward the base of a *calimbor*. He landed, and I followed his lead. My landing wasn't smooth. I had to dig my bare heels into the moss to bring myself to a full stop. I was out of practice.

If Ace had been here, he would've made such fun of me.

Thinking of my brother made my spine turn as solid as the trunk of the giant tree. Silas led me straight through the door at the base. If I wasn't mistaken, it used to house a candy shop. My brother must've requisitioned the *calimbor* and turned it into a government facility. I wondered where the candy shop had gone? Higher up? Could ground-dwellers inhabit the upper floors now?

Before entering, I took in the spirals and thought back on my idea of adding ziplines between the trunks. After the portal stamp was fixed, I would work on this.

With Kajika.

My heart performed a small pirouette.

I'd been gone two weeks. I imagined someone had been keeping him and my brother up to date on my state. As I passed through the wide door set in the trunk, I bumped into a girl.

"*Gatizogin*," she said, before her mouth slackened and her slanted brown eyes became almost round.

I smiled. *You are excused, Magena,* I thought, not that she would hear me.

"Lily! *Gejaiwe*, you are alive!"

She thought I was dead? I felt my eyebrows writhe. Did I even still have eyebrows, or had they fallen out along with my hair? I touched my forehead. They were still there, and so were my lashes.

"We didn't dare speak of your condition in case—" Silas tightened the leather tie binding his ponytail. "In case..."

In case I didn't make it.

Footsteps resonated in the circular, cavernous hull of the tree. Five floors had been removed so the room stretched up and up. Only narrow balconies housing ribbon-like benches remained where the floors had once been. *Faelights* drifted around the dim space, casting more shadows than light.

"Lily Wood, in the flesh. Never thought I'd see you again." Gregor strode toward me, his black, fitted tunic making him one with the darkness.

You mean, you hoped you would never see me again, I signed.

Too lazy to learn sign language, my father had ordered his right-hand man to study it so he could act as translator.

Gregor smiled, and it crinkled his eyes and mouth. He'd aged in the last five months. I guessed it wasn't due to the passing time—I'd only been gone a Neverrian month—but rather, to the new regime. Just because my brother had kept him on as *wariff* didn't mean Ace was making Gregor's life easy.

"Believe it or not, I'm glad to see you, Lily," he said.

I didn't believe him.

He looked hurt, and the guarded expression reminded me of Remo. *Remo.* I would get to hold him soon.

"I need to meet with Negongwa, but I will see you later, Lily," Magena said, sidestepping me. She swung around more than once on her way out, her short black hair bobbing around her ears.

"Shall we begin?" Gregor asked, gesturing to the entrance.

I nodded, and we returned to the air field of portals.

"Pick one."

I soared up a hundred feet into the sky until I found the one that led to the boathouse.

"I should've figured you'd pick this one. Now set your hand on it."

I touched the slick surface, and my portal stamp flashed to life, but the portal didn't soften. Gregor produced a thumb-sized gold acorn from his tunic pocket.

Before he could begin, I lifted my hand and signed, *Does Ace know I'm alive?*

"He knows your body stayed whole, but he doesn't know you've woken up. Unless one of the courtiers traveled to Neverra. I heard your presence caused quite a stir this morning."

Can someone tell him before you mess with the lock?

"Ye of little faith." He clucked his tongue. "Now hold still so I can get to work."

I replaced my hand on the portal.

Gregor had always been cocky. As his forehead pleated in concentration, I prayed his cockiness wasn't overconfidence but true skill. He held the acorn over the portal and tugged on the short stem. A beam appeared from the bottom of the golden tree nut. Not a beam...a projection. A hot-pink pattern that matched the stamp on his wrist.

Carefully, Gregor spun the top and the frame encasing the pattern changed, curved. Then he spun the middle part, and the pattern nearest the outer curve—not yet a circle—changed. And then he twisted the bottom half, and the innermost array of lines swirled and set. The projection in no way matched the one on my wrist.

As the sky dimmed, faeries tried to approach us, but Silas kept them back. When a crowd formed, Gregor cursed in Faeli, then let out a shrill whistle, and a regiment of *lucionaga* streamed from the assembly hall.

"Tell them to get these voyeurs out of here, Silas," Gregor barked, and the *draca* obeyed. Soon we were alone again.

My fingers started to become numb from their inertia, but I didn't move them. The sun set, and the sky turned periwinkle. *Astriums* appeared in glittery streaks, and I marveled as though seeing them for the first time.

"Some people believe that those stars are the spirits of dead faeries."

I glanced at Gregor.

"Some people…" he repeated. "Not me. I wouldn't believe such a foolish theory."

I smiled at the *wariff* who was still twisting and turning, making the slightest of adjustments to each cog. The pink projection was starting to resemble my stamp in that it was now a circle. However, within that circle was a scattering of tiny etchings, not five distinct lines.

"How do you like your new house?" he asked a long moment later.

I frowned.

"Where you woke up…it's your new house. The queen had it built it for you." He lifted his hazel gaze to my face, but then lowered it again. "The larger one next to it is hers and Ace's. She offered to have one built for me, but I much prefer living at the apex of my *calimbor*. I can keep a better eye on Neverra from up there."

He let out a short breath, and I looked down, fearing the circle he'd managed to attain had somehow turned octagonal, but it was still round. The reason he'd gasped was because he'd managed to create one line.

One out of the five.

Sweat beaded from his tawny sideburns, tracked down his angular jaw.

"Every courtier wants a house on the Pink Sea now, but Ace isn't allowing anyone else to live there. You should see the fortunes some people are willing to pay. I suggested they use all that money and head out to Tahiti and rent out one of those luxury houses on stilts. Way less macabre than swimming over an ancient prison if you ask me."

Gregor was rambling. Surprisingly, I didn't mind. It kept my mind occupied and it answered many of my questions.

"Yes," he murmured as twinkling *faelights* began to blink off in *calimbor* windows.

Neverra was going to sleep.

I looked down at the pink pattern. He'd managed to shape a second line.

"Your mother wanted to see you," he said after another lengthy silence.

My mother wanted to see me?

That was a first.

"Ace still has her on lockdown in his old apartment. She asked that you visit her."

I passed my hand through my hair, or at least through what was left of it. I patted the soft fuzz. This new hairdo would take some getting used to. I couldn't remember a time I'd worn my locks in any other fashion than long.

My fingers struck the dandelion clover. I untucked it and twirled it, watching the fluctuating colors. Gregor glanced at the flower.

"Cruz was a quixotic man."

Was... Pain fired across my breastbone. I pressed the flower against my nose and pulled its scent deep into me, and somehow, it cooled the blistering ache. Carefully, I replaced the clover behind my ear.

A stillness enveloped the world at nightfall, which was the reason it had always been my favorite moment of the day. When I was little, I would fly out my window toward the palace's floating garden and lie on the moss to look up at the *astriums*. Often, I would fall asleep there and be awakened by my brother returning to the palace at an indecent hour, or by a huffing Veroli.

"Three down, two to go," Gregor murmured. He sounded as though he could hardly believe he was succeeding. "When you see your brother, tell him I want a raise and a medal. In that order."

I snorted, and his lips contorted into a smile. To think Gregor Farrow had a sense of humor... Unless he was serious? Maybe he truly wanted a medal and raise, in which case he was a pompous ass. Then again, *if* he succeeded, I was certain he could ask anything of my brother.

I sucked in a sharp breath, suddenly realizing exactly what he would ask for—the abolishment of the law that prevented him from bringing his daughter and grandson to Neverra.

My intake of air made him look up, and then he glanced around the vast darkness. The faerie sentries bobbed in a wide circle around us.

Dropping his voice to a whisper, he asked, "How are..." He snuck a glance over his shoulder. Only Silas was close enough to hear, but he didn't seem particularly interested by our conversation. "How are they?"

A slow smile crept across my features.

With the hand that wasn't splayed on the portal, I formed the letters of Remo's name, then touched my index and middle finger to my lips and curled the tips to form the word, *cute*.

"I heard. What sort of name is Remo anyway?" he huffed.

I laughed. Gregor smirked, but his expression was pliant. Oh, he was going to *love* his grandson, name and all.

Never in a thousand years would I have expected to feel anything but antipathy toward the *wariff*, but there I was, feeling *something*. When Cruz and Ace had told me Gregor was joining in their fight, I was certain he would backstab both. Had he simply acted like a heartless tyrant to impress my father?

"Four," Gregor announced. He dug the heel of one of his hands into his eye sockets, then blinked. His eyes were probably stinging from concentration and fatigue.

Mine weren't stinging, but then again, I'd slept enough to last me a Neverrian week.

I watched the monochromatic isle fill with color as the sun peeked over the mountains. And then I lost sight of the land as my body swayed and fell hand first inside the portal.

Gregor had done it!

41

THE BOATHOUSE

J tumbled into the boathouse gracelessly, knocking my head and shoulders against the wooden bench. I half expected my brother to snicker, but my brother wasn't there. No one was there. I stood up and dusted my hands on my white gown, and then I strode through the empty boathouse, stepping right into a mound of deep snow.

As soon as it hit my ankles, it began to evaporate. I wanted to laugh, but then I spotted an elderly couple trudging down the beach with their dog. Considering the weather and the steam rising from my skin, I must've looked like I'd just escaped a kooky house.

I brushed my dust over my legs to cloak the steam but didn't bother changing the appearance of my white dress. Instead, I skipped through the snow toward the forest like a wild doe. Once entrenched in the tall pines, I checked my surroundings and leaped off the ground, hurtling through the air toward Kajika's house.

I landed on the deck that was also covered in several inches of snow. I raised my fist to knock but stopped, knuckles millimeters from the wood. What would he think of me? How did I even look? I suddenly became a self-conscious mess, but then I pumped steel into my spine and knocked.

A different hairdo didn't shut off your feelings for someone.

When the door opened, I let out the breath I'd been holding.

Menawa rubbed a fist into sleep-filled eyes, which made me wonder what time it was. The sky was light, which meant it mustn't have been too early. He pried his lids higher, forehead scrunched. Did he not recognize me? Magena had recognized me the instant she'd seen me. Then again, women were more observant than men.

My identity must've finally registered because his eyes became as round as the heads of the dandelion clover still tucked behind my ear. "Lily?"

I nodded eagerly.

"Y-You are back...and alive."

I didn't nod. Both were self-evident.

He raked his hands through his silky black hair. "Kajika is not here."

I frowned.

"He left for New York yesterday. His agent entered him in an apparently very significant tournament. UFC? KFC? Something of the sort."

I smiled. I didn't think Kajika would be fighting in a fried chicken tournament.

He touched my shoulder. "I do not know if it would be wise of you to go looking for him. For some time, he has been...bothered."

I cocked an eyebrow. Had Kajika not told his brother about us? Was that what was bothering the hunter? Or was it something else entirely? *Regret?*

Gwenelda padded to her husband's side. The second she saw me, recognition flared in her dark eyes. "The lock has been fixed?"

I'd forgotten they'd been stranded here. I nodded.

She sucked in a breath, then gripped Menawa's forearm. "We must go back. Today. We must go back today! Father must be desperate to see us."

"We cannot leave my brother," Menawa said.

"He can come with us now. Besides, he will not return until tomorrow. We can be back by then."

"Gwen—"

She placed a finger against his lips. "We will not be gone long." But then, as though remembering I was still there, she said, "Perhaps Lily could inform Kajika that the portals are fixed."

Was she suggesting what I thought she was suggesting?

"I am sure Lily Wood has more important things to do than collect my celebrity brother."

Gwen's high cheekbones rose with a placid smile. "*Twa*," she said.

Kajika hadn't taught me much Gottwa, but that word came back to me: *men.*

Twa indeed.

"Better hurry. His match begins when the sun sets, and it has been setting early."

As I took off, I heard Menawa asking his wife why she'd suggested I go fetch his brother. I didn't wait to hear her answer. I soared toward the graveyard.

I would never have thought that the sight of headstones could make me happy, but they did. I landed on the porch, a tad bit more elegantly than earlier, then worked on evening my frantic breathing. Slowly, I spun the handle, and the door creaked open.

Derek had taken to locking the door at night, but not during the day. Odds were my brother and sister-in-law wouldn't be in the house. The distinct scent of something roasting filled the house, as well as a steady stream of classical music. I started walking through the living room when the sound of a voice halted me in my tracks.

"What time do you thing you'll be home tomorrow?" Cat asked someone.

She was here!

I rushed toward the kitchen.

"Lily!" My brother leaped to his feet, his chair skidding backward.

Cat's whisk fell against the kitchen counter, splashing her with gravy.

Ace lunged toward me but stopped inches from my body, blue eyes aglow. Finally, he smiled. "Nice haircut."

I flicked his arm, and then he wrapped that arm and his other one around me. And then Cat squeezed between us.

Someone had started crying—loud, raucous snuffling. I thought it was me, but it turned out to be Cat. "Oh, Lily," she croaked.

"Cat, don't choke her. We just got her back."

I laughed.

She laughed. And then she ugly-cried some more.

"You might want to get changed before Derek comes back from his late lunch at Bee's. He might think you've gone off and married someone if he sees you in a white gown."

I wouldn't be staying that long. Not this time. I would most definitely come back to see Derek, though.

Cat slowly pressed away from me, and then she smiled, and smiled, lips wobbling. Ace gripped her shoulders that had started shaking too.

"She has been a bit emotional lately," he said, as though I wouldn't be able to tell from her blotchy face. "Lily, did Gregor— Are the portals—"

Of course. That's what I'd rushed over to tell them! I nodded frantically. Ace released a sigh that filled the entire kitchen, and then Cat spun around and clasped her arms around his neck.

Go, I signed.

My brother kissed Cat's forehead, then looked at me. "Aren't you coming back with us?"

My pulse hammered against my ribs. *Not yet.*

I waited for my brother to say something else, but he didn't. He just stood there, regarding me with his jaw set. He knew where I was going, and he still didn't approve. It hurt. I turned my back, refusing to let my brother's opinion spoil my mood, and marched to my old bedroom. Until I pushed through the door, I hadn't even considered whether my belongings would still be there. They were. Derek hadn't gotten rid of me.

It somewhat lifted my mood. I opened my closet door and tossed an outfit on the bed, and then I dug through the boot in which I'd stuck my cell phone. I turned it on, then marveled when the screen lit up. It still had battery. *Unbelievable…*

Still, I plugged it into a socket as I changed out of my white gown and into a more appropriate outfit—gray suede leggings and a white silk top that draped off one of my shoulders. I added my black knee-high boots…the ones with the spiky heels.

I felt a thrill zipping them up, perhaps because I never thought I'd see them, much less wear them ever again. I stopped by my bathroom next—*my* bathroom—and grinned, but the grin vanished from my face when I took in my reflection.

Without hair…without hair, I looked…*odd.* I removed the dandelion clover from behind my ear. It had wilted anyway, just like my mood. I laid it on the little vanity shelf, next to a bottle of perfume I'd bought in Paris, then I clutched the edge of the sink and gaped at the girl in the mirror.

I could create hair from *wita*, but Kajika could see through my dust. I could buy a wig, but wigs were so ugh.

I hung my head, and the tears that hadn't emerged in Neverra trickled down my cheeks, evaporating almost as quickly as they fell. I cried for my lost hair; I cried for the floppy flower; I cried for Cruz; I cried because my brother still didn't approve of the man whom I'd set my heart upon.

"What's with the pity party?"

I spun to find Ace leaning against the doorframe. I glowered at him, and he smirked.

"Nothing like an annoying older brother to stanch waterworks." One side of his mouth lifted, and he extended his arm. A folded square of paper flapped between his index and middle finger. "You'll probably need this."

I frowned at the paper. My stamp worked. I didn't need a page from Ley's book.

"For the hunter, dum-dum."

I jerked my head up so fast my neck cracked.

For a long moment, we looked at each other, and then I lunged toward him and hugged him as tight as I used to hug him when I was little, and he would sweep me out of the palace to take me galli-vanting through Neverra.

"I love you, lil' sis."

Not as much as I loved him. I finally pressed away from him.

"You look different."

I palmed my nonexistent hair self-consciously.

"Alive."

That hadn't been what I had been expecting Ace to say.

I slid my hand off my head and signed, *I look ugly.*

He snorted. "Lily, even if you tried, you wouldn't manage to look ugly."

I scrunched up my nose and pointed to my hair.

"It's different. Definitely not ugly. In a way it makes you look older, edgier, as though you belong on the back of a Harley."

I snorted.

"Look, I'm not the most objective person in the world when it comes to you, but I guarantee that you look better than 99.99 percent of the women out there, faeries and humans included. The only person who tops you is my wife."

I rolled my eyes.

"What? I said I wasn't particularly objective."

I shook my head, grinning.

Cat barged into the room. "I'm ready." She sounded breathless.

I never expected Cat to be excited about returning to Neverra. Then again, she'd built herself a fabulous new house. Or maybe her breathlessness had to do with my brother not being stranded from the faerie isle like I had been.

"Don't you look nice," she said, giving me a once-over.

"See, I'm not the only one who thinks this."

I made a face.

She handed Ace her bag, and then she strode to my vanity cabinet and opened it. She took out a black eyeliner, mascara, and a tube of lipstick. "Sit." She pointed to the bathtub. "Look up."

She poked my eye with the pencil, then rubbed her fingertip against my lid, and then she rolled mascara onto my lashes. She tortured my other eye next. Biting her lower lip, she studied my face, adding a touch of liner here and there. Then she capped the black pencil and decorated my lips with bright red lipstick.

"Can I object?" Ace asked.

"Nope," Cat said.

"She's going to garner way more attention than the hunter's," he said gruffly, which made Cat smile.

I had to admit, it made me smile too. Especially when I saw how serious Ace was.

"You're ready." She pressed the lipstick into my hands. "How are you getting to New York?"

Did everyone know about Kajika's match?

"The portals?" she suggested.

I hadn't even considered the portals. I suddenly worried that going through a portal would erase the ink from Ley's page, but then remembered the book had already traveled to Neverra and back, and the ink hadn't vanished.

I nodded, then chucked my cell phone, lipstick, and the piece of paper from Holly's book into my favorite Valentino purse.

"I just gave two more pages to Gwen and Menawa," Cat was telling my brother, while I speared a pair of diamond hoops through my ears. "We're running out."

"Not many people left to bring in."

"Just the Daneelies," Cat said.

"Not many will be coming, if any at all."

I wondered if more had happened since I'd left, besides Pete becoming a hunter. Had Quinn and Kiera resurfaced?

I wanted to ask, but I also wanted to get to New York as fast as possible. We took off toward the boathouse. Ace and I flew while Cat ran.

The door to locker number four was still gaping.

"Ready?" Ace asked Cat.

She nodded.

"After you, my queen."

Her hand shook as she raised it—she still didn't believe it would work. She pressed her palm against the back of the locker, and her portal stamp flashed, and then she was gone.

"I'm going to need an escort."

Right.

He extended his hand, and I clasped it. And then I pressed my fingers to the back of the locker, and we glided right through.

MADISON SQUARE GARDEN

*M*y brother's expression when he emerged from the portal would forever stay etched in me. Relief and joy. He wrapped an arm around Cat's waist and pulled her against him, tucking her head under his chin.

I leaped off the portal, but then doubled back and tapped Cat's shoulder. She looked away from the sea of courtiers who were slowly congregating around them.

I signed, *I love my new house.*

Her smile increased tenfold. "Come back quick, Lily." Her voice was hoarse with emotion.

I nodded, then soared up. I hadn't taken the Manhattan portal in a long time, but sort of remembered where it was. *Sort of* being the keyword. It took me three Neverrian minutes to locate the darn thing. Enough time for my pink-haired friend to flit beside me and ask me where I was heading.

I didn't answer her, just kept scanning the floating disks.

The second I saw train tracks, I dove down and through the portal. I bumped my head against a door. Cursing silently, I opened it and stumbled out of the technical panel onto a dusky platform.

"The train to White Plains will be departing in five minutes on platform one hundred and thirty two. Five minutes."

I rounded a staircase and was instantly swept up in a crush of bodies. Grand Central Station was always crowded, whatever the time of day or night. A man yapping into his cell phone bumped into me. I didn't think he would apologize or reach out to steady me, but he did both. And then he ended his call and slipped his phone inside his suit pocket.

"I am so sorry." The man still hadn't let go of my leather sleeve.

I'd gone with my brother's suggestion of adding a leather jacket. Not for warmth—I no longer needed clothes to keep me warm—but for style.

His eyes scurried across my face, then down my body. *Subtle.* Although I was surprised by his intense attention, I was also flattered. If a complete stranger found me appealing enough to spare more than a quick glance at me, then I couldn't be *that* hideous.

I shrugged him off.

Flustered, he scratched the back of his head. "*Wow.* I don't know what came over me."

I smiled to ease his distress and then I climbed the stairs, weaving through an even denser crowd. I felt more than one pair of eyes land on me as I strode through the cavernous concourse, and I suddenly wondered if perhaps I glowed. Nonsense. Humans couldn't detect faeries. Maybe my lipstick had smudged. I checked my reflection in my phone's photo app to make sure my lipstick was where it was supposed to be. It was, so I sped up, my heels clicking against the buffed stone.

Outside, I took off running, but then cast *wita* around me and sailed upward. Pedestrians would see a girl enter a restaurant, not a girl taking to the sky. I flew to the circular roof of Madison Square Garden, then lurched off it like Spiderman, casting illusion upon illusion. Once I'd landed on the sidewalk, I collected my dust and walked casually toward the entrance. I didn't have a ticket, and the man at the entrance said the match was sold-out.

I was about to tell him who I was when I noticed a ticket hawker a couple feet away. I walked to him and pointed to the ticket.

"Three hundred bucks, take it or leave it."

I was taking it. I fished around for my wallet, but I'd forgotten it in my haste. I dug through my bag, desperate to locate a stranded bill, but found nothing. The hawker lost interest.

I did something I never thought I would do...I created bills with *wita*. I tapped his shoulder and extended the three green hundreds. He inspected them, then tucked them into his back pocket and handed me the ticket. I hadn't *really* cheated him since they would stay in bill form until the day I died, which was probably going to be a long time after him.

I walked back to the ticketing counter and handed over my ticket. The man scanned it, then let me through. The excited hum in the stadium electrified my pace. I hurried up the stairs, taking them two at a time. A voice boomed from a loudspeaker, announcing Kajika's name and then his opponent's name, and then the crowd roared, cheering, whistling, chanting.

On the landing, I stopped to catch my breath and to take in the lit Octagon below. This was a far cry from the dingy ring back in the barn.

A hostess asked me for my ticket. I distractedly handed it to her, too busy peering over her shoulder. She gestured toward a seat in the middle of the stands. As I trailed her down, the hunter trotted in, bare-chested and glorious. The crowd went wild. I stopped to stare at him as he raised his gloved hands over his head to acknowledge his fans. I waited for him to spot me, but he didn't. I smiled to myself as I headed down my row, careful not to step on anyone's feet.

I took my seat and lowered my bag onto my lap just as Kajika's opponent erupted into the ring—a monstrous man with a body that looked carved from a *calimbor* trunk. The crowd cheered, but nowhere as loudly as they'd clamored for the hunter. That only amplified my thrill. Not that I thought the hunter basked in applause...I was pretty certain Kajika hated recognition, but it didn't prevent me from being proud of him.

The tournament started, and I could tell Kajika was holding back as he kneed his opponent's thigh, then later, as he delivered a flurry of punches. He barely broke a sweat during the first two rounds. He did let his opponent land a few jabs, I assumed for showmanship. During the third round, though, Kajika's concentration broke. He had his opponent clinched against the fence when his face jerked up and his gaze scanned the crowd.

I ducked behind my handbag. I didn't want to distract him.

The crowd jeered. I peeked over the top of my bag. Kajika was sprawled on the canvas, and his opponent rained blows over him. The referee broke them up. During his minute break, as a young aid squirted water into the hunter's mouth, Kajika scanned the stands again.

When his gaze slammed into mine, goosebumps scattered over my arms and legs. I couldn't tell from his expression how he felt about my presence. My heart held extremely still as the fourth round was announced. He pushed himself away from the ropes, still not breaking eye contact.

This time, he clobbered his opponent, no longer even attempting to make the fight look fair. During his next water break, he didn't look for me, didn't raise his eyes off the mat, and my pulse flattened.

The fifth round began and ended the same way the fourth had. That Kajika's opponent managed to walk out of the Octagon was a miracle. Kajika was awarded a bulky belt. Bright camera flashes twinkled around the stage and the clapping intensified. When the hunter still hadn't looked my way, I stood, my knees threatening to give out.

I wasn't sure what I had been expecting, but certainly not that.

I climbed up the stairs and then once through the doors, away from the cacophony, a long breath ratcheted up my throat. I eyed the doors I'd skipped through earlier, so inanely hopeful.

I started toward them, but stopped and turned. Had I been expecting that Kajika would scale the ropes and run to me? That he would swing me into his arms and take off with me in front of all his worshipping fans?

I checked the date on the ticket. It had been almost three weeks since I'd seen him. He had every right to be disconcerted by my return.

Besides, the hunter didn't do displays of affection.

I crumpled my ticket and tossed it in the trash, and then I sought out the entrance to the underbelly of the stadium.

I might not have been able to fight in a ring, but that didn't mean I couldn't fight for what I wanted. And I wanted the hunter.

43

LOCKER ROOM

*I*t took me a couple minutes to locate the path to the locker rooms. No one stopped me, but I garnered many suspicious gazes. When I noticed the badges flapping around the staff's necks, I whisked my hand in front of my chest and created a matching one. That lessened the attention coming my way.

I walked through what felt like a maze of hallways, trying to find a sign showing Kajika's name. But then my palm flashed, reminding me that I possessed the greatest tracking device. I curled my fingers and followed the direction it fed me.

I located him just as he strode into a room, trailed by a middle-aged man in a gray suit. His manager, I imagined. I didn't move for a long time, waiting for the suit-clad man to emerge from the room.

When he finally walked out, bellowing for someone named Jake, I took out my cell phone. They walked down the hallway, right past me. Although I felt the man in the suit glance my way, he didn't stop. I walked fast. Ran. A girl with glasses lifted her face from a clipboard to study me, so I slowed before she alerted the authorities.

Once in front of the closed door, I rubbed my clammy hands against my suede leggings, then spread my fingers around the knob and twisted. My ears buzzed and my forehead prickled. I thought of my hair again, but cast my worries aside and let myself in.

Kajika sat on a bench facing the opposite wall, his broad back to me. No muscle twitched underneath his dark skin. Only the dust adorning the top of his spine and one of his thick shoulders pulsed.

I closed the door.

"Look who returns." His voice was so low and gravelly it sent a chill up my spine. His biceps moved as he unwrapped the tape from his fingers.

You're mad at me.

He snorted, and it echoed through the small locker room. "I am not mad."

Then why don't you look at me?

"Because I do not want to." He coiled the tape and placed it beside him on the bench.

My heart clapped like the thunder that had echoed through the Daneelie barrack. *Are you disgusted by my appearance? Is that it?*

He shook his head.

Then what?!

Slowly he turned. At first it was only his neck and face, but then his shoulders pivoted and he lifted one leg, then the other. His expression was careful, guarded, distant almost. There was no frostiness in his gaze, but there was also no warmth.

I swallowed a breath. *You found someone else, didn't you?*

His eyebrows jutted.

You replaced me.

"I think you have us mixed up, Lily."

I crossed my arms and held them tight against my torso. *What is that supposed to mean?*

"Did you think I would not find out about your new engagement?"

My new engagement? To whom am I engaged?

His pupils pulsed. "You tell me."

I have been unconscious for three days and working on fixing the lock for one, so I'm not sure when I would've had the time to conjure the Cauldron and tie my essence with someone else's.

Kajika's cautious stare turned hooded. I liked hooded better than cautious. At least he was displaying emotion. "What did you do the remaining seventeen days?"

What remaining seventeen days?

"You have been gone for three weeks!" There was the heat I'd come to associate with the hunter.

Three human *weeks! That corresponds to four days in Neverra!*

The hunter sat up straighter.

Who told you I was engaged? I was still seething, still yelling into his mind, angry that he would put stock in such a rumor. Did he not know me? Did he really believe I would get myself a new fiancé?

His Adam's apple joggled in his freshly-shaven throat. "Your brother," he finally said. "Your brother told me you had decided to marry Silas. He told me I should move on."

The silence was crushing.

My brother... He'd made up a lie to drive the hunter away?

I was suddenly so angry with Ace I wanted to throttle him. *How could you believe I would do that?*

"I did not want to believe it, Lily, but he asked Silas to confirm it, and the faerie said you had been seeing each other for some time now." The hunter dipped his face into his neck. "I remembered the way you had looked at him the night I was attacked, so I did not question his word."

I let out a rough grunt. *Silas is a friend.* Well, until now. I was benching him as a friend until I got to the bottom of this. *I am not attracted to the* draca. *Never have been and never will be.* I trembled so hard my teeth clattered. *The only man I have ever loved beside you was Cruz, and well, he's no longer here.*

My fire swept through me in great, livid waves...not waves. Breakers. Breakers that were breaking against me...breaking me. Kajika shot to his feet, then lunged toward me. He gathered me against him and held me, waiting for the storm of my fury to pass. It took excruciatingly long minutes.

Long minutes during which the door to his locker room opened, bumping into my spine. He bit out some words that didn't register inside my overheated mind and shoved the door closed. I felt like my body had turned into a live wire. I expected to see smoke rise from my nose any instant.

Kajika tightened his hold on me, then began to whisper that he was sorry. Sorry to have believed it. If my body was scorching his, he didn't show it. Didn't add any distance. Didn't hiss through his teeth.

Slowly my rage ebbed, but I kept my arms crossed. Not that there was much room to uncross them. *Did you replace me?*

I felt a rough breath pulse against my shorn hair. "You are not easy to replace."

That doesn't answer my question. I squeezed my lids, wondering why I had to torture myself with this question. *Have you been with anyone else in the time I was gone?*

"I have been too consumed by indignation and despair to do much more than pick fights with people, in and outside the Octagon."

Was that what Menawa had meant about his brother being *bothered*?

Kajika snorted, then glided his long fingers up my spine and seized my neck, tipping it back so that my face was turned toward his. "That is putting it mildly. You broke my fucking heart." His thumb stroked a spot behind my ear. "You will excuse me if I break your brother's fucking nose the next time I see him."

Two curse words in a row. I take it you're a little mad.

He grinned, and that smile burned away the rest of my anger. "You have no fucking idea." He gazed long and hard at me.

I suddenly worried he hated what he was seeing, and I untangled my arms and diffidently palmed my bristly scalp. I wished I had taken the time to buy a wig; I wished I hadn't trusted my brother. He'd probably lied to me when he said I looked okay, hoping my shaved head would be so off-putting to the hunter that the latter would reject me. I lowered my eyes to his chin, unable to stomach the attention.

Kajika pushed my hands away, then slowly drew his palm over my head and back down to my neck, where he kneaded my pinching tendons. "You are even more beautiful than I remembered."

My gaze crept back up to his. He lowered his mouth toward mine but didn't touch my lips, just held them tauntingly close. I could smell the mints he must've crushed with his molars sometime before I'd arrived. I could smell the leather on his fingers and the sweat that had dried on his skin. I licked my lips, then tried to slant my mouth over his but he tightened his grip on my neck and held my face away.

"I am sorry Cruz died, Lily," he murmured.

That made me stop panting.

"But I am also not sorry, because I am a selfish bastard. I do not know if you will be able to forgive me for thinking this, but I wanted to be honest with you."

My heart stiffened, along with the rest of my body.

"Do you detest me now?"

Of course not, I whispered into his mind.

He released my neck and grazed my jaw with his torn knuckles, making me shudder. Cruz's face materialized behind my closed lids. I saw his lips move, heard him utter how he loved me in a hundred different ways, how he was sorry to have taken me for granted. I felt my heart shred all over again.

A tear slid down my cheek, and Kajika brushed it away. *Why did you have to bring him up?*

"Because he will linger in your heart for a long time. And I do not want you to ever compare us and find me lacking."

I would never, Kajika.

He ran the pad of his thumb over my bottom lip, then over my top one, and it raised goosebumps on all the parts of my body he hadn't touched. "Am I still allowed to kiss you?"

I nodded.

His mouth finally rested upon mine. For a while, we breathed each other in, and then his lips pried mine apart.

"Kajika, it's time for the press conference." The door behind us snicked open.

Without breaking away from me, Kajika smacked it closed, then pressed my body up against it to keep it that way. He leaned into me, one palm planted on the door and the other on the small of my back.

His kissing turned so rough it made me gasp. He pulled away. I tugged him back against me, inviting the roughness. I clawed at his shoulders, and he growled into my mouth. My fingers dug deep into his back, and he ground into me.

He had shown me tenderness. He had shown me honesty. And now he was showing me something else.

Something raw and carnal.

Something almost painful but that caused no pain.

"I have missed you, *ma mika. Gejaiwe,* how I have missed you," he murmured against my neck, embedding kisses into my skin.

A smile curved my lips as I let my head rock back against the door. *I can feel how much you've missed me.*

"What you can feel is how much my body has missed yours." He bucked his hips into me, then put some unwelcome space between our bodies.

I straightened my neck, a complaint teetering on the edge of my mind.

He dragged my fingers off one of his shoulders, then pressed them against his chest, right over his pounding heart.

"*This* is how much I have missed you."

The hand that gripped mine smoldered with my W.

44

THE PAGE

lthough it ripped me open to break apart, the pounding on Kajika's locker room door was relentless, and so was the accompanying barking that he was being completely unprofessional.

Kajika huffed as he peeled himself off me and readjusted himself. "One minute, Sam!"

The man stopped barking. "You have thirty seconds to get your ass out here."

I laughed quietly.

Kajika stared at me through his scruffy bangs. "You think it is funny?"

Your jaw is covered in my lipstick, so yes, a little.

His lips curved. I stepped toward him and hovered my hand over his jaw. *Don't freak out, okay?*

"Why would I—" He bounced away from my flaming palm, but not before I'd managed to burn off the red stains. He rubbed at his jaw as though I had scorched it. "A warning would have been nice. Do I still have skin?"

I rolled my eyes. *No, I burned it all off.*

"Might want to use some on yourself, smart-ass."

The slang sounded funny coming from the hunter. I raised my palm to my jaw and ignited it again to burn away any lingering red smears.

"Your thirty seconds are up, Kajika. I'm coming in. Don't you dare stop me!" The door flew open, and the suit-clad man I'd seen earlier barreled inside. He looked at me, and then at Kajika, and then back at me.

Even though Sam wasn't giving off any dangerous vibes, Kajika stepped in front of me.

"Who's she?" he asked.

"My mate," Kajika said, which made my cheeks burn.

"Your...*mate*?"

I tossed the word *girlfriend* Kajika's way, but he must not have heard me, because he repeated, "Yes, my mate."

My heart spiked. *People don't use that word, Kajika.*

"My future wife," he said.

Oh, skies, I was filled with fire, but I was pretty sure I was also *on* fire.

Someone whispered, "Isn't that Lily Wood?"

"Who?"

"Oh, Jake, you know nothing about everything."

I peeked sideways and spotted the girl with the glasses and clipboard standing beside the young boy Kajika's manager had talked with earlier.

She caught me looking and jerked her gaze down to her clipboard.

"I didn't know you were engaged," Sam said.

"Because it is none of your business. It is none of anyone's business."

I palmed my head, wishing I had hair to hide behind. *Couldn't you just have told him I was your girlfriend?*

"Girlfriend does not encompass what you mean to me, Lily."

"Oh my God, I was right," Clipboard-girl hissed. "It is Lily Wood."

Kajika glared at her. She backed up, lost her footing, but caught herself on Jake's arm.

Sam sighed, then extended his hand toward me. Kajika didn't move, and I didn't reach around him to shake it, so Sam lowered his fingers. "Well, nice to meet you, Lily. I apologize for interrupting your…reunion, but I have to borrow your fiancé."

"I do not feel like speaking with the press."

Color rose on Sam's face. "You signed a contract, son. You may not feel like chatting with journalists, but you're legally bound to do so, so come on."

Kajika grumbled.

I placed a hand on his back. *Go. I'll wait right here.*

"Because you think I am letting you out of my sight?" He spun and took my hand before it fell back alongside my body.

"Am I going deaf? Did she say something?" Sam asked Jake, or maybe he was asking Clipboard-girl.

The latter whispered, "She's mute, Mr. Hodge."

Kajika was looking down at me. "Unless you mind being around journalists?"

I've spent my life around them. Bring it on, mate.

A smile surged on Kajika's face. He tucked me under his arm, then told his manager that we were ready.

THE PRESS CONFERENCE WAS INTERESTING. The sports journalists acted like gossip columnists. Reporters asked me a hundred times when my brother's wedding would happen, and what had happened to my hair. I told Kajika to tell them I'd been sick, and that was the reason the wedding had been delayed. I hated to use a fake illness as an excuse, but it wasn't like I could tell them I'd been running low on fire.

After a half hour, we were finally ushered out of the press room.

"I'll see you in training in three days," Sam said.

"I am taking a week off." Kajika gripped my hand tighter.

"Fine." Sam huffed. "One week, but not a minute more."

Kajika nodded.

I almost suggested he quit, but that would be implying he could live off me, and I didn't see the hunter agreeing to that.

"Damn right."

So much slang coming out of that mouth.

"I am trying to learn to speak more like a thug."

I chuckled. *I'm pretty sure thugs use contractions.*

"I will work on that." He smiled. "Let me throw on some clothes, and we can head back to my hotel." He steered us into the locker room, then released my hand to grab a black t-shirt and black cargo pants from a hanger.

Kajika... I traced the new stamp on my wrist.

He tugged on his pants, then the shirt. "You do not want to go back to a hotel with me?"

No. It's not that at all. It's just... I'd like to take you someplace before that.

He eased a black fabric belt through his pants' belt loops, eyes cemented on mine.

I grabbed the paper from the bag, and extended it toward him, barely daring to breathe, so afraid he would refuse.

He took the paper from my shaky fingers, then smoothed it out. "Huh."

Is that a yes?

"Is your brother back in Neverra?"

Yes.

"Then show me the way."

Even though trepidation zapped up my spine, I smiled.

He stepped toward me and looped his arms around my waist. "*Ma mika,* I will not shoot an arrow through your brother's chest, but I do intend to give him a piece of my mind and perhaps a closer look at my fists, even if it wins me a stay in one of your *cupolas.*"

Cupolas *have been abolished.*

"Then I have nothing to fear."

Catori might have some objections.

"I do not fear Catori's wrath. Only yours." He kissed the tip of my nose. "Only yours, *aabiti*."

Aabiti?

"Mate."

I blushed, and he laughed.

The man who never laughed, laughed.

45

THE RUNA

$\mathcal{W}$e stood in front of the portal to Neverra. My feet ached from the fifteen-block walk in spiky heels, and I was short of breath, although that had more to do with nerves than exertion. The hunter observed the fuse box as though it were an Egyptian hieroglyph.

"I was wondering where my page had gone. I am relieved that you were the one to take it," he said, his white teeth gleaming in the semi obscurity.

I didn't take it from your house. My brother gave it to me.

He gave a soft grunt. "So *he* was the one to take it. Figures."

I tipped my eyebrows up. Would Ace have done that? I supposed my brother was capable of it. He liked to control people, and what better way to make sure that Kajika wouldn't arrive in his kingdom unannounced than to steal his ticket?

My irritation rose another notch. He was no better than our father…

Kajika tightened his grip on my hand. "That is not true, *ma mika*. Ace is not Linus. Linus would never have allowed my tribe to enter Neverra or settle there. Your father would have gassed us the minute we stepped out of our graves if he had not been too much of a coward to travel to Earth."

But Ace made you believe I was engaged!

"I know, and that is wrong, but I have had some time to think about it, and I believe he was protecting you from me. Sometimes it feels as though he considers you his daughter more than his sister. That is not to say I am not angry...I am furious, but a part of me understands."

A train full of evening commuters squealed onto the tracks next to us. In a couple seconds, the doors would slide open.

"How does this work?" He flapped the square of paper. "Do I have to press it against one of the fuses?"

This was really happening. *Any fuse. And, Kajika...don't let go of my hand, and don't move once you get through.*

"Why?"

I shot him a teasing smile. *You'll see.*

"I do not like to see. I like to know."

Just go.

Gaze cemented to mine, he touched the yellowed page to one of the fuses, while I pressed my hand against them. The symbol on my wrist ignited at the same time as a spark lit up the darkness, and the portal swallowed us whole.

KAJIKA DIDN'T HEED my words. The second we emerged from the portal, he lunged, and my hand ripped out of his. Pulse accelerating, I dove off the platform after him. Kajika said he couldn't die from a bad fall, but I didn't want to test his theory.

He fell faster than I could fly, and for a second, I thought I wouldn't be able to catch up, but then he smacked into another portal. He grunted as I reached him, face as pale as the paper crumpled in his bruised hands.

I told you not to move off the portal.

He grunted again, pushing himself up to his feet. "But you failed to mention why."

I bit my lip, worried he was angry.

"I am not, Lily." He raked his hand through his long bangs.

The sun was at the apex of the sky. Barely an hour had elapsed since I'd left, even though several had ticked by on Earth.

What do you think?

Faeries, who had been gliding nearby, approached. The hunter glared at them, and they backed away, but like fish around a lure, they didn't leave.

"It is...it is"—he tipped his head up—"the sky is purple."

Didn't I tell you that?

"And those trees." He gestured to the *calimbors*.

I let him take in my birthplace, feeding him the names of the places he looked at—the Pink Sea, the Five Cliffs, the Glades.

Your family has settled in the Valley between the Five—that's what we call those five cliffs for short.

"Where do you live?"

I used to live in the palace, but it fell when the mist fell. Cat and Ace built me a house on the Pink Sea. I pointed out the tiny bobbing edifice.

The hunter squinted at it. I couldn't tell what he thought. He was no fan of water, that I knew. Besides, if his family had settled in the Valley, he'd probably want to live there too.

"Lily, I do not care where I live as long as you are by my side."

A blush warmed my face.

"So tell me, how do we get down from here?"

I extended my arms.

He cocked up an eyebrow. "You will carry me down? I weigh two of you. Not two, three."

Don't be cocky, now. I wiggled my fingers, and he stepped into my embrace.

He was heavy, and I wasn't able to fly, but I was able to slow down our descent. We drifted as though attached to a parachute. Kajika's heart drummed frantically against my cheek, but soon it quieted, and his wound-up muscles relaxed. He pressed me harder to him, but it was no longer out of fear. At some point, he brushed his lips against the top of my head, and bliss over-whelmed me.

When we landed on the moss, I unclasped my arms from around his, but stayed close.

See, I didn't drop you, I said, feeling triumphant.

He offered me one of his rare smiles before craning his neck to behold the copse of portals. "It is unreal."

And yet it's real.

"Kajika! Oh, *Gejaiwe*, Kajika!" Magena leaped out of a *runa* that had been about to take off and raced toward the hunter. Limbs blurred with speed, she launched herself into his arms. He caught her and returned her hug.

Jealousy reared its petty head. Especially considering Magena had been Ishtu's sister.

Kajika set Magena down, then picked the hand that I'd balled at my side and pulled me against him.

"I cannot believe you managed to get him here," Magena sputtered, winded and grinning.

"She made sound arguments."

Magena snorted. "Uh-huh." She winked at me, and then gestured to the *runa*. I noticed Dawson standing beside the *volitor* basket. "I was just about to head to the Valley to see Negongwa about something. Want to hitch a ride?"

Kajika shot a scornful look at the *runa*. "In that thing?"

Magena smiled. "Dawson, think you can handle this guy?"

Although Dawson's face colored with a crushing blush, he nodded.

"The boy does not seem very certain," he muttered. "Besides he is almost as scrawny as Lily."

"The basket is made of a special wood that floats. He just controls the direction." She whipped around and started running, but halted when she realized we weren't following. "Come on, grumpy."

Would you rather I whistle for a lucionaga *to carry you? Or maybe you can climb onto Silas's back…*

The hunter narrowed his eyes, then pinched my waist. I laughed and rose onto my toes to kiss him. That elicited gasps and whispers from our thickening audience. Even though no faerie had strayed too close, they were watching us closely.

I think they're having a collective heart attack right now.

A corner of the hunter's mouth curled in satisfaction. Finally, casting piercing glares around him, he followed Magena.

She was already in the basket, giggling over something Dawson had told her.

"Hey, Lily," he said, before his gaze climbed up the length of the hunter's hulking figure. Terror scrunched up his features. "You're..." He tugged at his gray tunic collar. "Did you grow?"

When Veroli and Dawson had traveled to Earth, Kajika had met them, but briefly.

"His biceps certainly did," Magena said.

"That must be it." Dawson pushed his mop of blond hair off his freckled forehead.

"You *are* huge. I'm not sure you'll even fit through the opening of the wigwams," she added.

"Wigwams? You built wigwams?" Kajika asked.

"They're different than the ones we used to live in. Way neater." She patted the space on the bench next to her.

Kajika gave the faerie-made contraption another lengthy once-over.

"Will you ride too, Lily?" Dawson asked me, strapping himself back in.

I will fly next to you, I signed. I gave Kajika a little shove. *It's safe. I promise. Besides, I'll hold your hand if you're scared.*

"Scared? Me?" He shook his head. "You have me mistaken for a Seelie, Lily."

I pinched the taut skin at his waist in retaliation for earlier.

He finally climbed in, inspecting each inch of the basket. When Dawson lifted off the ground and the basket teetered, the hunter turned a little green.

I hopped off the ground and flew beside them. As we traveled across the sky, Magena talked and talked, mostly in Gottwa. Here and there, she slid in an English word. I drifted away from them, flying closer to Dawson.

Where is Ace? I signed.

"In the Valley with Negongwa and Gregor. They're updating the portal stamps. The old one is taking to Unseelie skin now that he has the lock."

Below us, the Pink Sea glimmered wildly. A shadow flickered beneath the waves.

He dipped his chin toward the shadow. "That must be Catori. She's been trying to teach me to hold my breath underwater, but I really suck at it."

I stared at her a moment, and then I unzipped shoes and tossed my bag and boots inside the *runa*. Like a pelican, I dive-bombed toward the shadow that recoiled so fast that by the time I opened my eyes, it had vanished. I kicked back toward the surface that had shifted from mirror-calm to agitated, probably to match Cat's mood. I scanned the wavelets for her, but she must've receded into the depths because no one had come up. I heard Kajika yelling for Dawson to get lower, but then I didn't hear anything anymore as I was swept under.

My heart rose into my throat. Instead of kicking, I turned to stone and sank. And then I stopped sinking, and a glimmering form rounded on me. I pressed my hand over my pounding chest, which caused Cat to break into a grin.

Even though the water slowed my hand movements, I signed, *You scared me.*

She shook her head, then signed the very same thing.

We kicked back to the surface. The second our faces broke over the surf, she pulled me into a quick hug. "Way to announce yourself, Lily."

The anxiety that sinking had caused me—propelling me to a time when it hadn't been playful—gradually retreated.

"Lily!" Kajika roared.

Cat looked up at the same time I did. "If it isn't the hunter who swore he would never step foot in Neverra," she said playfully.

Kajika was too busy glowering to respond. I knew what he was thinking because I was thinking the exact same thing. I wasn't even sure what had gotten into me to dive into the water.

"You were not thinking," he muttered.

"I feel there's a story there," Magena chirped.

Cat's smile was gone. "Did you just get here?"

I nodded.

"We're going to the Valley. Want to come, Cat?" Magena asked.

"I'll go get changed and meet you there."

I rose above the water, steam curling off my body.

"Unlike some of us, I don't dry instantly," she said.

I smirked, and then I didn't, because I was thinking about my made-up engagement.

Kajika put my thoughts into words. "Catori, were you aware of the lie your mate fed me?"

Her forehead, which looked more like hammered copper than tiny scales, furrowed.

"Ace told me Lily had gotten engaged to Silas."

"He said what?" Her voice was as sharp as her shine.

I sighed, relieved she wasn't in on the lie.

"Why would he do that?" she said.

"I am guessing it was to keep me away," Kajika said.

Magena piped up. "This is the most entertainment I've had since the day Catori vanquished the mist."

We all looked at Magena. At least one person thought this was fun.

Cat must've decided she didn't need to dry off, because she caught ahold of the bottom of the *volitor* basket, scaled it, then leaped inside. She wrung out her hair. "Dawson, take me to my husband."

Dawson's eyes darted around anxiously. Poor guy was probably thinking this would be his last run as a *runa* driver. He rose and the basket rose with him. And then we were flying over the *panem*. I stared down at the dandelion clovers and my heart contorted. I raised my face toward the sun, willing its bright rays to blind me.

Would this ever get easier?

When I tipped my face back down, my gaze collided into Kajika's. His lips were pressed into a soft line.

"With time, Lily," he said, just loud enough for me to hear. "With time, it will become easier."

But time passed so slowly in Neverra...

"When you lose someone," Kajika said, and Cat and Magena stopped chatting, "time comes to a standstill everywhere."

A faraway gleam appeared in both girls' eyes. Both had lost loved ones. Cat had lost her mother and Blake. Magena had lost her sister and countless others.

For the first time since I'd fallen for the hunter, my jealousy of Ishtu waned. He had loved her like I had loved Cruz, but both were gone, and we remained.

We remained...

THE TRAVELER

*A*lthough I'd headed to the cliff before leaving Neverra, I hadn't yet seen the Valley, hadn't yet witnessed the Gottwas' new settlement.

Huts made of the same pale-gray rock as the cliffs peppered the perfectly round valley like stone igloos, circling a huge edifice made of curved glass filled with concentric, raised beds of soil.

The Gottwas had built a biodome? Did they fear our farmers would refuse to sell them their wares, or were they setting up competition? Then again being self-sufficient was a laudable quality.

By the biodome's entrance stood a cluster of people and bodiless Unseelies, their smoky forms weaving through the settlement. Did they live here too now?

I turned to look at Kajika, wondering what he could be thinking. But he wasn't looking down at the Valley. Something had caught his attention on one of the stone ledges cut into the sides of the cliffs. A *capra* slithered there, or perhaps a *quila* had taken flight? A tuft of blue grass swayed, hiding whatever animal had passed through it.

I stared back below. Several people had turned to look up. My gaze caught on one face. I dove ahead of the *runa* into the Valley and straight for the person that face belonged to—my brother.

The second I landed beside him, I moved my hands to form words. *How could you?*

Ace gripped my wrist and pulled me aside, away from Negongwa and Menawa, with whom he'd been discussing skies only knew what. I snatched my hand away.

"It was a test, Lily," he said, his voice low. "I wanted to see how much you meant to him, because you mean the world to me, and I didn't want to see you get hurt."

My heart shook in my chest. I wanted to sign a thousand words, but my fingers trembled so much I couldn't even form one word.

He reached out and squeezed my quivering shoulder. "I'm sorry, okay? I should probably not have gone as far as to concoct a fake engagement."

You think? I managed to sign.

He sighed, and it bulked up his chest. "Maybe it was a shitty way of apologizing, but the page from Ley's book—"

That you stole from him!

"Stole from him? I may be a bastard at times, but I'm not a thief."

"Ace Wood!" Cat sprang toward him.

Ace cracked his neck from side to side as though gearing up for a fight. Cat did seem exceptionally angry. Her wet hair flogged the air as she strode over toward my brother, still clad in her black one-piece swimsuit that made her look like a sexy action figure.

She poked him in the chest, and Ace raised his palms. For an entire minute, he let her talk—yell at him. And then he wrapped his hand around her still poking fingers and lowered them. "Got it out of your system?"

"How could you do this to them? Would you have appreciated if someone did that to you?"

He tipped his face to the side and studied her a moment. "Someone did do that to us."

That quieted Cat.

He leaned toward her and although he spoke softly, I heard every word. "And next time you yell at me, wear some clothes. Your outfit is very...distracting."

Spots of color appeared on Cat's cheekbones.

Kajika had stepped out of the *runa*, but he hadn't moved toward us. He was still scanning the rocky ledges.

"If anyone gets to be mad at me, it's Kajika. And Lily...but she's already spoken her piece. Kajika?" Ace called out to him loudly. "If you have something to say, I'd rather get it over with now."

The hunter finally looked away from the ledges and approached us. Every few seconds, he halted and glanced upward.

What is it? What did you see?

Ace was scanning the jutting ledges too now, and so was I.

"What's going on?" Cat asked, eyes pinging from us to the rock.

I walked over to the hunter, who still hadn't answered me, and took his hand in mine. *What is it, Kajika?*

He ripped his hand from mine and lurched toward my brother and Cat. They both stumbled back in surprise. *Lucionaga* zoomed through the settlement. They grabbed Kajika by the biceps and hauled him up.

Kajika tore his arms out of their grasp. "You useless people, protect your king and queen."

That's when I noticed the arrow protruding from between his shoulder blades. He reached around and yanked it out just as another arrow soared through the purple air from the exact spot Kajika had been watching.

It struck a *lucionaga* in the thigh.

The guard let out a blood-curdling scream that warbled as he fell over, driving the arrow further through his leg. Smoke rushed out of his wound like a geyser. The arrow hadn't hit his heart, but if it was infused with Unseelie blood, it didn't matter.

No one helped him, all too intent on shielding my brother and Cat. I rushed to the *lucionaga* and tried to pry the arrow out of his flesh, but my fingers kept catching fire. Hands scooped me up and dragged me back.

I fought back, until I heard Kajika's voice in my ear, "Do not touch it, Lily."

Just as the guard exploded into ash, Kajika spun me around and sheltered me against his chest. For a second, he held me there, murmuring words my buzzing eardrums didn't register, and then he screamed Gwenelda's name, and I thought she'd been hit, but then she was there, next to us.

"Keep her safe!"

He released me, and it felt like a knife had sheared me away from him. I stumbled against Gwenelda.

Kajika! I scanned the chaos around me for him, but he'd blurred away. Gwen was staring upward, her square jaw set in a hard line. I followed her line of sight and finally saw my hunter scaling the cliffs alongside his brother. While Menawa had a quiver full of arrows strung across his back, Kajika was weaponless.

Panic overwhelmed me, and I turned to Gwenelda. Although her features were tense, she wasn't trembling like I was. How I yearned for her calm. No part of me was calm. Not my mind, not my body, not my heart. All of me was as chaotic as the Valley.

Gwenelda ushered me toward the *lucionaga* surrounding my brother. Cat broke out of the circle and dashed toward us.

"Who did this, Gwen?" Her voice was shrill.

"I do not know, Catori." Her gaze had risen from Menawa and Kajika to a spot a couple ledges up from them. "I do not know."

She squinted. We all did.

And that's when I saw him. The man who'd launched an attack on the king.

Cat gasped, because she'd seen him too. "How did he get here? Who let him through?" She was yelling now, frantic.

And that was when it hit me. Not an arrow. Thank the skies, not an arrow. But the realization of what had happened to the hunter's missing page.

My brother hadn't stolen it; Pete had.

*a*t some point, my brother broke free of his guards and soared into the sky so dizzyingly fast that it took his *lucionaga* terrible seconds to catch up.

Cat watched her husband blast upward without screaming his name, but her lips quivered. I assumed she was too frozen with fear to speak, or perhaps she didn't want to distract Ace's focus.

Menawa had reached the ledge from which the arrows had been shot. The long blue tufts of grass shivered at his feet. Where was Kajika? I searched the wall of rock for his form, my extremities tingling with dread.

Ace landed on the lip of the ledge beside Menawa. Something glittered in my brother's hand—a weapon forged of dust.

No one moved for so long that I pushed off the ground. I wasn't planning to intervene, but I wanted to see what was happening. I needed to see. It was visceral.

Gwenelda's hand wrapped around my ankle and held me back like a child holding onto the string of a balloon.

"He will never forgive me if something happens to you, Lily."

But I couldn't just stand there.

"Please," she begged, and I started to drift back down, but then a wild, gravelly scream shook the Valley.

Gwen's fingers uncinched, and I bounded upward, leveling off at the ridge just in time to see my brother's glittery sword slice into Pete's waist. The man writhed against Kajika, who had him pinned to his chest.

"Who sent you?" Ace growled.

"No one!" Pete screeched. "No one!"

"You really want us to believe you're working alone?" Ace asked calmly.

Could my brother be right? Could the Daneelies have ordered this attack?

"It was all me. Only me!" Blood had blotted into Pete's navy t-shirt and soaked into his jeans. It stank up the air.

Kajika caught me staring. Although his eyes sparked with fury— probably because I'd disobeyed him, or maybe he was furious with Pete...I hoped it was the latter—he didn't yell at me to return to the Valley.

He let me watch.

Let me approach.

The crescent scar that spanned Pete's cheek writhed as he grunted, wringing his body, trying to break free from Kajika. He could try all he wanted—there was no breaking free from the hunter once he'd caught you.

I knew this firsthand. Unlike Pete, though, I wasn't looking to break free.

"Who gave you access to the portals?" Ace asked.

"I did," Kajika suddenly said.

I gasped.

The hunter was so far beneath the ledge that I couldn't read his expression. "I had a page from Ley's book, and that page was stolen from me. I did not report it, because I thought you had taken it from me, Ace."

You could've led with that.

The hunter's eyes flashed to mine.

"Why would I— *Oh*." My brother's pinched shoulders relaxed the merest bit.

Pete squirmed again, and Kajika tightened the arm he'd wrapped around the man's throat.

"We let you into our home," Menawa hissed. "We taught you our ways, and this is how you repay us? By trying to kill Ace Wood?"

"How did you get down from the portals?" Ace asked, voice as rough as sandpaper.

Pete wheezed, clawing at Kajika's arm. The hunter must've loosened his grip, because Pete managed to blurt out, "I jumped."

"And no one saw him?" Ace skimmed the faces of the guards bobbing around him. "Or did someone help him?"

A volley of protests rose from them in a cacophony, matching the one below me in the Valley where everyone had congregated around Cat and Gwenelda and were squinting to see what was happening.

"What did he do? Brainwash you? Just because one of your people married him, it doesn't make him a virtuous person. He's a murderer! Just like his father and his grandfather. A fucking murderer!" Pete yelled.

"We are all murderers," Menawa said in that thunderously calm voice of his. "We have all killed, Pete. But we have also learned to set down our weapons and use words instead of arrows and dust."

"Fat good that did you. Look at where the lot of you are living. Ostracized in a fucking valley."

"We chose this place. We were offered a *calimbor*. We were offered the Glades. We picked *this* site. No one forced us to live here," Menawa said, but then shook his head. "Why do I bother explaining this to you? We owe you no explanation, Pete. We owe you nothing."

"Not even mercy, oh peaceful warrior?" Pete bit out, but then his cheeks rounded and flushed as Kajika flexed his arm.

Menawa didn't let Pete's taunt rattle him. Instead, he calmly turned to Ace, "What would you like us to do with him, *Massin*?"

Massin… Even to the Unseelies, my brother was considered a sovereign? Since the Hareni was built, no Unseelie had spoken the term, always referring to the Neverrian kings by their first names.

For a moment, the only noise that could be heard across the Valley was the swaying of the long grass and the soft wheezes coming from the traitor's flapping lips.

Then Ace said, "I will let Kajika decide his fate. After all, it was Kajika who was tortured and stolen from."

Tension thickened underneath that dark ledge as the hunter weighed my brother's invitation. His gaze moved off Ace and onto me. Was he trying to see if killing the man would frighten me? Even though I hated the idea of inflicting death, I hated the idea of letting Pete live more.

"The only way for a hunter to kill another hunter is to behead him. I do not care to behead you, Pete, but I also do not care to let you keep your life after all you have done. So I will show you mercy by asking Ace Wood to drive his sword of *gassen* through your black heart." Kajika stroked the man's scar. "Even though you deserve far worse than a quick and painless death."

My brother squared his shoulders. Had he expected not to be involved in the outcome?

"You might want to get out of the way, then. Wouldn't want to nick you with my sword." He glanced over his shoulder at me, then focused back on the hunter. "Lily would never forgive me."

Kajika smirked, and then he released Pete and shoved him toward my brother, whose sword was already brandished. Ace extended his arm, and the blade slid right through Pete's chest.

When blood gushed, I spun my face away, stomach lurching just from the slick sound. When the smell reached me, I dropped back into the Valley, landing in a crouch beside Cat.

"They killed him?" she asked.

I gritted my teeth to hold back the vomit burning my throat.

Cat stroked my hunched spine. "Who killed Pete, Lily?"

Who'd killed him?

I did, I signed.

"What are you talking about? I was watching you... You didn't take out your dust."

I'd brought this upon Pete, the same way I'd brought this upon my brother and Kajika. Had I never gone looking for Daneelies, blood wouldn't have been spilled.

Cat knelt beside me. "What happened up there?"

Hands scooped me off the ground, then nestled me against a warm, wildly beating chest. "I told you to stay by Gwenelda's side, *ma mika*. I knew this would not end well."

I swallowed back my bile. *This is all my fault,* I whispered into his mind.

"Lily—" he murmured.

I should never have gone looking for people who didn't want to be found.

His eyes reflected the stacks of stone ledges tufted with long grass. "Men like Pete...they do not turn evil overnight. There was evil lurking within him. Trust me, I experienced it firsthand. He took immense pleasure in butchering my body."

I scrunched up my nose, still not feeling very blameless even though his words did ease some of my guilt.

"And, Lily, if people do not want to be found, they hide better. Perhaps we caught them unawares, but they could have left Lake Superior. They could have left the country, settled somewhere far. They did not."

I bit my lip. He ran his thumb over my mouth to dislodge my teeth. "Do not blame yourself."

"So, how do you like my kingdom, *ventor*?" My brother had landed beside us.

Cat rushed over to him, a black blur of hair and swimsuit. When she arrived, she looked at Ace and touched his face as though to make sure he was whole. He kissed her forehead, then draped an arm around her shoulders.

"It is not without pleasant surprises, *pahan*."

My brother's lips kicked up into a grin. "Wouldn't want it to get to boring around here, or you'll leave, and my little sister will hold me accountable."

Color must've returned to my cheeks, because Kajika deemed me strong enough to be set down.

He laced his hand through mine. "Except I would leave with her."

"In order to leave, you'd need a portal stamp. And I know just the man who can make that happen. Shall I go introduce you to him? I think you two will hit it right off."

Cat turned on him. "He saved your life today, Ace. Be nice."

"I *am* being nice. I'm offering him a way to come and go as he pleases."

Kajika studied my brother's expression. "This is not a trick, *pahan*?"

Ace's smile fell, and he grew so serious that I suddenly saw my father in him. "Kajika, you did save my life back there. And you've saved Catori's a few times also. I may not seem grateful, but I've been keeping track. Not many people on Neverra or on Earth can claim their king owes them something, but you can. I do owe you tremendously. But that debt vanishes if you break my sister's heart, got it?"

Slowly, the hunter's lips bent into smile. "Got it, *masseen*."

"It's *massin*, not *masseen*. Just stick to Ace? At least you don't butcher that word."

I looked at Cat, and she at me, both of us confused by this peculiar exchange.

"Cat, why don't you give Lily a tour of our water villa and organize some lunch for the four of us?" Ace cocked his head toward the *wariff*, who was debriefing the *lucionaga*. "I'll go introduce Kajika to Gregor."

I gaped at my brother. We were going to have lunch, all four together? When I'd gone through the portal, I'd assumed we would claw at each other's throats, and it would end in tears...not in a home-cooked meal.

"Gregor and I are already old friends," Kajika quipped.

"I forget you are even older than I am."

"I thought you forgot nothing."

Ace chuckled as both men began to stroll through the Valley toward the *wariff*.

We listened to them banter—yes, however unbelievable, they bantered. The layer of frost that had wedged itself between them the minute they'd met had finally thawed. It was as though Pete's death had brought them together in some strange, perverted way.

And perhaps it had.

Or perhaps it was my guilt attempting to turn something horrible into something good.

Cat clasped my hand and squeezed it. I squeezed it right back.

EPILOGUE

amily isn't always fashioned from rainbows and butterflies. Sometimes it's forged from spilled blood and peculiar alliances.

This was how my family came to be.

We were a curious mix of people. The only thing we had in common, besides all of us being faeries, was that we would lay down our lives for each other, like Kajika had done for Ace that day and like my brother would do for him someday in the future.

Because our futures stayed intertwined.

I'd always longed for a happily-ever-after, because I was told that's what happened at the end of faerie tales. Not even in my wildest dreams would I have imagined that my happily-ever-after would rise from a rowan wood casket one dark, wintry night.

Up next:
Amara and Remo's story in
RECKLESS CRUEL HEIRS.

WHAT TO READ NEXT

Don't miss out on my next release by signing up for my newsletter here or on WWW.OLIVIAWILDENSTEIN.COM

If you enjoy enemies-to-lovers stories with alpha males and heroines who know their own mind, then you'll love my wolves.
Start *The Boulder Wolves* series with
A PACK OF BLOOD AND LIES.

How about a witchy, slow-burn romance? Travel to the coldest and mistiest town in France with a ragtag crew tasked with bringing magic back to the world in **OF WICKED BLOOD.**

Or head over to the City of Lights with my angels in **FEATHER** for a modern and darkly romantic *Romeo & Juliet* retelling.

ACKNOWLEDGMENTS

Acknowledgments are the most extraordinary thing to write for they signify two great accomplishments in an author's life. The first is: I wrote an entire book (it still seems unreal to me each time I put that final period on a manuscript, and *Raging Rival Hearts* is my ninth book! Will this feeling ever cease, I wonder?). The second is: I have *many* people to, as this part is called, acknowledge.

First and foremost, thank you to you, my readers, for your devotion, support, and enthusiasm. Cat, Ace, Lily, Kajika, and I are extremely grateful and lucky to have you.

The others to whom I am forever thankful are my brilliant editor, Jessica Nelson, my awesome proofreader, Josiah Davis, my incredible cover designer, Alessia Casali, my squadron of kick-ass beta readers, my author friends whose advice is always invaluable, and my family, who allow me to hide out in my writing cave (even on weekends).

Even though the story has come to a close, I have one last book in store for this series: *Reckless Cruel Heirs*. It will feature a certain little baby from this book (fully-grown by the time you'll meet him) and another faerie baby (can you guess whose?). I cannot wait to write it!

Be sure to sign up for my newsletter to stay up to date on all the happenings.

SIGN UP on www.oliviawildenstein.com

ALSO BY OLIVIA WILDENSTEIN

YA PARANORMAL ROMANCE

The Lost Clan series

ROSE PETAL GRAVES

ROWAN WOOD LEGENDS

RISING SILVER MIST

RAGING RIVAL HEARTS

RECKLESS CRUEL HEIRS

The Boulder Wolves series

A PACK OF BLOOD AND LIES

A PACK OF VOWS AND TEARS

A PACK OF LOVE AND HATE

A PACK OF STORMS AND STARS

Angels of Elysium series

FEATHER

CELESTIAL

STARLIGHT

The Quatrefoil Chronicles series

OF WICKED BLOOD

OF TAINTED HEART

YA CONTEMPORARY ROMANCE

GHOSTBOY, CHAMELEON & THE DUKE OF GRAFFITI

NOT ANOTHER LOVE SONG

ROMANTIC SUSPENSE

Cold Little Games **series**

COLD LITTLE LIES

COLD LITTLE GAMES

COLD LITTLE HEARTS

ABOUT THE AUTHOR

USA TODAY bestselling author Olivia Wildenstein grew up in New York City and earned her bachelor's in comparative literature from Brown University. After designing jewelry for a few years, Wildenstein traded in her tools for the writing life, which made more sense considering her college degree.

When she's not sitting at her computer, she's psychoanalyzing everyone she meets (Yes. Everyone), eavesdropping on conversations to gather material for her next book, and attempting not to forget one of her kids in school.

She has a slight obsession with romance, which might be the reason why she writes it. She's a hybrid author of over a dozen Young Adult love stories.

oliviawildenstein.com
olivia@wildenstein.com

Made in the USA
Columbia, SC
06 November 2021